The Map Colorist

Also by Rebecca D'Harlingue

The Lines Between Us

The Map Colorist

A NOVEL

Rebecca D'Harlingue

SHE WRITES PRESS

Published 2023
Printed in the United States of America
Print ISBN: 978-1-64742-547-0
E-ISBN: 978-1-64742-548-7
Library of Congress Control Number: 2023907751

For information, address:
She Writes Press
1569 Solano Ave #546
Berkeley, CA 94707

Interior Design by

She Writes Press is a division of SparkPoint Studio, LLC.

This is a work of fiction. Names, characters, places, and incidents either are the product of the author's imagination or are used fictitiously. Any resemblance to actual persons, living or dead, is entirely coincidental.

For my beloved grandchildren,
Lily and Oliver,
as promised

Historical Notes

The *Atlas Maior*, printed by the Blaeu printing house, was the largest and most expensive publication of the seventeenth century.

The Dutch East India Company (*Vereenigde Oostindische Compagnie*) is generally referred to as the VOC. The Dutch West India Company (*West-Indische Compagnie*) is referred to as the WIC.

Prologue

Amsterdam
June 1699
Anneke

If he had known how it would end, my father would have struck the paintbrush from my young hand. Even so, my mother would have quietly retrieved it, saying she was teaching my brother and me a useful skill. What she would not have said was that the income she made from map coloring allowed us to live a more comfortable life, concealing the fact that my father was not as successful an artist as our circumstances might imply.

The coloring meant different things to each of us. To my mother, it was not only a chore that she carried out as part of her housewifely duties. It also allowed her to, in some small way, take part in the artistic world to which she had aspired. To my brother, it was a spark for his imagination. Where were these places that we so tirelessly transformed? What kind of people lived there?

For me, the task itself was sheer joy. The colors, the beauty I could create, insured that I never resented the work asked of me. I even dreamed of drawing my own maps. This desire would come into play in the unraveling of our lives, but I embraced it, and with it, all that was to come.

Chapter 1
1646

Every night before drifting off to dream, Anneke and Lucas prayed, snuggled into their box bed, and listened to their father's tales of Africa. Sometimes he spoke of the different peoples his group had come across and of the houses on stilts he had seen. Sometimes he spoke of the heat and the quick, heavy rain. Sometimes he spoke of the terrain, difficult and beautiful. Then he would stop speaking, as though he were there again, and the children often wondered whether he wished himself back in those lands, so different from their home of Holland with its dikes and windmills in a never-ending battle to keep the sea at bay.

When Anneke and Lucas asked him to describe the food, he always spoke of the fruit: bananas, coconuts, melons, and tamarinds.

"It is not just the taste, my children, but the feel of them in your mouth."

"And what is that like, Papa?" they would always ask.

"Like the cool of the night and the warmth of the sun. Like biting into everything sweet in life." Anneke would whisper to herself, "tamarind," and she felt those sensations within the beauty of the word.

"But what do they really taste like, Papa? Name something we have that is like them," seven-year-old Lucas would insist, and his sister, all of a year older, would roll her eyes. But the only answer Isaac ever gave his son was, "Like nothing you have ever eaten."

Most of all, the children loved to hear of the strange beasts. There were large cats with spotted coats that ran faster than any horse, and those that seemed a strange breed of horse with black-and-white stripes.

"There are mysterious enormous creatures with long tubes connected to their heads where one would expect a nose to be!" their father would say, and the children would gleefully cry out, "But that is just an elephant, Papa—an elephant with a trunk!"

"Just an elephant!" he would say. "But you cannot imagine what it is like to see one."

"We've seen pictures, Papa. You've even drawn pictures for us."

"So I have, children," he would say, and his mind would wander to the suspicion he always felt that his drawings might not accurately portray things he held only in his memory.

"Still," he would continue, "you cannot imagine how thrilling it is to see a real elephant! Before you were born, before I went to Africa, there was a real elephant brought to Amsterdam. Her name was Hansken. The great artist Rembrandt van Rijn himself made many drawings of her, so fascinating did he find her. She was brought from Ceylon and so was a bit different from the elephants I saw in Africa. Even having seen her, I was not prepared for the first time we came across elephants, some using their trunk to pull branches from the trees to feed themselves, some taking up water with their trunk to drink. These elephants were larger than Hansken, with much bigger ears, and they had huge curved tusks coming from their mouths."

"Were you frightened, Papa?" Anneke always asked, though he had answered her many times.

"No, sweet one. I wasn't, but I don't know why."

The children were vaguely aware that there was a hint of obsession in their father's tales, though they would not have known how to name it. They had been very young when their father had left them and their mother, Lysbeth, for Africa. He had been part of the 1642 expedition when Jan van Herder had gone to meet with the king of Congo, Nkanga a Lukeni, called Garcia II by the Portuguese. They had gone to Mbanza Congo, called San Salvador. When his mission there was completed, van Herder had pushed his group further, and they had traveled inland to the river Kwango, proceeding in a northeasterly direction.

It had been like a new world opening to Isaac. Everywhere there were wonders, and sometimes terrors. His task had been to make sketches of the land and of the animals and of the peoples. And he had done so at a frenzied pace for weeks on end. There was so much to see and record, and Isaac wondered how God had created lands so different from all he had known that they seemed not to belong to the same world at all. Isaac had used his talents to record all that he could. He wanted his countrymen to see what he had seen. But he also wanted more. He wanted to be recognized for what he would bring home. He wanted to be accepted as an artist, and perhaps even to be respected by the scholars of the day. He, who had come from a humble background, longed for this. Perhaps he could gain fame.

Fate would not have it so, however, and he consoled himself that it must not have been God's will. On the ship's journey home, they were caught in a storm. Isaac had brought his satchel with all of his drawings onto the deck when he had gone up to sketch some of the sailors. The storm approached quickly, and he ran to help the seamen as best he could. After the storm, he searched for the bag everywhere, but his efforts were fruitless. Abandoned, it must have been swept overboard.

When he went below deck to the area he shared with some of the other skilled men, there were papers scattered on the floor near his hammock. Picking one up, he saw that it was a page of the copious notes he had written about the land itself. They must have fallen from his satchel when he had gone on deck before the storm and so were saved from oblivion. So distraught was he at the loss of his drawings that he barely looked at the pages he gathered up. He guarded them for the rest of the journey, but gone were his dreams of glory. Who now would know the name of Isaac van Brug?

Chapter 2

July 1652

As did so many in the city, Isaac and Lysbeth worked in their home. Isaac did his paintings, and Lysbeth colored maps. Like most colorists, she worked anonymously. No buyer would know whose hand had applied the hues that brought a map to life.

From the time their children were very young, Lysbeth and Isaac had believed that they should be educated. Isaac had especially insisted that this should be the case for Lucas, and Lysbeth had adamantly argued that Anneke should not be left behind. Lysbeth's coloring helped to pay for better schools so the children would become proficient at reading and writing, and even learn mathematics. For their part, the children did well in their studies and enjoyed their lessons.

When Anneke and Lucas reached the ages of fourteen and thirteen, Lysbeth decided that she would add more to their education by teaching them to color. She explained which colors to use on each part of the map. Yellow and occasionally crimson defined the outline of the map. Roadways were red and white, or yellow shadowed with burnt umber. Red or yellow, or sometimes green, marked the borders of places. Lysbeth's plan was to get Anneke and Lucas to such a skill level that they could do the basics and she could devote herself to the more elaborate, and more satisfying, decorations found on most maps: cartouches, scrollwork, botanicals, gargoyles, costumed figures, scenery, the compass rose. In this way, they would increase the family's income and security, for one never knew what the future might bring.

At first, Lysbeth drew simple maps for Anneke and Lucas to color.

Sometimes she would copy the major parts of a map that she was working on, but more often she would draw a map of a fantastical place: the land of the green men, the land of the purple cows, the land of the giant trees, the land of magical creatures. Though Anneke and Lucas sometimes felt that their mother thought of them still as young children to be amused in this way, they happily forgave her this common mother's error, and the tedium of the work was eased for all three of them. Anneke and Lucas would ask their mother to draw decorative elements that went with the names of the places, and sometimes they suggested imaginary places.

"Draw the land of the eels, Mama," Lucas would say, and they would all laugh since Lysbeth had a particular aversion to eels and would never cook them.

"You know that they live in water anyway, Lucas," she would say, and he would reply that she could draw a map of the sea.

"How about a map of the land of handsome men, Mama," Anneke would ask, and their mother would raise her eyebrows, smile, and set to work.

When Lysbeth thought it was time to practice on real maps, she spoke to the pressman at the printshop. Might she have some maps that had to be discarded, perhaps some that had been wrinkled in the press? They were just for practice for someone she was teaching to color, she assured him, and she would destroy them once they had served their purpose. She was rewarded with several prints of a map of Portugal.

Anneke and Lucas hovered next to her when she unfurled the defective maps, as though she were revealing a treasure. Following their mother's lead, Anneke and Lucas began by covering the hills of Portugal with a thin layer of tincture of myrrh. For the woods, every tree was marked with a fine pencil dipped in grass green, made of copper green tempered with gamboge. As they worked, Lysbeth praised or gently guided her children, reminding them to mimic her work as closely as they could.

They painted the names of the cities and towns in red to make them stand out. When that was dry, they worked on the border of a province, again using the green, making sure the paint was no thicker in one spot than in another. To refine the line, when the paint was almost dry, they took a clean pencil dipped in water and went around the line again, until giving the illusion that it grew fainter at the edges. Then they repeated the process with another province, this one yellow, and the next a crimson made from cochineal.

When Lysbeth compared the three completed maps, she found that each was slightly different. "We will begin again, children. Yours must look the same as mine. There is a required uniformity to this work."

"But you didn't color everything according to the general guidelines you had told us before, Mama," Anneke protested.

"That is true, child, but each map is unique. You will learn what is called for with more practice."

"Will we never be able to use our own ideas, Mama?" the girl persisted.

"You have just started, Anneke! How can you even have notions of your own? Perhaps someday you will have the wisdom and freedom to stray a bit from the usual color schemes, but for now, you must learn to do exactly what is expected." Then, turning to her son, she said, "What do you say, Lucas? How do you feel about coloring your first real map?"

"Where is Portugal, Mama? I would like to go to Portugal," Lucas responded. His mother noted both that he had not answered the question and that he was anxious to leave her for a place totally unknown to him.

"Perhaps someday you will venture out, Lucas. For now, let us try again." With that, Anneke and Lucas turned to the paints that Lysbeth had prepared. There would be no income from their use this day, but she told herself that she was investing in their future.

They practiced thus for several months, some days passing more pleasantly than others. At times, the discipline required to sit working for hours after they returned from school caused Lucas to complain, and Anneke's patience with the standard color scheme waned. But the atmosphere was never greatly tainted by these protests, and for the most part, concentrating on a common task seemed to bring the three closer together.

After six months of practice, Lysbeth deemed her students ready and got up the courage to speak to Heer Alders at Blaeu's printing house, whose maps she painted. She told him what she had been doing and held her breath until he asked, "Why are you telling me this, Vrouw Plettenburg?"

"Because I would like to start them on coloring maps for the House of Blaeu, Heer Alders." She had hoped that her value as a colorist would weigh in her favor in this request, but she was just about to look down and admit that her idea was unreasonable when Alders replied. "Very well. You may begin them on some simple maps for which they can do just the basic, prescribed coloring, and which we sell to those who can afford no better."

"Thank you, Heer Alders!" Lysbeth said, smiling while he informed his assistant of the new plan.

Over the next year, Lysbeth became ever more aware that each of her children was developing a particular style, and so she decided that it would be more satisfying, and in fact more efficient, for each to work on a project from start to finish. This precluded any disagreements on how to proceed, for under her tutelage, Anneke and Lucas had gained confidence enough to sometimes question their mother's plan, though they did not stray far enough that she needed to correct them. If they did their own maps, the work would feel more integrated in its presentation, though few others would have the sensibility to discern this.

Lysbeth noticed that while Anneke gave meticulous attention to all parts of the map, she excelled at coloring the decorative elements, whether it was scrollwork, plants, animals, human figures, or buildings. After a time, she began to use colors other than the conventional ones for the map itself, choosing hues to match the scheme of the embellishments.

Lysbeth feared that Anneke's fanciful plans risked her work being rejected, and each time it was not, Lysbeth questioned her own technique. Still, she told herself that she, too, incorporated artistry into her work. After all, she believed that she could have been an artist in her own right if she had ever been given formal training. She looked at her husband's creations and felt that she could at least have equaled his efforts, although she loyally kept these thoughts to herself.

Even though Isaac did sell some paintings and was a member of the St. Luke's Guild for painters, his work was not admired enough to attract any apprentices, who would not only have paid a fee but also helped with tasks such as preparing the canvases and mixing the paints, eventually working on the simpler parts of a painting which the master would then finish. This extra income and aid to efficiency were what allowed other artists to earn more than Isaac ever could.

The family could have survived on what Isaac earned, but Lysbeth wanted the comfort and security that the coloring allowed them. She knew that Isaac held himself the true artist of the family, and he poorly concealed the disdain he felt for the efforts of his wife and children. However, the extra income gave people the impression that Isaac was more successful than he was. This result, he did not disdain.

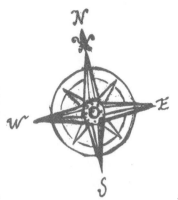

Chapter 3

January 1655

As his family labored over their maps and colors one dreary afternoon, with less light than they might desire, Isaac interrupted them.

"I have an announcement." Lysbeth and Lucas immediately looked up from their tasks, Lysbeth from care for her husband and Lucas happy to take a break from work that to him had become tedious. Anneke, however, was so immersed in her map that her mother nudged her to get her attention, and it was clear that she only reluctantly raised her head. Noticing for the first time that her father had entered the room, she said, "Oh, hello, Papa." They all indulgently smiled, accustomed to Anneke's ability to shut out the world around her.

"As I was saying," Isaac continued, "I have an announcement."

"Yes, husband, and what is that?"

"I have decided that Lucas will go to the cartography school in Leiden to be trained as a surveyor and mapmaker. Thanks to the sacrifices we have made to give the children a good education, I feel that he will succeed. One of my patrons has been kind enough to see to it that he will find a place there, and I believe that it would be a reliable and respectable way to make a living." Having uttered the few sentences he had prepared, Isaac waited to see how his family, especially his wife, would react to this news.

"Oh, and which patron is that, dear husband? Did he come up with this suggestion on his own?"

"The patron is Heer Leendert. You may recall that he was pleased with the painting I did of his small country holding. When I told him of Lucas's interest in maps, he mentioned an acquaintance who teaches at the school, and things progressed from there."

"My interest in maps? My only interest in maps is that I wish to visit the places they portray. Why would I wish to draw them? After two years of coloring, I have had my fill of sitting before a table with a representation I care nothing about," Lucas dared to respond.

"Lucas!" his mother said. "We owe much to the maps we color!"

"This could be your chance to travel, Lucas, as you've always wanted to do, though Mama and I would miss you in the workroom," Anneke put in.

"Yes! Perhaps you could be taken on by the VOC or the WIC as a cartographer. You could learn to survey and to make valuable contributions to what is known of the world!" Isaac added.

"I do not know that the mapmakers always do the traveling," Lysbeth quietly said. "They are often just going by observations done by those who have explored the areas. Is this, husband, your real desire, that Lucas will create a map from your notes on Africa?"

"And if it is, what of it? There is no shame in a son being of service to his father."

But Lucas had heard the word "survey" and knew that this would at least enable him to forsake the confines of this room.

"I would be happy to study, Mama! I think I would do well with surveying. Even if I didn't get to travel for it, I could surely get a job with one of the *waterschappen.*"

"That's right," Isaac said, embracing this newfound enthusiasm in his son. "The water boards always need accurate measurements."

Lysbeth realized that she could not oppose both her husband and her son, and even Anneke seemed willing to have Lucas leave them. In truth, it was good to see Lucas excited about something. For a long time, she had seen his unhappiness but knew not how to address it.

"Very well, if you are set upon this. But surely there must be fees to be paid at the school."

"I would be willing to do extra coloring, Mama, to help give Lucas this chance!"

"That is good of you, daughter, but neither of us could do enough to compensate for both the loss of Lucas's pay and the extra cost of schooling and living in another city. I have heard that there are also such classes here in Amsterdam."

"But, Mama, I want to go to Leiden!" Lucas proclaimed.

"What we want and what is possible are not always one," Lysbeth said. "You are well past the age of having learned that."

"Perhaps Mama is right, Lucas," Isaac said, conceding this point since his main desire was for his son to be trained. "Wherever you attend classes, it will open much wider vistas for you in the future."

Thus was the family set upon a road whose end they could not see.

When the day came for Lucas to begin his new pursuit, both Anneke and Lysbeth had mixed emotions, though neither spoke of it. They would see him when he was not at school, but the years of toiling together with a common purpose had seemed to give their lives structure and meaning and a certain intimacy. Still, they had each noticed Lucas's discontent and hoped his absence would lighten the atmosphere of the workroom.

It seemed so at first, but as the weeks passed, each became ever more immersed in her own painting, uninterrupted by Lucas's sighs or comments. While Anneke seemed to take little note of the change, given that she had always been able to shut out all but the colors, Lysbeth came to feel that she was losing both of her children. She knew that this was the fate of all mothers, as children grew and found their own way, but now she understood that she had somehow thought she would be shielded from this feeling of abandonment. They had worked together so closely for so long, and she had felt that it would always be so, that they would continue into the future, never changing. Of course, if she had been queried, she would have said that she wanted her children to make lives of their own, to have families, to give her grandchildren. But these were thoughts for the future, not the longings of the present.

Added to this, Lysbeth harbored another feeling, and one that she did not like to look at too closely. With Lucas's work table empty, there were only the efforts of herself and Anneke to compare, and she could not escape the obvious. Anneke had surpassed her mother in skill, and not only in skill, but also in artistic sensibility. Lysbeth found this difficult to accept, and also somewhat of a puzzle. If she could recognize her daughter's proficiency, why could she not cultivate it in herself? She was envious of her own daughter, and she felt both shame and resentment.

For a long time, Lysbeth had hoped that working as a colorist would somehow lead to an ability to create other works, but no such magic had occurred. Over the years, she came to tell herself that, contrary to her expectations, the coloring had inhibited her own creativity. It had taken her eyes from a world of reality, which might have been portrayed by her brush, to one of artificial lines and standard figures. Her purpose was to enhance the map's function of providing information. If she could also make it beautiful, that was a bonus, but as the years passed, the coloring was often a task and nothing more.

At times she allowed herself the added grievance that she had sacrificed her ambitions for those of a husband who was, at best, an undistinguished painter. If they had lived elsewhere, perhaps it would not have been so apparent, but they lived in a place and time of truly wondrous artists. Not all had achieved fame, but she could see that many far surpassed her Isaac's offerings.

These were her thoughts on the dark days. She scolded herself for criticizing her husband's work, and for envying her daughter's. She could not stop the judgment from springing to her mind, but she could control her tongue, and so she found that she could forgive herself.

On days when Lysbeth found the silence of the workroom most pressing, she would talk to Anneke about the past. She would tell stories of Anneke's and Lucas's young childhood, as every mother does; how Anneke had decided to decorate the walls with paint while her mother was putting baby Lucas to sleep; how although Anneke had been a fussy eater as a child, she always loved, rather inexplicably, any kind of stewed fish, as long as her mother seasoned it with pepper, mace, and some crushed rusk. While these stories were ostensibly about the children, they focused on Lysbeth's own reactions to them, both at the time and now, softened by memory.

Lysbeth knew that when Anneke was absorbed in working on a map, she only half-listened to these stories, and one day, feeling lonely, she wanted Anneke to pay her greater heed. Lucas had always made what they needed to mix the paints, and when he left to study cartography, the task fell to Anneke. Now Lysbeth pulled Anneke away from her coloring by saying, "We are getting low on the tartar lye, Anneke. Please prepare more."

"Oh, Mama, must I? Don't you think we have enough for today?"

"No, we are getting too low. Come, we can talk while you work."

"But do we even have the tartar, Mama?"

"Yes, Anneke. I purchased some yesterday from the apothecary. You go get the basin and water, and I will stir up the fire."

Rising from her work table, Anneke left the room. She had come to understand why Lucas hated this chore. She had always enjoyed the step of actually mixing the colors, which each of them did on their own, depending upon the demands of the map they were coloring. Making the tartar lye, however, did not offer the intrinsic pleasure of experimenting to achieve a desired color.

Anneke returned with the basin of water and found the white tartar, the best that was available, and at such a price that she could not waste it by performing the procedure incorrectly. As Anneke put some of the tartar on a half sheet of brown paper, her mother began to talk about Isaac's journey, the inspiration for the many nighttime stories he had regaled his son and daughter with when they were young. Even then, Anneke had felt her mother had not shared her children's enthusiasm for Isaac's tales. Slowly, over the years, as they had each labored over their maps, Lysbeth had at times revealed the struggles she had endured those years when her husband had been away. She knew that he had faced hardships of a different sort, but they were of his choosing, and his enthusiasm for the trip had hurt her.

As Anneke began to tightly wrap the paper with the tartar on it, Lysbeth told of the day in late 1641 when Isaac had come home to announce with unsuppressed delight that he had been chosen to accompany Jan van Herder on his diplomatic mission to Garcia II, king of Congo. Lysbeth had been stunned into silence. Her husband seemed to have mistaken her reaction for excitement for him, and he had embraced and kissed her, assuring her that this would be the making of him, and thus of their family.

"I am only twenty-four. I have so much ahead of me! Is it not wonderful, wife?" Lysbeth recalled him saying. And all she had done was nod.

"I was a year younger than he, but it seemed that I was feeling the responsibility of our two children more strongly. Being seventeen, twenty-three might seem old to you, Anneke, but can you imagine yourself in just a few years, married and with two children to care for, alone for two years?"

"Why did you not tell him how you truly felt?" Anneke asked as she looked up from her task.

At first, Lysbeth did not answer and just looked pointedly at the rolled-up paper in her daughter's hands. Anneke went to the basin and thoroughly wet the paper, then walked over to the fire and plunged it in. Both she and her mother watched the paper. As it turned red, Anneke used tongs to quickly remove it from the fire and plunge it back into the basin of water.

"Because I loved him," Lysbeth finally replied to her daughter's question as Anneke rubbed the paper until it fell into pieces.

"But you had Lucas and me to care for, and he was set to leave you for two years!" Anneke protested.

"It's true. You were only four, and Lucas three. But I think that you may mistake my meaning in saying that I loved him. I do not mean that I happily sacrificed myself for his happiness, though there was some of that. I could see how uplifted he was with this new chance. He had big dreams, then, of becoming a famous artist, and he saw this as his opportunity to become known. His illustrations were to be but the beginning, the thing that would bring him to the attention of important people, people who could offer him commissions."

"But none of that happened, did it?" Anneke replied in a small voice without raising her gaze from the pieces of paper before her.

"No. You know the story of the storm and the loss of his drawings. Sometimes I wonder if they ever existed."

"Mama, how can you say that?" Anneke had never heard her mother say something that seemed so disloyal.

"Oh, I suppose I don't really mean it. It's just that his never-ending tales have taken on the feel of something from his imagination, nothing more real than his desires. It hardly matters now, does it? I did not protest when he said that he would go because I was afraid that I would lose him if I did. His dreams were so important to him. Men have that luxury."

"And that is how you began to do the coloring for the House of Blaeu?"

"Yes. Your father had been given an advance before he left, and that was to tide us over. I don't think your father ever dared to try to calculate whether it would be enough, for what would he do if he knew that it was not? I hired a young girl to help with you and Lucas." Pausing, she added, "You know, I had dreamed of becoming an artist myself."

"Yes, Mama, and I've seen the drawings you do for yourself, though you seek to hide them from us, as though you are ashamed. I never asked you about them because I did not want to intrude. They are good, Mama."

"Not good enough. Perhaps if I had more training, things might have gone differently, but your father came along, and I loved him, and I knew from early on that to compete with him would not make for a happy marriage."

"So, when Papa left, you turned to coloring."

"Yes. I had done some coloring in my parents' home, and I hoped that eventually I would be able to design some of the cartouches, but that never came to be. Blaeu's started me on a trial basis, and I slowly gained their approval. As you know, it is not easy work. Our backs and arms ache at the end of the day, but we cannot deny that this work is more pleasing than other jobs that might be open to women. Do you know that I get a secret pleasure from the colors left on my hands at the end of the day?

"So, we made it through those years, and when your father returned, he was downcast. At first, I was angry. How dare he not be joyful to be home with his wife and children? But then he told me of the loss of the drawings, and of his despair at having lost that chance for recognition. He still had his written notes of the journey, and he said that he had done some surveying also. I was surprised at this since I hadn't known he had any training as a surveyor. He just said that there was another in the group who had taken it upon himself to teach him, both during the long hours on the ship and as they traversed the land.

"I encouraged Isaac to seek out the map-printing houses, to see if they might have someone who could use them to make a new map of the area. He said that he tried Hondius and Janssonius, and Visscher, too. But he would not go to Heer Blaeu, or even to anyone who worked there. I thought it was his pride that would not let him go there as a supplicant because I worked there and I was a lowly colorist."

Anneke noted some bitterness in her mother's voice at this last and felt the truth of it. "I didn't know he did any surveying on the trip. He always talked only of his 'notes.' I didn't realize that they would be more detailed."

"At one point I encouraged him to try to get work here as a surveyor. It would have made for a steadier income. But he said that he wasn't formally trained, and besides, he was an artist."

"Still, even after all these years, he hasn't given up on the dream of wanting his notes to be made into a map, has he?'

"No, and so he has decided to raise a cartographer. He has transferred his dreams to Lucas, as you saw. Poor Lucas, set upon a course for which he has no desire, and at which he seems incapable of excelling."

Anneke did not respond immediately. Returning to her task, she walked over to another shelf, took down a long, narrow glass, and put the crumbled, burnt paper pieces into it. If she had done it correctly, the black would settle to the bottom in a day or two, and she would pour off the clear lye into a glass with a stopper.

"Why do you say that about Lucas, Mama?"

"I hear you in the evenings sometimes, Anneke, you and Lucas. I hear you trying to explain to him something that he doesn't understand, though I don't know how you can have this knowledge."

"I read his school books and class notes, and I am able to help him with some of the concepts. But, Mama, I am only feeling my way. The lessons on translating notes and measurements into a map seem easier to me than they do to Lucas, though the mathematics is sometimes beyond me. Lucas is better at the surveying lessons, learning to use the instruments and making the calculations, but he could use help with that, too. He also laments that he has no instruments of his own, for if he did it would help him understand the surveying concepts better."

"Even I didn't realize just how involved you are with Lucas's lessons, Anneke. Are you sure of what you say, about Lucas needing help?"

"Yes, Mama. You can ask him yourself."

"It seems to me that if your father wants Lucas to succeed in this, perhaps he should pay for a tutor to come to the house to help him."

"Oh, that would be wonderful, Mama! And I could learn, too, couldn't I? I would so love to understand how the maps, which we can only decorate, came to be."

"We will have to convince your father."

When Lucas returned from his classes that day, Lysbeth told him of the plan to ask Isaac for a tutor. At first Lucas seemed embarrassed that his mother knew of his difficulties, but that was soon outweighed by the possibility of getting help. Lysbeth also mentioned that Isaac had done some surveying on the van Herder excursion and might possibly have surveying instruments. It was decided that Lucas would bring up the request for instruments to Isaac, and Lysbeth would broach the subject of a tutor.

"Papa, I didn't know that you had done surveying on your trip to Africa," he began. "Mama told us that today."

"Yes, well, I only had a bit of training, not the fine opportunity that you have. There was a surveyor on the trip who saw my interest and helped me some."

"Do you still have any of the instruments, Papa? It would be a great help to me to have some of the tools that we talk about in class. I know that I could understand their use better if I had some to practice with."

"I had no instruments," Isaac answered quickly. "I borrowed those of the surveyor on the trip. It was he, after all, who was hired for the work. The surveying was just something to add interest to the trip. My true calling has always been my art."

"There is another thing, Isaac. I believe that it would be useful for Lucas to have the aid of a tutor," Lysbeth said. "Thanks to the profitable commissions you have gotten lately, we have been able to put savings aside, and this seems a very worthy way to use that money."

"But why do you need a tutor, Lucas?" Isaac asked his son.

"Well, it would be helpful, Papa. Some of the boys have a stronger background than I do, especially in mathematics. Besides, Papa, it would be a kindness to Anneke, for she is also interested in my lessons," Lucas replied. It seemed to Anneke that he was unable to admit that she had helped him.

"Anneke? Why would she need to learn this? She could never become a sworn land surveyor, and who would ever hire a girl to do the work of a cartographer?"

"But, Papa," Anneke broke in. "You have often said that having knowledge is better than not having it. My learning could do no harm, and maybe Lucas and I could help each other."

"If you really want Lucas to succeed on this track that you have set him upon, Isaac," Lysbeth said, "then I believe that we should do whatever is necessary to ensure that end, especially now that he is showing an interest. And if we are paying a tutor anyway, there is no harm in Anneke listening to the lessons."

"Very well. But Anneke is just to observe the lessons. She is not to interfere in any way, even with questions."

"I won't, Papa, I promise! I'm sure that Lucas will get more from the lessons than I will, but I can at least pick up something." As Anneke said this, she thought about what her mother had told her that day and wondered if women must always hide their talents so as not to make the men they love feel that they are less.

Although the subject matter for the surveying and the cartography classes overlapped to some degree, Lucas was most interested in surveying, and he urged the tutor to spend the bulk of the time on those subjects. Anneke was more interested in the actual putting together of a map, and it was true when she told the tutor that Lucas needed more help in that area. The mathematics was the most difficult aspect for both of them, but it was as important for a surveyor as it was for a cartographer, who must understand how to utilize the measurements made by the surveyor.

Anneke was not always able to keep her promise of not interrupting with questions, and in truth, the tutor did not mind occasionally focusing his attention on his student's pretty sister, with her auburn hair and green eyes. He was only a few years older than she, and Anneke did not disdain using his obvious interest in her to get her questions answered, for as her learning progressed, the idea began to blossom in her mind that she might use her father's notes to create the map he had always dreamed of.

After a year and a half, Lucas was doing well enough in his classes that he no longer needed the tutor's help, but Anneke begged him not to tell their parents, for then her learning would halt. Lucas loved his sister, and though he did not know to what use she hoped to put her knowledge, he agreed to carry on with the pretense of needing help. The tutor saw what was happening, but he was happy to continue teaching the pair, for the extra stuivers helped make his life more tolerable.

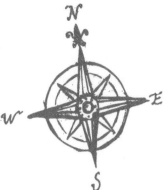

Chapter 4

February 1658

His three years of study had done nothing to quench Lucas's thirst to travel to the places that maps depicted. When he was younger and his days had been spent coloring maps that were drawn by others, the only way he got through the task was to imagine himself in the place he was coloring, though he often knew nothing about it. His surveying and cartography lessons had sharpened and refined his curiosity. One might hear information about the places that were being explored by the Dutch, but it was not the kind of detail he craved. Anyone who talked about the colonies spoke of opportunities, costs, labor, resources. They concerned themselves only with the potential for profit.

Lucas yearned to stand in those far-off lands. Were there hills or plains? Was there water everywhere, as in Holland, or was there desert? What was the exact color of the sky? What did the air feel like? Beyond this, he longed to know about the inhabitants of such far-flung places. He thought back on all the evenings when his father had spoken of his travels in Africa, and he wished that he had asked more about the peoples. What did they look like? What were their customs? How did the sound of their language touch the ear?

He felt constrained even in his ability to imagine. How could he conceive of a land that was completely different from his homeland? Were there other lands where one escaped the city to see a field of windmills constantly pumping water to maintain the integrity of the polders, those lands stolen from the sea?

Were there great cities like Amsterdam in those other places? He had heard of the settlements the Dutch had founded under the auspices of either the VOC or the WIC. The colonizers probably attempted to recreate their homeland wherever they found themselves, but surely the place itself limited that ability, and surely the native people placed their own stamp on what they were recruited to build.

Lucas also longed to discover other beliefs. In his homeland, even though the Dutch Reformed Church aimed to control the creeds of all, there were those who professed other Protestant beliefs. There were even Roman Catholics. Still, the God and Savior that they all worshipped was the same one. Even the Jews believed in the God of the Old Testament. Who were the gods of the places that he colored on a map? What virtues were most exalted and what vices most reviled?

The time came when Lucas felt that he must escape the confines of his limited experience. He could question no more, not without making an effort to find answers. So it was that one evening he broke the silence during the family's meal.

"I've signed on to a ship with the WIC," he said.

Isaac's knife clattered onto his pewter plate and Lysbeth stared at their son.

"What do you mean, you've signed on to a ship?" Isaac said.

"Just that, Papa. I've signed on to a ship that will go to Africa. It is due to sail in two days."

"Two days!" Lysbeth said. "How can that be?"

When he didn't reply, his sister asked in a subdued tone, "How long have you known this, Lucas?"

Lucas looked down at his beer and replied. "I've known for a couple of months."

"And you are just now telling us?" Isaac asked in a louder voice.

Lucas now looked at his father. "I didn't tell you sooner because I didn't want to hear all of the arguments for days on end. I've committed myself, and there's nothing to be done."

"But I'm your father!"

"And I'm a man, Papa! I am eighteen!"

"A man who still lives in my house!"

"I will remedy that in two days."

"And what of your schooling? What of the money I spent paying for a tutor?"

"Oh, if it is about the money, don't worry. I can do surveying."

"And you think that you will have the chance to do that by signing on to a ship? Has anyone said that you will be able to do anything other than fulfill the duties of a common crewman?"

"Yes, Papa. One of my teachers put me in contact with a surveyor who is going. He has gotten permission to take me as his assistant, so I won't be a common crewman. We will leave the ship when it reaches the fort at Elmina, and we will travel out to get more information that will supplement the current WIC maps of the area. It will be a much shorter journey than going on a ship to Batavia, so we will hopefully have fewer hardships on board."

Getting no response, he continued more gently, "I need to see something of the world, Papa. You always talked of your travels in Africa. Is it so surprising that I want to go?"

Isaac seemed taken aback at this, as though his fascination had been his own, and he could not see that others might harbor a desire to see new things, though he himself had planted this seed in his son.

"If you have signed up, then there is nothing to be done," Isaac finally said, looking down.

"That's right, Papa," Lucas said, standing and leaving the table without seeing the stricken looks on the faces of his mother and sister.

When Anneke later found her brother in the small storeroom on the upper floor, Lucas looked at his sister with misery in his eyes.

"Why must you go, Lucas, and why must you leave on such a sour note between you and Papa?" Anneke gently asked. "Why do you find it so easy to argue with him?"

"And why do you and Mother constantly flatter and cajole him?"

"Because he is the head of our family, and we owe him respect."

"Yes, he is the head, but if it were not for our labor, he would not be able to fancy himself the artist, looking down on us from his superior status. I have to go, Anneke. And it is not just to escape. You know that I have always had a longing to see foreign lands."

"But I will miss you so, Lucas!" Anneke protested. "And what of Mama? And even Papa? You know that he loves you, even with his vanity."

"I know, Sister, but if I stay, I fear that I would say something to sever the bond between Papa and me forever. I will return. It is not as though I have signed on as a settler in one of the colonies. I will only be gone two years."

"Two years. I don't understand why you resent him so, Lucas."

"That is because you have the kinder heart that sees goodness, in both Papa and in me, in far greater measure than may actually exist. I must do this, Anneke. I must."

Two days later, as he had said, Lucas left to join his ship. His mother and sister wept when they bade him farewell and wanted to walk with him to the docks, but he said that he could not begin his life among men as a boy who brings his mama and his sister with him. Isaac did not offer to accompany him and gruffly said goodbye, but Anneke saw the tears in his eyes as he embraced his only son.

Anneke knew that when Lucas had packed his bag, he had slipped in some of the surveying tools the family had purchased for him for his studies. He hadn't put in very many personal items so that he could include his surveyor's chain, compass, level, and alidade. As he walked along the canal in the direction of the docks, Anneke stared at his receding figure, trying to fix in her mind the image of her brother's outline, carrying his odd-shaped bag, distorted by the hopeful tools within.

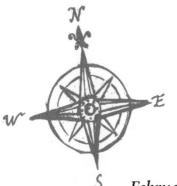

Chapter 5

February–December 1658

The first days after Lucas's departure passed slowly for those who had been left behind. Anneke and Lysbeth worked mostly in silence, and Isaac, who had rarely interrupted them in their work, found himself leaving his studio to see how his wife and daughter fared.

They did not speak much of Lucas. When they did mention him, Anneke noticed that Isaac seemed caught between anger at his son for making such a momentous decision without consulting him, and wonder—and perhaps envy—that Lucas would find himself on the shores of Africa. Most days, Lysbeth's cheerful words belied the sadness in her eyes. Anneke knew that her mother keenly felt Lucas's absence.

Anneke missed her brother, but she also grieved for the end of the lessons, and perhaps a bit for the end of her queries to the handsome tutor. He had said that she could contact him if she had questions, but she could hardly envision herself being so bold, or devising the circumstances in which they could meet. So, as she colored the work of men she had never known, she imagined their process. What were the notes they had worked from? How specific were the details? How much had they simply guessed when information was lacking?

She had learned a great deal of how the process worked, and she could only hope that it was enough for her to create the map her father had spoken of for so long. She would keep it a secret, both because she planned to surprise Isaac with it and because she was not yet confident enough in her talent and skill. She did not want anyone attempting to dissuade her from at least trying, for she feared that she might be vulnerable to their arguments.

Several months after Lucas had gone, Lysbeth heard that Heer Alders had been replaced and that a new director, a master colorist himself, was overseeing the colorists at Blaeu's. She hadn't met him, though, since she usually only went to the shop to drop off completed maps or to pick up new ones, and she seldom lingered. Anneke asked her mother whether the change would affect their work, but Lysbeth replied that she had worked under several different men over the years and they rarely bothered to involve themselves directly with colorists at their level.

As it happened, however, the new director was paying close attention to the maps brought to him by those who worked at home, and he began noticing the different styles coming from the house of Lysbeth Plettenburg. He had been told that her children, Anneke and Lucas van Brug, also colored for Blaeu. He had taken to separating the maps from that household into two piles, determined by their styles, knowing nothing of those who worked so diligently on their assignments. Then one day, he sent a message to the father of the family, Isaac van Brug, asking him to come to the printing house. At first, Isaac was incensed at what he perceived as the colorist's temerity, summoning him in this manner, and even considered not complying. But Lysbeth convinced Isaac that they could not afford to ignore a request from a representative of the business that helped to support them.

So it was that Isaac van Brug presented himself at the printing house, a place the other members of his family could have found in their sleep but whose threshold he had never deigned to cross. When Heer Meyert, the master colorist, ushered him in, gushing praise for the work of his family, it was difficult for Isaac to hide his surprise. "I am told that your wife, Vrouw Plettenburg, has colored for this house for many years," he began.

"That's right," Isaac curtly replied.

"And that your children are also working for us as colorists?"

"That was true, but my son, Lucas, stopped when he became a student at the cartography school three years ago, and now he has gone to sea."

"Ah, that would explain it."

"May I ask what you think that explains?"

At this, Meyert reached for two piles of maps on his desk. "I have been taking a careful look at the work of all the colorists since I came here. I had noted two different styles of coloring coming from the van Brug house, and having been informed that there were three colorists, I was somewhat perplexed. Can you look at these and tell me who in your family colored each stack?"

Although Isaac rarely took the time to seriously examine his family's coloring work, he did know his wife's style, as she had been coloring for many years. He knew in his heart that his wife had considerable talent, but he was astounded to see the level of skill in the other stack of maps, which must have been colored by his daughter. Seeing several completed maps together, he understood that her level of accomplishment was far above what he had realized. He didn't know what was valued as a map colorist, but as an artist, he appreciated the precision of the work and the subtleties in color use that she had been able to achieve within the limited scope of the given task and materials.

"This stack must be those done by my daughter, Anneke," he finally responded.

"I see. And how old is your daughter, Heer van Brug?"

"Old enough to have colored these!"

"Please, do not mistake my meaning, Heer van Brug. I am not implying that she is too young. As we can both see, her work can be judged better even than that of your esteemed wife. The reason I ask your daughter's age is that we would like to offer her a more advanced colorist position."

"What would that entail?"

"Well, under my supervision, she will be given ever more

important assignments. In order for me to keep a close eye on her progress, and to give her help when it is called for, she would need to work here, at the publishing house, rather than in your home."

"I don't see how my daughter working within the proximity of so many men at the printing house can be at all acceptable."

"But would not the fact that there are so many people working here, as well as others going in and out all day, ensure her security? If anyone were disrespectful, there would be many to witness it."

When Isaac still hesitated, Meyert added, "Perhaps you can discuss it with your wife, Heer van Brug. After all, she has worked for the House of Blaeu for many years, and she knows that we run an honest and honorable establishment."

The suggestion that he needed to consult his wife in his decision-making annoyed Isaac, but as he needed time to think this through, he took his leave, promising that he would inform Meyert soon of his decision.

"This is a wonderful opportunity for Anneke!" Lysbeth said when Isaac told her of his meeting with Meyert. "She will receive further training, a higher wage, and, being in the shop, she could even come to the attention of Heer Blaeu himself, who might assign her to some important coloring commissions."

"But why does she need to do this? She is a girl. Isn't it her destiny to become a good wife and mother?" Isaac asked.

"And am I not a good wife and mother, though I have been doing this work for many years?"

"Of course, Lysbeth, but you have always worked within the shelter of our home."

After a moment, Lysbeth replied, "You speak of Anneke becoming a wife and mother, but we do not have enough saved to give her the kind of wedding feast and celebration that we would like. Some of her extra income could be put toward that." Then, looking her husband in the eye, she added, "Besides, it could be that she will need to contribute to the financial well-being of her future family."

"Very well. You and Anneke have my permission to call upon Heer Meyert at Blaeu's."

"Wouldn't you care to accompany us, husband?" Lysbeth asked, now that she had prevailed.

Isaac didn't respond as he left the room and headed for his studio.

As Anneke and Lysbeth made their way along the Bloemgracht to Blaeu's the next day, each was lost in her own thoughts. Finally, Lysbeth broke the silence.

"Well, daughter, it seems you have made quite an impression."

"We will see what Heer Meyert has to say, will we not? It could be that Papa exaggerated or misunderstood. Maybe he was not even referring to my maps, but yours. After all, you alone taught me everything that I know."

"You need not say so, child. We both know that your eye and skill have passed me by. I am not saying that I am not proud of my work, but it does not stand out in the way that yours does. My maps are more practical, emphasizing the utility of the map, rather than just its beauty."

"Do you think that my techniques obscure the information of the maps, Mama?"

"Perhaps they do not obscure, but I do not know whether they emphasize."

"And what did you think of Lucas's work, Mama, if I may ask?"

"Lucas's heart was never in the work itself, but in the places he imagined as he colored. I always feared that he would leave us, that he would answer the call of the sea. It is so easy for our young men to leave, with the lure of adventure the VOC and the WIC seem to offer. Who knows what exotic ports he dreamed of?"

"I hope that once he returns from this trip, he will decide to stay here. I do miss him."

"As do I, my dear. It is a tribute to you and your brother that, even through years of working so closely, you have maintained the love you owe one another. Not everyone would have gotten along so well in such circumstances."

"Perhaps it is because we never wanted the same things and could be content with the other's accomplishments."

Pondering this, mother and daughter entered the printing house of the great Joan Blaeu.

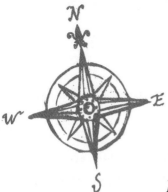

Chapter 6
December 1658

As they stepped inside the printshop, Lysbeth went to find someone to tell Heer Meyert that they were there in answer to his summons. For a few moments, Anneke watched as her mother fruitlessly searched for someone who seemed willing to interrupt his work for long enough to listen to and obey her request. Anneke's attention was soon drawn to the printing presses, however. Previously, when she had come to the printing house, she hadn't stayed long enough to take much notice of those who labored there. Now, as she imagined herself working on the premises, she took in so much more. She could almost taste the sharp tang of metal from the engraved copper plates heating by the fire. The odor of the vine black ink daubed onto the copper plates bore ghosts of the vegetables that had been burnt to make the charcoal used for the ink. The familiar trace of wood from the press and tables blended with that of the dampened paper. Overlaying it all was the stench of bodies straining.

The roller presses dominated the room, almost as tall as a man and wider than the length of a man's arm. On each side a sturdy frame held a crossbar, and between these supports was a flat surface that extended out each way. On this lay the heavy roller, which exerted immense force onto the paper and copper plates. Anneke briefly wondered whether a hand or an arm had ever been crushed beneath its power. The roller was lowered and the plate and paper moved forward when a pressman turned the huge crossed bars on one side of the press.

There was a pressman working at each station, but her eyes settled on one in particular. It was evident that great strength was needed for the task, and since the young man wore no doublet, she could see his muscles bulge from his shirtsleeves. Even so, he clearly exerted every bit of his brawn to rotate the crossbar that moved the roller. With both hands on the arm of the cross that was closest to him, and a foot on the arm below, he pulled the wheel toward him. It slowly moved, and the paper and plate were brought forward to pass underneath the roller and emerge on the other side, another printed map to be hung to dry.

The pressman's face was as wide at his jaw as it was at his forehead, and his nose seemed slightly large, but it was a pleasant face. As he pulled on the arm of the cross piece, his eyes looked upward as though the sights of the printshop might distract him from the concentration of his energy, and his mouth was open as though in a silent scream. Or perhaps it was a prayer. As another map rolled out, there was a moment's rest as the next paper was applied, and then he was called upon to again repeat his Sisyphean task.

Work requiring strength and agility was an everyday part of life, but not so prevalent in Anneke's life that she was unimpressed. In her home, it was the quiet, delicate work that prevailed, and though she knew that this, too, took its own toll, it was more the slow, building ache from bending over a map, the occasional sharp pain or numbness of the hand, the headache that sometimes came from the constant odor of the coloring agents. Sometimes her face would even ache, and she would be reminded of the many times her mother had scolded her not to grimace so at her work, that it would cause lines to appear before her time. It was not that she disliked her work, but simply that she seemed incapable of maintaining a serene countenance when she was so completely engrossed in the coloring of a map.

Looking at the pressman again, she could see that lines were form-ing on his face, though she could tell from his body and his eyes that he was young. That would make sense, too, for an apprentice could be used for this relatively unskilled task. She hoped that he would be allowed to train in something less wearing before his face prematurely became that of an old man.

Her observations were interrupted as she saw a man approaching and greeting her mother, who then led him over to where Anneke stood.

"Heer Meyert, this is my daughter, Anneke van Brug. Anneke, Heer Meyert, the master colorist," Lysbeth said.

"Good morning, Juffrouw van Brug. It is a pleasure to meet you." Anneke looked up at the tall, slender man. His hair was thinning but he was not as old as she had imagined he would be, and she thought that he must be quite talented to occupy such a lofty position.

"Good morning, Heer Meyert," she said as she gave a brief smile.

"Let's go somewhere a bit quieter." He led the two women to a small room that was cluttered with maps, paints, brushes, folios, and even an unfinished globe. He did not close the door, but the objects seemed to absorb some of the din from the printing room.

"Please, sit down." He directed them to the two chairs while he looked around and finally settled himself on top of a barrel. Anneke could tell that this simple courtesy impressed her mother, but it also put him at a greater advantage as he looked down upon them from the height of his makeshift seat.

"So, Juffrouw van Brug, your mother informs me that it is you whose maps I spoke to your father about," Heer Meyert said as he looked at Anneke intensely but not unkindly. "Although I have not been in my position long, I have made a great effort to acquaint myself with the work of the colorists that we employ. For some reason, our records had not been changed to reflect that your brother no longer colors for us, and I was surprised that I could discern only two styles. I had no way of knowing who had done which maps, and I confess that I assumed the more accomplished ones to be the work of your mother or brother. I was a bit humbled at learning that this was incorrect."

"A very natural error," Lysbeth rushed to say.

"You do not need to try to salve my pride, Vrouw Plettenburg. I assure you, I hold myself in high enough esteem," Heer Meyert replied with an upward curve of one corner of his mouth.

"I find your use of color, Juffrouw, to be most interesting, though somewhat unorthodox. Many of our wealthier clients purchase our colored maps for the aesthetic pleasure as much as for the information they convey. I must admit," he added with that same half-smile, "that some of our engravers see the work of colorists as obscuring their efforts. I understand their concern to some extent, but I am here to sell maps, and to sell them for as high a price as we can get."

"I do believe that our efforts can often enhance rather than detract from the information given in a map," Lysbeth couldn't help saying.

"As it happens, I agree. But that is a debate that we will never win with the engravers. Now, Vrouw Plettenburg, as I told Heer van Brug, I would like to propose that your daughter come to work here, at the printing house, so that I may more closely guide her and watch her development as a colorist. I daresay that I may even learn something." Now his smile was full as he looked at Anneke.

"Well, what say you, Juffrouw?" Heer Meyert asked.

"Might it be possible to know a few more details of what the work here would entail?" asked Anneke in a low voice.

"You would come here each day, except for the Lord's Day, and you would do your coloring work here. I, as well as others I might call in, will observe you."

"How much would you pay her?" inquired the ever-practical Lysbeth.

Heer Meyert's reply showed that he had both contemplated and prepared for this question. Answering Lysbeth's inquiry, but addressing Anneke, he said, "Well now, that would depend upon what you accomplish. Heer Blaeu has given me permission to offer you double the number of stuivers you are presently paid per map. In all fairness, however, I would caution that you might not be able to finish maps as quickly, as you would occasionally need to discuss what you are doing with me or others. On the other hand, I believe that your raw talent would be developed here, to your advantage and ours. In addition, you would not have the distractions of working in your home."

Anneke thought that the distractions of the printing house, as she had already seen, would be far beyond those at home. Still, they might find a quieter corner for her to work in. This time, her voice was less timid than before. "It is questionable whether the distractions would be less, and I would forgo the loving atmosphere of my own family's home."

"I do have other colorists that I am interested in. If you do not wish to accept my most generous offer, then I pray that you take up no more of my time," Meyert said as he began to rise.

"We did not say that!" Lysbeth intervened. "Please, we must talk this over with my husband. Can you allow us two days to decide?"

"Two days. Past that, I will find someone who will appreciate my offer." With that, Meyert stood and left the room with a muttered, "Good day to you!"

Despite his clear irritation with them for not giving an immediate answer, Meyert had given them two days, and Anneke, having seen her mother's interest in his offer, felt confident that they would be returning with a positive response.

As she neared the press room, Anneke glanced over and saw that the young pressman she had noticed when they arrived was no longer there. With some surprise, she noted her reaction to this. How could she think of some young man she had seen for only minutes when she had just learned that her life might take on a whole new direction? Perhaps she was just a silly girl, after all.

As she lingered near the door to the street, her mother having taken a moment to speak to an engraver she knew, Anneke heard from behind her, "Excuse me, Juffrouw. Might I be so bold as to ask whether you were looking for me?"

"You? Why would I be looking for you?" a flustered Anneke replied. The lines of concentration she had seen on his face before had now relaxed. She noticed the clear blue of his eyes and briefly wondered how she would mix paints to achieve it.

"Though I was at the press when you entered, I felt your gaze on me. It is so seldom that we get a young woman such as yourself in the printing room that I couldn't help but notice you. My name is Daniel, by the way."

"I don't know what you think you saw, but I was studying the press. Good day to you!" Anneke turned and hurried toward the door, and although she knew there was no other way that she could have properly responded, she still regretted rebuffing the engaging young man with the good name.

For his part, Daniel was not discouraged but rather amused at the young woman who had so clearly been watching him as he strained his muscles to work the press. Perhaps, once he had noticed her observing him, he had exaggerated his movements a bit. He had vaguely recognized her as someone he had seen enter the shop before to pick up or drop off maps. But today he had noticed her as soon as she had entered the printing room. It was not just the auburn hair that flowed below her cap, but everything about her seemed more alive with color. Her bodice was an emerald green, its sleeves a paler tint of the same hue. Her skirt was a bright blue, and though Daniel hardly considered himself an expert on such things, it seemed to him that this was both an unusual combination and one which not everyone would carry off as well as did this young woman.

When he had gotten close enough to speak to her, he noticed that the green of her bodice matched her eyes, and that through her hair she had woven a blue ribbon that echoed the color of her skirt. Even more than this, he had seen the way that, despite her words, it was as though she were assessing when she looked at him, and found him pleasing. And he, in turn, found that he was pleased.

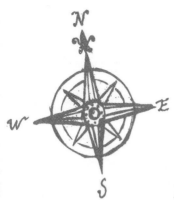

Chapter 7

February 1659

While Anneke worked at Blaeu's during the next two months, she found herself sneaking looks in Daniel's direction. At night, she often thought of him and wondered what it would be like to spend time with him away from the prying eyes of those at the printing house. This was the first time she was attracted to a young man who seemed to return her interest. There were young men at her church, but none of them seemed to take any notice of her. Occasionally, she had tried to gain the attention of some particular boy while her parents conversed with the other church members of their generation as people gathered outside for a few minutes each week after the service. Either the fellow had not been receptive or she herself had decided, after a few minutes' dialog, that the young man did not, after all, catch her fancy.

Anneke understood that she was more serious than many of the other girls her age, and although she sometimes participated in their chatter about the boys of the neighborhood, she knew that she was looking for more than they were. The pressman took up more of her thoughts than she could logically explain. Yes, he looked strong and had an appealing face, but his weren't the kind of good looks that the other girls would appreciate. Perhaps it was his attention to his work at the press, or perhaps it was the way he looked at her as though he were seeing only her.

Slowly they became better acquainted, finding moments to speak to one another. Still, Anneke kept in mind what her mother had said the first time Anneke had mentioned the kind young man. Lysbeth had reacted with a mix of pleasure and worry.

"It's nice that you've met someone that you can talk to at Blaeu's, Anneke, but be careful," she had said slowly.

"What do you mean, Mama? Why be careful?"

"You know a young woman must always maintain a reputation that is beyond reproach, and you need to be particularly careful at your place of work. It is unusual enough for a woman to be working there, is it not? You don't want to give anyone a chance to gossip about you."

Anneke had been taken aback for a moment, but she knew the truth of what her mother said. Still, she couldn't help but reply a bit archly, "I will act with propriety, Mama. You need not have reminded me of that." But she knew that her mother's caution had not been unwarranted.

Now as she approached the printing house, Anneke wondered how she would put her promise into practice. She certainly didn't want to give anyone reason to talk about Daniel and her, but how could she change her behavior without Daniel feeling rebuffed? Though she had known him but a short time, she decided he was the sort of man who would respond best to frank speaking. When she entered the shop, she noticed that he was, as always, already at his press. There was really no excuse for her to approach him then, and should she do so, it would cause curious glances from the others working in the shop, the exact thing that she wished to avoid. Even as she glanced his way he smiled at her, and she looked away.

When he had a brief reprieve from the press, Daniel came over to the table where Anneke was preparing her paints for the day. She understood that Daniel had carefully timed things in order to have a few moments to speak with her. In her time at Blaeu's, Anneke had learned more about the printing process itself, including what was required to ready the next map to be printed. The copper plate was heated and the ink was applied with a dabber, a round, wool-stuffed sheepskin pad with a wooden handle. The lampblack and oil ink were pounded into the lines made by the engraver. Whatever happened, the next plate needed to go into the press as soon as it was ready. There were always orders waiting and no time to waste. Woe to the pressman who let the press lie idle while a prepared copper plate awaited. Each time Daniel stepped away to talk with her, he took a small risk.

"Good morning, Anneke," Daniel said with a smile. Although this was not unusual, Anneke thought only now that Heer Meyert might object to a distraction from her work as well as his. Besides, the informality of the way he addressed her, and indeed of how she had been addressing him, might be open to misinterpretation.

"I cannot stop to speak to you now, Heer . . . Heer . . ." She realized she didn't even know his family name.

"Teller," he replied with a look of hurt and confusion. "My name is Daniel Teller."

"Perhaps we can visit a bit when we are eating our midday meal."

"Yes, perhaps we can," Daniel replied coolly and walked away.

For the rest of the morning, Anneke was distracted from her work, something which rarely happened. When she noticed that Daniel had taken his break to quickly eat the meal he had brought, and that he had not come over to her but stood talking to a worker who was hanging a wet map that had just come out of the press, she quickly got her own food and quietly approached him. He did not appear to notice her, or acted as though he didn't, and she didn't feel comfortable inserting herself into the men's conversation.

As she turned to walk away, Daniel addressed her. "Juffrouw van Brug, a moment please." She turned, and as he walked toward her, she led the way back to her work table.

"Is there something you wished to say to me, Juffrouw?" Daniel asked.

Remembering her resolve to speak candidly to Daniel, Anneke plunged ahead. "Oh, please, Daniel. I'm sorry if I seemed rude earlier. It's just that my mother reminded me yesterday that people might misinterpret our conversations. I, and you as well, cannot have others gossiping about us."

"Misinterpret? What do you think they might make of our innocent exchanges?" Daniel asked, though Anneke was certain that he knew perfectly well what she was talking about. He just wanted her to feel uncomfortable after the earlier snub.

"You know what I mean, Daniel."

"Yes, I do. They might think that I am interested in seeing you as more than just someone I work with, and they would be correct. But I see that you are in the right. We cannot just grab moments from our work to talk. I would like to see you outside of work. Our February weather keeps the canals frozen. Might you go skating with me? I believe that is often allowed by girls' parents."

Anneke was surprised but pleased at this suggestion, which seemed as though he must have had it planned. "Perhaps my parents would allow that. I'll ask this evening and let you know tomorrow."

That evening, Anneke did not wish to broach the topic at dinner. She preferred to speak to her mother alone. Even though it had been her mother who had advised her against appearing unduly interested in any of her coworkers, Anneke hoped to convince her that this was an acceptable outing. After all, many young people went skating as an innocent way to spend time together. She also hoped that Lysbeth would speak to Isaac for her.

"Mama, Daniel, the young pressman I told you about, has asked whether you and Papa might permit me to go skating with him," Anneke began.

"Oh, has he now?"

"Yes, I told him what you said, that we shouldn't be seen talking together at work so much, not that we ever spend more than a few minutes."

"Well, it sounds like you decided to be honest with the young man. I think that was the right way to go about things, Anneke, especially if you like him. No one likes to be shunned for no apparent reason."

"I do like him, Mama! From the first day, I noticed him. He is strong, and a hard worker—"

"Except for when he is talking to you . . ."

"Yes, and we both realize that we don't want to be seen as shirking our duties, or even be distracted from them. That is why Daniel suggested we meet outside of the printing house."

"That seems like a sensible solution."

"Oh, yes, Mama! Daniel is very responsible."

Smiling, Lysbeth said, "It seems that you know him well for someone you've only spoken to in stolen moments."

Blushing, Anneke did not reply.

"I suppose it will be all right. After all, your Papa and I went skating together in our early days. Your Papa will have to approve, of course."

"Mama, could you ask him for me?"

"I don't know why you are hesitant, Anneke. Your father finds it difficult to deny you most of what you wish for." Somehow, Anneke understood that asking permission to allow a young man to spend time with her was different from every other request she had ever made of her Papa.

"Please, Mama," she pleaded.

"Very well, Anneke. I'll speak to him."

Later that evening, as Anneke rested in her bed cupboard, she heard her father's voice rising. It was much louder than the quiet whispers she usually heard from her parents.

"A pressman?" Isaac had said to Lysbeth. "A pressman? Surely our Anneke is meant for better than that. Besides, she barely knows this young man."

Anneke strained to hear her mother's response. If felt odd and disrespectful. The whole family slept in the same room, and for her entire life, she had studiously ignored whatever she heard from the other family members' bed cupboards. It was the only way to give any impression of privacy in the close quarters in which most Amsterdam families lived.

"She has had some weeks to get to know him," Anneke heard her mother say, "and she is convinced that he is sensible. Besides, Anneke has a mind of her own, Isaac. I think that if we try to stop her from seeing him, she will still find a way. I would rather know the circumstances in which they meet. Besides, being a pressman is honest work, and perhaps he has ambition to go higher in the printing house. At least we know that he works for a reputable and stable business."

"I had hoped for something better for her, perhaps an artist," her father had said. "I know many young men in the St. Luke's Guild."

Anneke was surprised to hear her father say this, for until the night when he had told them of Heer Meyert's suggestion, he had never mentioned anything about her possible future as a wife. Now that she thought about it, she realized this was unusual among her peers.

"An artist's lot is not always so secure," Anneke heard her mother reply, and the silence that followed told her that her mother had won.

As Anneke walked to Blaeu's the next morning, she pondered the condition that her parents had placed on the skating expedition. "We must, of course, meet this young man, Anneke," Lysbeth had said. Daniel would join the family after the church service on Sunday so that Lysbeth and Isaac could meet him. Lysbeth had said she was inclined to approve of Daniel since she had observed him at Blaeu's from time to time and he seemed like a conscientious, serious young man.

When Anneke arrived at the printing house, she immediately sought Daniel's gaze, and it seemed that he had been waiting for her, for he looked over from his press as she entered. She gave him a smile, which she hoped told him that her parents had agreed. As soon as he could get away, he came to her work table.

"Your parents have given their permission?"

"Yes, they have. They want to meet you, and they suggested that you find us after church on Sunday. It seems only a formality. I doubt they will wish to linger for very long, and after that, you and I can depart."

"It is only natural that they would wish to meet me, although I feel as though I am already somewhat acquainted with your mother, from having often seen her come and go."

"Yes, and she already has a good impression of you."

"What church does your family attend, Anneke?"

"We go to the Nieuwe Kerk. And you?"

"I have been attending the Oude Kerk, but there is no reason I cannot change. I go alone since my parents live in Leiden. The churches are only about a ten-minute walk from each other, so it makes little difference to me."

Anneke gave him a broad smile, and Daniel returned to his press.

All during the preacher's sermon, her foot resting on the bag containing her skates, Anneke's mind wandered, imagining what it would be like to spend the afternoon with Daniel. As soon as the service was over, she hastened to the door, urging her parents to hurry along. Lysbeth smiled at her daughter's enthusiasm, but Isaac didn't seem quite sure what to make of it. As soon as they left the church, Daniel was at her side. Anneke smiled at him and turned to her parents.

"Papa, this is Daniel Teller. Daniel, this is my father, Isaac van Brug."

"Good morning, Heer van Brug! It is a pleasure to meet you."

"Heer Teller," Isaac managed, adding a smile when Lysbeth nudged him with her elbow.

"Mama, Daniel Teller. Daniel, my mother, Vrouw Plettenburg."

"Hello, Daniel. I've seen you at Blaeu's, but it is nice to finally meet you."

"I feel the same, Vrouw Plettenburg. It is nice to be introduced." At this there was an awkward pause, which Daniel sought to fill. "And I would like to thank you both for giving your permission for Anneke and me to go skating together."

"See that you behave properly, young man, and escort my daughter back to our home in no more than two—"

"Three hours," Lysbeth put in.

"Thank you, Mama and Papa!" Anneke said, leading Daniel away as he called back, "I will take very good care of her, Heer van Brug."

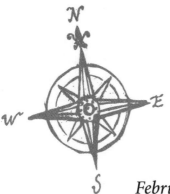

Chapter 8

February–October 1659

As they made their way to the Herengracht, Daniel took Anneke's bag and flung it over his shoulder to join his own. When they got to an entry point, they sat down and took out their skates, the long blades curving upward in front like the prow of a ship. Daniel quickly had his skates on and stepped in front of where Anneke sat, leaning down to assist her. Not since she was a little girl had anyone thought it necessary to help her with this task, but the small kindness strangely touched her. When Daniel put out his hands to help her up, she happily grabbed onto him, and they stepped onto the ice.

At first, they skated side by side, their hands clasped behind their backs and leaning forward slightly. Anneke felt the cold against her cheeks as she and Daniel sped on. Like everyone else, she had put on extra woolen layers beneath her ordinary clothes. She had not found it too warm in church, as it was almost as cold inside the building as out. Now she reveled in the freedom of skating with Daniel. She looked at the other skaters gliding past, long chains of people holding onto the waist of the person in front, older people being pushed along in armchairs on runners, children supporting themselves on chairs they pushed in front of them, and couples with their arms around each other's waists. Her eyes lingered on these last, and as though he had read her thoughts, Daniel skated closer, put his arm behind her, and clasped her waist. Her extra clothes made his touch barely perceptible, but that did not diminish her excitement at this gesture that felt so intimate.

Just as the cold seemed to be creeping through to her skin, Daniel steered them toward one of the tents the innkeepers had set up at the canal's edge.

"They have a sweetened brandy here that is delicious. Will you try some?"

"That seems extravagant, Daniel."

"Today is a day for extravagance," he said, and Anneke again had the pleasure of feeling cared for. "How about if we share one?" she said, and Daniel found her a place to sit by the fire and warm her hands while he went to the tent for their drink.

"I am enjoying myself very much, Anneke. This is so much better than stealing moments at Blaeu's to talk. I feel as though everyone is observing us, especially after your mother's warning. Here we can be ourselves."

Anneke smiled and nodded, and once they had finished their drink and were sufficiently warmed, she followed Daniel back onto the ice. Before she would have wished it, it was time to head back to her house. At the foot of the few steps to her door, Daniel took her hand and squeezed it.

"Thank you, Anneke. I hope that we can have such an outing again soon."

"As do I, Daniel." Giving him her warmest smile, Anneke turned and walked up the stairs to her door.

As she made her way to the printing house on Monday, Anneke wondered what Lucas would think of her skating expedition. Part of her felt that he would not have thought much of anything about it. Even before he left, it seemed that he had been pulling away from the family, becoming more absorbed in his own life. She had seen how he had changed when he had left the coloring room to attend classes. Still, she told herself, when they were together working with the tutor, it seemed the easy feelings between them had simply been transferred to the new situation.

Now she admitted that she may have only deceived herself. Clearly,

Lucas had planned his departure without confiding in her. That had hurt her, and it still did. *I don't need him, anyway,* she thought. *I don't care what he would think of Daniel.* But she knew it was not true. She missed her brother, who in some ways had felt like her ally. Mama and Papa had each other, and although she and Mama were close, it was not the same. She feared that when Lucas returned, they would not be able to recapture what they previously had. They would have had too many disparate experiences.

As the next days passed, Anneke kept wondering whether Daniel would repeat his invitation. She felt sure that he had enjoyed their time together, and she had shown and said that she, too, would like to see him again outside of work. They still stole moments to talk at the printing house, but no request came. Was he not what he appeared to be? Were there other girls that Daniel was interested in? Having had so little experience with men, Anneke realized that she might not be the best judge of these things. Just because Daniel paid attention to her didn't mean that he was seeing only her. Who knew what he did with his free time?

Her worries were put to rest when, after a couple of weeks, Daniel said, "If we wish to have more skating opportunities, we should perhaps do so soon. The ice won't last forever."

"I had started to think that you did not wish to spend time with me after all," Anneke blurted out.

The surprise she read on Daniel's face seemed genuine. "I didn't want your parents to think that I was too insistent on seeing you. I don't have much experience of such things, so perhaps I misjudged. I thought that I had made clear how much I enjoyed our time together. I take every chance I can get to speak with you here."

Anneke's cheeks reddened, and in the face of such honesty, she decided to be frank. "I haven't had much experience with men, so perhaps it is I who am ignorant of how things are usually done. But let's forget all of that now. When do you think we should go, Daniel?"

"I was hoping for this Sunday. Do you think your parents would approve?"

"I don't see why not. They gave their permission before. I will speak to them tonight, but let's plan for another day on the ice!" Daniel's smile and the tender look in his eyes reassured her in ways that even his words had not accomplished.

As it turned out, things were not quite that simple. This time Isaac insisted on a chance to spend more time with Daniel, and Lysbeth agreed that, rather than skating, he should come home with them after church on Sunday and share their midday meal.

"I would be honored, and I will be glad to get to know your parents better," Daniel said when Anneke shared the news. She felt a little hurt at this, realizing she had expected him to be disappointed that they would be deprived of time with just the two of them. Then he continued. "Anneke, I want your parents to like and trust me. I want them to feel comfortable with us being together." Anneke smiled, and the plan was agreed upon.

After church on Sunday, the group of four hurried to the van Brug house, the sooner to escape the cold. Isaac mounted the steps and opened the door, silently holding it for the other three to enter.

"Welcome to our home, Daniel," Lysbeth said.

"Thank you, Vrouw Plettenburg. It was most kind of you to invite me."

Since, as in many Amsterdam homes, the first room to be entered was that of the family business, Isaac's paintings festooned the walls. It was here where he met with those who might be interested in having a painting done, or even purchasing one of those on display. Anneke held her breath as Daniel entered. His reaction here would strongly influence Isaac's attitude toward the newcomer. Slowly the young man walked around the room.

"Anneke had told me that you are an artist, Heer van Brug, but I feel it is a real privilege to be able to see so many of your paintings. If I may give an opinion, they are very fine indeed." Receiving only an affirmative grunt from Isaac, Daniel continued, undaunted, as he walked back to a portrait of the family. "Naturally, I am drawn to this one," he said with a smile. "This is your son, Lucas, away at sea now?"

"Yes, that is Lucas." Isaac seemed to relax a bit. "Come through to the other room now. We want to get to know you better if you are going to be spending more time with our daughter."

Anneke grimaced at Isaac's somewhat abrupt manner, but Daniel seemed content to follow Isaac's lead.

"Of course, Heer van Brug. I completely understand. Is there anything in particular you would like to know about me?"

"Who are your people? What are your plans? Why do you want to spend time with my daughter?"

At this last, Anneke was a bit hurt. Was her father implying that she was not worthy of a young man's attentions?

"I am from Leiden, and my parents still live there. My father has a junior school in our home, and my mother often helps him. They teach reading, writing, and mathematics. They usually have ten or twelve students."

"You did not wish to help with the school?" asked Lysbeth, who had great regard for learning.

"My father and mother manage very well, and I wanted to try my hand at something else. I had a friend who moved to Amsterdam and said that there were more opportunities for young men here. With my parents' blessing, I came here about three years ago. I eventually found my place at Blaeu's. At first, I was just an errand boy, but I have now been a pressman for two years."

"And is that the height of your ambition?"

"No, sir. I hope to rise to other positions at Blaeu's. I have schooling, and I would hope to become more involved with the business aspect of a printing house, either at Blaeu's or elsewhere."

"Well, it does seem as though you have some ambition. And as to my last question?"

"Surely you know how delightful your daughter is, Heer van Brug. She is intelligent, sincere, and thoughtful. I very much enjoy her company."

Anneke glowed at Daniel's praise. He had said nothing of her looks, and though she knew it to be vanity, she wondered if he found her pretty.

Just as Isaac began another question, Lysbeth interrupted him. "Really, husband, I think that Daniel has stood up well to your queries. Let us have our meal now. We can surely get to know more of one another in comfortable conversation."

Isaac acquiesced, and they passed a pleasant few hours. Isaac remained more aloof than his wife, but Anneke had heard that it is sometimes hard for fathers to accept the young men who show an interest in a beloved daughter. She forgave her father for his manner and appreciated her mother even more.

After Daniel left, Lysbeth said, "He seems a very good young man, indeed." When Isaac only grunted, Anneke couldn't help but ask, "And what did you think of Daniel, Papa?"

"I suppose your mother is right."

That would have to be enough, Anneke realized. They would not object to further outings with Daniel.

Over the next few weeks, Daniel and Anneke skated most Sundays, with Isaac and Lysbeth even joining them several times. It seemed to Anneke they did this to demonstrate, perhaps especially to Daniel, that they were dutiful parents who kept a watchful eye over their daughter. At first the older pair was a bit tentative on the ice, but before long they were gliding along with everyone else and seemed to pay but scant attention to the young couple. Anneke felt certain that her parents loved each other, but, as in all marriages, there were periods of disagreement. Now, on the frigid canal, she was happy to see the two so clearly enjoying each other's company.

On these occasions, Daniel seemed never to lose sight of where Isaac and Lysbeth were, and Anneke wondered why she did not command all of his attention. One day, however, there was an incident that made her grateful for this habit.

"Watch out!" Daniel called, and Anneke, looking in the direction of Daniel's stare, saw what was about to happen. Isaac and Lysbeth skated blithely on, not having heard the warning and unaware of the group of young men who were clearly engaged in a race. As the youth on the edge of the group neared Isaac, Isaac looked up but saw him too late. The two collided, sending Isaac sprawling to the ground, along with Lysbeth, whose waist he had been holding.

Daniel and Anneke had already started toward her parents and reached them in time to hear the young man mutter, "They should have been more cautious."

"How dare you say that? It was clearly you who were at fault!" Anneke yelled.

"And who are you to have a say?" The young man blustered, skating very close to her and pulling himself up to his full height.

Daniel, who had been helping Isaac and Lysbeth to their feet, now skated to Anneke and said quietly, "Please, leave this to me, Anneke." There was something in the seriousness of his tone that led Anneke to turn her back on the boorish young man and skate over to her parents. Now the three of them stared back at Daniel as he stood very close to the man, speaking to him quietly and calmly. The youth slowly took on a less belligerent stance, finally turning and skating away.

"What did you say to him?" Anneke asked when Daniel returned.

"I simply showed him reason," was all that Daniel would say.

Isaac and Lysbeth were sore but not seriously hurt. After that day, they did not again accompany the young pair. Though Isaac and Lysbeth cited their bad experience as the reason, Anneke noted that they did not seem to think the ice was so dangerous that they forbade her from skating. Daniel had proven himself a caring and capable companion for their daughter.

A few weeks later, Daniel suggested that they skate to Leiden. At first, Anneke said that she could not be out so long, but he assured her that it would only take them an hour and a half or so each way. He said that he hadn't suggested it earlier because he had wanted to be sure she was a strong enough skater. Hearing the compliment, Anneke agreed, though she was still somewhat worried about the time. When they reached Leiden, Anneke asked if they should turn back.

"Please, not yet, Anneke. I would like for you to meet my parents." Feeling foolish that, in the excitement of the adventure, she had forgotten that they lived in Leiden, she quickly agreed.

"Of course, Daniel. I would love to meet them." His obvious pleasure at her response warmed her heart. They soon exited the ice and placed the skates in their bags. Daniel led her to a narrow house not very different from her own except for the sign above the entry: "Otto Teller: Here Children Are Taught." They climbed the four steps to his parents' door and Daniel knocked.

"Do they know we are coming?" Anneke asked anxiously as they waited for someone to answer.

"No, it is a surprise." Anneke didn't have time to feel nervous, for the door opened, and a woman with Daniel's squarish face exclaimed with obvious pleasure, "Daniel! How wonderful to see you, my son!"

"Hello, Mama." As the woman stepped aside for him to enter, Daniel motioned for Anneke to precede him. When she entered, she also saw a man lingering close, obviously Daniel's father. The front room bore the marks of the owners' profession, with a large chair in front of rows of benches and shelves with stacks of quills, ink pots, and books. Anneke had only a moment to take it all in, for she was ushered through to the family's main room, and Daniel's mother warmly greeted her.

"I am Geertruyd Mauritz, Daniel's mother. And this is my husband, Otto Teller. Welcome to our home."

"I am Anneke van Brug. I am very happy to be here, Vrouw Mauritz and Heer Teller."

"Welcome, Juffrouw," said Daniel's father with a kind smile. Anneke remembered Daniel telling her that his father's students held special regard for him, for he was more patient than most.

"Mama, Papa, this is the girl I wrote to you about." Anneke blushed to hear that Daniel had told his parents about her.

"I assumed as much, Daniel. It is not every day that you bring home a young woman," his mother laughed as she embraced him.

"Come, come. You must be very cold, skating all the way from Amsterdam. I will find you something warm to drink, and I have some sugared biscuits with dried cherries, and some cheese. You must have something to give you strength for the return trip."

Over the course of the next hour, Daniel's parents showed a courteous curiosity about Anneke. It was clear that they knew something of her from Daniel's letters. When Anneke and Daniel left, she turned to him. "So you have written to your parents about me."

"Yes. After all, your parents know me. It seemed only right that my mama and papa should know something of you."

Anneke nodded and smiled, warmed by the implications of Daniel wanting her to meet his parents.

As the weather grew warmer over the next months, Daniel found new ways for them to be together. Often, they would walk or visit at Anneke's home. Once they had even gone on an all-day trip to the countryside, sharing a wagon with some of Daniel's friends from the printing house and their guests. This had been a surprise for Anneke, though Daniel had gotten permission from her parents for the extended excursion. Food was brought for morning and afternoon snacks, but they stopped at an inn for the midday meal. All of the planning that had clearly gone into the day touched and impressed Anneke. Most of all, she loved being able to spend so many hours with Daniel, and she wondered what it would be like to be with him all the time.

As fall set in, the opportunities for outings diminished greatly, such that Daniel and Anneke rarely saw each other away from the printing house. Daniel's parents had decided to close their school, saying that they were getting too old to handle so many children. Otto's new plan seemed no less demanding, as he had decided to open a bookshop. Daniel's aid was required for this. Every day that he did not work at Blaeu's, he made the trip to Leiden to help with the preparations, and then work in the shop. "I am sorry, Anneke, that we cannot see each other now, but I owe my parents whatever help I can give."

There was little Anneke could do but accept the situation, but as the weeks and then months dragged on, she began to question Daniel's feelings for her, and hers for him. She did not yet know it, but her life was about to change in ways that would push these worries aside.

Chapter 9
November 1659

Anneke closed the printshop door on the cold November wind, and as she made her way to her large desk, already piled high with the maps she would color for the week, she didn't notice the stares of the others as she passed. She was already lost in the world of color, rethinking the scheme she should use on the map that she had recently begun. She didn't see the look of the apprentices who were hanging the newly-printed maps to dry or carrying in wood for the fire. She was even blind to Daniel's gaze, though he stepped away from the press and started to follow her across the room until he heard Heer Meyert tell Anneke that Heer Blaeu wished to see her immediately.

"But what can he want?" she blurted without thinking. "Do you know, Heer Meyert?"

"I am not certain, though I have an idea. It is nothing for you to worry about. One of our wealthiest patrons called Heer Blaeu to his home the other day, and he went." Heer Meyert seemed impressed, both by the summons and the attendance.

Finding this to be no answer at all, Anneke put down the satchel with her midday meal and walked toward the door of Heer Blaeu. She wished that she was wearing her nicer lace collar, the one she wore on Sundays, but her mother had always discouraged her from using that one when she was working at the printer's. "You do not want to get paint or ink on your best collar. Besides, Heer Blaeu might start wondering whether he is paying you too much, that you can afford something so fine." Anneke had thought that Heer Blaeu would not have bothered himself to take such careful note of the details of her attire, but she had finally understood why, for all these years, her mother had never worn her better clothes when going to the printing house.

As she reached his office, Anneke tentatively knocked on the doorframe. Heer Blaeu seldom had his door closed, except when discussing something that he wished to keep private. Everyone at the House of Blaeu assumed that the open door signified a desire to always know what was going on in his establishment more than an invitation to interrupt.

At the sound of the knock, however, Blaeu turned from the table by the window, where he stood studying an engraving he had just acquired.

"Ah, Juffrouw van Brug, come in. Close the door behind you, please. Come sit down." He pointed to a lovely carved chair across from the large table at which he sat. The surface was stacked with papers, a seeming testament to his importance. "I have something to tell you which may have a great effect on your future. No need to look alarmed. I mean that it will be of benefit to you, and to me as well." Hardly imagining how anything having to do with her could possibly be of advantage to the powerful Joan Blaeu, Anneke made no reply.

"Heer Meyert tells me that he is very pleased with your progress and that together you have worked to add more precious materials, including silver and gold, to some of the maps for our important customers."

"Yes, Heer Blaeu. Heer Meyert has been very generous with his time in helping me."

"He has done so at my direction."

"Of course, Heer Blaeu."

"Well, one of our best clients desires a colorist to work in his home and do more elaborate decorating on many of the maps that he has purchased from us. You know many of the wealthier men of the city seem to search for ways to display to others their exalted level of success. For many it is paintings, for some curiosities from over the seas, and for some it is maps. As you know, there are other map printers in our city with whom we compete. The gentleman of whom I speak has always purchased from the House of Blaeu. I would like to repay his loyalty by granting his wish and lending him one of our expert colorists, namely, you, Juffrouw van Brug."

"May I ask if there are other colorists you are considering, Heer Blaeu?"

Blaeu frowned a bit at this unexpected response. "No, there are not. I asked Meyert to give me samples of our three most advanced colorists. Of course, the other two are men who have been with us for many years. When I showed the samples to this patron, he chose you."

"Did you tell him our names, sir?"

"No. Although he has been loyal to us, as I say, I did not wish to tempt him to go directly to any of my colorists."

"So, when he made his choice, he did not know that I am a woman." Anneke did not doubt her own ability but had worried the client might have chosen her precisely because she was a young woman, a young woman who would be in his home.

"No, he did not. He made his choice based solely on your work. When I told him your name, he showed no hesitancy in employing a woman. In fact, he seemed amused by the novelty." Blaeu paused. "I will not require this of you, Juffrouw. If you wish to simply continue as you are, I will still employ you. Heer Meyert told me of your father's discomfort at the thought of you working here at the printing house, among so many men. I wonder whether he will allow you to go into a private home. You may tell him the patron is a man who is highly respected. He is married, and there would always be servants about the house. Still, should you accept this offer, you should be careful in that household."

"May I ask the client's name?"

"It is de Groot. Willem de Groot."

"Thank you. I will speak to my parents, Heer Blaeu," Anneke said, then rose from her chair to leave Blaeu's office. She wondered if his caution was of a general nature, as her mother's had been, or whether there was a more specific reason behind it.

If she had seen Daniel after leaving Heer Blaeu's office, she would have told him about their employer's offer, but she did not see him, nor did she look for him. She had tried to be patient with Daniel for continually putting his duty to his parents above his desire to see her. After all, he was just being a responsible son, a trait that all admired. Still, she couldn't help but feel a bit triumphant that now she also had something that might require her complete attention.

"I was at the guild hall today, and I believe I may have a lead on a new commission," said Isaac, beginning the nightly recitation of his day. During this dinner ritual, everyone quietly listened as Isaac shared each moment of his day. No one ever questioned that this was how things should be. It had simply always been so. When Anneke had visited other homes for dinner, she was surprised to see that there was not much talk during the meal. She found this strange, and she was glad of her family's custom since everyone contributed to the conversation after Isaac finished.

As she filled everyone's pewter plate with the mutton, vegetable, and prune hutspot she had prepared, Lysbeth ventured a casual response.

"That is good news, Isaac." Lysbeth always tempered any enthusiasm at such announcements, in case the commission never came to fruition.

"What type of painting would it be, Father?" Anneke asked.

"A burgher wishes a portrait of himself, and if he is satisfied with that, there might also be one of his wife." No one commented on this, for everyone knew that, at least for artists of Isaac's talent and reputation, there was a fine balance that must be attained between realistically portraying the person and presenting them in a flattering light. Too realistic and the less-than-lovely subject might be offended. Too complimentary and even the vainest patron would protest that the depiction looked nothing like him.

It was all well and good for someone like Rembrandt van Rijn to paint his subjects as they really appeared, in all their human imperfection. No one would ever question how he had depicted anyone, for who would dare to critique the master? But for such as Isaac, there was always the chance that the portrait would be deemed unacceptable.

"When will you find out whether you will receive the commission?" Anneke asked, receiving an admonishing look from her mother.

"I hope within the week," Isaac replied gruffly. It was clear that he no longer wished to discuss the subject. "How did your work go today?" Isaac asked of the table in general, as he did most evenings.

"Fine," Lysbeth and Anneke replied, knowing this was all the response he really wished to hear, and indeed he seemed to be concentrating on dipping his bread into the juice of the stew.

Nevertheless, Anneke said, "Heer Blaeu called me into his office today."

"Oh?" Isaac looked up, refraining from passing judgment on this pronouncement until he heard more details.

"I believe it is good news, Papa and Mama. Heer Blaeu says that he is very pleased with my coloring. You know that Heer Meyert has been allowing me to use more expensive colors and has even been training me in the technique of adding gold and silver to the maps I work on."

"That is wonderful, Anneke!" Lysbeth exclaimed.

Isaac only frowned. He said, "Those who request such embellishments only do it to show their wealth to their friends. They understand nothing of the aesthetics of real works of art."

Anneke dared to protest in spite of her fear that her father would deny her this opportunity, which she now realized she wanted very much. "Does everyone who buys a painting really appreciate it as you would have them do, Papa? Don't some of them also purchase the most expensive pieces they can afford so that they can show off their prosperity?"

"Anneke!" Lysbeth reprimanded, knowing that if Lucas had spoken this way to her husband there would have been a stern rebuke. Anneke usually managed to evade Isaac's irritation, but she had hit upon a sore topic.

"It is clear that all of this map coloring has blunted any artistic sensibilities you may have inherited from me, Anneke. If you cannot understand the difference between the creation of a painting and the mere decoration of a printed engraving, then I think you should keep your opinions to yourself!"

"I do not think that you consider what your criticism says of the work I also do, and that Lucas faithfully did. This is unjust of you, Isaac," Lysbeth said.

Isaac looked at his wife with some remorse but said nothing. After several moments, Anneke said, "An important client has asked that a colorist work on some of the maps he owns. I have advanced to such a degree that Heer Blaeu included me when he showed the client the work of his three best colorists. The patron chose mine."

"He chose the work of a young girl?" Isaac said. "Does that not seem rather suspicious?"

"Heer Blaeu said that he didn't tell him the names of the colorists. He chose me because of my work."

When Isaac didn't reply, Lysbeth said, "I do not think you can say no."

"Heer Blaeu said that he would not require me to accept," Anneke admitted, "but it is clear that I would advance no further if I refused."

"You have a talent, Anneke, and I am glad that Heer Blaeu recognizes it. If you wish to do this, I think you should," her mother said.

Still Isaac was silent as he pushed his empty plate away.

"There is one other thing," Anneke said. "The work is to be done in the home of the client, Heer de Groot." As her father finally looked up, she rushed on, "Of course, his wife will be there, and their servants. I will probably not even see him."

"I have heard of de Groot," Isaac finally said. "He also owns some fine paintings."

Anneke and Lysbeth said no more. That night, Anneke again heard her parents' soft voices. The next morning, her father said that she could accept the offer.

Chapter 10

November 1659

After much discussion, it was decided that Anneke would make her own way, unaccompanied, to the de Groot home each day. She was used to walking alone to Blaeu's, and de Groot's was not much further from home. The day before she was to start, Isaac had walked with Anneke on the Herengracht to look for the home Heer Meyert had described to her so she would feel confident that she could find it on the first day of her work there.

Making her way, Anneke went from trying to plan what she would say to trying not to think about what she was about to embark upon. Every few seconds, she remembered to look about her for the house that she and Isaac had located the previous day. She wondered whether she would actually meet the wealthy Heer de Groot. Perhaps she would be supervised by a secretary. Might his wife be the person to greet her? No, she thought that wealthy women didn't usually bother themselves with things like maps. If it were Heer de Groot himself, what should she expect?

Heer Blaeu had said to her, "You must be your most circumspect, Anneke, when you are with Heer de Groot. Behave as a proper young lady at all times." She had never given the printer any reason to think that she would behave in any other way. Was he just giving her an extra reminder, since she would in effect be the representative of the House of Blaeu?

She passed ever-grander houses and finally came to the de Groot home. As in much of the city, the gables were a distinguishing feature of each house. Many on the canal street had step gables, but de Groot's had a neck, or rectangular, gable, with a shell motif at the top. She ascended the few steps, noticing that the door was not painted the usual green but a lovely blue, and she smiled at this small rebellion. She lifted the heavy silver knocker and let it fall, startled at the loud reverberation. A kind-looking man, simply but neatly dressed in black with a hint of white at his neck, opened the door and gave her an inquiring look.

"My name is Anneke van Brug. I am the map colorist from the House of Blaeu."

"Ah, yes. We had expected a colorist, but I had not been informed that a young woman would be performing that service. Forgive me for saying it, but it is most unusual, is it not?"

"I may be young, but I have been a colorist for many years, and Heer Blaeu would hardly have sent me if he did not think me capable of the work," Anneke replied with more boldness than she would have done had she more time to consider.

Smiling, the servant replied, "Of course you are correct. Forgive my impertinence."

Not knowing whether he was joking to imply that it was possible for a man employed in a house such as this to be impertinent to one as lowly as she, she tilted her head and kept silent.

"I am Warner. Please, come this way, Juffrouw." He stepped aside and gestured for her to enter. "I will tell the master that you are here."

"Oh, but surely it is not the master himself to whom I must speak!" Anneke burst out.

"And why not? He is the one with the interest in the maps. Just remember, Juffrouw, you have been sent here by the House of Blaeu, who has shown such confidence in you." Warner smiled, having echoed her own words.

Leading her to an upper level of the house, he finally indicated the room in which she was to wait. "I shall inform Heer de Groot that you are here. I believe that he will be anxious to speak with you immediately."

Anneke stepped into a room like none she had ever seen. She had been prepared for grandeur, having seen glimpses of the other rooms they had passed, and the entrance itself had been finer than she could ever have imagined. But this—*this* room was like a wonderland. Even in the House of Blaeu, she had never seen so many maps displayed at once. Everywhere she turned, there were maps on the wall. Nearly every surface of table, desk, or chest was covered with opened atlas folios showing yet more lands. Anneke had submerged herself in maps for so many hours of her life, and yet nothing had prepared her for this astounding profusion. The effect was almost dizzying, as though she were caught in a world which was not the three-dimensional one of a room in a building in Amsterdam, but rather a two-dimensional universe in which one might wander anywhere on earth simply by entering its representation.

Anneke could see nowhere that she might sit until the otherworldly sensation passed, and so she began to slowly walk around the edge of the room, looking at the maps on the walls, holding onto the edges of the furniture to keep her grounded in the reality of the space. Many of the maps had been colored, and her expert eye noted the high quality of the work done in each.

In the corner was an enormous celestial globe, transporting her even further from her current time and place. She knew how globes were made, for she had seen the gores being printed at Blaeu's, but the magic with which they had been fit together to create the perfect sphere, the seams barely discernible, added to the room's marvel.

As she finished her circuit of the room, she realized she had been there for almost an hour, lost in the lands depicted. Heer de Groot was not all that excited about meeting with her, it seemed, to make her wait so long. As she had no prior experience dealing with men of de Groot's stature, save perhaps for Heer Blaeu himself, she didn't know whether his behavior was an insult to her or simply to be expected.

In all, the atlases must have contained hundreds of maps. It seemed that many had been printed decades ago, and although Heer Blaeu had spoken of Heer de Groot's loyalty, she realized that there were also maps here from other printers. She knew that different maps of a given area would often be the same, or only very slightly altered, even if they had come from different printing houses and were reproduced many years apart. Copying maps from other printers, and even purchasing their copperplates, was the way that things had always been done; entirely new maps were rarely added. Thus, within all of these atlases, there might well be many copies of the same map, simply contained in a different folio.

With the thought of why she was here, she now began to look more closely at the various maps lying on all the surfaces. Most of these were not colored but were simply the black imprint. The printing itself was well done, the lines crisp and clear. She wondered if any of these were to be part of her assignment here. How would her work proceed? Would de Groot choose individual maps for her to work on? Considering how fine this room was, she began to wonder whether she would, in fact, do all of her coloring here. Surely Heer de Groot, when he understood what would be involved, would not wish to have her work in these surroundings, with the untidy mess that would be created, no matter how careful she might be. The more she thought about this, the more she convinced herself that working at Blaeu's would, indeed, be possible.

"What do you think of my collection, Juffrouw van Brug?"

Spinning around, Anneke saw a tall, thin man in his early thirties dressed in rather flamboyant clothes, but of such obvious quality that they avoided mere vulgar ostentation. His fine doublet was struck through with gold threads, and under the slashed sleeves, one glimpsed golden-colored silk. His breeches were of black velvet, and the canion rolls at the tops of his stockings were trimmed with lace so exquisite that Anneke briefly thought that it was wasted in such a lowly spot.

"I am sorry if I startled you," came the deep voice again. "I had thought you were expecting me," he continued with a wry smile.

"Oh, yes, I . . . I was just lost in . . ."

"My world of maps?"

"Yes, that is precisely it."

"But you have not answered my question. What is your opinion of my collection? I am interested in the thoughts of an expert such as yourself."

"It is most generous of you to term me an expert. It seems to me that 'collection' hardly seems an adequate word for what you have here. From what I have seen, it is an astounding array showing both the depth and breadth of the entire state of cartography of our time."

"Beautifully put, and I thank you for the compliment. When one has devoted as much passion and expense to such a hobby, it is most gratifying to hear it praised. Forgive me, but I haven't yet properly introduced myself. I am Willem de Groot, and you are Juffrouw van Brug, I believe?"

"Yes, Heer de Groot. It is an honor to meet you."

"The honor is mine, I assure you. When Heer Blaeu told me the identity of the colorist whose work I had chosen, I was momentarily dubious. So young, and a woman? But your work spoke for itself, as I had already seen. Besides, both Heer Blaeu and Heer Meyert assured me that your skills and your artistry are among the best in Amsterdam today. And if you are among the best in Amsterdam, then you are among the best in the world. Is that not so, Juffrouw van Brug?"

"The way you phrase it, sir, I can only reply in a boastful manner, else impugn the fame of our city's entire artistic community."

"Well said, and testifying to a maturity of understanding beyond your years. You are, indeed, an unusual young woman. But, let us get to the subject at hand. As I told Heer Blaeu, I would like to hire you on a trial basis, for even though you have the testimony of the House of Blaeu as to your worth, I am a man who needs to observe things for himself.

"We shall begin with one of the maps that is, perhaps, less important to me, and I would like to see what you are able to do with the paints that you most commonly use. If you do well, we will proceed to more complex—and costly—methods. Heer Blaeu tells me that you have used some of the more precious paints, such as ultramarine, and that you have applied both gold and silver. That is so, is it not?"

"Yes, Heer de Groot. I have been trained in the latest mode of using the finer embellishments available."

"Excellent! I see my maps not only as information but as the kernels of works of art in themselves, their beauty coming to fruition only by the most meticulous and harmonious use of color and fine metals. I have seen some of the maps in the collection of my friend, and your employer's acquaintance too, I believe, Laurens van der Hem. He has had some very fine work done on some of his maps, and I confess to a feeling of envy. It seems that every time I see him, he speaks of his continuing quest to find the best colorist in Amsterdam. Indeed, given the quality of his collection, I wonder at his feeling that he needs to continue searching. But you are to be my secret, Juffrouw van Brug. I am placing much hope in you and your abilities."

"Thank you, sir. I shall do my utmost not to disappoint."

"Very well. Let us begin our experiment."

For the next half hour, Anneke listened to her new employer's monologue about what map to start with, arguing with himself about which one he would be willing to sacrifice should Anneke's skills prove to be a disappointment, yet not wishing to expend her time and energy on an inferior map should her talents prove to be as praiseworthy as Blaeu had claimed. Finally, he settled on one.

"I see that you have come with a case. Do you have everything you need to start today?"

"I do have my materials, but I wonder, Heer de Groot, if it wouldn't be better for me to work at Blaeu's. You know, there will be a great many things I will need to spread out. I will need to make the tartar lye and the gum water. That will require not just the ingredients, but also glasses, shells, and water, and I would need to use the fire. I suppose I could make those at home or at Blaeu's and transport them here. But that does not even begin to speak of what I will need to make the colors." Anneke had spoken this last so rapidly that she felt out of breath. As de Groot only gave her a crooked smile, she continued. "And this is such a magnificent room! How could I bring all of that in here? And there is hardly any place to work, with maps everywhere."

As de Groot still said nothing, she faltered. "Or perhaps you don't mean for me to work in this room at all, but in some humbler room of the house," she finished weakly.

When she had remained silent for several moments, de Groot finally spoke. "Oh, no, Juffrouw. It is here you will do your work. In my home, and in this room. I had hoped that you would find it inspiring, with all of these maps."

"Oh, it is! It's just that—"

"Do not worry, Juffrouw. I myself will move some of the maps to make space for you, and I have servants to clean any mess you might make."

Knowing that she was defeated, Anneke said, "I do have what I need to make a bit of a start today if you wish it."

"Splendid! Let's proceed then. Will that table there suffice for your needs to begin?" He pointed to the largest one, whose top was somewhat angled and with a ledge at the bottom, though it was not as vertical as a painter's easel. When she nodded, he began removing the maps from it, stacking them on top of those on other tables. Anneke waited, and once the table was cleared, he placed the chosen map on it and looked at her expectantly. "Well, there you are! Tell me, how will you start?"

The map he had chosen was one of Helvetia. Anneke noted that he had not, by any means, chosen an easy depiction for her to begin. Still, she had colored this map several times before, both at home and at Blaeu's. It was a popular map. It was a map that required a fair amount of work due to the many geographical features depicted, mainly the area's many mountain ranges.

"I am assuming that you wish to have more coloring, rather than less, done on your maps. I mean to say, I intend to first paint the mountains of the map, if that meets with your approval," Anneke said.

"I leave it entirely in your hands, Juffrouw. You see the types of coloring I have seen fit to purchase previously, so let that be a general guide to you, if you wish. However, part of why I was interested in your work was that I noted that you have something of your own unique style."

Nodding, Anneke got out the materials that she would need. She had brought only a few prepared paints with her, but one was a copper green that would serve well for the mountains. She carefully took out the stoppered vial and a camel hair pencil in a duck's quill. Setting the glass on the table, she pulled out the stopper, taking care to hold the vial tightly as she did so. Next, she dipped the quill into the paint, then stroked it against the side of the container so as not to have so much paint that it would drip onto the map. Repeating the procedure, she continued the coloring. Soon she was completely engrossed in her task. When she finished a section of mountains, she straightened and stretched her back. De Groot had stood next to her the entire time, and he also seemed to come out of an intense concentration.

"This is fascinating," he murmured.

"Really, Heer de Groot, this will take a very long time. I will not be able even to finish the mountain ranges today. Surely you must have more important matters to attend to," Anneke said.

"Are you trying to dismiss me, Juffrouw van Brug, from my own map room?" Anneke blushed, realizing that her statement could have been perceived as both rude and presumptuous, but de Groot was smiling. "I'm afraid you will have to get used to working with an audience, at least for a while. I am intrigued by this entire process."

"So you have not had a colorist working in your home before, Heer de Groot?"

"No, you are the first."

He looked into her eyes, but she looked away, dipped her quill again, and continued her work, trying not to let his presence distract her.

As she walked home later, Anneke went over in her mind everything that had happened. It was a startling beginning with a man she had just met, a man of great wealth and influence. He did truly seem interested in how she did her work, which struck her as most unusual. Normally, art collectors didn't pay much attention to the artist's process. She knew that from her father's experiences. De Groot was different in this respect. And he had eyes that shone like silver in the light, with dark hair to set them off.

When Anneke returned the next morning, de Groot was already waiting for her in the map room.

"What shall it be today, then?" he asked cheerfully.

"Well, I should continue with the map of Helvetia, though of course I will not be able to finish it today, as I will need to let certain sections dry before I proceed to other parts."

"Then would not the most efficient way be for you to color multiple maps at once?"

"Yes, that is what I usually do."

"Then we shall do that here, too."

Anneke was gratified to see that he already trusted her enough to have her start on another map, and while she worked on the Helvetia map, he chose the next one.

"Let's do this one," de Groot said, spreading out a map of the Belearides. It contained three large islands, the most important of which was Maiorca. On the left edge of the map was part of the eastern coast of Spain. She was familiar with the map. "This time, though, I want you to explain more fully what you are doing, if you please," he added.

"Of course, as you wish. Please give me a few moments to think through how to go about this." De Groot waited patiently, and her discomfort at having him observe her receded as she became immersed in the map. Finally, she asked, "Do you wish me to color the ocean also, or just the land features, the cartouche, and the decorative?"

"What would you suggest?"

"I would like to begin with a light wash of pale blue over the ocean areas. While that is drying, I can paint the outline of the map with umber."

As she began to work, de Groot watched her carefully. She prepared and applied the color for the ocean, then proceeded to the outline. He once interrupted her to ask whether she was ready for the midday meal, but she explained that she could not stop until the outline was complete, otherwise there would be a visible line where the paint had dried, even after she painted the rest.

When she finally announced that she would take a break and eat, she stood to take the food she had brought from her bag. De Groot looked at her strangely and excused himself to go to his own meal.

After she had eaten, Anneke began work on the Helvetia map again, and soon after that de Groot returned. She then checked the Belearides map to see whether it was dry enough to continue. Always de Groot sat at her elbow, his very presence a question about what she would do next. "I will color the hills and mountains on the islands and the mainland next," she said. "I'll use a copper green for them. For this work, I will use a somewhat drier brush. This will take quite a while, so it is the last thing I will be able to do today. I imagine that it will be somewhat tedious for you."

Without replying, de Groot simply smiled and stayed by Anneke until she finished for the day. "What will you do tomorrow, then?" he asked as she was clearing her materials away.

"I will do the borders of the islands and the mainland. I will outline them in black, then, when that has dried, I will do an inner line of another color, perhaps sienna for Maiorca, cyan for Menorca and the mainland, and cerise for the other small island. If I can do all of that tomorrow, I will work on the cartouche, the heraldic devices, and any other decoratives on the following day."

"Very well, Juffrouw. Until tomorrow," de Groot said, and Anneke felt gratified at the ease with which they already spoke to one another.

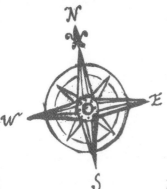

Chapter 11

December 1659

Anneke had been working at de Groot's home for more than three weeks before she met his wife. She hadn't known how to feel about this since she had never had personal contact with such a wealthy woman. Was it strange that the mistress of the home didn't meet her sooner, or was Anneke making too much of her own importance? Perhaps it was to be expected that such a grand lady would not waste her time on such as she. Then, one day, as Anneke and de Groot were bent over a map while she explained what she was doing and planned to do next, de Groot's wife swept into the room, her silks rustling.

"Ah, my dear, here you are," she said. "Closed up with your colorist, I see, and dead to the rest of the world."

"Juffrouw van Brug was just explaining to me how it is that she plans to color the cartouche on this map, and—"

"Yes, yes, yes, spare me the details. But aren't you going to present the young lady to me?"

"Pardon. Of course. This is Anneke van Brug. Juffrouw van Brug, this is my wife, Helena Kregier."

"It is an honor to meet you, Vrouw Kregier," Anneke said, torn between a polite nod and a slight curtsey, and managing only to look awkward.

"Not at all, my dear. You have no idea how relieved I am for Willem to have someone else with whom to talk about his maps. It is a passion for him, but for me, it has all become rather tedious."

Not knowing how to respond to what seemed to Anneke a rather personal and unkind comment, she said nothing.

"Oh, don't look so serious, Juffrouw! Willem knows that my interest in his maps has long since been exhausted. That is why I fully supported his idea when he said that he planned to ask Blaeu if he had a colorist in his employ who could come here for an extensive commission." Here Vrouw Kregier paused. "I did not realize that the colorist would be a young woman, and so lovely."

Anneke bent her head and wondered whether the lady was somehow jealous, but she pushed this thought aside. How could such a beautiful, elegant woman feel threatened by her?

"Really, Helena, you are making our young colorist uncomfortable," de Groot protested.

"Oh, I'm sorry, Willem! I shall henceforth be more careful of her feelings. Well, it was very nice to make your acquaintance, Anneke, if I may call you that. And now I must see to the kitchen staff, as I have some friends coming for the midday meal today. Perhaps one day you can join us?"

"It would be an honor," Anneke replied, sure that the offer was not sincere but was perhaps meant to give her false hopes of joining such august company.

"Enjoy your friends, Helena," de Groot said in a tone that felt like a dismissal.

After Helena left the room, de Groot said, "I am sorry if she made you feel uncomfortable, Juffrouw. My wife is not always sensitive to the feelings of others."

"Not at all. She was most courteous," Anneke replied. She realized that she was not used to the ways of folks such as these, but she did feel fairly certain that Vrouw Kregier was skilled at walking the fine line between graciousness and disdain.

The days passed quickly at de Groot's, and Anneke became ever more involved in the work. It didn't take long for the collector to completely trust her skill, and he told her that he wished her to use the very best colors available. After another month, he said, "I believe that you know how to apply gold to the map, do you not? I have seen it done on some of my friends' maps, and it is quite beautiful. Cost is of no consequence." Then he amended his statement with a wry smile. "Actually, I should admit that the more precious the materials, the better, for that will increase my prestige with my fellow map enthusiasts."

"Yes, I was trained at Blaeu's to add precious metals. Still, it has been a while, and I am hesitant to immediately begin on one of your maps. I would like to practice on a sheet of paper before applying it to a map. That would, of course, waste some of the gold, but I believe that it is better than trying it first directly on a map and risk ruining the entire work."

"I trust your judgment on how to approach it. You may buy what you need at the shop, as you have done for the other materials, on my credit there. How is the gold sold?"

"One purchases gold leaf in the form of a tiny booklet, no larger than the palm of my hand, of very thin sheets of gold. A sheet is then ground on a rubbing stone with honey, water, and salt. Then it must be washed until thoroughly clean. This will yield a very small amount of liquid gold, which I will store in a shell. A bit of vinegar can then be added to improve consistency."

"It seems you understand the process well. Please commence as you think proper."

Any illusions Anneke had that she would at times be able to color at Blaeu's, or even work alone in de Groot's home, were soon dispelled. He was always in the room when she was there unless he had pressing business to attend to. At times, he even brought his papers into the room and worked on them while Anneke continued to transform his maps. To say that he hovered would not be accurate, for that would have implied that his attention was unwanted. In fact, as Anneke got more used to his presence, she found that she relished the inherent compliment he paid her by his intense interest, and she understood that, at least in part, it was she herself that held him.

It was more than his confidence in her ability and his appreciation of her skill. He was open to some of the more unconventional recommendations she sometimes made, such as when she suggested a shade of purple for the compass rose, the cartouche, or figures on the map, and even some of the boundaries. Though the color was rarely used in maps and hardly prominent even in Dutch paintings, he declared himself enchanted with her use of it. She felt that he held her in esteem and showed it each day in subtle changes in his tone of voice, his look, and how he stood near her when they discussed a map. He never made her feel uncomfortable. He made her feel valued.

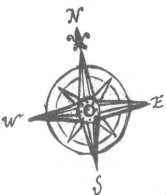

Chapter 12
December 1659

De Groot's maps were not all that occupied Anneke's thoughts. Her success at Blaeu's, and now at de Groot's, had given her the confidence to do even more. She would do it. She would create her own map.

At night, after everyone was asleep, she would sneak into her father's studio to look for his notes on Africa. It had taken several nights of searching, but finally she laid her hands on what must be the papers he had talked about since she was a child. It occurred to Anneke that it was odd the papers, which seemed to loom so large in her father's mind, would be stashed in such an obscure spot. It didn't matter, though. What mattered was that she had found them.

She took them to the loft room, where she had already decided to work, since the other family members rarely ventured there. She knew it would take all of her knowledge to interpret the papers and then use that information to produce a map. That was her goal, though, and repeating it to herself made it seem somehow more attainable.

Over the next weeks, her understanding of what she had found improved. She was able to decipher the surveying notes, slowly recalling what she had learned from Lucas's tutor. It took a while to figure out which general notes corresponded with the more detailed surveying notes for any specific area, but she was finally confident that she had succeeded in correctly matching the various pieces of information.

∾

Soon after mastering Isaac's notes, Anneke began stealing into her mother's workroom to look for discarded maps that she could practice with. She first came across the old maps that Lysbeth had gotten from Blaeu's for Lucas and herself to work on when they were first learning to color. This hint of sentimentality on her mother's part touched her, and it also gave her a pang of guilt for the deception she was engaging in. She told herself there was no harm in what she was doing, and Lysbeth would also appreciate her father's happiness and pride when Anneke produced the map.

She knew where her mother kept maps that had been ruined in the painting process for one reason or another. This rarely happened, but when it did, the family had to pay Blaeu for the map. Although the maps were now useless, Lysbeth had been loath to throw out something that she had paid for. This served as a boon for Anneke, as it was these maps with which she could now begin her practice.

To start, she used the technique common to mapmakers who wished to copy, alter, or add new information. She went along the lines, making pinpricks. Then, placing it over another paper, she rubbed soot on the top sheet. When she removed it, she could connect the dots made by the soot to make the lines of the new map. Anneke did this twice in order to get the feel of the necessary precision. Next, she began copying maps, now freely sketching what she saw. Finally, she started to draw from memory the many countries that she had colored dozens of times over the years. Perhaps she went through this exercise more than was necessary, postponing the moment when she would have to begin the real work of translating her father's notes into a map.

Mostly she drew on old copies of the broadsheet her father always bought, *Tidings from Various Quarters*. In this way, she spent nothing, but since the pages were covered with print, she finally admitted to herself that she could not continue straining her eyes trying to distinguish between the printed words and the lines of the maps.

When she and Lucas had taken their lessons from the tutor, Isaac had approved the purchase of paper for their work. One day, Anneke asked her mother if she might have paper to practice what she had learned, lest she forget it all from lack of use. She described how she had been using the newspaper on which to write and how she was afraid of damaging her eyesight if she continued.

"It is harder to justify the cost without Lucas being here," her mother had at first replied. But seeing the disappointment in her daughter's eyes, she continued. "You know, Lijsbeth Philips, who, along with Jan Bouman, runs the newspaper that your Papa buys, is an old acquaintance of mine. If she could let us have some of the remains or partly damaged paper from the print each week, I'm sure that she would give it to us for very cheap, and perhaps even free. It wouldn't be high quality since it's only broadsheet paper, but would that suit you?"

"Oh, yes, thank you, Mama!" Anneke replied, again momentarily wondering at what she did not know about her mother's past. She had heard her talk of "another Lysbeth I knew when I was a girl, who spelled her name differently," but Anneke had never imagined that it was a person with such a profitable and well-known business.

Vrouw Philips had been happy to see her old friend and was more than willing to give Anneke some paper each week if she just went to her printing house to retrieve it. Anneke spent many happy evenings working on her maps, now on paper with no underlying reports of tragedies or triumphs.

Anneke's skill increased through these exercises, but she needed to concentrate more specifically on the area relevant to Isaac's notes. When she returned from de Groot's each day and greeted her mother, Anneke would ask what she had worked on. To some extent, it was an unnecessary question, as whatever maps Lysbeth had colored that day would be lying in plain view to dry. Still, Anneke talked with her mother as she walked around the room, studying the results of her mother's labor. If Lysbeth noticed this new pattern of specific interest, she did not question it. She was just glad to have her daughter's company. After the first few days of this, Anneke began to ask Lysbeth what maps she had yet to begin. She was careful to keep her inquiries casual, wanting them to sound more like an interest in her mother rather than in the maps themselves.

That this was yet another deception, Anneke tried to ignore, just as she did when she entered her mother's workroom at night to borrow maps of Africa. Occasionally she found a map of the entire landmass, but at times there would be something more specific to the areas she needed. The route Isaac had traveled with van Herder's group had begun on Angola's northwest coast, at Mols Fort near Luanda. The group had then entered Congo and proceeded in a northeasterly direction until around the area of Mannebacanÿ. Whenever she found a relevant map, Anneke would take it to her loft room and copy as much of it as she could. She would concentrate on boundaries and place names. For areas marked with many small drawings of mountains or trees, she just drew one, then a line around the area that should be filled with that symbol.

Since she worked at night, she required extra candles, which she secretly purchased with the pay she received from de Groot. When she began to fear that she was dangerously straining to see, she allowed herself to light even more candles. She hated watching her investment melt away, but what use would a colorist with diminished eyesight be?

Shortly before dawn, when the embers in her foot warmer had long since turned cold, she would again sneak into her mother's workroom to replace the map in the spot she had taken it from. She would then sleep for two or three hours and begin her day. When Lysbeth asked her if she had not slept well, Anneke would put on a feigned look of ignorance and ask why her mother would make such an inquiry.

Sometimes Anneke was able to borrow the same map on consecutive nights, but if her mother began to color it, she dared not take it for fear of smudging the coloring. One evening she surveyed the stack of maps that she had copied, all at different levels of completion. She berated herself for not having realized it before. She needed to work on one map only and add details to it as she found more information on other maps. This would allow her to have a more complete plan to which she would add the new material, as well as allowing her to sleep more. Now she spent more of the money from de Groot to purchase better quality paper.

As she worked, she was pleased to discover her ease with names in different languages. While she had not paid special attention to this as she colored, she must have absorbed a degree of familiarity with the varied labels. This would serve her well, as some of the designations from her father's papers were in Dutch, some in Portuguese, and some in a language she could not identify. As she copied these onto her map, she wondered about the people who had decided what each place would be called. If the names were in Dutch or Portuguese, what did the people who lived there call their home?

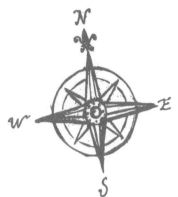

Chapter 13

February 1660

Two years after he had left, Lucas returned from Africa. Anneke was delighted to finally have him home again, and Lysbeth was noticeably relieved that he had returned unharmed. Isaac, however, was a bit subdued, and Anneke hoped that he was not still harboring some resentment at Lucas's having signed on to the WIC without asking his permission. As Anneke soon noticed, Lucas himself didn't appear to be glad to be back. It just seemed that he had no enthusiasm for his home. Anneke put it down to exhaustion. Surely it had been a trying two years, and perhaps her dear brother just needed to rest.

Lucas dutifully answered questions from their parents, but he volunteered no information. Anneke forbore from querying him, thinking that perhaps if left alone, he would soon be ready to tell them more of his adventures.

A week later, after Anneke had helped her mother with the dishes from the evening meal and their parents had sat down, her father to read and her mother to sew, Lucas suggested that they go for a walk along the canal.

"At this hour?" Anneke had asked.

"Isn't this Amsterdam, the bastion of good citizens?" he replied in a tone that prompted Anneke to try to discern his level of sincerity.

"And if the citizens misbehave, there is always the night watch," she said, trying to sound playful, but meaning it as both reassurance and warning.

"Please, Anneke." This time, there was no doubt that her brother spoke in earnest.

She nodded and headed for the door, reaching for her cloak to guard against the cold and fog. Although she had lived along a canal all her life, she always associated a chill with the dark waters, even on the warmest of evenings. This night it took no imagination to know the cold would be piercing, and Lucas reached for his mariner's jacket, which had protected him so many nights on the black and empty sea.

Lucas got the candle lantern. It was the law that every twelfth house was to hang a candle lantern to help light the street, but it was hard to enforce. As they stepped out the door, they were happy to have their light to descend the stairs. Anneke looked ahead for the next light, as she always did, each one successively becoming her goal.

"Mama does not look well," Lucas began.

"In what way?" Anneke asked, surprised that this was what Lucas so urgently needed to say.

"She is thinner, Anneke, and she is pale. Have you not noticed?"

"I suppose you might be right, but no, I hadn't noticed. If there is a change, it has been so slow and subtle that I took no note. You, who have been gone, might be more likely to be aware of it. Or, are you sure that you are not simply misremembering Mama's appearance?"

"I don't think so," Lucas answered, and they walked in silence for several moments, catching bits of other conversations as couples passed them.

"You know, Mama took it much to heart when you left us. Although after a while she did not speak of it as much, I know that she pined for you. It hurt me too, you know, especially that you kept it from me. I had always thought you and I were close."

"So we were, but, Anneke, I just couldn't risk Papa finding out and somehow preventing me from going. I had to keep it to myself. I had to go, Anneke. You know that I always longed to see foreign shores."

"You didn't trust me? You thought that I would betray you?" Anneke asked.

"No . . . Yes . . . I feared that you would. You have always been so close to Papa."

"I would not have, you know," she replied in a gentle tone, "but I do hope that your thirst for adventure has been satisfied and that you won't feel the pull to leave Amsterdam again." Getting no reply, she said, "There is something that you did not share with Papa and Mama."

"You're right, of course. Oh, Anneke, you speak of my adventures. How could you not, after hearing all of Papa's tales of his time in Africa? But it was hard work, punctuated by moments which I would rather forget. You cannot imagine what the conditions were like on the ship. I thank God that I was not a common seaman, for I don't know whether I could have endured the conditions that they suffered. Because I was assigned to work with the surveyor, even on board the ship we had better provisions, and a space somewhat to ourselves. Some of the crew died from the dreadful food or illnesses on the ship. But even that was not to be compared to the suffering our country-men inflicted upon the natives of Africa, buying and selling them, and stuffing them into ships to be taken to the New World.

"Yes, there is much that I did not tell our parents, nor will I burden you with the details of the cruelties I have seen, and of which I, too, have been guilty. You do not want to know the depth of the depravity of our illustrious merchants. If you did, you would never be able to enjoy the riches that they bring to these shores. I do not wish you to think less of me, Sister, so I will refrain from listing our heinous sins against God's children. I know our preachers would say it is all a part of God's plan, but that does not ease my soul! Rather, it makes me doubt the truth of anything they say."

They walked on a few more paces, listening to their steps upon the cobblestones. Anneke had never given these things any thought. She had no reason to, not having witnessed what her brother had. "Let us speak of something else," Lucas said then. The wind picked up and Anneke noticed that there were fewer people on the street. He said, "You must be doing well to afford such a cloak."

"Perhaps you do not recognize this as mother's cast-off. I have merely added a bit of fur trim. Besides, I have earned everything I have, and more," Anneke said quickly, sensing a rebuke in his remark. "You know nothing of my life these two years."

"I am simply trying to say that I am impressed with your accomplishments."

"Thank you." Then, after a moment, she said, "So, did you do a lot of surveying, as you had hoped?"

"Yes, and I have learned a great deal. The surveyor was most kind. He not only taught me when we were doing our work on land, but he also tutored me during the long, empty hours at sea. I feel that I am capable now of doing what is needful to become a sworn land surveyor."

"That is wonderful, Lucas! I'm so happy to hear that, and Mama will be happy, too, to know that you do not intend to take to the sea again."

"No, and that is why I have pulled you into the cold night." An unwelcome whiff from the canal floated past them, and he paused for a moment. "I understand that you have risen at Blaeu's and you work for this Heer de Groot, who must surely be a man of great influence. You could help me, Anneke."

Anneke stumbled and Lucas caught her by the arm, but she jerked away.

"What is it that you are asking me, Lucas? Back such a short time, and already looking to use me?"

"But isn't that the way of our family? From a tender age, our parents used us to make extra money. It didn't matter whether we wanted to or not. It was mere luck that each of us found something of interest in coloring the maps. The work shaped both of our futures."

Anneke walked along in silence, wishing she had another layer beneath her clothes to guard against the cold night air. "That was done from need. I see no need in you."

Now Lucas's voice grew colder than the night. "Need? Papa could have done something else, accepted that he was not an artist of the first rank and worked in trade or some other business."

"I've come to see that it is more complex than that. It is also that Mama wished for a few finer things that our income could provide. She didn't want to just scrape along, but we could have made it with what Papa provided."

"You are always seeking to defend Papa! Mama coddled his ambitions while stifling her own. I believe that she could have been a better artist than he." After a few more steps, Lucas added more quietly, "And you are the best of us all."

"So now you seek to cajole me with flattery? How little you know me, Brother." With resignation, Anneke added, "Perhaps I should have expected that after your long absence."

"It is not flattery if I speak the truth. We all know it. Even those at the House of Blaeu recognized it, just from your use of color. And now this Heer de Groot must think very highly of you to keep you working there for so long, unless there is some other reason."

Anneke said nothing. She should be insulted at what Lucas had implied, but she herself had wondered whether she had become the attraction to de Groot, and she knew that part of her hoped it was so. "What is it that you want, Lucas?"

"Only this—for you to use your influence with Blaeu or de Groot to help me to get a surveying position. I would like one fairly close to the city. I don't want to be stuck out somewhere in the countryside where all I do is measure polders for the *waterschappen*."

"And did you never think that I might sometime wish to use whatever slight influence I might have for myself, Lucas? I am not just an instrument for others' advancement."

"To be truthful, Sister, no. I did not imagine that you would need to ask for favors. Are you not satisfied with what you have attained? What else could you desire?"

"Because I am just a woman? Is that what you mean, Lucas?"

"Well, yes. You are on your way, Anneke. Isn't it fitting that I should start to advance in the world? I may someday wish to marry and have a family of my own, and I would need to have a position that would enable me to properly care for them."

"You are wrong, Lucas. I do have hope for accomplishing something for which I will need the help of those who have looked favorably on my work."

"What is it? Could it not wait?"

"I have no intention of begging repeatedly of those who have shown me favor." Feeling both her own anger and her brother's disappointment, Anneke added, "Come. The candle in the lantern is getting low. I am freezing and it has been a long day. Please, let's turn round and speak of this no more tonight." Lucas bowed his head. They turned and hurried home in silence.

As she sat down for breakfast the next morning, Anneke couldn't help but note that, as she had been doing since Lucas's return, Lysbeth had again served the more costly wheat bread, not the rye that was their usual fare. There were also two kinds of cheese this morning. As always, there was beer on the table, but today there was also buttermilk.

"This is a delicious breakfast, Mama," Lucas announced with his mouth half full.

"It is not much, but I do not know how you ate on board the ship and in foreign lands, so I want you to have a taste of home," Lysbeth said.

"Rather, a taste of something a bit finer than home," Anneke muttered. She didn't know if they hadn't heard or only pretended not to.

"Well, Lucas, you have been home for a week. I haven't seen that you have done much. What are your plans? Surely you do not intend to remain idle much longer," Isaac said as he sat down at the table.

"And if he does spend a few more days at home, I would think he has earned a rest," Lysbeth remarked.

"It's all right, Mama and Papa. No need to worry. I have a plan. I intend to become a sworn land surveyor. I learned much in my time away."

"Well, if you could achieve that, it would indeed be something to be proud of, and you would earn a good wage," his mother said.

"Yes. I do need to get my qualification and find a position. It would help to have a connection somehow."

"Might the surveyor from the ship help you?" Isaac asked.

"He has already signed onto another ship and will be leaving in a few days. It could be difficult finding a position," Lucas said, staring at his sister.

"This is delicious cheese, Mama," Anneke said, avoiding her brother's gaze.

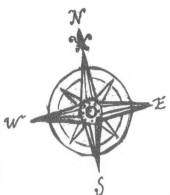

Chapter 14
February 1660

De Groot's wife, Helena, had taken to entering the map room most days. Anneke didn't know what to think of this since she had declared her complete indifference to the maps. But then Anneke began to notice that Vrouw Kregier didn't actually seem to pay much attention to the maps. A pattern emerged in which she would give her husband a brief greeting and then sit and talk with Anneke for a few minutes. After a time, de Groot would remind his wife that Anneke was there to work, and she would gracefully take her leave.

Anneke wondered whether Vrouw Kregier had begun to suspect that her husband found something of interest in his map room other than the maps themselves. Although she constantly reminded herself that he was married, Anneke couldn't deny that there seemed to be some feeling between de Groot and herself. Would his wife one day demand that Anneke do her work elsewhere? While that would harm her position with Blaeu, and she did love the type of coloring she was able to do at de Groot's, it would bring an end to this tug of feelings for her patron.

It only increased Anneke's speculation about Vrouw Kregier's motives when she was surprised one morning by Helena inviting her to take the midday meal with her and her friends on the following day.

"Yes, I've been telling my friends of Willem's talented colorist, with whom he spends most hours of every day. They would very much like to meet you, Anneke."

"Yes, of course, Vrouw Kregier, it would be an honor," Anneke replied.

"Wonderful! It's arranged then," Helena said as she left the room without even a farewell for her husband.

Walking home that day, Anneke wondered whether she should tell her family about the invitation. She didn't want Lucas to see this as yet another opportunity for her to gain influence. Neither did she wish to tell her mother. Somehow, it seemed cruel to share yet another interesting aspect of her new life.

Now, after Lucas's comments about Lysbeth looking thinner and pale, Anneke studied her mother more carefully. Lysbeth never complained of any malady, though, and so Anneke told herself that she saw no great change in her mother's appearance. Still, Anneke saw her loneliness and her great pleasure at seeing her daughter return each day. Although Isaac was home painting much of the day, Anneke knew that there was not the same feeling of companionship as the two women had felt together. Anneke had missed her mother's presence when first she started at Blaeu's, but she soon became immersed in her work there. Now that she was working at de Groot's, those days of toiling at home with her mother seemed a distant past.

At times she found herself pitying her mother, and she was ashamed. If her mother's life had been different, she might have come closer to her dream of being an artist. Anneke tried to tell herself that her mother's life was a result of her choices, mainly of the choice to marry Isaac, but she didn't know whether that was true. It was extremely difficult for a woman to gain success as an artist. Her own level of success, Anneke reminded herself, was due to any talent she had inherited from her parents, and to her mother's patient teaching.

No, she would not mention the luncheon invitation.

Despite her decision of the previous day, Anneke found that she could not keep secret the gathering she had taken part in at the de Groot's home that day.

"I was most honored today to be included at the midday meal of Heer de Groot's wife, Vrouw Kregier, and her friends," Anneke announced at dinner as she looked at the soup she was stirring in order to cool it. She heard someone sigh and knew that it could have come from her father or brother, even her mother. She was aware that she spoke too much of the wonders of the de Groot household, but she could not help herself. It was all so strange and new to her, and sharing it with her family seemed the only way to make it real, to make it an actual part of her life.

"Oh?" her mother finally replied obligingly.

"Yes, I was most surprised and delighted when Vrouw Kregier came into the map room yesterday to invite me. It seems that I am something of a curiosity to them."

"So you are an oddity on display for their amusement?" Lucas interjected.

"Why must you be so critical? Perhaps they find it intriguing that a woman may earn her keep through her artistic talents!"

"Oh, please, Anneke," Lucas said. "You are at best a curiosity to them, at worst a lowly laborer. Did you not learn that in all the years of our youth spent doing the anonymous work for Blaeu to sell to his clients?" Anneke couldn't help but attribute his bitterness to her refusal of doing him the favor he had asked. That did not excuse him for the implied insult to their mother.

"Say what you will, Lucas," Anneke responded, "but you speak from ignorance. I know how I am treated in that household. It is with respect for what I do."

"I hope that your perceptions are correct, Anneke, but do not rely on them too strongly, or I fear that you will end in disappointment," said her father.

Anneke wondered what caused his remark—whether it was his own bitterness at his inability to achieve the status he had aimed for or a real desire to spare her the pain he had come to know. She chose to believe that it was the latter.

"Tell us about the meal, my dear. Were there many delicious dishes?" her mother asked.

"Oh, yes! It was wonderful. There was a delicious chervil soup cooked in sweet milk, egg, and butter. Then it was poured over white bread. Can you imagine using fine white bread in that way? Next, there was fresh mutton cooked with prunes and mint, served with artichokes and carrots. There were also oysters stewed with verjuice, butter, and mace. Finally, there were both fruit tarts and marzipan!"

"It sounds like a feast, indeed," Lysbeth commented, trying not to feel as though Anneke's enthusiasm was an implied criticism of their own meals. "And what of Vrouw Kregier? Is she pleasant? Did any of her guests converse with you?"

"Vrouw Kregier always now greets me when I happen to see her as I enter or leave the house, and she comes to speak with me most days when I am working. She was most gracious to me today, as were her friends. They asked about my background and how I had come to be so accomplished at such a young age. Of course, I told them that my father is an artist and my mother taught me my craft from an early age."

"And how did they respond to that?" inquired her father.

"I must admit that they did not have too much to say. I took it to mean that they have very little understanding of the life of artists, or even of the work that I am doing in Heer de Groot's home."

"Was it a pleasant time for you, daughter?" asked her mother.

"Yes, it was, and I never felt like I was on display, Lucas. I was content to listen to the ladies' conversations, to enjoy the good food, and to savor the elegance of the room. There was one thing that was most entertaining. One of the guests had brought a little African boy with her. He waited upon her and everyone was delighted with how well-trained and attentive he was. The lady said that he was almost like her little pet. His skin was so black, and his hair was like lamb's wool."

"You are a fool, Anneke!" Lucas burst out. "Do you not understand what you were seeing? That child is a slave!"

"What are you talking about? Slavery is not legal in the Republic!" Anneke said.

"The buying and selling of slaves within the Republic is not allowed, but you know that the VOC and the WIC are deeply involved with slavery in other parts of the world, enslaving people and using them, transporting them, selling them."

"I do not think that this is appropriate dinner conversation, Lucas!" their father intervened.

"Not appropriate? To tell the truth? Anneke, did the lady say how this child came to be a member of her household?" Lucas asked.

"She said that her husband had brought him home with him after one of his trips for the WIC," Anneke said.

"That means that the child was purchased, torn from his family. He was bought and brought here. What do you think will become of him, Anneke? What use will be made of him when he is no longer the lady's darling 'pet'? It is hard to imagine anything for him other than a life of hardship and degradation."

There was no reply to this, and his family understood that Lucas had learned hard truths in his time away. Hard truths that no one wanted to acknowledge, for why should they be different from other Amsterdamers who did not question too closely the source of their city's prosperity?

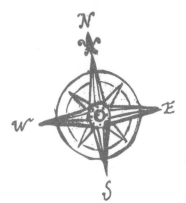

Chapter 15

March 1660

As the days passed, Anneke became ever more absorbed by the challenges of the maps she colored. She and her employer seemed to constitute their own world, replete with the countries, cities, towns, and islands—colored and uncolored—that surrounded them. Indeed, their world was even richer than the physical world in which they existed since in this artificial place, there were many maps of the same places, sometimes identical except for the coloring. They were surrounded by Swedens, Norways, Russias, Englands, Scotlands, Spains, and Portugals. There were several copies of Visscher's splendid *Leo Hollandicus*, with Holland portrayed as a lion rampant. Depictions of the East Indies, the Mogul Empire, the Japanese Empire, and the Holy Land took them further away. Even the Americas were represented with maps of Chile and Peru, Brazil, and the colony of New Netherland.

About a month after Anneke's midday meal with Helena and her friends, de Groot pulled out maps of Africa. Anneke tried to display only the level of interest that she would normally show when he selected another map to be worked on. There was one of the entire continent as well as some of more specific areas. Most intriguingly, there was also a map which, de Groot informed her, had originally been printed the previous century and contained West Africa, the Kingdom of Congo. He did not know whether there were more current maps to be found of the area.

De Groot wanted to start with the map of Africa, and as excited as she was about that prospect, she wished that he had chosen the one with the Kingdom of Congo, as that more specifically reflected the area of the map she had begun to work on in the loft room of her home. The Africa map would take several days to color. Anneke proposed leaving the ocean uncolored, and when de Groot asked whether that would then cause the ships and sea creatures depicted to look as though they were floating in air, she replied that she would do a pale blue wash just around the base of the figures. Having satisfied him, she said that in this case, she would begin by painting the continent itself, which would be entirely filled with color—aqua, rose, and yellow—placed such that the different regions would be easily discerned. As she began her work, de Groot again seated himself so that he could observe her every brushstroke. It seemed to Anneke that he was sitting slightly closer today, but she couldn't decide how she felt about that. Certainly, she made an effort not to show that she had noticed any change.

Coloring the sections of the continent took several hours, and as she announced she could do no more that day, de Groot himself reached for her cloak to help her on with it. Their hands touched. It was too obvious to simply be ignored, and Anneke rushed to fill the moment. "Tomorrow I will outline each region in a darker shade of whatever color I have used today. Then I will work outward from there on the following days, painting the ships and creatures in the sea, then the figures on the side panels. Next, I will do the small landscapes in the top panel. Finally, I will do the border of the map in ochre." Here she paused for breath, and de Groot, looking into her eyes said, "Whatever you wish, Anneke." She turned and left the room.

Anneke was disappointed to find de Groot was not at home the next day. While he seemed to place the utmost importance on the embellishment of his maps, and his presence in the room while Anneke transformed them, there were times when business concerns kept him from indulging himself in his passion. Anneke told herself that it was all to the good that de Groot was not there, for she could take out the map of Africa, and the one of the Kingdom of Congo, and begin to make copies of them. She knew they were slightly different from the ones that she had purloined from her mother's workroom, and she wanted to compare the depictions. She did not know yet how she would decide which one was correct where the information was in conflict. Being printed more recently did not necessarily mean a map had been created more recently, or even that it was more correct if it were.

Anneke began to trace the map she had started on the previous day. Although she had not tried it with her mother's colored maps, she had hoped that if she were very careful, there would be no damage to the coloring. To her dismay, however, she quickly found that the process could smudge the paint, so she stopped the attempt. While she believed that only her trained eye would discern the adulteration, she feared that de Groot's obsession with the maps might give him greater powers of observation than one would normally expect.

She set to work drawing a copy but dared not spend too much time on it, since she would need to show de Groot what progress she had made in coloring. Over the next days, she found times when de Groot was out that she could continue with her sketches, which she kept hidden in a drawer under some maps that he never looked at.

Each time she was engaged in this work, she feared being discovered. If Warner or one of the other servants came in, perhaps to bring her something to eat or drink, as was their habit, she felt sure that they would not pay enough attention to what she was doing to know that this was not one of the many steps that were involved in the task of coloring a map. She believed that the same could be said of Vrouw Kregier, who had always pointedly ignored the details of Anneke's work. However, if de Groot came in unexpectedly, he would definitely question what she was doing. And what could she tell him? Although she knew that at some point in her scheme she would tell him of her secret project, now was not the time. Besides, how would he react to her working on something of her own during time that he considered to be exclusively his?

Unfortunately, Anneke had misjudged the mistress of the house. One day, when she entered the room while Anneke was concentrating on her copying, she showed herself to have been more observant than she had pretended to be.

"Oh, Juffrouw," she said, startling Anneke. "I have never seen you do that before. Whatever are you doing? Why, it looks to me as though you are making a copy of that map. Now, why would you need to do that, I wonder."

It took Anneke a moment to recover from her shock and to pull her thoughts from the map she had been so intent upon.

"Oh, I am making a copy of the map so that I may practice some of the more difficult aspects of my coloring, such as adding precious metals."

"But I'm sure that Willem told me that you had become proficient in using gold and silver. Surely you would not now waste such expensive materials on a mere practice copy," Helena said with a smile, and Anneke berated herself for telling such a transparent lie.

"No, I—"

"It doesn't matter. In fact, it gives me pleasure to know this secret of yours. It suits my purpose precisely," Helena said, and turning, left the room.

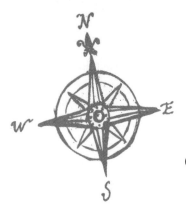

Chapter 16

March 1660

As Heer Blaeu had said that she should come in occasionally to report on her work at de Groot's, Anneke headed to the printing house. While there, she could also get some supplies. Her underlying purpose, however, was to see Daniel.

She hadn't seen very much of the pressman since starting her work at de Groot's. She felt uneasy about this, but after all, Daniel was as much to blame as she. He was still spending all of his free time traveling to Leiden to help his parents, whose bookshop was taking longer to get established than they had hoped. Anneke was also busy, and if she were honest, she knew that she had not missed Daniel as much as she might have were it not for the attraction she couldn't help feeling for the map collector. *The married map collector*, she reminded herself. But she also excused herself. One could not help emotions, as long as one did not act upon them.

When she entered the shop, she saw that Daniel was not on the press at that moment, and she went over to talk to him. "Good morning, Daniel!" she said, somewhat surprised at her own surge of happiness at seeing him.

"The same to you, Juffrouw van Brug," he replied with a wary smile. "It has been weeks since I have seen you here. Whatever might you want from a pressman?"

"Stop it, Daniel! It is true that I have not come into the printshop very much, but neither have you made any effort to see me."

"You know why that is, Anneke. My parents—"

"Yes, I know, and I understand, but it is unfair of you to take that cold tone with me."

"You are right, Anneke. It is a pleasure to see you now, at least. What has brought you here today?"

"I need to speak to you about something serious."

"Oh? And what might that be, my dear Juffrouw?"

Anneke wished she could simply tell him that she wanted to speak with him because she enjoyed his company, but what she had to say would show that to be false.

"Daniel, I have seen you speaking in friendly terms with one of the engravers, Heer Klopper. Though I have greeted him when I've seen him, he won't even deign to speak to me. I don't understand why."

At the unexpected question, the traces of Daniel's smile vanished. "Why do you care about whether Klopper speaks to you? I only talk to him because he seems interested in the work of the press, probably concerned we will somehow not do justice to his engravings. He does have some degree of power here, more than I do, at any rate, so I want to be on good terms with him. I hate to tell you, Anneke, but I don't think he likes you. I think he is a bit jealous of your success, of the attention that Heer Blaeu has paid to you. Besides, I've heard him say that colorists muddy the clarity of his engravings."

"How can he say that? We enhance his work! I, for one, am most careful to respect the lines of the engraver. I do think that most of the customers who purchase the colored versions of our works care less about the accuracy than they do about the beauty, and the prestige of having colored maps, but that fault cannot be laid at my feet. I know something of the skill of the cartographer, of the exacting precision that goes into the drawing of the map. I can only hope that in his engraving, Heer Klopper is as faithful to their work as I am to his."

"Peace, Anneke! I did not criticize your work! I am only reporting what Klopper says since you seem eager to be his friend."

"Oh, Daniel, it is not his friendship I want but his skill."

"Has your father now decided that he wishes to have some of his drawings engraved? I'm sure Klopper would not be interested,

Anneke. I'm also certain that Heer Blaeu would not look kindly upon you stealing the time of one of his engravers. Besides, why not just go to the guild? There are dozens of engravers in the city. I'm sure that your father could find one to suit his needs and his price."

"It's not for him. It's for a map, Daniel. It's a map that needs Klopper's skills."

"What are you talking about? Why would you need him to engrave a map? We're all surrounded by hundreds of maps!"

"This would be a new map, Daniel, a new map of a part of Africa. I know that Heer Blaeu is working on a tremendous new world atlas, and I was hoping that this map could be included."

"Have you lost your reason, Anneke? That is not how these things are done! You know that most of the maps will be ones that Heer Blaeu already owns, or that he will buy from other printers. Few of the maps in the atlas will be new. He may want to include some new maps, but it is he who will decide upon them, not Klopper, and Heer Blaeu will get them from scholarly cartographers, not a girl colorist."

"And how is it that you know so much, Daniel? You are yourself just a lowly pressman!" As soon as she said the words, Anneke regretted them.

Her remark had not angered Daniel. It had humiliated him, and she knew this to be the less forgivable sin. He had disparaged her place as a colorist, but he himself had in the past said that her position was higher than his.

"I know so much because I have been here for years. I study people and what they do. I try to understand how things work. I don't want to be a pressman forever, Anneke. My body wouldn't allow me to, even if I did."

"I am sorry, Daniel. I spoke without thinking."

"How could you even have such a map, Anneke?"

She didn't want to lie to Daniel, but neither did she wish to reveal to him that the map would be of her own design, taken from her father's careful notes of his journey in 1642. Although he had expressed admiration for her color work, he would never believe that she could produce a map on her own, and she feared that his disbelief laid bare would sever something between them.

"It is from something of my father's. He would very much like to see it printed, to become a part of the great atlas. I was asking for him." In a way, it wasn't a complete falsehood, but she said it with the knowledge that Daniel would misconstrue her meaning.

"Then I think that your father should look into it himself, Anneke." As she turned to go, Daniel reached out to touch her arm. "Anneke, I do miss you so very much. I am sorry for these harsh words between us. Usually, I leave right from the printing house on Saturdays and go straight to Leiden, then return Sunday evening. Perhaps I could leave early on Sunday one week instead, and you could accompany me. The boat ride is very pleasant, and though I would be busy when we are there, at least we would be together. I know that my parents would love to see you."

"I don't know, Daniel. I don't know whether my parents would allow me to be gone all day with you. When we went to Leiden before, at least it was not for so long. Besides, being only March and still quite chilly, I cannot think that it would be so enjoyable on the boat."

"Perhaps in April? Perhaps you could ask your parents then?"

"Yes, perhaps I could."

As she tossed and turned in bed that night, Anneke tried to stop the constant questions about her connection to Daniel. She did have feelings for him, but there was no denying that the lack of opportunities to spend time together had left her less confident about any future there might be for the two of them.

Unable to resolve this, she forced herself to think about who might help her get her map printed. Daniel had been right in saying that approaching the engraver was impossible. As the light of dawn crept into the room, she came up with another approach. She would look to someone else in the vast world of map printing, someone with whom she might have more in common, who would be more amenable to listening to her.

Another colorist, but one with more experience and prestige than she, might see his way to helping her. Over the years, she had heard her mother mention other colorists that she knew who belonged to the St. Luke's Guild of painters. There was Frans Koerten, who was an engraver and cartographer as well as a colorist. He was older, though—much older than her parents, even, and she doubted he would have time for a young woman still to prove herself. Her mother had also spoken of Johannes Vingboons, who was Lysbeth's contemporary and an accomplished colorist and artist. Anneke also knew that he colored for Blaeu.

Anneke wondered how she could possibly contact Heer Vingboons. The maps that he received to work on, and those that he had finished, were delivered by courier. She had seen him enter the printing house only once, and that was to go directly to the office of Heer Blaeu and to leave shortly thereafter. She could hardly ask Heer Meyert how to get in touch with Vingboons, for what excuse could she possibly give? What she wanted from Vingboons was a way to go beyond the authority of Meyert, to present to Heer Blaeu himself a new map to be included in his *Atlas Maior*.

She had thought of asking at the guild, but she was still hoping to gain membership as a master colorist someday, and she didn't want to jeopardize her chances with unfounded gossip about her asking how to contact a man. It occurred to her to ask her brother Lucas to help her. It seemed that he was no longer angry with her for refusing to assist him since he had acquired contacts in his pursuit of receiving his qualification and had been working in a new position for a few weeks now. His days were busy, but he could more easily inquire about Heer Vingboons. No one would think anything of his questions. He might not be enthusiastic about the task, but surely he would be willing to help her in the pursuit of fulfilling a lifelong wish of their father. She would seek a chance to speak to him after the family dinner, for which he was still almost always home.

It was difficult to have a private conversation in the main room, where, as in most families, everyone ate, slept, and sat when not occupied with their work, so Anneke asked Lucas if he cared to take a walk with her. He was reluctant at first, pleading fatigue from a long day. When he was doing fieldwork, it was physically tiring. In addition, and even when they were back in their work office, there was an emotional weight, as Lucas was still in the stages of proving himself. At her intense look, however, Lucas gave in and wearily rose from his chair.

After donning cloak and jacket and getting their lantern, they descended the steps to the pathway next to the canal. There were other people strolling, but the brother and sister were able to keep sufficient distance from them so that their conversation would not be overheard.

"Well, Anneke, what is so urgent that you had to tear me away from a restful evening?"

"Lucas, you know how it has always been father's dream to have a map made and published from the notes he saved from his trip to Africa with van Herder?" Anneke began.

Lucas looked at her with surprise, but responded, "Of course! He spoke of it so often when we were young, but I haven't really thought about it in years."

"Well, you remember how I particularly liked the cartography lessons with the tutor?" Anneke asked.

Lucas chuckled. "It's all right, Anneke. We can both admit that you helped me with the cartography work. I am past feeling shame at that. I did well in the surveying lessons, and it is that which I now pursue. But why do you bring that up?"

"Lucas, since December I have been working on creating a map using Papa's notes. I am making good progress."

"What? How? How is it that I knew nothing of this? What does Papa think? And Mama?"

"That's just it, Lucas. They don't know about it. Have you not noticed how sometimes in the evening I excuse myself from the family, saying that I need to go work in the loft room since I need total quiet to finish some maps? I have said that I am worried I am not working as quickly as I should, and so I bring work home to make more progress. I always take care to carry a large folder, which could contain a map that I am coloring."

"Anneke! I cannot believe that you have been capable of such an elaborate ruse!"

"But it is for a good cause. Can't you see that, Lucas? I have only done all of this in the service of trying to make Papa's dream come true."

"Why not tell him, then?"

"At first I feared that I would not be capable of producing a credible map, and I didn't want to disappoint him if that proved to be the case."

"But how did you even begin? I know that you understood the cartographic art better than I, but I cannot imagine even attempting this, Anneke!"

"You know that we have done many maps of Africa in the past, and so I felt a certain familiarity. I copied maps that Mama had for coloring, and I have also been able to copy a map of Africa in Heer de Groot's collection." Before he could react to this, she rushed on. "There is something else that I need to tell you, Lucas. I must tell someone! I've tried to put it out of my mind, but I've not been able to. I don't quite know what to make of it."

"What is it Anneke? Don't be so mysterious."

"Some of Papa's papers appear to be in a different hand, especially some of the more precise notes that contain surveying information."

"Do you mean that Papa has been telling us an elaborate lie all of these years, saying he had the information to make a map if only someone had the skill to do it for him? That was the whole reason he sent me to school, so that someday I could make his dream come true! And now you are telling me the notes aren't even his?"

"I'm not exactly saying that, Lucas. I tell myself that there must be an explanation for the difference in writing. Remember when Papa once told us that he had injured his hand on the expedition and it took a while to heal? Perhaps that explains this. Perhaps he dictated his notes to someone. Perhaps someone copied his notes for some reason."

"Did you not ask Papa about this, Anneke?"

"How could I, Lucas? It would have been to reveal my entire scheme to him, and I so want this to be a surprise! Besides, I really don't want to tell him I took his papers without having a completed map to show him, though it is far from certain that I will be able to get anyone to print it. I don't want to raise his hopes only to have them dashed."

"What does that matter, Anneke? You are too concerned with his pride. You and Mama always have been. What of the truth?"

"I have told myself that he is the true author of the notes and that somehow, someone else wrote them down."

"You are telling yourself a fabrication that you know cannot be true."

"I don't care, Lucas! I know that you do not feel about Papa the way that I do, and perhaps for good reason, but I intend to do this one thing for him. You know that he has lived a life of dreams just outside his grasp. If I can make this one come true, I will!"

"And what of Mama's dreams, Anneke? Did she not sacrifice her talent to serve his?"

"The story is more complex than that, Lucas. What Mama did was from love, from her need to keep our family together, and from her own doubt in her talents, too."

"I don't see it that way, Anneke, but I know there will be no convincing you. You have always been Papa's special child."

"As you have been Mama's, but that is not what is important here. Besides, you know that each of them loves us both. So how can you wish to deny this great gift that I want to give Papa?"

"And if it is a gift built on a lie? I would not have thought it of Papa. Do you know, I always wondered why he didn't take his notes to a cartographer and ask that a map be made. Now I understand. They were not all his notes, and that would be immediately discovered. How do you know, Anneke, that he will thank you for this? He will know that you have discovered his secret. Will that not bring him shame?"

"If he sees his map in print, I think that joy will overcome any other feelings. Besides, Mama said that when Papa first came home, he did take the notes to some map printers, though not to Blaeu."

"How do you know he told the truth? And maybe he claimed not to have tried Blaeu because he feared that Mama would discover his deceit. Even if this works, it will be one more open secret that will be kept. All of us afraid to speak of it, afraid of unbalancing the family."

"At least Mama need never know." At the look on her brother's face, Anneke added, "I do think that she will be happy for him, Lucas."

"If you say so, Anneke. There is something else, though. Do you not remember what I told you of what I had seen in Africa, of how our merchants bought and sold the people there? What if your map gives them more information to broaden what they are doing? How could you be a part of that, Anneke?"

Anneke did not answer at first. "I confess that I had not thought of that, but surely the WIC has its own maps, does it not? Maps that they keep secret?"

"Yes, I assume that they do," Lucas conceded.

"Then my map will only be giving information to those not involved with the heinous trade of which you speak," Anneke said.

"Perhaps," Lucas said slowly.

"Papa always says that knowledge is better than ignorance, does he not? Surely that is the case here. Is it not a good thing for more people to better understand a small part of the world?"

"I will not argue with you further, Anneke, though you have not dispelled my worries."

By the time they reached home, Anneke had abandoned the idea of asking for her brother's help.

Chapter 17

April 1660

Since Anneke had realized she must herself discover where Vingboons lived, she began stopping by Blaeu's more frequently on her way to or from de Groot's. She knew the colorist did not go to the printing house often, but after several weeks, her efforts were rewarded when she heard someone say, "Heer Vingboons, it is nice to see you. We don't usually have the pleasure."

"Yes, the man who normally delivers my completed maps was ill today, and it is so lovely out that I decided to come myself."

Anneke quickly stole a glance at the speaker. She then hurried to get the supplies that she needed and slipped from the printing house. She waited for Vingboons to leave and followed him until she saw him enter a house on the corner of Sint Antoniesbreestraat and Salamandersteeg. She was sure he had not seen her, but even so, she was somewhat shocked at her bold behavior. Still, she would now be able to send him a message asking for an appointment. She knew of a boy in her neighborhood who could be paid to deliver notes. All she had to do was describe to him where to find Vingboons's home. She could even accompany him part of the way if needed. She would tell him to wait for an answer, if possible, so that she need pay him for just the one trip.

She knew from talk at Blaeu's that Vingboons was unmarried but lived with his parents, so there would be no impropriety of appearing at the home of a single man. In the note she wrote to him, she introduced herself as a fellow colorist for the House of Blaeu. She included the information that Heer Blaeu had chosen her to color maps for Heer Willem de Groot. She hoped this would give her more prestige in his eyes and he would thus be more likely to grant her request for an interview. It was only later that she worried Vingboons might instead see her as a competitor and thus be disinclined to help. Nevertheless, he had replied that he could receive her in the studio at his home any afternoon that was convenient for her.

As she stood before Vingboons's building, Anneke thought that the narrow home looked much like her own. She wondered whether he wished for more daylight for his coloring work, as she often had. Somehow this thought of mutual problems helped to dispel some of her nervousness. She knocked on the door, and when a maid answered, Anneke announced her name and reason for being there.

As she was led into the front room, it was obvious that this was not where Vingboons worked, but rather where he displayed some maps that he must have colored, as well as watercolor images of exotic-looking places, which she had not expected to see. She was absorbed in one of these when someone behind her said, "Juffrouw van Brug, I believe." As Anneke turned, she saw a man of middle age approaching, a man whose face hinted that he might have been handsome in his youth. He wore neither a smile nor a frown, but perhaps a look of curiosity.

"Yes. You are Heer Vingboons?"

"One and the same. Do you like my watercolors?" he asked, and Anneke felt that it was more than a hope for praise, but rather a sincere request for her opinion.

"Oh, very much! I haven't seen many works done in watercolor, apart from the maps we color, of course. Most who paint landscapes use oil, do they not? I am intrigued that you have achieved such satisfactory results and a depth of color it is not easy to achieve with watercolor."

At this Vingboons did smile. "I am so relieved that you approve. I have heard good things about your work as a colorist, though you seem quite young to me."

Anneke was surprised and gratified by the other's praise. "I have worked as a colorist since I was quite young, under the tutelage of my mother."

"Ah, yes." The joy seemed to fade a bit from his countenance. "Your mother is Lysbeth Plettenburg, is she not? But I am surprised you do not mention your father, Isaac van Brug. He is an artist himself."

Anneke told herself that she should not have been surprised that Vingboons was aware of her family. After all, as a member of the St. Luke's Guild, he would at least have heard of her father, and he would know her mother's name as another colorist at Blaeu's, though she was not sure how he would know that Isaac was married to Lysbeth.

"You are, of course, correct, Heer Vingboons, and I perceive that it is this which prompted you to reply to the note from a young woman unknown to you."

"Even had I not made the connection with your parents, one who has already come to the attention of Heer Blaeu—and not only to his attention, but has even been recommended by him to a wealthy client such as Willem de Groot—would have commanded a courteous reply on her own merits."

Anneke tried to look modest at his praise. Still, she sensed something else underlying his magnanimous words. Not wishing to press her request too soon, she decided she could satisfy her curiosity, and perhaps ingratiate herself even further, by referring again to the paintings.

"May I ask what places the paintings depict? Are they real or the fruit of your imagination?"

"Oh, they are real, my dear Juffrouw. I am working now on this one," he said, leading her over to a painting on an easel. It is a view of Cochin on the Malabar Coast of India," he said, and she saw a painting of water, a town wall, and a mass of rooftops, not unlike the impression one would get of a European town. "You see that there are many spires. Those are the churches the Portuguese have built there."

"And this one, Heer Vingboons? What does it represent?" inquired Anneke, pointing to another painting, this one in blues and greens, with fewer buildings than the newer scene, and two green hills that looked like a seaman's tall woolen hat.

"Ah, that is Havana, Cuba. I originally painted and sold that scene years ago, but I was so fond of it that I decided to keep a copy for myself."

Anneke could well understand this. She, too, was drawn to the vibrancy of the colors.

"But there are so many paintings here, Heer Vingboons! Surely you have not traveled to all of these places yourself?"

"No, no, of course not," he answered with a laugh. "I but paint from what others have told me. I use reports and sketches from those who have traveled there with the VOC and the WIC, masters, helmsmen, merchants, and even humble crewmen. You would be surprised how many men wish their observations to be made known to a wider public, and they see my paintings as a way to do that."

"No, Heer Vingboons, I would not be at all surprised. But do you somehow note the names of those from whom you procure this information?" Anneke asked.

"I will admit that I do not, Juffrouw, for that would be most difficult. Most of the images are based on various sources. For some, I have no sketches to work from but only the descriptions that others bring to me, and I must trust that they are faithful observers. At times I have a rough sketch, but I refine it with other reports."

"I find it surprising that men are so willing to have their names lost as contributors to your work. I would have thought they would seek some reflected fame."

"I think they find satisfaction enough in knowing that they have contributed to the spread of knowledge about all the places we Dutch have been," Vingboons answered.

"That is very generous of spirit. Do they then see the finished work?"

"Many of them do come back later to see how I have rendered their information. They are usually happy with what I have done. It is also gratifying that others who have been to these places have found my depictions accurate."

"They are also beautiful, if I might venture to say so, Heer Vingboons."

"Thank you, Juffrouw van Brug. I am pleased that you think so. I have seen some of the maps that you have colored, and I value the opinion of one who is so young and yet so talented. I feel happy that I have hit upon this work. We Dutch are curious about the world, which has allowed us to prosper. There is, happily, a good market for my work."

"Indeed, at times it seems that our appetite for the exotic is insatiable."

"What an astute observation in one of such tender years. I see that your insight goes beyond the mere work of coloring."

"Now it is I who thank you, Heer Vingboons."

"But enough talk of my work. What has brought you here today? How may I be of service?"

"I do hesitate to ask, since what I seek is a great favor. I would not ask on my own account, but I am engaged in a project that is dear to the heart of my father."

"Your father?" Vingboons said, the warmth receding from his tone. "What is this project of which you speak?"

"Well, when my father was a young man, he had the opportunity to accompany van Herder on his mission to Congo in 1642. He was brought on as an artist to sketch what he saw. Unfortunately, his sketches, those of the peoples, the land, and its animals, were lost in a storm at sea. However, his notes on the places that they visited, how they were situated, what they were called, and so on, survived. He has long wished to use this information to add to the current map of the area, which has very little detail. Using that information, I have been able to draw a new map, and I was hoping that I could prevail upon you to use your influence with Heer Blaeu to get him to look at my map." Here Anneke paused, having noted the way Vingboons had seemed to stiffen in his chair.

"So this desire is more your father's than your own, Juffrouw van Brug?"

"In so much as his dream, repeated so often since my childhood, was my original motive, yes, but—"

"You need explain no further. I was happy to hear you out when I thought the favor was for you, but now, I'm afraid I am put off." Vingboons's gaze drifted away from her, and his eyes looked as though he were examining something Anneke could not see.

"But it has become my most fond wish! To have a work of mine put into the world, perhaps even included in Heer Blaeu's plans for a major atlas. Surely that would be a dream fulfilled for any interested in cartography."

"I thought that you were a colorist, not a cartographer in your own right. How could you be?" Vingboons asked with a bit more gentleness in his voice.

"I am a colorist, but that doesn't mean I can't be more! My brother attended classes in surveying and cartography. He also had a tutor to help him with his lessons, and I studied along with him. He took to the surveying classes, and he pursues that career now. I found the cartography lessons particularly fascinating, and after coloring so many maps, it seemed to come to me naturally."

"I can believe that you are an exceptional young lady, what with already having risen in the estimation of the House of Blaeu. Nevertheless, my answer is the same. I will not help you."

"But why? Why do you refuse me?"

"Ask your mother, Juffrouw. Ask Lysbeth." He walked from the room, leaving her to find her own way out.

Anneke paid no heed to those she passed as she made her way home. She couldn't imagine what Vingboons could have meant when he told her to ask her mother. Was there some secret past between them? Did her father know about it? But how was she to find out, and did she really want to know?

Yes, she wanted to know, and her mind was already constructing a fabrication to ask Lysbeth about Vingboons. She couldn't tell her mother the real reason for her visit to the artist because she still didn't want her mother to know about the map. It wasn't only that she didn't trust her mother to keep her secret from her father, though she didn't. It was also that persistent nagging in the back of her mind about the notes that appeared to be in a different hand. She had told herself that there was a reasonable explanation, but she didn't know whether Lysbeth would accept it, and she didn't want to find out.

By the time she reached home, she had come up with the fiction she would use with her mother. She went straight into the workroom to find her bent over a map.

"Mama, I must ask you something."

Normally, Lysbeth would have calmly continued painting, not wishing to interrupt the flow of the work. But today, sensing something in her daughter's tone, she immediately turned to her.

"What is it, Anneke? It's not like you to interrupt me so abruptly."

"I'm sorry, Mama. It's just that I met someone at Heer Blaeu's today. Johannes Vingboons was there, and Heer Meyert introduced me to him. I knew of him, of course, but I had never met him. He didn't seem very friendly, but he was polite enough when I asked him whether I could ask his opinion about some coloring issues. We found a quiet corner of the printing house. He didn't seem very enthusiastic about addressing my questions, but I thought that perhaps he was just a quiet sort of man. I had heard how much Heer Blaeu respects his work, so I asked whether he would ever be willing to look at my work, and if he approved, commend me to Heer Blaeu. He replied that he had heard I already worked with an important collector and thus did not require any recommendation from him.

"It occurred to me that he might be envious of the success I had already achieved, but I really did think that a word from him to Heer Blaeu could only enhance my standing. I was not willing to give up on my request, but before I could think how to proceed, he asked me whether I was not the daughter of Isaac van Brug and Lysbeth Plettenburg. I was surprised that he knew of you both, but then I suppose he would have heard of a fellow guild member and of a fellow colorist at Blaeu's. Of course, I said that I was your daughter, and then he said the strangest thing, Mama. He said, 'Ask your mother why I won't help you.' That's all he said, and then he turned and left."

Lysbeth looked at her hand and seemed surprised that it still held a brush. She instinctively looked down at the map to make sure no paint had dripped onto it. Anneke held her tongue as her mother carefully put the brush down, then slowly stood and walked to the window. When she spoke, it was as though she were addressing the passersby in the street below and not her insistent daughter in the room.

"Yes, of course he knows my name, and that of your Papa. I knew him years ago, before I had even met Isaac. Johannes and I were beginning colorists at the same time. Neither of us was steadily working for Heer Blaeu yet, but we would occasionally be given a map. We would sometimes see one another, picking up or dropping off a map, or perhaps just lingering, hoping that we would get an assignment, until someone would tell us to leave.

"He began to seek me out. He came to services at the church of my family so that we could speak there. Eventually, my mother even allowed me to go skating with him, where we had the kind of privacy that brings, though one be in the midst of crowds. He even began to speak of marriage."

"But you've never spoken of this, Mama!"

"No, a wise wife does not speak of a former admirer, and somehow it seemed disloyal to even tell you children there was a man I had feelings for before your father."

"But what happened?"

"I met your father, of course. A real artist! How romantic that seemed. He was kind, and like no one I had known. And he was handsome. Who knows what turns the head of a young girl?"

"What did Heer Vingboons do?"

"What could he do? I told him that I no longer wished to see him, that I had met someone else, someone whom I felt I was meant to marry. Johannes was bitter. I do believe he truly loved me, and one could say that I had used him ill. Still, I would not have guessed that he still harbors this feeling against me."

"Perhaps it is not against you, Mama, but rather against Papa."

"When one is married, that is the same thing."

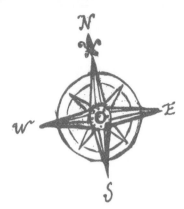

Chapter 18

May 1660

As Anneke made her way to the de Groot home, she saw some signs of spring and realized that it was already May. She had not asked her parents about a boat trip to Leiden with Daniel. He was still going there, as far as she knew, but she had only seen him for brief periods when she had gone into Blaeu's for some other reason. Neither had he seemed insistent, and she wondered whether his feelings were cooling.

Upon her arrival at the de Groot home, however, her thoughts of Daniel fled. She looked forward to another day of working on the maps and discussing her work with de Groot.

At first, maps had been the sole topic of the discussions between Anneke and de Groot. He would tell her the overall effect he wanted and she would make suggestions. He asked if she had seen the maps of Dirk Jansz van Santen, a young colorist like herself whose work he had seen and who showed great promise. When Anneke replied that she had not seen them, he seemed to reflect for a moment. Then he said that it was just as well, that he wanted her to paint from her own ideas and not be influenced by the work of another. Anneke could not help but bask in the implied compliment, especially coming from a man of such wealth and sophistication.

Over the six months that Anneke had been there, their conversations had gradually become more personal. When De Groot urged her to call him Willem, Anneke at first resisted, but after a while, it seemed unduly formal and even awkward to continue addressing him as Heer de Groot. Although she could never point to any one comment that Willem made, she nevertheless could not shake the feeling that there was some measure of going too far, of becoming too familiar. He was, after all, a married man. It wasn't that she objected to their exchanges. On the contrary, she looked forward to them. However, one day the mood seemed to change.

De Groot had chosen a map titled *Hibernia Regnum, Vulgo Ireland.*

"Today, Anneke, I would like to try to see for myself what it feels like to color a map. Never fear, I have no thought of replacing you! I simply wish to experience the coloring in a personal way." Anneke, though surprised by the request, nodded in agreement. He said that he particularly liked the copper green color she sometimes used, and he would like to paint much of the map with that color. She replied that they would also need to use some other colors in order to distinguish the regions, but many could indeed be copper green, and they could also outline the whole in a deeper shade of that color, which would be quite striking. When de Groot said that he wished to help make the paint, Anneke went to the shelf that she had taken over for her supplies to make sure she had everything she needed.

"Very well," she said, "but you realize that we may not even get to painting today as the procedure to make the color is rather time-consuming." Once he said that he understood, she continued. "Please ask for someone to bring us some linen so that we can cover our mouths." When the young maid, Agneta, with a bit of a quizzical look on her face, had brought the pieces of fabric, Anneke continued. "We start with one Amsterdam pond of verdigris," she said as she pointed out the small scale she had been using and handed de Groot the verdigris. "This is from Montpellier, since that made in other places tends to fade. Next, we add three ons of cream of tartar," she said, pointing to the correct container. "Now we hold the linen to our mouths to breathe through as we beat the two substances to a fine powder."

At first, de Groot disdained using the linen, but as he ground the powder, he quickly realized his error, brought the cloth to his mouth, and from behind it smiled ruefully at Anneke, who couldn't suppress a small laugh.

"Next we add two mingels of water, and we must heat it over the fire until it reduces to half the volume." As they waited for this, de Groot betrayed his impatience. "How much longer will this take?"

"Well, after it cools, we must put it into a glass and let it settle until the liquid becomes clear. Then we will probably be able to use it for the first part of our coloring, but later, when we wish for a darker shade to outline, we will need to set it on a chafing dish over coals until enough of the liquid again reduces to get the color we need." When she saw his look of frustration, she smiled again, and couldn't help adding, "Of course, we will need to test the color, for if it shines too much it is not correct, and we will need to start again."

"Stop!" de Groot said. He grasped her forearm before immediately realizing what he had done and removing his grip. "I am sorry," he said, "I was moved by artistic fervor."

"It is nothing," Anneke said softly and looked away. "We will work on some other project for which I have the colors ready." She swiftly moved to find a map she had been working on and for which the colors were prepared. De Groot said he did not wish to continue on something she had already begun, for fear of ruining it, and he found a less precious map to practice on. All afternoon they worked, with de Groot demonstrating no particular talent for the task. Finally, in frustration, Anneke put her hand on his to guide it, as she recalled her mother doing in her own early days of learning to color. Neither seemed to notice the touch when it happened, and it was only when she removed her hand that there was an awkwardness for a few moments, only to reappear when she again took his hand.

After another day of practice, de Groot declared himself ready to color the map of Ireland that he had chosen. Although Anneke knew him to be far from adequately prepared, she said nothing since it was, after all, his map. They began with the areas to be painted copper green, she pointing out which regions to paint so that no adjacent areas would be the same color. After that had dried, they painted some areas a pale rose, then the last sections a light yellow. Finally, de Groot said that he was exhausted and was sure he had reached the limits of his capabilities. "Finish it for me, Anneke," he said, throwing up his hands. Anneke simply nodded and set the map aside. "We will let this dry for now." She would finish it another day, when he was absent. She could perhaps repair some of the worst areas of the coloring, although dried watercolor could be unforgiving. At least she could enhance the beauty of the map in coloring the cartouches.

Later, as she was preparing to leave, de Groot asked her to sit for a moment.

"Anneke, you know that I greatly admire your work," he began.

"You have been kind enough to say so, and I am very grateful for your continued interest. Heer Blaeu even told me that you praised my skill to him. That can only help me, even after I have finished my work here."

"Oh, Anneke, I value you for more than just your artistic talent," he said.

This was the first time he had spoken this way, but it was not as surprising as it would have been prior to their days of his brief apprenticeship.

"Heer de Groot—"

"Oh, come now, Anneke! You have been calling me Willem. Please do not regress to that level of formality. There is nothing wrong with our friendship. I have given over my map room for your work. I visit you here. At any time, a servant could interrupt us, and so in a sense, we are not really alone, are we? Naturally, if someone else is with us, then we address one another more formally. Does that not suit you?"

"Yes, I suppose that it does," Anneke murmured. But if they were to act differently when alone, that seemed to her to be the beginning of a dangerous road.

Just then, Warner entered. "Vrouw Kregier asked me to remind you that you have guests arriving shortly, Heer de Groot."

"Yes, thank you, Warner." Then, turning to Anneke with an apologetic smile, he said, "Goodbye, then, Anneke."

As she cleared the day's mess, Anneke wondered whether there had been something more that de Groot had meant to say to her, and she felt relieved that they had been interrupted. Of course, he was always a perfect gentleman with her, even when she had touched his hand with hers, which some might have taken as an invitation to familiarity. After all, he was a married man, so surely there was nothing more personal that he had intended to say. At times, though, Anneke had sensed that perhaps de Groot and his wife did not live in complete harmony. Nevertheless, she understood that even in marriages which seemed happy, such as that of her parents, there were still underlying complaints, and perhaps even resentments. It was how the couple managed these feelings, she supposed, that made for a marriage in which each partner was, at least, content. But then, the happiness of de Groot's marriage should not matter to her.

Chapter 19
May 1660

Anneke arrived early at the de Groot home the following day and left a note, explaining that she had forgotten to mention she would be going to Blaeu's, as he had asked her to report on her progress with de Groot's maps. This was not strictly true, for Blaeu had named no specific time but had simply sent a message through her mother that she should come by sometime to tell him how the coloring was going.

When she arrived, Daniel was at his press, unaware of her presence. His muscles tensed as he pulled on the crossed bar. Anneke looked away, feeling that she had intruded by watching him so frankly when he didn't see her. After a moment, one of the men spoke to Daniel and he looked over to where Anneke stood. She had not walked through the room yet to see if Heer Blaeu would be able to speak with her. She met Daniel's eyes, and when the printed map had emerged from beneath the roller, he stepped away from the press and walked toward her.

"You should not leave your press, should you?" she asked him.

"No. I shouldn't. I want to talk to you."

"I must speak with Heer Blaeu if he is here. Perhaps I will still be here when you have a minute free," Anneke said, feeling guilty at her own brusque manner.

As it happened, Heer Blaeu was not at the printing house that day. Anneke spoke with Heer Meyert instead, but since he had not been directly involved with Anneke's placement at the de Groot home, he seemed to have little interest in hearing about it.

"I am sorry, but you will have to return another day. For now, I see that there is someone who does seem to wish to talk to you. Perhaps you can spare him a few minutes."

Anneke was a bit taken aback by his disinterest in the commission, but even more, she felt embarrassed that Heer Meyert had referred to Daniel as someone to whom she owed her time. They had not been as discreet as she had thought, apparently, or else Daniel had shared details of their outings. She walked over to a corner where Daniel did, indeed, seem to be waiting for her. If she went over to him, everyone would see them conversing, but if she walked on, they would also notice the slight. At least the noise of the printing room would hinder anyone from overhearing them.

"Hello, Daniel. It's good to see you."

"It has been quite a while, hasn't it, Anneke? But I suppose that you are too busy now with your commission to have time for me."

"Come now, Daniel, don't be silly."

"Oh, I'm silly now." Then, in a gentler voice, he said, "I've missed you, Anneke."

"I've missed you, too, Daniel."

"Have you, Anneke? Have you really?"

"Yes, Daniel, I have," Anneke answered, only partly because she knew that was what he wished to hear. "But you are still helping with your parents' bookshop, are you not?"

"That is what I wanted to say. Things are going better there now, and I will have some free days. Do you think that we could spend time together on Sunday?"

"I would like that, Daniel. I will ask my parents, but I'm sure it will be all right. Plan on meeting my family Sunday after the church service."

"Until then, Anneke."

"Yes, until then, Daniel." She left the printing house, struggling to define her feelings.

∽

When Anneke had asked her parents about her Sunday plans, they had insisted that Daniel come for the midday meal. They knew he had been helping his parents, and to them, that seemed a sign of a good young man. Anneke again stopped by Blaeu's to tell Daniel. He seemed happy at the suggestion, and she wondered whether he was disappointed that they would have no time alone.

"What do you think we should prepare for Daniel's visit on Sunday?" Lysbeth asked on Friday morning.

Anneke started a bit. "I'm sure that anything will be fine, Mama."

"Yes, but do you know of anything that he particularly favors?" Lysbeth persisted.

"No, I suppose I don't really know," Anneke was a bit embarrassed to admit.

"Well, tomorrow you can help me prepare some things. We cannot wait until Sunday if he is to come right from church for the midday meal."

"But I had planned to go to Heer de Groot's tomorrow."

"You can take a Saturday to stay here and help with the preparation."

"But what will he think?"

"Who? Daniel?"

"No, Heer de Groot."

"Why should he think anything, Anneke? I doubt he will even notice your absence. Surely he has more important things to occupy his mind than whether his map colorist has come on any particular day."

"Very well, Mama," Anneke quietly replied, feeling uncomfortable that she had never shared with her family the fact that de Groot was almost always in the room while she worked. Nor did she tell Lysbeth now.

Anneke didn't sleep well that night, and when she went into the kitchen in the morning, Lysbeth was already working on preparations for the meal she would serve the next day.

"What are you working on, Mama? I assumed you would just make a hutspot tomorrow."

"I decided to make something a little different. I was able to get a bit of fresh pork, which I will mince and put into a dish with peas and turnips."

"Why so much trouble, Mama?"

"What is wrong with you, Anneke? I would think that you would be looking forward to Daniel's visit and that you would want us to prepare something special for him. You seem to show less interest than I would have expected. You seemed smitten with him from the early days of going to Blaeu's, and your father and I have been most indulgent in allowing you to skate with him and go on outings with other young people. Has something happened to change your feelings?"

"Oh, I don't know, Mama. Since he has spent so much time in Leiden over these past months, it has been difficult not to feel that we have drifted apart."

"But surely what he has done for his parents is all to his credit."

"Oh, I know that, Mama, but it is hard not to feel neglected."

"I would have thought you wise enough to overcome that feeling. But I suppose that wisdom cannot always dictate to the heart, especially when you are young."

"And it's not just that, Mama. He is a nice young man and he can be fun, but he is not, oh, I don't know . . . interesting."

"Not interesting? What do you mean? Do you require that he entertain you in some way?"

"It is just that his world seems so limited, Mama. He talks about Blaeu's so much, and he is just a pressman."

"That is good, honest work. Besides, didn't you tell us that he hopes to advance at the printing house? Everyone must start out somewhere, Anneke. Goodness is the most important thing to look for in a husband."

"I know, but you have Papa, who is good, and is also an artist. You yourself said that was partly why you chose him over Heer Vingboons, because being with an artist would be more exciting."

"I do not wish you to speak of Heer Vingboons, Anneke!" Lysbeth replied sharply, startling her daughter.

"I'm sorry, Mama. It's just that I don't want to live my life constantly hearing talk about the mechanics of printing and how one might advance within that small sphere."

"I imagine that you are exaggerating and that Daniel talks of other things, too. You could also introduce other topics, you know."

"I suppose you are right. With Papa, though, you could understand his desire of wanting to be an artist."

Lysbeth did not reply for several moments, busying herself with preparing the apples she would stew for the next day. "Yes, but the very fact that I once had dreams has made things difficult. It requires a very generous spirit, Anneke, to rejoice in someone else's success on a path that you yourself had hoped to tread. It is especially difficult if one's own work helped to support the other's pursuit."

Anneke looked away from her mother. Perhaps in another time and place, her father's work might have been held in higher esteem, but Holland was filled with extraordinary artists. "Are you resentful of Papa, Mama?" she eventually dared ask.

"I would not go that far. I love your father, and I cannot lay all of my disappointment at his feet. It is almost impossible for women to gain recognition for their own work. And besides, I have seen your talent, Anneke, and even just in our coloring work, mine pales in comparison."

"I'm sorry, Mama," Anneke said quietly.

"I do not mean to exaggerate my disappointment, daughter. I am only saying that perhaps you see our marriage in an idealized light, and this causes you to have unrealistic expectations." Then turning away, she added, "Come. Help me cut these apples."

Anneke quickly lost track of what the preacher was saying the next morning. She was thinking about Daniel and why she had made so little effort to see him lately. Here, in the house of God, she had to be honest with herself. Her change in sentiment was not completely caused by Daniel's absence. There was also the tug that she felt toward Willem. It was probably just that she felt flattered by his attention. *This is hardly something I should be thinking about in church*, she told herself. De Groot was married. There could never be anything more than friendship between them, and even that would leave them both open to temptation. She resolved to rediscover the fondness that she had once felt for Daniel, and yes, the excitement of their first encounter, when he had approached her with his piercing blue eyes and the strength his body seemed to exude, tempered by his gentle manner.

As the service finished and everyone filed out of the church, Daniel approached.

"Good morning, Anneke. Heer van Brug, Vrouw Plettenburg, it is very nice to see you again."

Anneke's "Hello, Daniel" was lost as her mother said, "It has been a long time since we have seen you, Daniel, but Anneke has told us of your dedication to your work at your parents' bookshop in Leiden. We are happy that you will be able to join us today."

Daniel showed himself very appreciative of the special trouble that Lysbeth had obviously gone to in preparing the food. He commented on each course and especially praised the delicious pancakes Lysbeth served at the end of the meal. At every moment, Daniel showed himself to be the kind and thoughtful young man that Anneke knew him to be. He did speak of his work at the printing house and of his hopes for the future there, but Anneke had to admit that this topic had been broached by her parents. It seemed that they were taking his interest in Anneke more seriously than she was ready for.

When the visit came to an end, Daniel thanked Lysbeth and Isaac for their hospitality and said he hoped he would be able to see them again soon. Anneke walked him to the door, and as he stood just inside, he said, "You didn't have very much to say today, Anneke."

"I hardly seemed to matter, what with all that you and my parents had to say to each other."

At the look on his face, Anneke tried to soften the sting with a smile, but it was too late. She knew that she sounded like a petulant child, but she only added, "Goodbye, Daniel. Thank you for coming." He had no choice but to bid her farewell and leave.

That night, she thought about her attraction to Daniel when she had first seen him at the printing house. She recalled the times they had been skating together, when there had been thrilling moments, not just speeding along with all the other skaters, but being with Daniel in particular. She loved the care she had heard in his voice, how he had taken her hand or quickly moved to help her if it seemed she might trip over a bump in the ice. She thought of their outings during the summer, which he had always planned with such consideration. But they hadn't had discussions as detailed and particular as those she had with Willem. She feared that Daniel would never be able to understand her work the way that Willem did. There were intriguing depths to Willem that she did not understand. She felt that there was much less to comprehend with Daniel, that his was a simpler soul. Perhaps this type of man would be easier to live with, but she didn't know whether ease was what she longed for. It didn't matter, she sharply reminded herself. Willem was a married man.

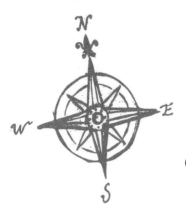

Chapter 20

July 1660

Upon returning to the de Groot home the next day, Warner informed Anneke that Heer de Groot was not at home, and he accompanied her to the map room.

"Heer de Groot left instructions that you are to continue with your coloring. He was surprised at your absence Saturday. He said he had most particularly wanted to talk to you about one of the maps since he knew that he would not be here today. Nevertheless, you are to continue as you have been going."

"Thank you, Warner. Heer de Groot hadn't told me of his plans."

"And why should he, Juffrouw?"

"Indeed, Warner. Why should he?" Anneke replied, with an uneasy feeling as she watched the servant disappear.

In the moment when Warner had said that the master was not at home, Anneke had felt a mixture of relief and disappointment. She had wanted to see him, but she had also felt nervous. What would the tenor of their conversation be? Was she sensing something from him, some desire? And what of her feelings for Daniel? *This is ridiculous,* she told herself. *There is no reason for me to even think of Willem and Daniel in the same way. Willem may be interested in me, but he is a married man. Any future with him is impossible.*

As she approached the map she had been working on, Anneke wondered whether Willem had already planned to be away or if he had left because he was angry about her absence two days before. Surely her imagination was exaggerating her importance to him. Was the feeling of disapproval that she got from Warner only because she had disappointed his master, or was he criticizing something that he had sensed between Willem and herself?

She donned the smock that she always wore when she was coloring. When she had first come, it had been newly laundered and white. Now it was covered with spots of paint, and she had felt embarrassed when de Groot had recently commented on it. She had stammered that she should have thought to bring a clean one, but he had said that he found the mix of colors enchanting, a symbol of her life as an artist.

She began her work, the only way she ever knew to forget the problems of the moment. It was hours later when she realized she had not thought of Willem or Daniel at all. When she packed up her things, she included the smock, which she had resolved to wash.

When de Groot returned the next day, there was no unease between them as a result of Anneke's absence. He spoke as though taking up a previous conversation. "Anneke, I tried to say this to you the other day, but we somehow got off the subject that I wished to address. You have been working here for eight months, longer than I had originally envisioned when first I spoke with Blaeu about hiring a colorist. However, I had not foreseen how much I would appreciate your skill in embellishing my maps. I admire you very much, Anneke, and so I would like to do something for you."

"But you have already done so much for me, giving me this commission. Well, of course the commission is through the House of Blaeu, but you have generously shown your satisfaction with my work. It will mean the world for my career as a colorist. Perhaps someday I may even join the Guild as a colorist on my own account and be able to accept commissions myself."

"But I didn't think most guilds, including the Guild of St. Luke, allowed women," de Groot replied, temporarily distracted from his original comment.

"Well, the guild does represent those who work in other arts, not just painting. For example, embroidery is represented, so women are accepted under that group. Even for artists, it is not completely unheard of. Well, perhaps it is here in Amsterdam, but my mother told me of a painter, Judith Leyster, who was admitted as a master to the Guild of St. Luke in Haarlem when my mother was just a young girl. Also, women colorists can sometimes be admitted."

"Nevertheless, entrance into a guild is beyond even my influence. But that is not the type of thing that I mean when I say that I want to do something for you."

"I know that, and I wasn't suggesting you should use your influence in that way."

"No, you weren't. But isn't there something you would like, Anneke? Something that I could do for you, or buy for you? Something that would show my regard? Perhaps there is something that I could do to help you in your advancement as a colorist. I would expect nothing in return."

This last remark, far from reassuring Anneke, seemed a gentle hint of danger. Anyone would suspect that a wealthy man offering to do something for a young woman would expect some sort of payment from her. Still, she saw a way that he could help her realize her dream, if she acted with great care. As she took time to ponder, de Groot, with a true note of concern in his voice, said, "Have I offended or frightened you, Anneke?"

"No," she hastened to reply. "And there is something I might ask of you."

At that moment Warner entered. "Excuse me, Heer de Groot, but Heer Bayard is here to see you. He says that he has just come from the Stock Exchange."

"Oh, very well," de Groot replied, giving Anneke an apologetic look before leaving. Having been abandoned, disappointment pricked her. De Groot might think her request presumptuous, but if he could help her get her map printed, she was willing to take that risk.

As soon as she had settled her things in the map room the next day, de Groot entered.

"Good morning, Anneke," he said warmly, and Anneke felt relieved. As the morning progressed, and de Groot did not speak of his offer, she sought to remind him of the previous day.

"I hope that your business with Heer Bayard went well yesterday."

"Oh, yes, of course. Nothing you should concern yourself with. When I am with you, I wish only to think of this undertaking of ours. I hope that you will permit me to call it our project, although we saw that my efforts were hardly worth the map and paints expended. No, you bring all of the talent and the work. I must be content with providing the supplies."

"Without which, there would be no project," she replied with a smile. "Besides, you encourage me to choose the finest materials, and that does make a difference to the beauty of the map."

Anneke continued coloring the map that was laid out on her work table. As he sometimes did, Willem looked through his collection as she worked. In this way, he knew which map he wished her to work on next. By the end of the day, de Groot had not returned to the topic of doing something for her, and it was a frustrated Anneke who left his home.

Over the next several days, as Willem did not speak of his offer, Anneke decided it had been but the thought of an idle moment and he had no intention of carrying it out. She had come close to convincing herself that this was for the best when, a couple of weeks later, he returned to the subject.

"Anneke, you know how much I admire your work. It is not just that, but spending time with you has added greatly to my daily pleasures. You may not credit this, but when one has acquired the kind of wealth I have, just getting more of it loses some of its luster. Business used to offer me excitement, but that has lessened, as even a gain doesn't have much more meaning for me than does a loss. It is all inconsequential when seen in the context of the whole. Observing you, how you are so serious in your work and how your decisions become something beautiful that also enhance the maps, has given me a reason to look forward to each day. It is a fascinating process, and you are at the center of it. Please do not feel that I speak too personally. It is your skill that I admire, and yes, that admiration leads me to a fond feeling for you, as one feels a sort of kinship with a writer who seems to understand one's soul. Please, Anneke, allow me the gratification of doing something for you to show my appreciation."

Anneke took a few minutes to respond, pretending an intense concentration on her work. Finally, Willem said, "Can you not even answer me, Anneke?"

She put her brush down and looked into those silvery eyes.

"I have thought of something that you could do for me, but I am hesitant to mention it. I fear that it is too great a favor."

"Please tell me, Anneke."

"Very well. I believe I have told you that my brother, Lucas, attended classes in cartography, although he took more to the surveying lessons. What I did not tell you is that I studied his lessons, too, for he had a tutor to help him, and I was allowed to sit in on those sessions. For some reason, the cartography lessons came naturally to me."

De Groot looked at her in confusion. "Is it that you wish me to aid your brother, then? But I wish for you to be the recipient of my generosity."

"It is not for my brother, and what I ask will cost you nothing, but it is something that only you can give. I want you to use your influence for me. Please, let me explain. When my father was a young man, he went on the van Herder expedition to Africa. Have you heard of it?"

"The name seems vaguely familiar, but I can't say I remember any details," Willem replied, making no attempt to conceal his bewilderment.

"In 1642, van Herder led an expedition to meet with the king of Congo. The group then traveled in a northeasterly direction. My father went as an artist, hired to make drawings of everything they saw—animals, plants, peoples, and the land. During a storm, his sketches were swept overboard. But his extensive notes on the route that they took were not destroyed." Here she paused to give de Groot a chance to comment, but he simply looked at her. "The notes are now being used to draw a map of the region of Congo and Angola."

"Your brother is creating a map?"

"No. I am."

Incredulity was clearly etched on de Groot's face, and Anneke knew that if he put it into words, she would hate him.

"That is quite a story, Anneke. Clearly, you are a young woman with more secrets than I could have imagined."

"Yes, it is a secret. Only my brother knows of the map, and now you."

"I am touched that you have shared it with me, but I admit I do not really understand why."

"I do not know whether you have heard, but Heer Blaeu is planning the printing of a new atlas. It will be the largest ever printed, requiring several volumes. Most of the maps, as is the custom, will be reprints that he already has, or that he will purchase from other printers, but I believe that Heer Blaeu would like to add some new maps. I want mine to be one of those." Anneke stopped. Having heard herself explain it aloud, she only now grasped the enormity of what it was she hoped for.

"That is quite an ambition," de Groot said slowly. "And how do you propose to bring this about?"

"That is the favor that I ask. I would like for you to use your influence with Heer Blaeu to include my map in his atlas."

"Anneke, I think that your estimate of my power far exceeds its reality."

"I do not believe so. The map is good, Willem. I know that it is good. Surely you have faith in my ability to judge maps."

"I have no doubt of your aesthetic appreciation, but what of the informative aspects of the maps?"

"I have the notes to prove the worth of what I include in the map! Surely it will be an improvement over the blank parts on current maps, which are filled with fanciful drawings when no facts are known about the area."

"I shall have to think on this, Anneke. As much as I admire you, I do not wish to appear the gullible fool, urging Blaeu to take on the work of a young woman who has never even left Amsterdam."

"But most of the cartographers have not done the travels themselves! They also work from the observations that others have made. My source contains not only descriptions but distances and measurements to determine the location of places."

"And all of this in your father's notes? Is he a surveyor, then? I thought him an artist only."

"He said there was a surveyor in the group who taught him a lot," Anneke said. Then, wishing to make her claim more credible, she added, "I imagine that they worked together on the more exacting measurements. Please, you said that I should tell you something you could do for me. This is it. I wish to keep this from my father until it is a reality. I want to surprise him, to show him it was I who was able to make his dream come true of seeing his notes become a map."

"So in reality, this is something I would be doing for your father," de Groot pointed out.

"Not just for him! Ever since I attended my brother's lessons, I have dreamed of creating a map myself. I love being a colorist, but how much more wonderful to create the map itself. If Heer Blaeu were to include my map, wouldn't that give me credibility? In the future, it might encourage others to come to me with information they had and ask me to draw a map for them. Think of it! Even the coloring of those maps would become more satisfying, as I would know precisely the creator's vision."

A new look had come over Willem's face, one of both surprise and skepticism. "I never imagined the extent of your ambition," he said with something of distaste in his tone. Gone was the look of the art patron, flattering and indulging his artist.

"Of course, I could only ever hope to accomplish this with your most generous help. I have only dared to mention it because you pressed me to know of something that you could do for me."

"Your request is hardly in the line of what I would have expected from a young woman. I have learned that you are not frivolous, but I thought perhaps you would like an introduction to other potential patrons," Willem said. "Or even to an appropriate bachelor."

Anneke tried to hide her reaction to this last comment. She had, indeed, been a fool, she told herself, to ever think he could be interested in her as a woman. He had been prepared to cavalierly hand her over to another man.

Perhaps de Groot mistook her silence for stubbornness or displeasure. All he said was, "I shall have to give this considerable thought."

He had begun to leave the room when Anneke said, "Also think of the favor that you would be doing for Heer Blaeu. New maps, with truly new information, could only add to the prestige of his atlas."

As he exited the map room, all he said was, "I wonder if he will see it that way."

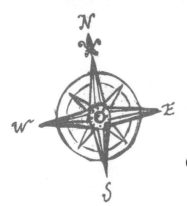

Chapter 21

July 1660

As though she had been waiting for her husband to leave, Helena entered the room moments later and shut the door. A closed door to the map room was unusual, and Anneke thought the servants would wonder about it, but privacy was clearly more important to Helena in that moment.

"Anneke," she said, approaching the table where the colorist sat. "Do you remember the day that I saw you tracing Willem's maps?"

"Yes, and I explained—"

"Come now. There is no need for you to invent a reason for what you were doing. I don't care. Besides, I have thought of a better way to convince you to join in a little scheme of mine."

"What scheme is that, Vrouw Kregier?"

"Oh, come now, Anneke. With what we are about to embark upon, you must call me Helena." At this remark, it seemed to Anneke that the other woman's features had shorn some of their beauty and had come to resemble those of an innocent-looking calico cat playing with a cornered mouse.

"I am going to tell Willem that since the day that you joined us for our midday meal, some of my friends and I have become enchanted with the idea of learning something of how to use watercolors. Here we have an expert at our disposal, and surely he can spare you a few hours a week to give lessons to my friends and me. However, one of these friends has a sister who is unable to go out due to health reasons, so the lessons must take place at her home. I daresay that Willem might even believe this could someday lead to my taking an interest in his colored maps."

"Of course," Anneke said, allowing herself to breathe more freely now. "I am no real expert in painting the kinds of pictures that you and your friends might be interested in, but I would be happy to teach you what I can."

"Oh, you misunderstand me, my dear," Helena said with a soft laugh. "There are to be no lessons. Do you honestly think that I would wish to engage in such an activity? If I want a painting of something, I will commission one, and it would be in oil, hardly in watercolor."

"Then I don't understand, Vrouw Kregier."

"Surely you are not as naive as you pretend to be. I have somewhere else that I would like to go, and I wish to have a plausible reason." Then she added, "I have my own desires to pursue."

Anneke was shocked as she understood the type of desires those might be. She felt embarrassed at the woman's open brazenness but knew that her answer had to be direct and clear. "I'm sorry, Vrouw Kregier, but I don't see how I can help you to deceive Heer de Groot, not after all that he has done for me."

"You will see when I tell you that if you do not consent to my plan, I will tell my husband that some items have recently gone missing and that this seems to have begun shortly after you began to come here."

Anneke stared at the woman, stunned at such audacity. "He won't believe you," she stammered. "He trusts me."

"Do you honestly think that he trusts you above me? Can you not see how besotted he is by my beauty? It may be that he loves me only in the way that he loves his maps, as something beautiful to show to his friends, but he will not wish to lose me. His interest in you is the same, you know. You help to satisfy his passion for these horrid maps, which he brags about to his fellow collectors. He can have no other thought for you."

Anneke's heart wanted to contest this, telling Helena of de Groot's offer to do something for her, but all she said was, "I will think on it."

"I shall expect your answer tomorrow. I will contrive to speak with you in private if Willem is here. If your answer is no, I shall explain to Willem that, unfortunately, you had to be put out of the house for your thievery."

She left the room and Anneke sat perfectly still, as though she had just awoken from a nightmare, afraid to stir in case the movement would make it all real. But it was real. Would Willem actually believe this lie of her? She hoped not, but one could not rely on hope.

If she were not complicit in Helena's vile plan, Willem would never speak to Heer Blaeu about her map. She would be cast out as a thief, never even able to color maps again. She would shame her whole family. Her mother would lose her position with Blaeu's, and her father might never get another commission. Might Lucas even suffer, so new and still to prove himself as a surveyor? Might his employers decide that the brother of a thief cannot be trusted?

No one would believe her denials. What thief would not deny guilt? Surely her family would believe her, she told herself. But even of this, she could not be certain. If they were all ruined along with her, they would need someone to blame, and she would be the one to hand.

Anneke slept little that night, repeating the same thoughts over and over again. She longed to be able to ask someone for advice, but who could she ask? She thought that Lucas would tell her to quit at once. He would tell her Helena would never follow through on her threats, but he had not been there. He had not dealt closely with the rich and powerful as she did now. Besides, he would give little weight to the fact that if she quit, it would bring an end to her dreams.

Although her mother didn't know of the map that she was creating, she did understand the importance of Anneke's coloring assignment at de Groot's. Lysbeth might find Helena's threats more credible than Lucas would, and she would understand all the possible repercussions if Helena followed through, but how could she tell her daughter to do something dishonorable?

And Daniel? His free days were again spent in Leiden, so she wouldn't even have a chance to ask him his opinion, but it was just as well. She didn't want to imagine what it would be like to tell Daniel. She wouldn't want to shatter his good opinion of her, and she feared that if he knew she was contemplating the deception, he would never see her in the same light.

No, she must decide for herself. Again, she returned to the question of whether Willem would give credence to the lie Helena would tell him. Her fate would depend upon him choosing to believe her over his own wife. Even if he were inclined to doubt his wife, would he wish to cause the turmoil to his household that would result from such a choice? He could always get another colorist, but how could he restore peace to his household once it was lost? As daring as he might be in the choices he allowed Anneke to make in her coloring, he did not seem like a man who would take risks with his home life. Though she had not witnessed tenderness between Willem and Helena, she knew that, like all Amsterdamers, he valued an ordered home life.

Even if he believes me, he will choose her falsehoods over my truth. She would comply with Helena's demands.

When she arrived at the de Groot house the next day, she found that, once again, Willem was not at home. As she settled into her routine, arranging the maps and preparing the paints she would work with that day, Helena entered the room. This time, she did not even bother to close the door.

"Have you decided where your interests lie?" she asked Anneke.

"I will do as you say," was the only reply the mistress took time to hear, as though she had known what it would be. Smiling, she left the room.

Helena had wasted no time, for when Anneke arrived the next day, Willem immediately greeted her with, "So, even my wife has taken a fancy to your work, Anneke! She wishes for you to teach her and her friends something of watercoloring. I must say, I am surprised, but perhaps that explains why she has taken to visiting us here in the map room more frequently."

Not knowing whether Helena had told him that they had already spoken, Anneke didn't reply.

"You should feel honored. It is unusual for my wife to allow anyone to tell her what to do, and surely you will have to do that in the course of your instruction. I would love to see it, but I understand that the lessons are to take place at the home of a friend who has difficulty getting around. I don't remember if Helena actually mentioned a name. Did she tell you the lady's name?"

"No, she didn't," Anneke said, relieved to know, at least, how she was to respond. Helena had told Willem that she had spoken to Anneke about the "lessons."

"It was kind of you to agree to do this. I don't imagine it will be of much interest to you," Willem said, as though she could have denied the request. "Well, I know that there is very little that I can deny my wife, so I imagine you found it to be the same." Anneke couldn't tell whether he was implying that he, and also she, found Helena so lovable that no one would want to deny her anything, or whether he meant that she brooked no disagreement once she had set her heart upon something.

"It will be my honor to teach the ladies."

"I must say that I'm not thrilled at the idea of you taking time away from your coloring for me, but I imagine that your students will tire of it soon and then I will have you all to myself again."

Anneke was startled at this last phrase and told herself that he only wanted her for her coloring. She asked herself how long Helena's dangerous game could last. Clearly, Helena had tired of her husband's attentions, so must she not also quickly lose interest in her lover?

"Perhaps I could find another way to make up some of the time," Anneke said, but Willem gave no indication that he had heard what she said. Instead, he asked her to show him what she had accomplished while he was gone and what her plans were for the day.

Even the coloring could not fully occupy her mind, and she berated herself again and again for deceiving this man who had done so much for her. He had shown her kindness, and even respect. It was not just that she was betraying him. It was worse. She was making it possible for his wife to betray him.

At the same time, she wanted him to agree to her request. It had been a week and he had not returned to the subject, but she had been loath to broach the matter herself. In part, it was fear that he would retreat and deny her request if he felt she was pushing him. In part, it was because she had felt a change in him when she had asked him to intervene with Blaeu, and she wished for a return to how things were before she had been so bold. He had shown no hint of the awkwardness between them that morning when he had talked with her about the lessons for his wife, but she herself had needed to control her reaction to what he was saying. He was unknowingly becoming complicit in a most vile hoax against himself.

Although Helena seemed confident her plan would be successful, Anneke did not share her sentiment. She felt it was inevitable that the scheme would come to light, and still she saw no way to escape the trap that would surely ensnare them all.

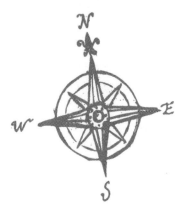

Chapter 22

August 1660

Anneke told herself that she must get de Groot to agree to her request and act upon it before Helena's treachery, and her own, became known. She felt sure that, once he had spoken to Blaeu, de Groot would not take back the request. If he did, he would need to explain why, and surely he would not wish to expose his wife's infidelity.

When he entered the map room, Anneke could see that gone was the ease with which he had spoken to her yesterday about the painting lessons. For one quick moment, she feared that he had already discovered Helena's deception even though they had not yet acted upon it.

Since she already felt his discomfort, she decided there was no point in trying to regain the relaxed nature of their interactions.

"It has been over a week, and I wondered whether you have come to a decision with regard to my request?" As she saw the swift look he gave her, she immediately felt she had been too hurried and too blunt.

"I see that you are, in fact, the ambitious young woman you showed yourself to be. I was mistaken about you, Anneke. At first, I was disappointed that you did not seem to comply with the image that I held of you, of a talented young woman grateful to be given an extraordinary opportunity. Upon sober reflection, however, I find that this new aspect intrigues me. You are not what I had imagined you to be."

"So you are not angered at my audacity? I feared that you were."

"Angered, no. Well, perhaps slightly at first. But as I say, I see now the error of my judgment."

"So you will help me?" she couldn't help but blurt out.

"I will help you, yes, but with conditions."

Anneke sat very still. In her naiveté, had she misjudged this man? She suddenly remembered Heer Blaeu's warning to her to be careful. "Conditions?" she said softly.

"Yes. Well, actually, one condition."

"Oh?"

"Yes. I wish to tell Blaeu that the map is by your brother."

"What? But, why?"

"You yourself told me that your brother has cartographic training and that he has sailed to Africa."

"But this is not based on anything he did there! Nor did he help me with the map. This is my work, not his!"

"I know that this is not what you wanted. But can you not see it from my side, Anneke? If I go to Blaeu and ask him to do something for a lovely young woman, a young woman who has been working from my home, with whom I have spent many hours without anyone else present, what do you imagine he will think?"

As Anneke made no reply, he continued. "You say that you wish this as a surprise for your father, so this will accomplish that more easily. Blaeu is much more likely to agree to this if he thinks that it comes from a man—someone who currently works as a surveyor, has traveled to Africa, and has some formal training in cartography."

Despite her efforts, Anneke's eyes filled with tears. "Yes, it will fulfill my wish for my father, but was it so much to ask that I receive some recognition? Must I simply work in obscurity so that others may benefit, simply because I am a woman?"

De Groot thought the answer to this was obvious, so he did not injure her further by asserting the truth of the situation. *Yes, because you are a woman.*

As soon as de Groot left the map room, Anneke packed her things and silently slipped out of the house. She had no heart for work today. If this neglect angered Willem, so be it. She could not help it. Until the moment when he had announced he would only help her by denying any chance of recognition for her work, she hadn't fully realized how ardently she had wished for it.

She had tried to tell herself that she created the map for her father, that she had used her favor from de Groot for him. Now she had to admit that she had only been lying to herself. She wanted to be recognized as a cartographer. She wanted it to be known that she had created a map in the *Atlas Maior*. She wanted to use that acknowledgment as a means to acquire commissions to do other maps, maps that she would design. She could oversee the engraving to make certain it remained faithful to her work. She could color her maps in a way that fulfilled the promise of what they contained. New information. New information about a small part of the world.

When she arrived home early, she told her mother that she had returned because she didn't feel well. Lysbeth was ready to believe this, as Anneke did look as though she might be ill. With her hand on her daughter's forehead, she said, "You do not seem to have a fever, but you should rest."

"Yes, I shall rest. I think that I will go lie down on the pallet in the loft room. It is quieter there, and I won't disturb you or father."

"You won't disturb us, dearest," Lysbeth said.

"Please, mother, I prefer it," Anneke said as she began to mount the narrow, winding staircase.

When she entered the room, she at first simply sat and stared, going over the morning's revelation again and again. It was as though it were a wound that she could not leave alone but unceasingly poked and prodded. Finally, she fell into a fitful sleep, as though she must make real the reason that she had given her mother for her retreat. When she awoke, she saw by the light that she must have missed the midday meal, and she vaguely remembered her mother entering the room, then silently leaving again.

She had to do something to occupy her mind. Perhaps some sort of solution would come to her if she lost herself in work. She took out the map she was creating. She needed to finish it so she would be ready when de Groot said that he would speak with Blaeu. And he must ask the printer soon, before Helena's deception came to light.

Trying to enter her map and leave the worries of this world behind, Anneke looked at all that she had accomplished. The most challenging part for her had been following the surveying notes and doing the mathematical calculations to place the named spots in the correct location. There she had written names such as Allagoa and Zimbozin and Enscon and Beequa, and Rio Zaire for the large river.

Nine times her father had written "tollhouse" in his notes, and she had added these to the maps: *Tolhuÿs*. Sometimes there was a name with it, as in Kikacko *Tolhuÿs*, but other times there was no specific designation. There was also a place that said *De huijse opstaken*, and Anneke wondered why people would build their houses on stilts. Were they afraid of flooding? Was it as a defense against wild animals or people who might harm them? Her father had provided no hint of explanation.

There were many areas with tiny drawings of mountains and even smaller ones of trees. It had taken a long time to fill this in, for she wanted the mountains to have a similar look without being uniform in appearance. To the west of the African coast was the Ethiopian Sea, and in this she had drawn three ships, two above the name and one below.

There was a cartouche at the top, a rectangle with a scroll around the outside, with the scale drawn in the middle. There was another in the lower left corner with the title of the map. It was in this area that the cartographer's name was usually placed, and she tried not to think about how it would eventually read.

As she had seen on many of the maps she had colored, she drew a decorative around the outside of this cartouche. It featured two men, an elephant, and a rhino like those she had seen on other maps of Africa. As she put the finishing touches on the drawing, she noticed that the elephant had a fearsome aspect, and she wondered if this were an accurate depiction of that creature.

As she worked, an idea came to her. Perhaps Willem would agree to saying that she and Lucas had made the map together. This was far from ideal, but if it was all that was possible, it was better than not having her name attached to the project at all. Even if both men agreed, her name would most probably be lost if a man was named as the cartographer, for who would seriously believe that a woman could ever play a part in the creation of a map? Some might see it as an eccentric desire on Lucas's part to include her name on his work, the result of an overly indulgent brother.

Still, this was the best solution she could think of, and she did not have the luxury of time to mull over the situation and come up with other ideas. First, she needed to tell Lucas what she had asked of de Groot, what he had proposed, and what she had thought of to alter the plan. So, when she deemed that it must be close to the time for her brother's return, she quietly slipped downstairs and out the door. She would wait for her brother to come, and she would tell him that she needed to speak to him most urgently.

It was not long before she saw a familiar shape approaching in the dusk. She went to meet him and beg him to take a walk with her.

"Not this again, Anneke," he said. "I am exhausted."

"But it is very important that I speak to you right away!" she insisted.

"Very well, but can we not speak inside? Why must we trod along every time you want to tell me something?"

"I do not wish Papa and Mama to hear what I have to say. Please, Lucas!"

"Very well, Anneke, but let us go up to the loft room. No one will hear us there, and I can at least sit down."

"Then let me sneak in first. I have been there all day. I told Mama that I did not feel well. She doesn't know that I came downstairs."

"You haven't been at the mansion today? No wonder you have the energy to go for a stroll. You have been relaxing, for I see no evidence that you are truly unwell."

"You are correct, but I will explain all later. Ask Mama where I am, and when she answers you, tell her that you will come to check on me and sit with me a while before dinner if I would like some company."

"I don't understand all of this plotting, Anneke, but I'm too tired to argue with you."

When Lucas entered the loft room, Anneke quickly explained every-thing that had happened between her and de Groot, and she told Lucas of the compromise she wanted to propose. She had worried he would interrupt her before she finished, but he only sat and stared.

"So, Lucas, may I tell Willem that he may say that the map has been designed by both of us?" she finished.

"No!" Lucas found voice to say. "There are so many problems with what you have just said that I do not even know where to begin. Did you not hear me when I expressed my feelings about a map of a part of Africa? I did not argue with you further, but that does not mean I do not harbor grave misgivings. And now you wish to put my name to it? Even aside from that, I must ask, what have you done, Anneke? What have you done to make de Groot promise such a thing? I cannot imagine that it is anything honorable."

Ignoring her brother's first objection, because she had no answer to it, she did not temper her anger at his question. "How dare you, Lucas? How dare you make such an assumption about your own sister? Have your years at sea so sullied your mind that this is your immediate conclusion? Can you not fathom that a man might actually respect me and my work and wish to show his gratitude?"

"Frankly, Anneke, no, I cannot. And nor would the gossips. Surely you are not so innocent to think that others will not draw the same conclusion that I have. And why do you call him Willem? A slip like that would give people even more fodder to believe the worst of you."

No, I am no longer as innocent as I was, Anneke thought. *Vrouw Kregier has changed me in more ways than I wish to admit.* Still, what she said was, "But don't you see? That is why de Groot demands that the map be attributed to you. It is a way to put off the speculations."

"And what would people think of me? I am a surveyor and have training as a cartographer. What would people think of me that I had to lean on my sister for help in such a project?"

"Oh, Lucas! Can you think only of yourself? You speak of cruelties and injustices that you saw when you were gone, but can you not see the injustice of denying me this simply because I am a woman?"

"You had claimed that you wanted this for Papa," Lucas replied. She looked as though he had slapped her, but she could not deny the truth of what he said. "Was that but an excuse all along for your insistence on doing something you were not meant to do?"

"And why was I not meant to do it? You yourself have said that I was more adept at the cartography lessons than you were. Why must I be denied this?"

"Because of who you are, Anneke. Yes, because you are a woman. We all must accept the place that God has given us."

She did not know how to respond to this. Did she not believe that God had made her who she was supposed to be? Did his plan for her only include what was usually meant for a woman of this time and place? She rebelled at the thought, but that would leave her on her own, with no comforting knowledge of the inevitability of fulfilling God's plan. But, she told herself, if she had this desire and this talent, maybe God had planted those within her. Maybe he intended for her to do something exceptional.

"How do you know that this isn't God's plan for me, Lucas? Why would I feel this? Why would I have this skill if it weren't for him? Perhaps this is what I am predestined to do."

Now Lucas hesitated. "I don't know, Anneke. I don't know. I just feel that you are treading a dangerous path. I fear some dire consequence, for you, and perhaps for all of us."

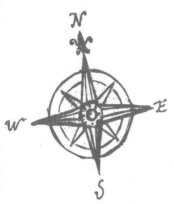

Chapter 23

August 1660

Anneke's mind let her think of nothing else after Lucas left her. She couldn't face her family at dinner. She quickly descended to show her mother that she wasn't ill, and to say that she was just tired and not hungry. In the bustle of putting dinner on the table, Anneke managed to slip away with some bread and cheese. Lucas's warning, this echo of Willem's sentiment, that she could not be named the map's creator because she was a woman, in turns discouraged and enraged her. Although Lucas had rejected her proposal, Anneke told herself that it was for reasons that held no worth. His objection that people would be suspicious of what she had done, or of what people would think of him, or of her proper place in the world, seemed insignificant in the face of what the world would gain by accepting her map, and with her name on it.

It wasn't just selfishness or ambition on her part. She did want to give her father something that he had always desired. Though he hid it behind his pride, she felt his disappointment in his own accomplishments. This would be something lustrous. Then it occurred to her that Isaac, too, would need for men to know that he had been instrumental in bringing about this map. Did she dare suggest to de Groot that he also be included in the map's attribution? She thought he might object less to the addition of her father's name than to that of her own. She also understood that if two men were to be named, there was an even greater chance that hers would be ignored. Still, she had to risk that, especially if she continued to embrace the notion that she was doing this for Isaac and not only for her own benefit. Having done her best to assure herself she would be able to convince de Groot to do as she asked, she fell asleep.

In the light of day, it was less easy to have faith in her plan, but Anneke told herself it was all she had. It seemed as though the words with which de Groot and Lucas had sought to discourage her had only inflamed her desire to see her own name on the map. She had, in truth, begun the map as a surprise for her father, but the predominance of that sentiment had changed as she worked. She loved the work itself, even though she had needed to do it clandestinely, at least as much as she reveled in her coloring, and she knew that she was good at it. Her confidence grew as she proceeded, and she saw that the map that she was creating was of a high quality. And who to judge better than she? Apart from cartographers themselves, and perhaps engravers, who knew the intricacies of a map better than a skilled colorist?

One such as she not only added beauty to the map but improved the viewer's ability to grasp the information therein. Borders and names and landscape features were more immediately identified by the coloring she did. And the beauty of the colors would cause the onlooker to study the various aspects of the map, to linger for a longer time. A colored map seduced in a way that no plain black lines could do.

As she approached the de Groot home, she again rehearsed what she would say to Willem. He would expect an answer to his proposal, and she did not want to delay. When Warner opened the door and led her to the map room, she was relieved to see that de Groot was already there, waiting for her. As soon as Warner left them, he turned his questioning eyes to her.

"Well, Anneke, have you learned to be content with the suggestion I made yesterday? I hope that you have, for it is the only way I can see of granting your wish."

"I have and I have not. I would like to make a slight adjustment to your idea."

"I will listen, but I warn you that my skill in negotiation is a large part of my success as a businessman." He gave her a half-smile, but Anneke didn't know whether it was meant to intimidate or reassure her. Still, she reminded herself, he was the one who had offered to do something for her in the first place.

She forced herself to look into his eyes. "You said that you wished to say that Lucas did the map. I would like to add my father's name, and also my own. Surely the objections you offered yesterday to having my name as the sole attribution would no longer apply if my brother's and my father's names were also listed."

His response was slow in coming, but he finally said, "And your father and brother would agree to this?"

"It is still my wish to keep this as a surprise for my father. I am certain that he will be thrilled when he learns that his dream has been made real."

"And your brother?"

"He will not object once it is done," she quickly replied, not at all certain that this would be the case. He might say that she had used him, but he was the one who had said that is what their family did.

"Very well, Anneke. I accept your proposal, but I must tell you that I am not happy with it. It is only because I said that I would do a favor for you, one of your choosing, that I will go ahead with this. I wish that I had never offered."

"Thank you." Anneke was torn between her feelings of hurt and relief. She should have better understood that he had probably simply wanted to buy her something. That would have been easy for him. He did not like her demands upon his actions. But he had accepted, and that was what mattered.

When it seemed that Willem had indeed abandoned the map room for the day, Anneke decided to do a task that would not require a high level of concentration. Looking at her supplies, she realized she was getting low on gum water. She would need gum arabic to prepare more, though. She didn't have any, but there was a drysalter a few blocks away. Her cloak was still damp from her walk in the misty morning, but she retrieved it from where it was drying near the fire and left the map room. Seeing no one about, she didn't bother to leave word. She didn't believe that Willem would return, and no one else would care where she was.

When she started walking, she realized that she didn't remember the precise location of the shop. A rosy-cheeked woman who was carrying a large covered basket gave her directions and she found the shop with no trouble and entered.

"You're the young woman that goes to de Groot's every day, are you not?" the shopkeeper, a fellow of middling age with an inquisitive face, greeted her.

Somewhat taken aback at having been recognized, Anneke nodded. "How is it that you know?"

"Oh, I've noticed you passing by. Of course, you don't pass directly by, but when I'm not busy, I like to stand in front of the shop to get some air and greet potential customers as they pass. When I look up the street, I can see those who walk by."

"There must be many times when you are not busy to have happened to notice me going by," Anneke said with less than extreme courtesy.

"Oh, but you pass by twice a day, don't you? Once coming and once going, though it's usually in the morning that I see you. I get here quite early. I don't sleep as well as I once did, you see, and I get everything ready, then I must wait for someone to decide they need my wares."

"But how did you know that I go to de Groot's? You cannot see that from here."

"Now that's true, but I'm not the only one to have noticed you, am I? You are a lovely young woman, and you often carry a type of large folder. We don't often see that, and I will say there's been speculation about what is in the folder, and what you do at de Groot's house."

Deciding that since there were clearly tales going around about her presence in the neighborhood, it would be best to tell this man what her business was so that he could snuff out any disparaging musings about what she might be up to. "If you must know, I am a map colorist and Heer de Groot has commissioned me to color many of the maps in his large collection."

"Is that so? And you a woman, and a young one at that."

"Indeed, although I have worked for years for the House of Blaeu. Can you now help me with my purchase?"

Anneke took the gum arabic for which she had come, and left the clerk to spread the word among the local gossips that he knew why the young woman went to de Groot's house.

When she returned to the map room, she realized that she had probably gotten more than she needed, but she could just use a bit at a time to make the gum water she would require for the next couple of weeks. Needing more water than what was always provided for her painting, she ventured from the map room, hoping to catch one of the servants. Soon she saw the young maid, Agneta. Anneke knew that the best water would be spring water, but she simply asked the girl to bring her a small bottle of clean water. The maid seemed a bit flustered to be approached, much less to be asked for something, but she seemed excited, too, and soon returned with the requested item.

"Oh, Juffrouw, are you going to use it for your painting?"

"Yes, I am. I will be making gum water, which I will mix with the paint. Thank you for bringing it to me. Would you like to see what I will do with it?"

"Oh, no. I'd best be getting back to my regular duties," the girl said, leaving the room but then turning to say, "You're welcome."

After beating the gum arabic on a wooden surface to make it dissolve more easily, Anneke placed it into a clean bottle and added the water. She shook it, set the bottle aside, and reminded herself to shake it a few more times that day. Once the gum arabic had completely dissolved, she would strain the liquid through a rag and put it into a stoppered glass bottle. The mixture would last for a month, and she hoped that she would still be there when it was time to prepare more. She was considering what to do next when Vrouw Kregier entered the room.

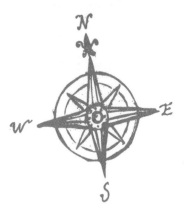

Chapter 24

August 1660

"I do not know what you and Willem talked about this morning, but he did not seem particularly pleased. Though I don't believe he had planned to leave the house today, he brusquely informed me that he needed to go out and I need not expect him to be home for several hours. I sent a message to my friend through a trusted servant, and I have just gotten his reply that he is ready to receive me as soon as I can go to him. So, we begin, Anneke."

"Begin?"

"Come now, you have agreed to this. Do not pretend that you do not understand my meaning. You will pack up some things that you might bring for a painting lesson, and we will leave together."

"But what if Heer de Groot returns and wonders where you are? Where I am?"

"I have told Warner that we are going to the home of Celia Hartgers, a friend of mine who will say that we have been there if that ever becomes necessary. She actually does have an invalid sister who lives with her, making it necessary for our 'painting lessons' to be at Vrouw Hartgers's home," Helena said, smiling as though at her own cleverness.

"But how do you know that you can trust this woman, this Vrouw Hartgers?"

"Oh, Celia? I have done favors for her, and she knows that I will again. We ladies must stick together, you know, Anneke."

Anneke merely nodded and gathered her things to leave. She

followed Helena out and saw a carriage waiting for them. Before she could think, she said, "I didn't know that you had a carriage."

"Naturally we do! Willem seldom uses it. He complains that the streets are so crowded that it is faster and more pleasant to walk. Come, climb in," she added as they approached the carriage.

"But am I to truly go with you?" Anneke asked, a trace of panic in her voice.

"Of course not, foolish thing, but we must be seen leaving together. We will go to Celia's home and enter it. I will tell the coachman not to wait but to return home, in case Willem needs him. I will give him a time to return for us. After he leaves, I will walk to my destination. It is not far. You will wait for me at Vrouw Hartgers's. Her husband maintains an extensive library, and I daresay one such as you will find amusement in reading while I am gone."

"But what will the servants think?"

"Oh, stop asking so many questions! I'm sure that my friend has thought of everything. You needn't worry. Come now!"

Anneke stepped up into the coach. She had never been in one before, but her nervousness prevented her from feeling any excitement. She was embarking upon a road not of her choosing, and there was no going back.

When the servant showed Helena and Anneke into the main room of Vrouw Hartgers's home, Anneke was surprised at what she saw. Having spent so many days in the de Groot home, she had thought that all of Helena's friends would live in homes just as extravagant. It was ironic that she found herself disdaining Vrouw Hartgers's furnishings since they were far superior to those of her own family. There really was no comparison. This home had more similarities to Helena's in the level of evident wealth than to her own parents' modest house, but still, there was a notable difference. Here the furnishings had worn or faded colors, and the tables and chairs had a heavy, solid, traditional feel as opposed to the lighter, more elegant lines of de Groot and Helena's French-inspired home. There were a few paintings on the walls, but they were not first-rate. The artists' skill levels were closer to her father's, Anneke thought, then felt a pang of guilt at this disloyal notion. On the whole, this home was like a map that was merely printed, finely done but not remarkable, whereas the de Groot home was like an exquisitely colored map.

When Vrouw Hartgers entered the room and greeted Helena, Anneke's impression was strengthened. The woman's bodice and skirt were made of silk, but not of the same quality as Helena's. The collar and cuff were trimmed with lace, but hardly of a finer workmanship than Anneke's own best set. Vrouw Hartgers clearly hoped to make an impression, but her garments did not compare to the wealth and sophistication of Helena's. In fact, Anneke found it difficult to believe that Helena, who so prided herself on her lofty station in the city of Amsterdam, should befriend such a woman as Vrouw Hartgers. It was in that moment that Anneke began to wonder whether Vrouw Hartgers was also someone whom Helena used in order to satisfy her own desires.

"My dearest Helena," Vrouw Hartgers said, approaching Helena, who seemed to withdraw a fraction.

"Hello, Celia. The arrangements have been made, and I would like to leave as soon as possible. This is the van Brug girl that I told you about. She will remain here until I get back so that the coachman will see us leave together."

Anneke thought she perceived some resentment from Vrouw Hartgers at Helena's peremptory tone, but who was she to judge? She had seen so few interactions between women like these. Still, she did just then recall that Vrouw Hartgers had not been a guest on the day Helena had invited Anneke for the midday meal, so perhaps this woman was not of Helena's inner circle.

"Very well, Helena. She can keep Ursula company while you are gone. It will be a relief for me to get a rest from her unpleasant mood." As Helena left, Anneke thought she discerned already a look of lust in her eyes.

"What am I to call you then, Juffrouw? I certainly don't intend to constantly address you as Juffrouw van Brug," Celia said.

"My name is Anneke, Vrouw Hartgers."

"Well, Anneke, follow me and I will introduce you to my sister, Ursula," Celia said, leading her up the winding stairs to a plain room where the visitor saw a woman not much older than herself sitting with a drab-colored blanket wrapped around her legs. The woman's chair had been positioned by a small window, thus affording the invalid the bit of sunlight that found its way between the surrounding homes.

"This is my sister. You may call her Ursula. Ursula, this is Anneke. She will sit with you a while."

"Who is she, and what is she doing here?" Ursula asked, giving Anneke only a cursory glance.

"You don't need to know that. I should think you would be glad for someone to talk to," Celia said as she left the room.

As uncomfortable as Anneke felt in this unwelcoming house, she found it in herself to feel a momentary sympathy for the seated woman. As hemmed in by her lack of choices as Helena had made her feel, it was clear this woman's life was infinitely more constricted.

"Well, come closer," Ursula said, and Anneke complied. "What are you doing here, then?"

Assuming Celia did not wish her sister to know the real reason for her presence, Anneke simply said, "I arrived with Vrouw Helena Kregier."

"Oh, that one. And she is not even doing me the courtesy of coming up to greet me?"

"I'm afraid that she has already left. I'm sorry."

"What do you have to be sorry for? I doubt you have any control over what she does. My sister thinks Helena is her friend, but Celia is a fool. There is not much that I can see from the confines of this room, but even I understand that Helena Kregier only uses her. She plays on Celia's ridiculous desire to enter into the upper echelons of Amsterdam society. I daresay that even you can see that the wealth of Helena's husband far exceeds that of my brother-in-law. Celia will never reach such lofty heights."

Not knowing how to reply to this extremely frank analysis, Anneke said nothing.

"How do you even know Helena?" Ursula said. "You are clearly from a family of only modest means. What use has Helena put you to?"

Choosing to answer only the first question, Anneke said, "Heer de Groot employs me as a map colorist in his home."

"He does, does he? You hardly look the type."

Anneke didn't bother to hide the note of anger in her voice. "I received the commission through the Blaeu printing house, for whom I have worked for years, and for whom my mother works. I resent the implication of your remark."

"Calm down, Juffrouw! I apologize that my mind went to such a place. I fear that my assumptions have been sullied by knowledge of the intrigues of my sister and Helena."

"You know of it then?" Anneke blurted out.

"Yes. I perceive that you are not a willing part of their plan. How has she forced your obedience?"

After a moment, Anneke replied. "Helena said that she would tell Heer de Groot that I had stolen something if I did not comply."

"Despicable woman! And it is such as she that my sister wishes to court. It sickens me." Then, after a pause, she said, "But come, pull a chair closer to me and sit down. Perhaps you will forgive my insults and indulge me with the pleasure of your company."

Glad to find that this woman seemed to sympathize with her predicament, and feeling that the time would pass more quickly in conversation with her, Anneke gave a small smile and said she would happily join Ursula while she waited. As they talked, Anneke learned that Ursula had not always been as she was now. She had at one time been married and had a child, but her husband and daughter had both died of a fever. Shortly after their deaths, she herself had "tumbled from a window" and broken her legs so badly that she could never walk again. Anneke did not question how such a fall could have taken place.

Anneke was so engrossed in Ursula's story that she was surprised when Celia abruptly appeared at the door to announce that Helena had returned and it was time for Anneke to leave.

"Thank you for your company, and for telling me about yourself, Ursula," Anneke said, taking the woman's hand in her own. "I imagine that I will see you again, but I know not when."

"Although I understand that the reason for your visit is shameful to you, I am selfishly still happy that I will have further chances to converse with you," the woman said from her chair as Anneke was ushered from the room.

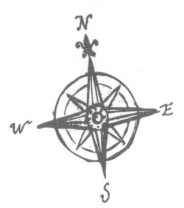

Chapter 25

August 1660

Another night of restlessness. Even though she had known that she would be called upon to fulfill her part in Helena's deception, Anneke had somehow hoped that the day would never come; that surely Helena would not be so bold as to enact her plan; that surely she herself would not need to play a part in it. But she had, and it weighed on Anneke even more than she had feared it would. It was she who was making Helena's sin possible. Anneke told herself that perhaps her part in the evil was lessened by the slight relief that she could offer to Ursula with her company, but this did nothing to alleviate the feeling that she, too, was stained by Helena's adultery.

And what would Daniel think if he were to learn of her part in this disgraceful conduct? They had seen each other only a few times since the day he had come to the midday meal at her family's house. It seemed that his parents' demands on him had not decreased as much as he had expected. Now, with what she had done, she instinctively drew back from the idea of seeing him, for she would feel ashamed.

Sometime in the night, Anneke began asking herself whether she should abandon her commission and never again enter the de Groot home. She now felt so trapped there, and a chance of escape, of just leaving the sordid trickery, was very tempting. Each time, though, she came back to the reasons she would not leave. It would mean the end of her father's dream, and hers, to bring a new map into the world. Not only that, if she were to leave, Blaeu would dismiss her for displeasing such an important client. Her mother might even lose her spot, in spite of all her faithful years of coloring Blaeu's maps.

Further, from spite, Helena might well go ahead with her plan to tell Willem that Anneke had stolen something. Even though Anneke thought it possible that Willem might suspect she had concocted the story, Helena's vanity would never allow her to imagine that Willem would doubt her. Besides, Anneke felt certain that Helena's desire for vengeance against Anneke would overtake all other considerations.

So it was that Anneke ate little for breakfast and left the house without even telling her mother goodbye. She didn't feel that she could fully face her, hiding what she now had to hide.

When she arrived at de Groot's, part of her marveled that Warner showed her into the map room as always, with no difference in his manner toward her. And, indeed, why should he not? The disgrace that Anneke felt was not visible for all to see.

Although she told herself that she shouldn't, as she had never done so before, Anneke inquired after Helena. Being told that the mistress would probably keep to her room that day, Anneke didn't trust herself with any response, trying to hide her relief.

While she was anxious to hear from Willem about whether he had spoken to Blaeu, she was glad that he was not in the map room when she entered. She would have time to compose herself, to immerse herself in work, so that when de Groot did come in, she would not need to look at him directly. After a brief greeting, he often simply watched her in silence for some time, not wishing his presence to unnecessarily distract her. She retrieved the map she had planned to work on the previous day before Helena had dragged her away. Remembering that she had begun the process to make gum water, she went to the shelf and stirred the bottle.

"Ah, I see that you are already hard at work," Willem said as he entered.

Anneke didn't know whether Helena had told him they had been out the previous day or whether she would have to explain why she had made no progress. She wasn't certain he would notice, but she feared he would. She got her answer when Willem said, "So, I hear that you and Helena went to Celia's home yesterday."

"Yes, we did."

"Did Ursula also participate in the lessons?" he asked, and Anneke hesitated, hating to directly lie to him. She was spared the immediate necessity for it when he added, "Oh, yes, I suppose she must have, since that was the reason for having the lessons there." But then he asked, "How did the ladies do?"

In response to Anneke's "It's difficult to say," de Groot merely laughed. "Ah, you show yourself to be the tactful young woman that I already knew you were. Well, you shall have to work all the harder today to make up for your absence yesterday, even though it was due to my wife's whim rather than any neglect on your part. Don't worry, Anneke. I doubt there will be many more lessons. Helena quickly loses interest in any activity for which she is not the focus of attention. For now, I must attend to some business. I shall return this afternoon."

Anneke nodded and began to prepare the colors she would need for the morning's work. She decided to finish the borders and the cartouches on the map of Ireland that de Groot had begun. After attempting to mitigate the ill effects of his work, she finally abandoned the map in frustration. She was absorbed in her own work when, as had happened every day after her first month there, food was brought in to her for the midday meal. This was much simpler fare than what Anneke had eaten with Vrouw Kregier and her guests, and Anneke imagined it was the meal the servants ate. Still, it was always very good and usually included soup, meat or fish, and salad or fruit. She was happy she did not have to bring something with her or walk home to take her meal there. Besides, Lysbeth did not always pause long enough in her coloring to make very much at midday, though it was considered by most Amsterdamers to be the main meal of the day. The offerings seemed even more acceptable to Anneke since de Groot often ate with her, foregoing a fancier meal with his wife.

All day, Anneke had waited for de Groot to return and tell her whether he had spoken with Blaeu. Finally, as the day's light started to wane, he appeared. In the afternoon's long hours, she had decided she would ask him. She had no confidence that Helena's scheme would continue to remain secret, and she worried about how Willem would react if he found out. Looking up from her worktable, she said, "May I ask whether you have spoken to Heer Blaeu?"

His reply was sharper than she had hoped. "Do not press me on this, Anneke! You know that I am not happy with what you have proposed, and I have no desire to rush to Blaeu's and perhaps make a fool of myself. Besides, in my surprise at your initial request, and then your changes to my stipulation, a most essential factor quite slipped my mind."

"And what is that?" Anneke asked somewhat meekly.

"I would like to see the map! How am I to recommend something sight unseen? If I were to do that, I would indeed deserve any scorn that might come my way. I have often praised your work as a colorist, Anneke, but your ability to create a map is not a foregone conclusion. No, I must see the map for myself. I must judge its quality as best I can, and perhaps even ask some other map enthusiasts I know to look at it."

"Oh, no, please! You must not do that!"

"What? Not even ask to see the map?"

"No. I understand your desire to see the map, and I will show it to you. But please, I beg of you, do not show it to others. What if word of it got out? I want it to be something completely new, something to astonish."

"Are you not perhaps exaggerating the effects that one map can have?" Willem asked, now with a gentler tone.

"That could be. But my map will be a new one, and given that so many times the maps that are printed are just the same ones previously put out by that house, or purchased or copied from another printing house, a new map is something to be noted. Especially one of a part of Africa."

"You may be right, and it will create a small stir. I do not know.

I will admit that I am often impressed by your understanding of the map-printing business in our city. When you first came, I expected you only to add an additional dimension to my maps, the beauty, and sometimes clarification, that color can bring. I will admit that you are more knowledgeable than I had anticipated."

"Thank you," Anneke said. She was flattered but knew his admiration would not mean he would recommend her map without first studying it himself.

"Nevertheless, you must bring the map. Do not allow my offer to do you a favor persuade you that I will let go of this requirement. I will not grant your wish at a risk to my own reputation. Besides, I will need to bring the map with me if I am to go to Blaeu's."

"I understand. Will you give me a few days?"

"Have you not finished it, then? You would have had me recommend a map that is not even complete?"

"It is not that! It is simply that I would wish to make a copy."

"Take as much time as you need, Anneke. It is you, not I, who wished to hurry this along." With that, he left the room, and for another day, she sensed his displeasure.

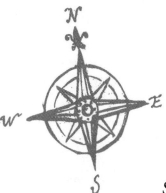

Chapter 26

September 1660

Two things overshadowed all else in Anneke's mind. She was terrified that her part in Helena's affair would be revealed. Even were it never brought to light, she felt dirtied by it, and though she reminded herself she could not have refused Helena's demand, that did not alleviate the disgust she felt for herself. She wished it to end, but she knew that would only happen when Helena grew tired of the game or when they were discovered. Anneke feared that even if Helena were to stop her deceit, somehow she herself would suffer. Her feeling of foreboding that it would culminate in disaster had prompted her to push de Groot into making the request of Blaeu soon.

Now she chastised herself for not having foreseen that de Groot would need to see the map, would need to bring it to the print house with him. What a foolish error! She had to fight off the doubt it threatened to cast over her confidence in her own ability. And it was a serious oversight, for she had misled de Groot into thinking the map was complete. It was close, but she still had some vital parts to finish. She also wished to painstakingly review the material she had used in its creation to make sure she had not misrepresented anything.

She would be putting her father's name to it, and Lucas's, and her own. Any obvious error would shame them all, but the greatest blame—she told herself bitterly—would be laid at her feet. She could hear the criticism now. *How could a woman create a map? Just allowing her to participate in the process was sure to invite error.* Even given that this was so, Isaac and Lucas would also suffer. Since Lucas's surveying position was linked to the art of cartography in the minds of many, his reputation could be ruined. She reminded herself that she had misled de Groot in this also, implying that Lucas had agreed to the attribution. And what of the consequences for Isaac? How would it reflect upon him to have his name attached to an inferior work, one riddled with mistakes? Even though his livelihood as a painter was not directly tied to the world of maps, his name would also be ridiculed.

Anneke tried to put these worries aside, promising herself she would make sure that her map was completely faithful to her father's notes. She did not let herself think that there might be a problem with her source.

Lost in her world of worry, Anneke was surprised when anyone in her family brought up something outside its realm. She half-listened to their conversations and answered only when roused from her private disquietude, as on the occasion when they were eating together and she heard her mother say, "Anneke, what is happening with Daniel?"

"Daniel?" Anneke repeated, as though she had never before heard the name.

"Yes, Daniel. What is wrong with you, dearest?"

"Oh, I'm sorry, Mama. Nothing is wrong. I am just tired."

"That's not surprising," remarked her father. "So many evenings, after having worked at de Groot's all day, you go up to the loft room. What is it you are doing up there, daughter? Is he demanding that you do work even outside of the normal hours of a working day? He seems to be taking advantage of you."

"It's not that, Papa," Anneke replied, and added without thinking, "I'm working on something for myself."

"Something for yourself? What could that possibly be?" demanded Isaac.

"Oh, it's nothing, Papa. I am just experimenting with some color mixtures and combinations of colors that I am thinking of using."

"That sounds interesting, Anneke," her mother said. "Perhaps you could show them to me sometime."

Anneke took another bite of her beet salad to give herself time to think. "The thing is, Mama, I've not really come up with anything I'm satisfied with. It's only something I hoped to try on some of the maps for de Groot. I don't think it's anything you could use for your coloring, as the work you do is much more restricted by accepted practices."

When she saw her mother's face fall, Anneke knew that she had hurt her mother and sought to soften her words. "Really, sometimes the demand from de Groot for innovation is quite tiresome, and I don't think that the quality of the resulting map will be as high as those that are more conventionally colored."

Even to her own ears, her words seemed disingenuous, and when she saw her mother's expression, she felt certain that Lysbeth had sensed her insincerity. She felt that an apology would only empha-size the insult, so not knowing how to repair the situation, Anneke remained silent.

"Well, if you worked in a more challenging and artistic medium, such as oils, perhaps I could help you. As it is, though, I hardly think it's worth my time," Isaac said. Perhaps he had meant to defend his wife against Anneke's insensitivity, but managed only to add to the insult.

Once Isaac and Lucas had left the room, Lysbeth sought to restore a semblance of harmony between herself and her daughter "I don't think you said what the situation is with you and Daniel, Anneke."

Grateful for her mother's generosity of spirit, Anneke replied. "Oh, Mama. I don't know. I like Daniel, but I rarely see him now. There is little call for me to go to the printing house, and you know yourself how busy I am. Besides, although he is still going to Leiden most of his free days, he could make more of an effort to see me."

"I understand, but maybe you should go to the printing house more often and speak to him in a way that shows that you are still interested. It is not unusual for young men to need a nudge. It may seem to him that his duties in Leiden are beyond his control, and it is you who are neglecting him by staying away from Blaeu's.

"He seems like a nice young man, and I think he could be a good match for you, Anneke. He, too, wishes to advance himself. Perhaps you should not treat his interest so lightly. If you do like him, you cannot just ignore him and expect he will be waiting for you. I thought it seemed as though he cared for you, but a man will only be so patient. There are other girls, I'm sure, who would happily receive Daniel's attentions."

"Please, Mama. Can we not talk of this? I understand what you are saying, but in truth, I have so many other things on my mind that I've rarely thought about Daniel. Does that mean something? I'm not even sure how I feel, so though you say I should make more effort to see him, maybe that would be unfair to him."

"Only you can know your feelings, daughter, but remember, there will be no line of men waiting for you when you decide that you have time for them. You do not want your chances to pass you by."

With mixed feelings of fatigue and irritation, Anneke said, "I am sorry, Mama. I cannot talk about this anymore. Please, excuse me." She left the table, leaving Lysbeth to wonder what it was that so occupied her daughter's thoughts.

"You are working on that map, aren't you?" Lucas's tone was accusing as he followed Anneke up the stairs.

"Yes, I am. You know that I am, Lucas."

"Why do you persist? Do you actually think there is any chance that Blaeu, or anyone else for that matter, will publish it?"

"I have reason to believe that it will be published, yes."

"You say this is for Papa, but why are you putting so much into something for a man who only disparages what you do?" Lucas asked, his voice rising.

"Fine!" Anneke replied, now matching his tone. "It's not just for Papa. I want this for me, too, Lucas. I want it for me. Can you not understand it?"

"Yes," he said more softly. "So, you are falling into our family's tradition of using one another. You are using father's notes and dreams as an excuse for your own."

"And why shouldn't I? If I am not supposed to have such ambitions of my own, then yes, I will adopt those of others to achieve my own desires." With that, Lucas left, and Anneke wondered if she was any different from Helena, taking advantage of people to achieve her ends. Lucas had accused her of adopting their father's dream for her own purposes. How much more appalled would he be if he knew that his name would also appear on the map?

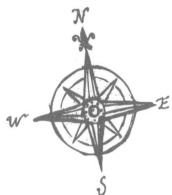

Chapter 27

September 1660

Anneke was surprised to find that de Groot was gone again the next day. She couldn't help but feel this was a sign of his displeasure with her, but there was nothing she could do. Perhaps if she accomplished a lot today, it would assuage his vexation. It crossed her mind that Helena might demand her assistance again, but she put this out of her mind as she chose which map to continue with and then prepared the paint she would need. By midmorning, she was so engrossed in her work that when Helena entered the map room, Anneke looked up in surprise.

"Ah, Anneke. Hard at work, I see. Aren't you the diligent one! Well, you will have to put aside your colors, for we are to have our lessons again today. I, too, have been busy this morning. I have sent and received messages, and everyone is ready to receive us." This she said with a lascivious smile, impossible to misinterpret.

When they arrived at the home of Vrouw Hartgers, things went much the same as before. This time, though, Anneke felt less awkward as she simply went right to Ursula's room.

"Anneke! I am happy to see you. I hadn't expected that you would come back so soon."

"Nor had I." Anneke's reply held considerably less enthusiasm.

"I am sorry. I know that you would much rather not be here, and I share in your considerable distaste for what is going on. That does not have to mean that we may not enjoy one another's company. I know that the benefit is much more to me than to you, but I would hope that visiting with me at least makes your wait less tedious."

Feeling she had done this woman a disservice with her attitude, Anneke said, "Of course, you are right, Ursula. Our conversation was the one pleasant aspect of my last visit, as I'm sure it will be of this one."

"Since your purported reason for being here is to give lessons in watercolor, I hope you don't mind that I've had some materials brought in so that you might instruct me in the rudiments of the art. I doubt I will be a very adept pupil, but then any of my efforts will only be for my own pleasure. I will not inflict my creations on anyone else."

"I think that is an excellent idea," Anneke replied with unfeigned sincerity. It would be a relief to have something to distract her from her reason for being here.

The two women passed a couple of hours pleasurably. Anneke chose a flowering tree as the subject, thinking that it would be something fairly simple. Ursula attempted to imitate what the younger woman showed her, and Anneke was generous with her praise. She felt sorry for Ursula, who clearly had few chances to do anything other than sit alone in her room. Anneke also wondered at her ability to seemingly accept her life as it was without turning to bitterness and accusation.

At first, the lesson brought a moment of peace to Anneke, away from the turbulence that engulfed her everywhere else. At de Groot's, there was his continued aloof manner and the daily tension over whether Helena would press her into service. At home, there was pressure to finish the map and the growing guilt that she felt over her dishonesty. She was lying to her parents about what she was doing in the evenings. Even more, she was deceiving them through her silence about the despicable part she played in Helena's ruse. They did not know she had told de Groot to use her brother's and her father's names when talking to Blaeu. They did not know of her burning ambition.

Within Ursula's room, Anneke briefly pushed her forebodings to the back of her mind. As they worked, Ursula asked questions. At first, they were general questions about Anneke's family and her experience as a colorist. She seemed to simply be showing a friendly interest when she asked more detailed questions. How did the experience of coloring maps at home, at Blaeu's, and at de Groot's compare?

Ursula's queries then naturally led to questions about people, and she would often pause her efforts to mimic what Anneke was painting. Each new bit of information seemed fascinating to Ursula. Anneke's father was an artist, and his name was Isaac. Her brother, Lucas, was a surveyor. Her mother, Lysbeth, was also a colorist, and her mother's family name was Plettenburg. Anneke attributed Ursula's curiosity to a hunger for more contact with the outside world, vicarious though that contact was.

After getting what details she could about Anneke's family, Ursula went on to ask about the printing house. Whenever Anneke tried returning them to the painting lesson, Ursula complied for a few moments but then laid down her brush and continued with what had begun to feel to Anneke like an interrogation. What was Heer Blaeu like? Did she have much contact with him? Was there someone she particularly liked? When Anneke mentioned Daniel the pressman, Ursula persisted in her questions until Anneke shared that she and Daniel had spent time together and that he had been a guest in her family's home. From her excited reaction, Anneke could tell that Ursula's view of what she felt for Daniel might surpass reality. Still, she hesitated to disillusion her since it seemed she gained pleasure from this romantic image. Finally, Ursula asked about the household of Willem de Groot and Helena Kregier.

"Helena and Willem seem to have an unusual marriage," she began.

"Do you know them well?" Anneke asked as she added flowers to her tree.

"I have met Willem on one or two occasions and Helena several times, when my sister is trying to impress them. I don't know how she thinks she will do that. I understand that their house is considerably grander than this one."

"It is true that it is quite imposing."

"Do you know, on the few occasions that they have been here, I have had the distinct feeling they would rather have remained at home. I wonder that my sister cannot sense this, but perhaps her desire to be included into their group of friends blinds her to what seems so plain to me.

"I am not so unaware as people assume me to be, simply because my legs will not hold me. I not only observe but have ample time to ponder what I have seen. And perhaps my reflections are not as colored by my own wants and desires as are those of someone like my sister. So, tell me, Anneke, what do you think will become of the de Groot–Kregier marriage?"

"I do not know that I can speak of it with any deeper knowledge than you seem to possess, and perhaps we should not speculate."

"Oh, come now," replied Ursula. "Do you not think that Helena, at least, invites conjecture by including so many of us in her affairs?"

"I am sorry, Ursula. I do not care to continue with this conversation." Anneke put down the brush she had been holding and headed for the door.

"So now your sensibilities are too delicate? You disappoint me, Anneke," Ursula called to the retreating figure. "I had judged yours a stronger character."

Anneke made no reply as she left the room. She started to descend the steps but paused partway down to calm herself. What had brought about this sudden change in the woman Anneke had thought was serene and wise, gracefully accepting the restrictions of her life? Or had this been Ursula's essence all along and Anneke had been too preoccupied with her own concerns to notice? She told herself that it seemed impossible, but could Ursula have had some nefarious purpose all along? With questions swirling through her mind, she carefully walked down the remaining stairs, lest her inner turmoil cause her to misstep.

Over the next days, Anneke struggled to put the strange encounter with Ursula from her mind. She continued working on the map in the evenings by the faint light afforded by her candles, but she told herself that she would need to find daylight hours when she wasn't at de Groot's in order to review everything.

They had not spoken of the map since de Groot insisted Anneke bring it to him before he would go to Blaeu. To an outsider, it would have seemed that their days continued much as they had done, but that was not so. Before, de Groot had told Anneke which maps he would like her to work on, and he would immediately ask for her plan. She would tell him that she needed more time to study the map, first to go through in her mind how she might color it in a more conventional way and then look for innovative ways to alter the coloring. Each map would offer different possibilities. This had become a familiar game with them. He would ask even though he knew what her answer would be. She would lightly respond with the words he knew were coming, and they would both smile.

Now, though, there was a different tone. His question held more of a demand, her answer more of a rebuke. He brusquely asked what she intended for the day, and she showed him which maps she would work on and told him how she would approach each one. Many days he gave her no new map, and though she knew he meant this as a sign of his displeasure, Anneke was relieved to have a respite from new maps constantly being added.

Each map took at least several days to complete, some longer, as each part, after being painted, needed to dry before another part was begun. Thus there was a constant shifting around of maps. She had taken to making notes of her plan for each one so as to easily take up where she had left off. When de Groot gave her a new map, she always made at least a small start to gratify him. Now she hoped to come closer to finishing those that were already in progress.

Whenever de Groot was absent, Helena pressed Anneke into service. When Helena next left Anneke at the home of Celia Hartgers, Anneke demurred when it was suggested that she should, as usual, go up to pass the time with Ursula. Celia did not seem to give any great importance to her sister's comfort and did not protest when Anneke thus deprived Ursula of her company. She did not even question the change.

After that, Anneke always brought a book to take her mind off the situation in which she found herself, now without the distraction of what she had perceived as a budding friendship. Perhaps Helena's use of her had made her more suspicious of others, but after Ursula's outburst, Anneke wondered if she, too, had some dark plan. Well, she would not give her the opportunity to fulfill it. Surely there was nothing she could do from the confines of her room.

To exacerbate Anneke's feeling of impending disaster, Helena's behavior was becoming ever more reckless. One day, she tarried longer than she should have, and they did not arrive back at the de Groot home until well after dark. This had not been their previous practice, and Anneke had been certain Willem would not credit Helena's weak excuse for why the "lesson" had gone on so long. "We were just so entranced by what Anneke was teaching us that we didn't even notice the passing time." Willem at least acted like he believed her, and Anneke wondered whether he was actually so trusting of his wife or simply wished to accept what she told him. Perhaps he didn't want to discuss it in front of the servants, and she realized that to him, she would fall into that same category. *How shocked he would be if he knew that I am more aware of his wife's passions than is he.*

Having so easily deceived her husband, Helena seemed bent on testing just how far his gullibility would extend, or maybe she had simply ceased to care. It was clear to Anneke that as Helena's assignations continued, she seemed ever less mindful of the impression she gave when they returned to her home. It might be that her hair was not as neatly arranged as it usually was or that her skin was flushed. One day, Anneke even noticed that Helena's lips seemed swollen and bruised. Surely Willem, and also the servants, would notice that she was taking on the look of a wanton woman.

As the situation became more obvious to her, Anneke became more panicked about getting the map to de Groot. As she reviewed what she had done, she felt a stab of panic the few times when she found she had committed some error that had to be corrected. What if there were other inaccuracies that she had missed? It was as frustrating as a nightmare, except that morning would bring no relieving reassurance that all was well.

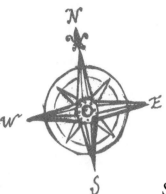

Chapter 28

September 1660

As she approached her home in the twilight, Anneke saw a figure who seemed to linger at her doorstep. He paced and kept glancing around, and when he saw her, he started to walk her way. As the man came near, she recognized Daniel.

"Daniel! What are you doing here?" she asked before she could think of a gentler greeting.

"What do you think I am doing here, Anneke? I came to see you."

"It is just that I am surprised."

"I have waited for you to come to Blaeu's, but you seem to have abandoned the printing house."

"I have been so busy, Daniel, and I thought that you had no free time anyway."

"Yes, you have been busy at de Groot's," he said bitterly. Then, in a tenderer voice, he said, "I care for you Anneke. I thought that you cared for me, too."

"I do, Daniel, but has your situation changed? Do you now have time to see me?"

"Yes, things are easing up with my parents' bookshop. I hope that they will be able to carry on now without so much help from me. May I see you Sunday? Perhaps we can take a stroll and find somewhere to eat." After a moment, he said, "I want us to get back to how we were, Anneke."

"I, too, would like to try, Daniel. I will see you Sunday then." Still,

Daniel might have hoped for more encouragement as he watched her turn from him and climb the four steps to her parents' door.

Once inside, Anneke told her mother that she had much work to do and excused herself from attending the evening meal with the family. At Lysbeth's anxious reply, she assured her mother that she would come down later and get some bread and cheese if she were hungry.

Going straight to the loft room, Anneke got out her materials to continue with the map. Despite her pressing need to finish the map, however, she found herself returning to her encounter with Daniel. She did care for him, she told herself, and perhaps she had been too abrupt. After all, his straightforward and caring manner offered an inviting refuge from the ugly complications of the de Groot home.

Anneke's parents had been visibly pleased when she told them she would be seeing the pressman. Anneke had enjoyed their time together, simply strolling and stopping for some food and drink at a cozy establishment Daniel knew. Although their stated goal of returning to their former feelings could have made for an awkward afternoon, they simply allowed themselves to show their pleasure at being together and to put from their minds any doubts from the time they had been apart.

Anneke returned home with a sense of hope about the future that she hadn't felt for weeks. She could see a time beyond the maze of her current problems, a time when she could live a proper life. It would still not be an ordinary life, however, for she would not let go of her ambition. She wished to be broadly recognized for her coloring, and she longed to continue creating maps. Once this map was published, surely she could find those who had information but not the cartographic skills to transform it into a map. Perhaps Heer Blaeu would even help her. Perhaps Daniel could be the kind of husband who did not feel diminished by his wife's success.

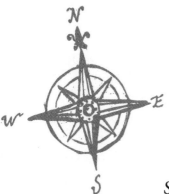

Chapter 29
September 1660

"I have finished my map," Anneke announced as de Groot entered the map room.

"Oh? Have you brought it?" he asked, and Anneke was gratified that he seemed genuinely interested. Perhaps he had forgiven her for the attribution demands. Perhaps his own passion for maps simply overshadowed all else.

"No, I haven't. I did not know whether you would be here today, and I didn't wish to bring it if you might be absent again." As she said it, she knew it sounded like a criticism, and she regretted that. She didn't want to risk his vexation again, nor did she wish him to ascribe her desire for his presence to anything other than her need for his help. She had quelled her feelings for him, which could never have come to anything. She had seen the results of Helena's blatant desire for someone outside of her marriage, and she was repulsed at the idea that she herself might have hoped for a more intimate bond with de Groot.

"I see. Well, we can take the carriage and go to your house today to retrieve it, if you wish. Otherwise, I will make sure that I am here tomorrow."

"Let us plan on tomorrow, then," Anneke quickly replied, having no desire to have to explain to her parents why this important man was accompanying her to their home. Besides, if Willem were home the following day, there was no chance Helena would demand her services.

∾

That night, Anneke reviewed her creation and decided it was the best that she was capable of doing. She felt that the map was a faithful depiction of the information in her sources, but she knew her opinion of her own work might be swayed by her yearning for it to be good. It was not merely her own perspective, however, for when she showed it to him the next day, de Groot also seemed impressed with what she had achieved, although he had frowned when he saw the title of the map and below it the names of Isaac van Brug, Lucas van Brug, and Anneke van Brug. She left the map with him in the hope that he would take it to Blaeu.

At the de Groot home the following day, she was told the master was not in and that he had left a note for her. She went to the map room, walked over to the window, and unsealed the note.

Anneke,

Now that I have seen the high quality of the map that you have produced, I am going to see Joan Blaeu today. I do not wish this strain between us to continue, and hopefully once this is decided one way or the other, we can return to our earlier ease.

Of course, neither you nor I have the expertise that Blaeu has, but I at least know that I will not be embarrassed to show him your map. We will see how he reacts to the attribution you have included below the title. I must repeat that this is not what I would have wished. However, having offered a favor, I feel that it is incumbent upon me to attempt to fulfill it.

Willem de Groot

Anneke folded the paper and stared out the window, trying to get her feelings in order. She was both excited and anxious about what would happen at Blaeu's. Now that the meeting was happening, perhaps at this very moment, she was unnerved by her own boldness in asking for her name to be included. Still, there was nothing she could do, and even if she were to be given the chance to retract her request, she would not have done so. She could see no other path toward making her way in the cartographic world.

She imagined how she would react when she heard Blaeu's answer. She did feel some trepidation at the thought that he might accept the map for the *Atlas Maior* with all three attributions. If he did, hopefully Lucas would see the advantage it would mean for him, even though he might be briefly angry with her for using his name when he had pointedly rejected her request. Certainly her father would be thrilled to see the fulfillment of his dream, and she did not think he would at all mind his name being included as one of its creators. He would see it as only his due, since the information used to produce it had come from him. And what would it mean to Anneke to have her name attached to the map? She longed to believe that it would open a new world of possibilities.

If Blaeu refused? When she thought of that very real possibility, she was flooded with disappointment, but underneath was also a feeling of relief. Lucas would never have to know of her duplicity. Perhaps there was even consolation in knowing that she would probably have to abandon the idea of creating more maps. Surely, even with having had a map accepted by Blaeu, it would be a constant struggle to find someone willing to trust his project to a woman. She knew that she already excelled at coloring, and she saw no reason why her success in that area would not grow. Anneke consoled herself with these thoughts and was starting to get out materials for the day when Helena entered.

"Do not bother with that now, Anneke. We must leave in a few minutes."

"Today? But Heer de Groot may return shortly. He only went to see Heer Blaeu. Surely we should stay home today."

Helena replied with scornful amusement, "Oh? Do you then know my husband's plans better than I? And what if he does return home before we do? It has happened before."

"Yes, but don't you think that we have been absent too frequently? Will he continue to believe that you and Celia and Ursula are so taken with watercolor lessons?"

"I would say that is my worry, not yours. Besides, have you not seen how he reacts to whatever fabrication I feed him? He makes himself blind to my faults and will also do so with my transgressions. To do otherwise would complicate his life, would mean he had to attend to something other than his business and his maps. And you." Helena spat out these last words. With a jolt, Anneke understood for the first time the depth of Helena's unhappiness, and perhaps a jealousy which had spurred her to drag down her husband's colorist. "Be ready to leave in five minutes."

Lost in thought, Anneke awaited Helena's return to Vrouw Hartgers's home. She had been so focused on de Groot talking to Blaeu that she had failed to imagine what would come after that. With a sinking feeling, she realized her excursions with Helena would probably continue no matter what happened with Blaeu. But how would this end? Surely Willem could not forever pretend he was oblivious to Helena's deception. It was even conceivable that Helena, in her desperate bid to gain her husband's attention, might tell him what she had done. Anneke had no doubt that she would also reveal her own part in the scheme. If Anneke tried to leave before that happened, Helena would tell de Groot that she was a thief.

There could be no happy ending to this story. Should she tell Willem herself? Should she explain how Helena had threatened her if she did not take part in her plan? At best, Willem would rightfully ask why she had not told him this before. At worst, he would see to it that she was disgraced. No matter what, she saw now that she could not hope to continue to work for him.

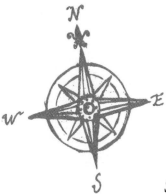

Chapter 30

September 1660

She knew what she must do. Anneke would go to Willem before he guessed the truth, before Helena could present her version of it. In telling him, she could not hide her part in the deception, but she hoped to make him understand that she had been given no choice. Surely his pride would prevent him from making his wife's behavior public knowledge. Once he understood what Helena had done, Anneke's part in it would seem minor. He may even be able to view her, along with himself, as Helena's victim.

She would not tell him immediately, though. First, she would give Helena a chance to discontinue the liaisons. They had not yet been discovered, and if she stopped now, perhaps all would remain forever secret. Surely even Helena must see that this was their only recourse. If she had to, Anneke would talk to Helena about her decreasing caution, about her recent untidy and improper appearance. Anneke felt certain the servants would soon become aware of their mistress's transgressions, if they had not already guessed. Perhaps Willem could pretend not to notice, but the servants would have no such compunction, and once they knew, Anneke felt certain that one of them would go to their master. Helena's manner inspired no loyalty.

When she arrived at the de Groot home, Anneke contrived to speak to Helena alone.

"Vrouw Kregier," she began. "I believe that it is only a matter of time, and probably a short time, until Heer de Groot discovers your disloyalty. Do you not think that it is time to stop? I beg this of you, for both of our sakes."

"Oh, it is 'Vrouw Kregier' now, is it? Do you not think we are on more intimate terms than that, Anneke?" Helena said mockingly. "And what makes you think that I care at all about you or your opinion? I have made you my creature, and thus you will remain until I have no further use for you. I will stop when I want to. In fact, I have begun to tire somewhat of the gentleman, but now I think I will carry on a bit longer just to show you who is mistress here."

Something in Anneke cracked. Fury surged in her for all the stress and worry she had endured because of this woman, and she said between clenched teeth, "Then I will tell Heer de Groot what you are doing!" Even in her rage, she expected that Helena would offer only another condescending remark, reminding her of all the reasons she would suffer at least as much as herself if their treachery were to become known. Anneke was taken aback at Helena's quick reply.

"Are you mad?"

Anneke saw more than fury in her face. She saw fear. The servants would hear if Helena shouted, but were that not the case, Anneke was sure Helena would be screeching.

"I am not mad. I am serious. I will tell your husband before your behavior comes to light. I will give him my side of what has happened. I believe he will show me mercy and will understand that whatever slander you tell him about me, it is but your desperation and vengeance."

"Anneke, you cannot do this," Helena said. It was as though the seriousness of her sin had suddenly become clear to her. "Do you know what they do to wives who commit adultery?"

In truth, Anneke did not know. She knew that the preachers spoke about its evils, but she knew of no consequence other than shame.

"They could leave me to whatever punishment Willem decides to inflict upon me. If he hands me over to the authorities, I could be fined, imprisoned, or banished! Can you ask me to accept that, Anneke?"

"But surely Heer de Groot would wish to keep it silent."

"Would he?" Helena said, a hint of hope now entering her voice. "I wish that I were as certain as you are. Though when we began, I boasted of my husband's great love and regard for me, or at least for what my beauty brings to him, I do not know how far that would go to protect me. His selfishness and pride might counsel him to keep this quiet, but he might act rashly, even against his own interests."

"Then stop now, Helena! Even if the servants have noticed something amiss, if they see no further evidence, surely they will keep quiet about any suspicions. Please, Helena! I truly did not know the possible legal consequences for what you are doing, but now that I do, I beg you to think of your own good as well as mine."

"How confident you have become," Helena said after a few moments, and her voice seemed calmer now. "I underestimated you, Anneke. I begin to see that there is more to you than I imagined, a part that even Willem has not seen, I daresay. You frightened me there for a moment, but I believe that you are right. Very well, Anneke, we will stop our 'lessons.' I didn't learn much anyway." With this, she left the room.

Anneke felt the tension in her body subside. It had been there for weeks, without her even noting the physical effects of her emotional turmoil. She was saved. Perhaps all really would be well. She had not predicted how Helena would react, neither her fear nor her acquiescence. Clearly Helena knew the possible consequences of her actions and had risked more than her husband's displeasure or God's punishment. Was her passion so strong? From some of the things she had said, Anneke thought that perhaps Helena's rebellion against convention, even at so high a potential cost, had been brought about by nothing more than boredom, or pique that her husband found other things more worthy of his time.

"It is agreed, Anneke," de Groot said as he entered the map room later that day. Anneke's mind was still in turmoil from her exchange with Helena. For a confused moment, she thought that somehow Helena had spoken to Willem.

"Blaeu has agreed to take your map. He was quite impressed with it, I will say. Once he saw it, he almost immediately said that he would like to include it in his *Atlas Maior*. In that moment, he didn't seem to care much about where it came from, though he did seem surprised at the attribution. I told him what you had told me of your father's notes, Lucas's studies, and your interest in those studies, and I said that I believed it had been a joint effort."

"But you know that is not true! I created the map! Could you not have told him that, at least? Even if my father's and brother's names were to be used, I had hoped that at least someone else would know the truth."

"I told you from the beginning, Anneke, that I would not take this to Blaeu as your creation. I do not think he would have accepted it. His initial interest would have been overcome by doubts. Even you must see that. To him you are a talented colorist, yes, but an untrained young woman. It would be asking too much of him to believe that you have transformed yourself into a cartographer."

Anneke mutely nodded her head.

"I had thought you would at least be a bit grateful, Anneke. I do not mind telling you that this entire thing has made me uncomfortable. At least Blaeu liked the map and didn't seem to think me a fool besotted by a young lady's charms for having brought it to him."

Anneke looked at him and said, "Why must this always be about what men think of women, that we have no more to offer than our bodies?"

"I find that phrasing somewhat vulgar, Anneke, but you must know the ways of the world."

"Yes," Anneke said resignedly. "Yes. And, thank you, Heer de Groot."

"Here is the map. Blaeu said he will contact your family about the transfer and financial arrangements."

Taking the map, Anneke said, "Perhaps I am overwhelmed with everything, but I find that I am not feeling well. Would you mind if I go back to my home? I shall return to the coloring tomorrow."

"I shall see you then," de Groot said as he left the room, and Anneke thought that in former times he would have shown some concern for her, might even have offered his carriage to take her home.

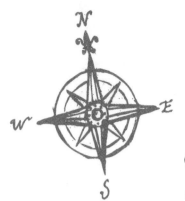

Chapter 31

October 1660

When Anneke arrived at de Groot's the following day, Warner looked shocked to see her.

"Oh," he said. "No one thought to send word. I think it would be better if you did not come in today, Juffrouw."

"But, why? Has something happened?"

"Yes. Please, return to your home. If Heer de Groot wants you again, he will send for you," Warner said, starting to close the door as she stood on the top step.

"Please, may I not speak with him?" Anneke said as she attempted to hold the door open. Then she heard Helena's voice.

"Is that her, Warner? Is that Anneke?"

"Yes, mistress," Warner replied. "Do not worry. I have told her to leave."

"No!" Helena screamed, coming toward the doorway.

"But, Vrouw Kregier, I do not think the master—"

"I don't care what you think, Warner," Helena replied in ever shriller tones. "Willem is not here. He has left for now. I must speak with Anneke."

Sensing defeat, Warner stood aside. Helena grabbed Anneke by the wrist and pulled her to a small but luxurious room that Anneke had never before entered. Having slammed the door behind them, she shoved a paper in Anneke's face. Taking it, Anneke read.

Heer de Groot,

I believe it is my duty to inform you of a most foul deception that is taking place. As you know, your wife is acquainted with my sister, Celia Hartgers. For these past weeks, my sister has shamefully played the part of go-between for your wife and her lover, whose identity is unknown to me. I do not wish to give the impression that my sister initiated the liaison, but she was a willing partner in Helena's plan.

I believe you were told that your wife, my sister, and I were receiving watercoloring lessons from the young map colorist, Anneke van Brug, whom you employ. What actually occurred was that Helena would leave the van Brug girl here, then she would be off to meet her lover. I do not believe that the colorist acted willingly, but surely a decent woman would not have played the part that she did, no matter what was threatened.

I hope that you do not think ill of me for bringing such scandalous behavior to your attention, but I felt that I myself could no longer remain silent without being considered complicit.

A virtuous woman,
Ursula Hartgers

Anneke read the note twice, then slowly lowered herself onto the nearest chair. "Has he seen this?" she whispered.

"Of course, he has seen it! Why do you think the house is in such turmoil? He must have shown it to Warner, who now seems to know all. I can't believe that he would show it to a servant!"

"Where is he?"

"After this was delivered, he came to me, threw it at me, and left. I've never seen him like this, Anneke. If he had flown into a rage, I would be less fearful. He said nothing. Absolutely nothing. When you and I spoke of stopping, I thought that I was exaggerating the real danger to me. I still thought that his pride would lead him to cover everything. Yes, he would make things unpleasant for me for a while, but soon he would again bury himself in his maps. I see now that I was a fool! Anneke, I am terrified that he will go to the *schout!*"

Anneke thought of the serious nature of going to the *schout*, who enforced the laws and prosecuted those who had broken them. Trying to allay Helena's fears and struggling to keep control of her own, she said, "Surely not, Helena. Surely he would not so ruin his own reputation."

"You did not see him. And he has told Warner! Soon all of the servants will have heard, and I know of at least one maid who will feel she must tell this to her church congregation. She will tell herself that it is her religious duty. All the while, she will be savoring the gossip and agreeing with others as they call me a whore!"

Anneke approached the frantic woman. "Helena, you must try to calm down! Continuing like this will only ensure that the whole household knows something is terribly wrong. It may already be too late to keep things from them, but you must not heighten the danger by your outbursts."

Either because she saw the reason in this or because she had exhausted herself, Helena stopped her pacing and sat down. "I don't know what to do," she said, "and I can't believe I am reduced to turning to someone like you for help."

Even in the moment, Anneke thought that if she were a more generous person, she would be able to overlook Helena's condescension, but she could not. In the midst of her shame and impending demise, Helena still thought herself superior to Anneke, and it was more than she could overlook.

"Yes, you have plunged me down into your depravity, so how, indeed, could I help you?"

The passing servants openly stared as she left the house.

Without having been aware of her steps, Anneke found herself at her own door. She had never been in such a situation before. She had no idea what to do. She only knew that she could keep this from her mother no longer. These past weeks, knowing how horrified her mother would have been to learn of Anneke's part in Helena's infidelity, she had held herself somewhat apart from Lysbeth. It was not only that she was afraid of letting something slip. Continuing with the easy manner they had always enjoyed seemed in itself a falsehood. How could she act as though there were nothing wrong? How could she lull her mother into a feeling that all was well?

So it was with mixed feelings that Lysbeth greeted Anneke when she interrupted her at her work, for she could see that something was terribly wrong, but she also felt a fleeting sense of happiness that her daughter's days of reticence seemed to have come to an end. There was some minor problem besieging her daughter, and she had come to her for comfort.

Lysbeth greeted her daughter. "Anneke, what is it, my dear? Come, sit down beside me." Even as she carefully laid down her brush and moved away from the map she had been working on, she sensed that her relief would be fleeting. Now that she looked fully at her daughter's face, she saw that it was ravaged.

"Anneke, what is it? You frighten me!"

"Mama, I—I do not even know how to begin! I have done something so shameful, so indecent, that I fear it will ruin us all!"

"What are you talking about?" Lysbeth said, and even from within her own misery, Anneke noted that her mother's face had gone pale.

What could have been explained in but a few sentences to an audience ready to hear such a tale took what seemed to Anneke like hours. Lysbeth could not believe what Anneke was trying to tell her. She could not conceive of such wanton behavior as Anneke was describing, much less her daughter's part in it. Finally, her questions came to an end, and it was Anneke's turn to ask a question, but this one would have no answer that could be given by a recitation of the facts.

"What am I to do, Mama? What will become of me? Should I tell Papa?"

"No!" was the swift reply. "I doubt we will be able to keep this from your father forever, but we must try to think things through before the time comes when he must learn of this. How culpable do you think Heer de Groot will find you in all of this?"

"I really have no idea, Mama. It may be tempting for him to lay a large part of the blame on me, if only to tell himself that somehow I was the one who tempted his wife into sin."

"I do not think that will be his reaction," Lysbeth said slowly. "This cannot have been Vrouw Kregier's first offense. To contrive such an elaborate plan seems to me to have required previous experience in deceit. Even for a man who has blinded himself to his wife's transgressions, surely Heer de Groot has not really been ignorant of the type of woman he calls his wife."

Anneke was shocked, both at the idea and at her mother having suggested it. The notion that this indecent behavior was Helena's habit had never occurred to her. Yet even in her surprise, she saw the sense of her mother's reasoning.

"You have often said that Heer de Groot seems to think highly of you. That should be to your advantage. Surely he can see that you were an innocent, coerced into this vile plan by the threats of an evil woman."

When Anneke didn't reply, Lysbeth said, "Heer de Groot has no reason to be displeased with you, does he Anneke?"

"I have done nothing shameful, Mama, but he has been less than happy with me of late."

"Why is that?"

"Oh, Mama." It was only now that Anneke began to cry, "I had such hopes! I wanted to surprise Papa. And yes, I was ambitious for myself, too! Now it will all come to naught! All because I was duped by that woman!"

"What are you talking about, Anneke? A surprise for your father?"

"You know how he has always talked about wanting a map from his notes on his trip to Africa? Well, I found Papa's notes and I created a map. It's a wonderful map, Mama!"

"How could that be, Anneke?"

"Remember how I always sat in with Lucas when he was being

tutored? I was good at it, Mama! I really understood it on a deep level, and it gave me the desire to create a map, not to just merely color the maps of others."

Oblivious to her mother's slight recoil at this belittling remark, she continued. "I should confess that I also stole into your workroom and borrowed maps of Africa that you were coloring. I am sorry, Mama. It is just that I so wanted the map to be good enough to be printed, printed in a real atlas. I wanted this for Papa, and I came to want it for myself, too, Mama!"

"But what does this have to do with Heer de Groot?" Lysbeth asked. Anneke noted with relief that, at least for now, her mother would not disparage her for having taken her maps without permission.

"I knew that no printer would accept a map if I brought it to him on my own. Women don't do such things. Even Heer Blaeu, who thought highly enough of my coloring to recommend me to Heer de Groot, would never be able to think of me as having the skill of a cartographer." Here Anneke hesitated, unsure of how her mother would react to de Groot's offer to do her a favor. "Heer de Groot seemed very taken with my coloring, Mama, and he even allowed—no, encouraged me to experiment with unusual color schemes. His maps are his passion, and he would spend most days with me in the map room."

"You never told me that, Anneke," her mother said in an implied rebuke that her daughter had kept this secret from her family. Anneke had told herself that she did not wish to boast of her success when her mother would never experience it. Even her father had not found a patron so taken with his work. She now admitted to herself that de Groot's behavior and attention could be construed as troubling, and she knew that was why she had not spoken of it before.

"There was nothing improper, Mama! You must believe me! It is just that he is so involved with his maps. One day, he said that he would like to do something for me. I don't know what he had in mind, and I even thought it would be a warning sign if he meant to give me an expensive gift. I put him off at first, but finally I told him that he could do me a favor."

"And what was that?" Lysbeth asked slowly.

"I asked him to request of Heer Blaeu that my map be included in his *Atlas Maior*."

For the first time, Lysbeth let out a gasp at the enormity of what her daughter had asked.

"And what did Heer de Groot say?" asked Lysbeth.

"Well, he was quite taken aback. I think he was shocked at the request, but even more so at the thought that I could have created a map."

"I must say that I share his surprise, on both counts, daughter."

"He also said he worried that it might look strange for a man to be presenting the work of a young woman, a young woman who has spent these last months in his home." Anneke's voice trailed off as she said this last. It sounded harsher now, and more damning, here in the presence of her mother.

"And well he might worry about that! Could you not see the danger in this, Anneke?"

"But I had worked so hard on it, Mama, so many hours up in the cold of the loft room, straining my eyes in the inadequate light of the candles. I wanted it so much! And I was angered that this would be his reaction, and perhaps even more that he could be right, that people would only see some scandalous cause for his request."

"People can be unjust in their suspicions, Anneke, but they are no less a threat for that."

"I know that, Mama, but the next day he said he would present the map to Heer Blaeu. He also said he would say it was Lucas's work since he knew Lucas was a surveyor. He thought Heer Blaeu would find him a more credible cartographer. I then said that Papa's name must also be attached to the map. That was the point of the map, after all, as a surprise for Papa."

"And did Heer de Groot agree?"

"Yes, but I told him that it must contain my name, also."

"And?"

"He was not happy, harboring the same objections as before, but I pressed him. I said that also having my brother's and my father's name on the map would surely erase any suspicions on Heer Blaeu's part, or anyone else's. He agreed then, but it was very grudging, and he has not been the same to me since."

"What did your brother say to this?"

"He was not altogether in support of the idea," Anneke replied slowly.

"What do you mean? Do you have his permission to use his name?"

"No," was the soft reply.

"Oh, Anneke, how could you do that?"

"Because I needed this, Mama! I wanted it with all my heart!"

"Nevertheless, to use the names of your brother and your father without their permission—"

"But it is to be a surprise for Papa! And surely Lucas will not object when he sees his name in a book that is bound to become famous. It will grant him great prestige."

"But mostly you were thinking of what it will mean for you, isn't that so, daughter?"

"Yes, Mama. But the map is so good! Even Heer de Groot, who has collected maps for years and has hundreds of them, sees that it is a very good map. On its merits, it has every right to be included!"

"Oh, Anneke! How can you know that? You do not know what will go into the new atlas."

"Oh, Mama, of course I do, and you do, too! It will be the same as the other atlases of the House of Blaeu or any of the other map-printing houses. It will mostly be maps that have been in Blaeu's previous atlases, or maps that he has purchased from other printers. Heer Blaeu should be happy to have a new map to include."

Lysbeth stared at her daughter in disbelief before replying. "Anneke, you have deluded yourself into believing that because you want it to be true."

"No, Mama. You are wrong," Anneke said, unable to keep a note of triumph from her voice. "Heer Blaeu has accepted my map."

"So you have cleverly tricked me in this conversation, Anneke. That is not worthy of you. You came to me and I thought it was advice that you wanted, not to show me for a fool."

"Oh, Mama! I am sorry! It all seemed to be part of the same story, and I am proud that Blaeu accepted my map."

"That may be so, Anneke," Lysbeth replied, "but that does not solve the dilemma with Vrouw Kregier. If anything, there is now more to lose."

When Anneke did not contradict her, she continued, "I shall have to think on this. Do not return to de Groot's tomorrow. This is a situation in which one must act carefully, but I confess I do not now see the next step."

An objection had sprung to Anneke's lips, but she thought better of it. Her mother and Warner had both given her the same advice, and she should heed it.

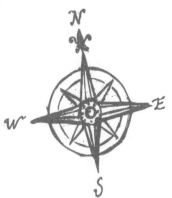

Chapter 32

October 1660

The map had caused quite a stir at the House of Blaeu, and before she even had the chance to speak to Anneke the next morning, Lysbeth received a note from Heer Meyert at Blaeu's asking her to come to the printing house at her earliest convenience. Lysbeth had lain awake most of the night going over and over her daughter's situation, never coming to any conclusion as to what was most likely to happen, much less what could be done about any of it.

When she saw the brief note of summons from Heer Meyert, she worried that the scandal involving Helena Kregier had already reached the printing house. If that were the case, it would mean de Groot either had not wished or had not been able to keep his wife's behavior hidden. She did not doubt that her daughter's name would also be implicated. If they were lucky, Anneke's name would be sullied by every gossiping tongue in Amsterdam but people would soon move on. If they were unlucky, it could be a disaster for her entire family.

Lysbeth left her home immediately, without even speaking to her daughter. She didn't know what she would say, and she had no desire to see her at that moment. Besides, she would know more about what was happening after she had spoken with Heer Meyert.

As she trod the familiar path to the printing house on Bloemgracht, Lysbeth found that she was not moving as briskly as she usually did, and she had to occasionally stop to catch her breath. She quickly put this down to her lack of sleep and emotional turmoil. She tried to imagine what Meyert would say to her. In addition to everything else,

Lysbeth was already mourning the loss of what had become almost a friendship with Meyert. He had taken a more active role with the colorists than any of the masters Lysbeth had known before him, and he seemed to take a special interest in her, although she wondered whether he was trying to ingratiate himself with her because she was the mother of a very talented colorist who might conceivably rise to a level higher than Meyert himself, even though she was only a woman.

Once she had dismissed that idea, she began to think that his kindness came from a genuine feeling, though she acknowledged that it might be pity, pity for the mother whose child's success had surpassed her own at such an early age. As time passed, however, Lysbeth came to believe that Meyert had genuinely taken an interest in her work. Now, though, that was surely all at an end. How could he respect a mother whose daughter was mentioned in connection with a case of adultery?

As she entered the printing house and walked toward Meyert's desk, she saw him rise, and his smile reached out to her. "Good morning, Vrouw Plettenburg," he began. "I hope that the tone of my note did not cause you to come with any undue haste. I should, perhaps, not have sent the messenger boy so early. It was just that I was anxious to speak with you."

This was hardly the response Lysbeth had expected, and she simply replied, "Not at all, Heer Meyert. I was happy to comply."

"Please, sit down," he said, pointing to the lone chair in front of his desk. "I simply wanted to congratulate you on the happy news." At Lysbeth's look of confusion, he continued, "Surely you are familiar with the map, the new map of Congo? The one that your husband and son created? Oh, and I believe that your daughter is also listed."

"Yes, I know of it," Lysbeth replied.

"Well, then perhaps I am in the happy position of giving you good news! It is a very impressive map, and Heer Blaeu was very grateful to Heer de Groot for having brought it to his attention. Heer Blaeu has already decided that it will be included in his *Atlas Maior*."

Although Anneke had already told her this, it was only now,

hearing of it from Meyert, in Blaeu's very establishment, that Lysbeth fully believed it. "I am pleased to hear it, Heer Meyert."

"But is this all the reaction you can muster to this news, Vrouw Plettenburg? I thought that for once I would see real happiness on your serene countenance. It is an honor for your family, you know. I can only think that it will help your son Lucas in his profession, and I understand that it has long been a dream of your husband's to have this map made from his notes."

"Naturally, I am pleased at the news, Heer Meyert, and I thank you for taking the time to talk with me about it yourself. It is just a bit of a surprise. Perhaps I did not have enough faith in the talent of my family."

"We thought it a bit strange that it was de Groot who brought the map to us, and I will admit to you, Vrouw Plettenburg, I was a bit wounded that you yourself had not brought it to me. I thought that we had come to have a mutual respect and even a proper regard for one another."

Lysbeth said nothing, so he continued. "However, we shall not worry about that now. I am simply happy for you, and for your family, of course. Oh, and I have not told you. Your family will be paid one hundred guilders for the map."

"So much?"

"It is a bit above the standard price we pay for a new map, but then I believe Heer Blaeu wished to show his regard for all of the work your family has done for us," Meyert replied with a smile, as though he were pleased to finally have evoked an excited response from her. But then she surprised him with her next question.

"The inclusion of the map in the atlas won't have any effect on my position as colorist, or Anneke's, will it, Heer Meyert?"

"No, of course not! I cannot imagine why you would even ask that, Vrouw Plettenburg," Meyert responded, with a puzzled look.

"It is just that I so highly value the work I have always done for the House of Blaeu."

"As do we, Vrouw Plettenburg, as do we. Surely you must know this.

If not, it is we who are at fault for not expressing it, though our continued use of your skill speaks to our opinion of your work." When Lysbeth offered no reply, he said, "Well, I do not wish to unduly detain you. I hope that coming here has not interfered too much with your day."

"No, no. I am grateful for your thoughtfulness in wishing to tell me this yourself. Good day, Heer Meyert."

Lysbeth barely heard his farewell as she made her way from the printing house, amazed at what she had just heard.

When she returned to her home, Lysbeth sought out her husband. She felt that, no matter what Anneke's wishes might be, it was her duty to tell Isaac what was happening, at least with regard to the map. She already felt guilty that she had kept from him Anneke's revelations of the evening before, and she would allay her guilt a bit by at least telling him part of what she had learned. She would not yet share her fears about Anneke's part in Vrouw Kregier's deception, for she hoped that somehow it would become resolved without the need for her husband to learn that painful truth.

She found Isaac already at work, and this touched her heart. Once again, he had high expectations for a commission that he had just received. Each time he seemed to truly believe that this, finally, would be the making of him. Part of her admired his optimism, but it only made it all the more painful to observe that as the painting progressed, even he could see that his skill level would preclude any such extraordinary outcome. Part of her felt anger toward him, that his stubborn belief in himself each time blinded him to the reality that this new commission would make for no great change in their fortunes. Part of her ached for him, for the disappointment she knew would come and from which she wished she could spare him. This morning, however, he was still filled with hope, and he greeted her with a smile and a kiss on the cheek.

"Good morning, my dear! Where have you been so early this morning? I looked for you earlier but saw that you must have gone out."

"I had received an early note from Heer Meyert asking me to see him at the printing house. I have just returned from there."

"Ah, so nothing of great import then. That is just as well, as I do not have time to talk long with you, my dear. I feel that I am at a crucial part of my work. It is going very well, don't you agree, wife?" Isaac looked fondly at his canvas.

"Yes, Isaac," Lysbeth murmured. He didn't notice that she hadn't even glanced at the painting. "Nevertheless, I would ask that you put down your paintbrush for a few moments and speak with me. I have something to tell you," Lysbeth replied. Hearing the note of insistence from his wife, Isaac did as she asked.

"You know how you have always said that you earnestly wished your notes on your trip to Congo could have been used to make a new map of the area?"

"Of course," Isaac answered, now a slight frown marring his earlier enthusiasm.

"And you remember that Anneke always participated in Lucas's lessons with his tutor when he was taking the surveying and cartography classes?"

"Now that you remind me, yes, I do remember that she had asked if she could sit in with them. But why are you bringing this up now?"

"Because Anneke has made that map using your notes. She told me about it last night—"

"What do you mean? Why didn't you tell me this then?"

"It seemed so incredible that I don't think I completely believed her, but that is what Heer Meyert wanted to see me about. He wanted to congratulate our family. The map will appear in the new *Atlas Maior* that Blaeu is working on."

"But how could this possibly be?" Isaac said, disbelief evident in his voice.

"Well, Anneke asked Heer de Groot to speak to Heer Blaeu about it. He was doubtful that Blaeu would take a map from Anneke, so he said that they must tell Blaeu the map was done by you, Lucas, and Anneke. In truth, he didn't even want to include Anneke in the attribution, but she insisted."

Isaac stumbled toward a chair. "You say that Anneke used my notes? She has gone through my things without my permission? How could you allow that, Lysbeth?"

"I didn't know of it! She said that she wanted it as a surprise for you, to see your lifelong dream come true."

"This cannot be!" Isaac said with a shaking voice, and Lysbeth was shocked that it seemed more from fear than any other emotion.

"No, Isaac, Heer Meyert said that the map is very good. It will do all of you credit."

"And Lucas knew of this?" her husband asked.

"Anneke told him of her intention. She admitted to me that he hadn't given permission for his name to be used, but I imagine that now he will be delighted."

"This will ruin me," Isaac said in a voice so low that Lysbeth strained to hear him. "This will be the end of me," he said as he left the room. A moment later, she heard the house door close.

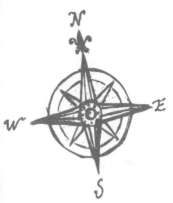

Chapter 33

October 1660

Over the years, as Isaac told of the surveyor who had helped him to grasp a bit of the craft, he had almost come to believe it himself. He had told his family that he had made specific measurements as a result of this learning and that, in addition to the copious narratives he had written about the places they saw, he had the material for what would be a wonderful new map of the area. He had seen no harm in this innocent deception. No one would ever use the notes, so no one would ever find out.

When he had first spoken of this, Lysbeth had encouraged him to take the papers to some of the map printers in the city. They would know of cartographers who could create a map. Surely they would be interested in a new map of an area about which so little was known. Isaac had told Lysbeth that he had gone to several of the map printers, though he never claimed to have seen Blaeu, since she could easily have discovered that this was a falsehood. In reality, he had not gone to see any of them. He just told her that no one was interested and pretended to be as bewildered by their lack of enthusiasm as was she. He had complained to her of the unfairness of the world, complained that once again he was being deprived of his due.

Hurrying down the street now, he tried to deny that this had become a familiar pattern in their lives. It was the world that was at fault, he had always said, not any lack on his part.

As he made his way to the house of Simon Janszoon, a home whose location he had known these many years, he told himself that once again circumstances had conspired to defeat him. Still, he now asked himself what had made him start Lucas in cartography and surveying classes. He knew that it had been with some vague hope of a map with his name on it. Had he so long told the story about his notes that he had put the truth of it from his mind? The truth that could now destroy him? The truth that the surveying notes were not his.

He came to the house, which he had passed many times over the years. It was not so far from his own home. He had been inside only once, shortly after his return from Africa. The visit had been a goodbye to the home's occupant, Simon Janszoon, who would soon set sail on another trip, this time for the VOC. He would be gone some years. Isaac wondered whether he had gone on other voyages after that. Perhaps he had obtained a position in Amsterdam or nearby so that he would not have to leave his wife again.

Isaac remembered thinking that Janszoon had a pretty young wife, and though Isaac himself had happily departed with van Herder all those years ago, he had wondered how this man could again be so ready to leave his spouse. Their visit had been filled with fellow feeling, and also regret. Isaac had lamented the loss of his sketches, and Simon had bemoaned the loss of his surveying papers. He had put so much work into them, but somehow they, too, must have been swept overboard, for he never found them after the storm that had washed away Isaac's sketches.

All of this Isaac now recalled in great detail as he lifted his hand to knock upon the surveyor's door. His first knock receiving no reply, he tried again. He waited, but as no one came, he tried a third time, becoming ever more agitated. He had hoped that he could quickly resolve the issue, though he had no clear idea of how that might come about. He imagined that Simon would be angry when he heard that he had been lied to, but it had been so many years ago. Maybe the sting would not be so sharp now. Isaac would offer to have Simon's name added to the map. Surely that would suffice to temper the surveyor's reaction. As these thoughts raced through his mind, he pounded on the door. Still, no one answered. He took from his pocket a small paper and a piece of black lead wrapped in string, which he always carried with him in case he wanted to sketch a striking scene or make a note for himself. He tore a bit from the paper and wrote:

> *Simon, we knew each other on the van Herder expedition. Something has come up which I believe will be to our mutual benefit. I hope to be able to speak to you soon. Isaac*

Although they had not seen each other for many years, Isaac hoped that he was striking a chord of friendship by using their given names only. He folded the paper, stuck it between the door and the doorjamb, and walked away. Feeling that he could not return home without having spoken to Janszoon, Isaac wandered along the canals, barely noting where he was, his distress providing him with a nervous energy. After a couple of hours, he found himself again before the Janszoon house. Expecting that this attempt would be no more successful than the last, Isaac knocked and was surprised when the surveyor opened the door himself.

"Yes?" he said, studying Isaac as though to ascertain who this man might be.

"Simon, it is I, Isaac van Brug."

"Isaac!" Janszoon exclaimed with a happy look of recollection. "Isaac, come in! I cannot believe it, after all these years!"

Not having been prepared for such an enthusiastic reception, Isaac could only reply, "Yes, I thought that I would come and see you." As he followed Simon into his home, he searched for something else to say. "I think you must have been gone on many voyages over the years, or surely our paths would have crossed."

"It is true, I have seen many parts of the world, Isaac, but for the past year I have resolved to stay here with my dear wife, Maria." As he said this, Isaac looked around the room. Shelves and tables were choked with objects that had clearly been obtained on the surveyor's voyages. There was even a cabinet with glazed doors through which outlines hinted at more precious items.

He also studied the man himself for a moment and thought how little he had changed. His face had more lines and a weathered look, but he moved with the strength and vigor of a younger man. Isaac guessed that both of these were the marks of a man who had spent much of his life at sea. What a contrast this was, Isaac thought, to his own pasty face and softened body, also the result of his lifetime's occupation of staying indoors and working at his easel. Then he noticed Simon looking at him, waiting for a response.

"Your wife must be happy to have you home after so many years apart."

"Well, there were always periods between the trips when I was at home, but somehow the call of the unknown always lured me away from my lovely wife. In truth, it was difficult at first being home and having no further travel plans to make. I think it was difficult for Maria, too. She was used to having her way, not that she no longer does," Simon added with an easy laugh. "Anyway, I did not leave her alone when I was gone. You may recall that even at the time of our expedition with van Herd, we had two boys who were already ten and twelve. Later we had a daughter, too. She and my wife are out doing the marketing for our midday meal. But what am I doing? I have given you no chance to talk. Surely you must have some reason for seeking me out after all these years. I am glad that you have, but I confess to being curious."

Now that he was here, Isaac found that he did not know how to begin. "Simon, do you remember the sketches I made, the ones that were washed overboard during that big storm?"

"How could I forget? We were united in our sorrow, you for your sketches and I for my surveying notes. Oh, I haven't thought about that in many years, though, Isaac. Surely you did not come to talk about that."

"Simon, I have come to confess something to you." At this, Simon's smile began to fade.

"Oh?"

"Yes, I will not blame you if you cannot forgive what I have done.

I am so ashamed, but something has happened that compelled me to come see you today. You may think this strange, but my daughter, Anneke, has created a map. My son, Lucas, is a surveyor like you. I wished him to also take lessons in cartography. To be frank, he struggled, and so I engaged a tutor to help him. My daughter, who I believe was jealous of what she saw as an unfair advantage being given to her brother, begged to be allowed to sit in on the lessons. I saw no harm in it, and though I paid no attention at the time, she must have studied the material intensely, for as I say, she has now created a map."

"That is interesting, Isaac, but I don't see what this has to do with me. I have no influence with anyone who would be able to put the map into print."

"No, that is not why I have come. In fact, the House of Blaeu has already accepted the map for their new atlas. It will, however, bear my name, and that of my son, as well as Anneke's."

"But that is something to be celebrated, Isaac! Why do you come to me and say that you have something to confess?"

"Because, without my knowledge, Anneke used what she believed were my notes to create the map."

"But your notes were just descriptions, were they not? How could she have created a map, much less one to be published by Blaeu, with such inadequate information?"

"Because there were surveying notes in with my papers," Isaac said. After a pause, he added, "Your surveying notes."

Simon's face became pale beneath the ruddiness. He looked at Simon in confusion. "But how can that be? My papers were lost."

"No, Simon, they were not lost. I have had them all these years."

"How?"

"In the chaos after the storm, I gathered the papers that were near my sleeping spot. I thought that they were only my own descriptions. I was so distraught over the loss of my sketches that I didn't notice your papers amongst all of mine."

"How could you not have been aware of them? You deliberately stole my notes!"

"No! I swear to you that I did not, Simon, though that makes my subsequent deception no less blameworthy. I hadn't the heart to look at the papers until well after we had arrived home. It was even after that visit with you here, the last time that we saw each other. I tried to forget my disappointment. I submerged myself in my painting, and it was not until weeks later that I had the courage to look at the notes. It was then that I discovered my error."

"Why did you not tell me then?" Simon asked in a husky voice.

"I did come to your home, but you had already left on the voyage with the VOC. By the time you returned from that trip, it had been so long that I had the notes in my possession that I told myself that surely you had by then put them from your mind." Not wishing to give Simon a chance to respond, Isaac rushed on.

"Things were also somewhat difficult at home. My wife was upset with me when I returned to her after such a long absence only to be suffering from melancholy due to the fate of my sketches. I saw that I was reduced in her eyes, and I made some foolish boasts to her about having information that could be made into a map, *should* be made into a map. She seemed to take an interest in this since, as you may recall, she herself is a map colorist. I even went through the pretense of telling her I had spoken to various map printers. I spoke of it as one more thing that should have worked out for me but didn't. I suppose that I spoke of this desire for a map in such terms that Anneke decided she would surprise me by creating one using the notes. And now, here I am."

"But this pitiful tale of what a weak man you are is hardly a reason to have kept my papers for all these years! I cannot believe that you deceived me so!" Simon's tone rose as he paced back and forth. "You have only come now because you feared I would learn of your treachery when the map comes out. Liar! Liar and thief! No! I will not stand for this!" Simon screamed and, turning suddenly toward Isaac, advanced with his hands outstretched, aiming for the throat of his erstwhile friend.

Isaac scrambled back in terror but was hindered by one of the large tables. The stronger man reached him and encircled his prey's neck with his sailor's hands, his whole body leaning into the task. Isaac was bent backward over the table, Simon's enraged face only inches away. Isaac pulled at the other's fingers, trying to loosen his grip but to no avail. He then chopped at Simon's arms to try to break the man's hold. He had barely any breath as he blindly reached for something with which to defend himself. Finally, his hand connected with a heavy object. He grabbed it, and even in his terror, he registered its sharp points. Raising it above Simon's outstretched arms, Isaac struck his attacker on the side of the head with every ounce of force he could muster. Immediately, blood began to pour from Simon's temple, and he had a momentary look of disbelief as he slowly sank to the floor.

"Simon! Simon!" Isaac cried, even as he knew that the other was past hearing. Seeing now that what he held was some type of sea shell, he dropped it. He stood and stared in horror at the man he had destroyed until he heard someone enter the house. With no thought but escape, he ran toward the door, almost bumping into the woman and girl whose shock allowed them only to move aside as this madman passed them.

Once on the street, Isaac had to restrain himself from running so that others would not notice his behavior. At any moment, Simon's wife would surely be out in the street yelling of the foul murder of her husband. Isaac could only hope that in her shock, and after all these years, she had not recognized the man who had destroyed the life she had known.

Chapter 34

October 1660

On the morning of Lysbeth's meeting with Heer Meyert, noticing that her mother had left, Anneke snuck out of the house. She had to go to de Groot's. She didn't see how her presence there could make her situation any worse, and she had to find out what he would do. If she simply waited at home, she would go mad.

Warner's manner today was subdued. He offered no advice but asked Anneke to wait by the door while he went to speak to his master. There were no sounds of distress coming from any of the rooms, and Anneke wondered what she had expected. Even Helena could not maintain her boisterous self-pity without some respite. However, the stillness was unnerving, and just as she was turning to leave, Warner returned.

"The master awaits you in the map room," he said in a flat tone, standing aside for her to pass.

Anneke had fallen asleep only as dawn approached, and she knew that her thoughts were not orderly. Her mind had reviewed the facts over and over without respite or reason. She wasn't even certain what she wished, if she even thought there was anything she dared hope for. As she reached the map room, she hesitated on the threshold. There was Willem, sitting and looking at a map as though it were any other morning. Still not feeling free to enter, Anneke said softly, "Heer de Groot." As she received no response, she raised her voice a bit and said, "Heer de Groot, Warner said that you would see me."

"Did he now? A yes to his inquiry seemed as easy as a no, though what could I have to say to you?"

"Please, Heer de Groot, please believe me when I say that I had no choice in the matter! Vrouw Kregier threatened that if I did not do as she asked, she would tell you I had stolen something."

De Groot looked at her as though she were some new map he had recently acquired but did not yet completely understand. "And you took her at her word?"

"I couldn't be certain, and I dared not risk it."

"You thought that I would believe her, Anneke?"

"I was afraid that you would. She is your wife, and people in positions such as mine are always the ones to be suspected."

"Have you not felt the favor I have shown you? Have I not done what you asked, even though it was against my better judgment?" Willem asked, and she could see more appeal than rebuke in his face. He continued, "I cannot understand why you thought that I would believe her. Besides, what would she gain by telling this fabrication? How would she know that you, then having nothing to lose, would not tell me of her treachery?"

"I . . . I suppose I didn't think of it in that way. I only took into account my position and hers, which is so far above mine. Besides, if I had told you of her demands, you could have had me cast out as a liar as well as a thief."

Willem studied her intently, then said, "I suppose I can understand your fears. You knew nothing of her past 'indiscretions.' How could you, when I myself have endeavored to keep them from the world?"

"I don't understand, Heer de Groot."

"No, you wouldn't, not someone with your innocent nature."

"Innocent no more," Anneke murmured, realizing her mother had been correct in her supposition that this was not Helena's first foray into adultery.

"If that is true, then the blame lies with Helena, and with me for putting my pride first. It was that pride which allowed her to continue with her escapades. She relied on that. Perhaps this time it will not serve her."

Not knowing how to respond and wishing to distance herself from the collector, Anneke began to wander around the room, again surveying the maps as she had done on the very first day she had arrived. Now she touched some of them, and she lingered over those that she herself had colored. They seemed to have been done by an altogether different person.

Willem watched her in silence until she said, "I shall have to leave. I will be sorry. I have loved the work here. It has made me feel more free than I have ever felt."

"Even though I so often sat at your elbow as you worked?"

"Yes. I was flattered by your interest in what I was doing, and even more by the license you gave me to pursue my own vision. That is something I could never have enjoyed at Blaeu's."

"I was intrigued by what you were doing, your use of color. I don't really understand why."

"Do you not?" Anneke said, and for a moment it felt like they were back on the neutral ground of discussing the coloring of a map. "Have you ever noticed that many of our painters use a certain color scheme? Well, how would you, when I'm not even certain of it myself, and I've never heard anyone else speak of it. There seem to be certain colors that our Dutch artists most prominently use in their works. There are often darkened hues of blue or green, and then an intense yellow, perhaps highlighted by red, and sometimes including rich browns. I don't think it is anything they consider. I think it is just something that everyone somehow feels, having absorbed it in a way from the work of others. Even we colorists usually heavily employ these colors. It seems to define who we are as a people. What you gave me was permission to try something else."

"I have never heard of that idea, and I believe myself to be fairly familiar with many of the works of our artists. My focus is on maps, but I have friends who are art patrons, and who have acquired from even the most prestigious. I shall have to pay attention in the future. It could help explain why your coloring has always seemed to me to be so creative, so stirring, so surprising."

"It could be that it is only my fancy, and I suppose that I shall never know whether you have come to agree with me or not."

"You will not stay with me, then? You will no longer work for me?" Willem asked.

"I did not think you would wish to see me after my part in your wife's deceit."

"Nor did I," Willem said. "But being with you, and discussing color with you again, I find that I am loath to forsake your company."

"I do not see how I could stay. I daresay that Vrouw Kregier somehow blames me for the letter from Ursula Hartgers, since I had become friendly with her."

"It remains to be seen how much sway my wife will have in our household in the future. I am tempted to tell the *schout* of her transgressions."

"But surely not!" Anneke burst out. "She is your wife, no matter what she has done. Vrouw Kregier told me that she could be fined, imprisoned, or banished! Would you have her punished so harshly?"

"So she knew what could happen, but she counted on me to protect her once again, did she? I tell you, Anneke, I have forgiven her too many times. Well, if I am honest, it wasn't forgiveness. It was my own cowardice in wishing to pretend that it had not happened. Each time, I withdrew from her more."

Though Anneke knew herself to be inexperienced in the ways of love and marriage, she wondered whether his increasing distance from his wife had not each time been the cause of her next betrayal. "No matter what you do, I shall have to leave," she said.

"Even if Helena is not here to torment you? I would never reveal your part in helping her. I believe—I have chosen to believe—that you were forced into it, as you say."

"If her affair becomes public, my part in it will, too. There are others who knew of it. In addition to Ursula and her sister, surely your own servants have surmised the truth by now. Besides, I could never come to the home of a man whose wife is not present."

"What will you do then, Anneke? Go back to Blaeu's?" Willem said in a voice tinged with sorrow.

"I'm not sure that Blaeu will have me back if your wife's transgressions become known. He may feel that I have been tainted by my association with this house and its shame." Anneke did not try to state it more kindly, nor to keep the bitterness from her voice. She had lost so much because of the strange workings of the marriage that festered in this house.

"I am sorry, Anneke. Truly sorry," he said, finally seeming to have resigned himself to the inevitability of her departure from his life forever.

"As am I," Anneke said. She thought to gather her things but realized they had all been provided by Willem as part of her work here. All that was left to collect was her empty portfolio. "Goodbye, Heer de Groot," she said, and barely heard his reply.

"Goodbye, my colorist."

Chapter 35

October 1660

As Isaac fled the scene of his undoing, at first he had to concentrate on which streets to take to return to his home. Once in a familiar area, however, his feet leading him where he needed to go, his thoughts were filled with the scene he had just left. He saw all of the details in his mind's eye, as though trying to remember them for a painting. But this was a painting he need not commit to canvas. It was seared into his memory. It had all happened so quickly that he could barely fathom how such an ending had come about. He could see the blood pouring from Simon's head and knew himself to be the cause, but only as though in some obscure dream where things come about without explanation. He hurried his footsteps, no longer afraid of being noticed by passersby. This close to his home, he was simply a man anxious to arrive at his own hearth. No evil would be construed from his haste.

He knew when he stepped into his home that he had somehow believed the past hour would be erased, as though it had never happened. But as the door closed behind him, the weight did not lift. If anything, it became heavier, as he knew that he would have to tell Lysbeth. Or would he? Should he try to conceal this from her? It would be better for her, he told himself. Maybe his misdeed would never come to light. What purpose would it serve for her to know that he was a murderer? But even as these thoughts battled in his mind, he knew he would tell her. He, the killer, needed to be comforted, and Lysbeth had always been the one to console him. It was strange, he thought, that she had not come to greet him when she heard the door, as was her wont.

He went to seek her in her workroom, and even in his extreme distress, he registered surprise to see Anneke there, looking around the room as though lost.

"Where is your mama?" he asked her.

"I don't know, Papa. It is unlike her to be out of the house at this hour. I was so hoping to speak to her."

"And what are you doing here?" he asked, as though at least solving this small mystery could somehow put the world to rights again.

"Oh, Papa, please do not ask me," his daughter replied, and it was a mark of his perturbation that he did not reprimand her for insolence. Neither had a moment to ponder this, for they heard the front door and went to seek the comfort of wife and mother.

"Mama, please, I must talk to you," Anneke said before Lysbeth even had time to remove the short jacket she had quickly donned before leaving the house.

"No, daughter, it is I who must speak to your mama most urgently. Please, leave us." Lysbeth followed her husband with only a concerned glance toward her daughter. Not knowing where else to go, Anneke went to the loft room. The stairs had never seemed so steep.

Once Anneke had left, Lysbeth anxiously asked her husband what was wrong, for there was a look of desolation upon his face unlike any she had ever seen.

"You will recall that you told me earlier of the map to be printed by Blaeu," he began, as though wishing to prolong the moment in which she still believed him to be a man incapable of murder.

"Of course, and you rushed out so quickly! What did you mean, Isaac, when you said the map would ruin you? I was so worried that I have been out wandering the streets looking for you."

Isaac took her cold hands into his and led her to the bench against the wall. Seating himself, he pulled her down alongside him. The enormity of what he had to tell her seemed more than he could bear, yet how could she begin to understand unless he started with his lies of so many years before?

"I have deceived you, Lysbeth, not with another woman, but with a lie these many years. I have deceived you, and now it has led to my undoing."

"What lie, Isaac? Please, speak more plainly!"

"Do you remember the notes I always said that I had from the van Herder expedition?"

"Of course, Isaac. We spoke of them just this morning. They are the notes that Anneke used to create the map. What is wrong with you, husband?"

"The surveying papers were not mine. They belonged to another man, Simon Janszoon, the surveyor on the trip."

"You have always said that he helped you with the notes. Why is this of import?"

"He didn't help me, Lysbeth! Listen to what I am saying! They were his notes. I stole them. Well, I didn't precisely steal them. It is just that they were mistakenly placed with my things after that storm at sea, and I never returned them to him. All of these years, I let him think they were washed overboard."

"But that is stealing, Isaac! How could you not have returned them to him?" Lysbeth said. He shrank from the censure in her voice over this offense, so much less grievous than that which he had yet to confess.

"That does not matter now—"

"But of course it matters! Anneke has used them in a map that Blaeu will publish, falsely believing—and falsely portraying—the source to be your notes. Something must be done. We must go to Blaeu immediately and explain that there was an error. That this Simon Janszoon must somehow be recognized as well."

"No! That we cannot do!"

"Why not?" asked Lysbeth, surprise and growing fear upon her face.

"No one else must ever know of the connection between us." Isaac hesitated, gathering courage to say what must be said. "I went to see him, Lysbeth. I went to see him to explain what had happened. I had hoped that he might agree to have the map go forward, with his name included. I was even willing to tell him that we would tell Blaeu the map was solely his, or even not have it printed at all."

"But how could you think that? It would break Anneke's heart! She has put so much into that map, and Heer Meyert says that Heer Blaeu was truly impressed with its quality. Anneke made that map to please you. She persuaded Heer de Groot to take it to Blaeu, at what cost to her, I do not know. She wanted to surprise you, but it could also open so many more opportunities for her. How can you think of simply saying you would throw all that away?"

"It doesn't matter anyway, Lysbeth," Isaac shouted, desperate to stop his wife's arguments and finish what he had to tell her. "Janszoon wouldn't agree to any compromise, because I didn't even get the chance to offer one. He was incensed that I had deceived him all these years, that I had his notes and never returned them, though I knew how crushed he was by their loss. Lysbeth, he was going to kill me. He came at me with his hands raised to my throat. He was strangling me!" Here Isaac paused, breathing heavily and gazing into a scene only he could see.

"What happened, Isaac?" Lysbeth whispered.

"I had to defend myself, Lysbeth! I had to! I reached for something and I hit him with it."

"Oh, Isaac! Is he all right? You didn't just abandon an injured man?"

"Lysbeth, he is dead."

With a sharp intake of breath, Lysbeth moved away from her husband. "You killed a man? You murdered a man over some notes, Isaac? How could you?"

"It was not over the notes, Lysbeth! He was going to kill me, I tell you! I had to save myself. Would you have preferred I let him strangle me in his rage?"

In that moment, her husband went from the murderer she had

briefly glimpsed to the flawed man she loved. She knew that she would do whatever she needed to, if only she could somehow help him escape the consequences of his actions. He had lied to her all these years, but how was he to know that a simple fabrication about some papers would lead to such disaster?

"Did anyone see you, Isaac? Can anyone identify you?" she asked, already becoming the logical, reasoning person they would need.

"His wife and daughter entered the house just after Simon fell. I ran past them out the door and hurried away. They may have come out to search for me after they had discovered Simon, but I didn't see them."

"But they saw you when you left the house? Would they have any reason to recognize you?"

"All those years ago, shortly after we returned from our journey, I did go to their home for the evening. But surely the wife will not have remembered me in that brief moment that I surprised her with my exit. And there is nothing to connect me to Simon, nothing that anyone else would know."

"But the wife and daughter did both see you. Surely they will be able to give some description of you. And those walking along the street might remember a man leaving the house in a hurry."

"I suppose it is possible," Isaac reluctantly conceded. "But what can I do?"

"Well, will you be content to sit home and wait to see whether the *schout*'s men will come for you?"

"What else is there to do? Any action I try to take might only succeed in making my association with him known."

Lysbeth grasped her husband by the upper arms. "You must leave, Isaac. You must run!" With that she left the room in tears, and her husband didn't know whether it was from sorrow or repulsion.

When Anneke heard her mother's steps upon the stairs, she went to meet her.

"Mama, I—" she began, but then she saw her mother's face.

"Mama, what is it? Has Papa learned of the situation with Heer de Groot and his wife? Was he very angry with me, Mama? What will he do?"

Lysbeth looked at her daughter in confusion, her mind still so wholly with her husband. Then she shook her head. "No, Anneke, it isn't that. Papa doesn't know about that. Something else has happened, but I cannot speak of it with you now. I have to think."

"But, Mama, that's what you told me about the situation with Heer de Groot, that you had to think. But you gave me no help, and I went to the house today." Surprised at observing no reaction to this from her mother, Anneke went on. "I told him that I had to leave, that I would never return to the house again. He seemed sorry to have it so, Mama. I think he does not lay great blame on me. The worst part is that he is thinking of telling the authorities about his wife's adultery."

At this, Lysbeth did react. "Surely not!"

"He says he may. As you guessed, Mama, this was not the first time Vrouw Kregier had deceived her husband. I think his rage with her may this time overcome his desire to protect himself from the shame. He did not seem inclined to allow my name to come out, but I do not know whether he could prevent it."

"I know that she has greatly wronged him, and you, daughter, but I cannot help but feel some pity for the woman," Lysbeth said. Then, as though turning away from a petty distraction, she said, "We shall just have to wait and see what happens, I suppose. There are much greater things to worry about now."

"What do you mean, Mama? Something worse than my situation with Vrouw Kregier?"

"Yes, child. Please, leave me in peace now." With that, she returned to her work area, though she did not take up paint or brush.

Chapter 36

October 1660

Isaac sat alone, staring at the painting he had once done of his wife and children. He had hung it on the wall to show prospective patrons his skill in painting a family portrait, but he could not now recall that it had ever succeeded in that role. If only he could return to a world where getting another client was his greatest concern! His wife had said that he should leave, run. But how, and where to? Surely he should wait and see. But if something happened, it would mean that it was already too late to escape.

Janszoon's wife couldn't have recognized him. It had been so long since she'd seen him. He told himself that nothing connected him to the man he hadn't seen in so many years—but then he froze. The note he had left! He had forgotten about that! What had become of it? Janszoon had not mentioned seeing it, and he had acted completely surprised when he opened the door. What could have happened to the note?

Isaac wasn't sure how long he had been walking after leaving the message and returning to the Janszoon home. If Simon hadn't seen it, had it simply fallen and been swept away by the wind? But then, Simon was not the only inhabitant of the house. Perhaps his wife and daughter had returned home before Simon, taken the paper and put it somewhere, then gone out again. Yet Simon knew that they were doing the marketing. If they had spoken, Maria clearly had not mentioned the message to her husband. Maybe he hadn't seen them at all and just knew this was the time they usually went out to make the day's needed purchases.

Whatever had happened to it, that paper connected him to the dead man. Even if Maria had not seen it, even if it had been blown away, someone could well have retrieved it. When news of the murder spread, and might even appear in the news sheets, someone would remember having picked it up, would remember Simon's name and his, and would report to the *schout*.

At least he had not put his family name on the note. Still, records of the van Herder trip could be checked for an Isaac. Lysbeth was right. He had to flee. It might take a few days for the news to spread, for someone to report having had the note, and for the authorities to check the records. If Maria had it, though, she would immediately hand it over, and then the time would be shortened. He must go or face a death that would be merciful if he were only hanged.

Anneke heard her parents' voices coming from behind the closed door of her father's painting room. At times she just heard the indistinct hum of general conversation, but now and then one or both would raise their voices. That was most unusual, and taken together with her mother's earlier preoccupied air, Anneke's anxiety increased. Straining to discern what they were saying, she crept closer to their door, loath to eavesdrop upon them but feeling justified by the circumstances.

"But what good would that do?" she heard her father say. "They will only find me there."

"Not if you give them a different name."

"And what could I do there? I'm no longer a young man. I know nothing of the skills needed for what one does there," Isaac objected.

"What does anyone know who agrees to go? You will learn what you need to do," Lysbeth said.

"But—"

"Why are you arguing, Isaac? Do you believe I want this? I am trying to think of what you can do, and I have no other ideas. Do you?"

"I suppose not." Anneke heard a familiar note of resignation in her father's voice.

"I could paint there," he said with a hint of hope. "After all, your old 'friend' Johannes Vingboons has found success painting such places, and he hasn't even traveled there himself." This time, amid whatever distress her parents were experiencing, Anneke heard the sarcasm and jealousy in her father's voice. Vingboons had not only admired Lysbeth, he had also been much more successful than Isaac himself had been.

"No! You cannot paint there! What if someone recognizes you from your style of painting?" Lysbeth objected.

"I will paint, Lysbeth! I must! It is everything to me."

"Above your family?" and now it was Lysbeth's turn to speak with bitterness.

"Of course not! But I am to forsake my family. You tell me I must. Leave me something, Lysbeth!"

In her shock, Anneke almost did not hear her mother's reply. "It is not I who has brought you to this point, Isaac. Do not blame me for saying what I think needs to be done. I do love you, Isaac, and this will break my heart, but not as much as witnessing your execution." With that, Anneke heard her mother's footsteps approaching the door, and she stood back as the door opened.

"Mama! What is happening?" she cried.

"Leave me alone, Anneke! You will know what is necessary when it is time!" Lysbeth pushed her daughter aside, headed to her work-room, and slammed the door.

Anneke climbed up to the loft to think but found that she got nowhere; over and over again, she repeated in her head the snatches of her parents' conversation that she had heard. When it began to grow dark, she went to sit next to the door to the street. Lucas should be home soon. She had not spoken to her brother very much since he had denied her permission to use his name. They were both very busy, and she felt guilty about including his name against his wishes.

But now she was shut off from her mother and father, and she needed to tell Lucas what she had heard. Surely she had misunderstood the meaning of her parents' words. Her mother couldn't have said the word "execution." Still, something was happening that would change all of their lives. Compared to this, her difficulties with the de Groot household dimmed. Though she had been waiting for him, she started when Lucas came through the door.

"Lucas!"

"Hello, Anneke! What are you doing? Were you about to leave the house?"

"Oh, Lucas, we must talk! Something horrible is going on with Papa and Mama."

When Anneke had told Lucas all that she had heard, he said, "This can't be, Anneke! You must have misheard. What can Papa have done that would require him to leave us? We must go and ask them!"

"Mama rebuffed me when I tried to ask her, and she has closed herself off in her workroom."

"Then let's ask Papa!" Lucas said, immediately heading for his father's painting room. When they got there, though, it was empty, and they could find their father nowhere. "He must have left the house," Lucas said with a puzzled expression. "Then we will have to ask Mama."

Lucas, however, had no more luck than had his sister. When Lucas tried to enter her workroom, he found that she had somehow blocked the door. He called through it, but she only told him to leave her alone, just as she had done with Anneke.

Neither of their parents appeared for dinner that night. Lucas and Anneke could not remember that ever having happened before. They made a quick meal of bread and butter, along with some cheese, and each headed to their sleeping nook, too drained to discuss the situation any further. When they arose the next morning, they found their mother already at work, with her door open.

"Your father has gone out," she told them calmly. "Do not ask me any questions. Tonight, we will tell you what is happening. Lucas, you need to leave for work, do you not? Anneke, I suggest that you try to find out whether anything further has happened with Heer de Groot."

"But how—" Anneke began.

"I don't know how, Anneke, but you must try. Our troubles come upon us from so many sources." With that, Lysbeth resolutely turned her back on her children in a dismissal they could not counter.

"What has happened with de Groot, Anneke?"

"Oh, Lucas, I can't tell you now," she replied wearily, but Lucas roughly grabbed her arm.

"Tell me, Anneke! How am I to go to work with two troubles hanging over our family? Troubles that I don't even know about!"

As Anneke gave him a brief account of her part in Vrouw Kregier's deception, Lucas's frown etched an ever-deepening line between his brows.

"How could you have done that, Anneke? It is so shameful!" he said in a subdued voice.

"Do you not understand that I had no choice, Lucas? No matter what we do, we are at the mercy of the rich! What if she had told de Groot that I was a thief, as she threatened to do?"

To this, he had no answer. Even though he was proud of the position he now held as a surveyor, he knew that the word of the rich would always carry more weight.

Then, as though compelled to reveal to Lucas all that she had kept from him, she continued.

"Lucas, there is something else that I need to tell you. Do you remember that I told you about the map that I made from Papa's notes? I told you that de Groot would only ask Blaeu to publish it in the atlas if your name were put to it as well as mine. Well, I told de Groot that he could put your name, and I asked him to put Papa's as well."

"After I told you not to use my name? How could you, Anneke? You know how I feel about that map. I feel like I hardly know you, with one deception after another."

"I had to, Lucas, or de Groot wouldn't have agreed!"

"I wish he hadn't! And what will it all come to now? Your name may be brought into the de Groot scandal from what you tell me, and now Papa seems to be involved in something dubious at best. My name will be besmirched by association with yours."

"Is that all you can think of, Lucas? How this will affect you? Please, Lucas! We must rely on each other now. Please, don't be angry with me," Anneke pleaded.

"You do not see your own selfishness in all of this, do you Anneke? Well, we shall see what this comes to. I must leave for work now. I have to take a canal boat to get to today's surveying assignment."

"Goodbye, Lucas." Staring at the closed door, Anneke asked herself whether Lucas was right, whether she had been selfish. Perhaps she had, but she would forgive herself, for who never puts aside care for others if one has a great ambition?

Chapter 37

October 1660

Surely if de Groot had taken public action against his wife, it would be included in the news sheets, Anneke told herself. She didn't think that today was a day when the sheets came out, though, and she felt that she must get some information. But how?

She hadn't become well acquainted with any of the servants at the de Groot mansion. Warner was too forbidding and would hardly welcome her questions. She had once asked the young maid, Agneta, for some water to make her gum water, but she hadn't spoken to her after that. She realized now that she had probably come across to the servants as aloof at best, too proud at worst. No, there was no one there who would tell her anything.

Vrouw Kregier's friend Celia might have some news. Perhaps Helena had confided in her. No, she would probably blame Celia for the letter Ursula had sent, though Anneke was certain that Ursula had acted on her own. Still, Anneke could think of nowhere else to try to discover some news. And the thought of confronting Ursula appealed to her, though it was against her better judgment.

Knocking at the door of the Hartgers sisters, Anneke panicked at the thought that Celia's husband might answer, for she had no excuse she could give him for her presence. Then she reminded herself that he had always been gone when she and Helena were there, which was always during the day. He must have been at his business, as he surely would be this morning. When Celia answered the door, she made no attempt to hide her dismay, and though she stepped back to allow Anneke to come in and escape the cold, her stance barred any further advance into the house.

"Juffrouw van Brug! What could you possibly want here? Haven't you done enough harm?"

"I? What harm have I done, Vrouw Hartgers?"

"All of this disaster with Helena. Surely you must bear some of the blame."

"I only aided her under threat of an accusation of thievery. Why were you complicit in her scheme? And it was not I but your sister who revealed the truth to Heer de Groot. Surely you know that."

At this, the woman's shoulders sank. "Yes, and Helena blames me as much as she does Ursula. But I didn't even know that Ursula had a way of getting messages out! She told me that she paid the cleaning woman to take it. My sister doesn't care what Helena thinks, but I feel cheated. I entered into her plan because I wished her to welcome me into her circle of friends. Now she won't even speak to me."

Anneke stared at the woman, who seemed to have laid her innermost thoughts bare. Celia clearly saw herself a victim, though she herself was to blame for her predicament.

"I suppose you would like to see my sister, though I noticed that the last few times you didn't bother to visit with her. She grated on your nerves after a time, I suspect. I never understood what either of you found of interest in such a relationship."

Not wishing to address the first part of Celia's comment, Anneke simply said, "Perhaps each of us was looking to pass the time. I would like to see her. But I have mainly come to ask whether you know if Heer de Groot has or will make Helena's adultery public. You must be as worried as I am that, should he do so, your part in the sorry affair will come out."

"Surely he wouldn't cause himself the embarrassment!"

"The last time I spoke to him, Heer de Groot said that he had tired of his wife's infidelities and he was considering reporting her to the *schout*. That's why I have come to see whether you know anything about that."

"I would have thought that you would know more than I. Helena always said that you and Willem spent a lot of time together." It would have been impossible for Anneke to miss the implication, but she didn't acknowledge it. Celia continued, "Can't you ask him his intentions?"

"As you might surmise, I have left the household for good. I no longer work for Heer de Groot."

"Well, at least that might make Helena happy. But what do I care now? I've tried to send messages, but I get no answers, and after all I did for her."

"Perhaps the servants don't deliver the messages to her. Maybe they even give them to Heer de Groot," said Anneke. She couldn't help but feel a hint of satisfaction at the other woman's increased distress as Celia walked over to a chair and said in a low voice, "Go up and see Ursula if you care to."

Even before Anneke reached the door to Ursula's room, she heard her say, "Ah, I wondered if you would have the courage to come."

"And what did you imagine I might say?" Anneke replied as she entered. Despite the fact that their last encounter had ended unpleasantly, and Anneke had avoided Ursula after that, she still felt a pang to note that her health seemed to have deteriorated. It was difficult to forgive her for what she had done, but Anneke found that, far from a harsh confrontation, she mostly wanted to understand.

"Why did you write the letter, Ursula?" she asked. "I thought we had the beginnings of a friendship. Surely you knew that I, too, would suffer consequences from the revelation. I explained to you that I had no choice in the matter."

"Ah, Anneke, but you did have a choice. You could have refused."

"And risked being called a thief?"

"You could have taken your chances. Surely de Groot knew something of his wife's deceptions. You don't really understand what not having a choice means, Anneke. Not having a choice is being unable to rise without assistance. Not having a choice is having to live with a sister who keeps me here only from duty. Not having a choice is accepting any visits thrust upon me because I cannot escape."

"Is that how you saw our time together?" Anneke asked.

"Didn't you?" Ursula accused.

"No. I will admit that at first our visits were mostly to help pass the time while I waited for Helena to return, and to take my mind off why I was here. But then I came to look forward to seeing you. I am sorry that our last meeting ended as it did."

"You say that now, but you never came to my room again. We had no chance to restore the harmony we had felt."

"I'm sorry, Ursula. I'm sorry that you feel that way. I'm sorry that you have so few choices in your life."

"I don't want your solicitude! I don't know why you seek to appease me. I've done the damage, and even if I wanted to, I couldn't undo it."

"Would you prefer my anger, Ursula? For I assure you that I could call upon it if you so desire. You have been the instrument of my ruin, for no matter what happens to Helena, I forfeit much."

"Do you think I care? You abandoned me! Get out! Get out now!" Ursula screamed. Anneke retreated, understanding that the woman had used the only means at her disposal to assuage her pain. She had built a shield against a hurt much older than their acquaintance by striking out at Anneke.

There was only one other place where Anneke thought she might find out whether Helena's infidelity had become known. De Groot was a longtime client of Blaeu's, so people there would recognize the name if they had heard about the fiasco with his wife. They also knew that Anneke had been working in the de Groot home. If they knew anything, they would be quick to ask her for details. It would be unpleasant, and she would have to be very careful how she answered their inquiries, but at least she would know whether Helena's actions had been revealed.

If she went to Blaeu's, she would see Daniel. What would he think of all of this? Sadness crept over her at his possible rejection, for she had come to believe that he would be a constant in her life. As she opened the door to the printshop, Daniel looked over to see the source of the cool breeze. He was helping to hang map sheets at the moment but left to approach her.

"Anneke, I am so happy to see you—but what is wrong?"

"Oh, Daniel, so much has happened. I need time to explain it to you, but not now. I hope that you will feel the same about me once you have heard it all," she said, embarrassed to feel tears seeping from her eyes.

"What is it, Anneke? You must tell me!"

"Not now. It is a complicated story, and I cannot speak of it while we are standing on the printshop floor in front of so many others."

"Very well. I am committed to helping a friend with something this evening, but might I call upon you at your home tomorrow evening?"

"Yes, Daniel, please do, though my family may be in turmoil."

"Anneke, you are worrying me!"

"I am sorry, Daniel. There is something going on with my parents that even I do not understand."

"Then perhaps I shouldn't intrude. Though I long to see you, should we wait a few days before meeting?"

"Oh, Daniel, please, no! Even being here with you now, I know that I will feel comforted by your presence, whatever may be coming." She looked at him with such intensity that he told her that others had started to observe them. At this, she stepped back from him a pace or two and assumed a more businesslike expression, but there was still urgency in her voice. "Daniel, has anyone mentioned Heer de Groot lately? Have you heard anything about him?"

Daniel stiffened. "De Groot? Why do you ask? Do you not see him every day?"

"I left his home a couple of days ago and will not return. Oh, Daniel, this is part of what I must talk to you about."

"Has he done something to you, Anneke? Are you all right?"

"No, Daniel, I am not, but it is not from anything he has done, at least not yet."

"You are talking in riddles, Anneke. Please tell me what this means!"

"I can't tell you here, Daniel. It is not what you may fear, but I do not even know yet how everything will end. I have not lost my virtue, Daniel, but I have done something of which I am not proud and which could lead to my downfall."

As he went to take her hand, she pulled away. "I must leave now, Daniel. If you still wish to see me, please come to my parents' tomorrow evening."

"I will come," he said as she walked away.

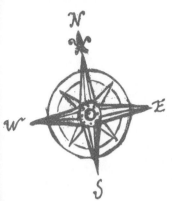

Chapter 38

October 1660

That evening, Isaac and Lysbeth told their children that they needed to speak to them. Anneke's and Lucas's fears were not allayed by the grim look on their parents' faces.

"Sit, children," Isaac said, pacing the room as one who may never rest again. "Tomorrow I will bid farewell to all of you," he began, and Anneke detected tears in her father's eyes. As both Anneke and Lucas protested, he raised his hand and looked pleadingly at his wife.

"Your father will depart tomorrow. We will tell the neighbors that he is traveling to Friesland for an important commission from a large landowner there who wants your father to paint some of the landscapes of his holdings, as well as to do a portrait of his family members."

"That is good news, is it not?" Lucas said, quickly. "We will miss you, Papa, but surely this is a good opportunity for you. It sounds like a large commission. Anneke had me so worried with bits of what she thought she had overheard."

"Lucas, stop!" Lysbeth said, looking at her husband to see if he would continue, but his eyes entreated her. "We will say that he is going to Friesland, but that will not be his destination," she said with a look that forbade interruption. "After three weeks, we will receive news that your Papa has been killed. We will be told that he fell off a horse the landowner had lent him to travel on the estate and hit his head on a rock."

Anneke sprang to her feet. "What do you mean, we will be told that he has died? This makes no sense! Why are you saying this?"

"In reality, your Papa will not travel to Friesland. Tomorrow he will board a VOC ship bound for Batavia," Lysbeth explained.

"No," Lucas whispered. "You know what I have said of life on a WIC ship. Surely it would be no better on a VOC ship! Papa, you cannot do it. And what will you do in Batavia? You are no administrator or farmer! I doubt you will find painting commissions there," he said, unable to keep a note of derision from his voice.

"I have no choice, Lucas, Anneke. I must flee. I am very lucky that I managed to get a spot on the ship. To go overland would have been difficult, and with less chance of escape."

"Why must you leave, Papa? I overheard something of what you and Mama said yesterday, but why must you go?" Anneke asked.

"Because I have killed a man."

Anneke gasped, but no sound escaped Lucas's lips.

"It was an accident. The man was coming at me. I feared for my life and I struck him on the head with a heavy shell. I did not intend to kill him, but the blow was fatal. I fear that the law will see only a man who has been killed in his home. Killed by me."

"Who is this man, Papa?" his daughter asked.

"Do you remember that I spoke of a surveyor on the expedition to Africa?"

"Yes, but that was so long ago," Lucas said.

"Anneke, your mother told me about the surprise you planned for me, the map you have created using my notes. I am deeply touched by your wish to do this for me, daughter, and your mother told me that Blaeu has said he will include it in his atlas with our names, and Lucas's, too."

"Oh, but it was to be a surprise for you, Papa!" Anneke protested, then returned to the moment. "But how is that connected to this?"

"Because, my dear child, the notes were not all mine. The more precise notes, the ones without which you could not have made your map, belonged to the surveyor. He thought they had been lost at sea during the storm that swept my drawings overboard. But I had them. I didn't realize at first that I had gathered them up with my own notes. To my shame, when I discovered them, I didn't tell him. All these years, and I didn't tell him. When your mama informed me of your map, I was afraid that he, Simon Janszoon, would learn of it and, seeing my name, would realize that only his notes could have made such a map possible.

"I went to see him, and when I told him of the situation, he was enraged that I had deceived him all these years, that I had let him think his notes had been lost. He came toward me and put his hands around my neck. He is a much larger and stronger man than I, and as I felt his fingers tighten, I knew that I would die if I did not act. In my desperation, I grabbed what came to hand and I hit him."

"Will they know it was you, Papa?" Lucas asked.

"When I arrived, Simon was the only one home, but as I ran out, his wife and daughter were entering. I met his wife only once, years ago, so it is doubtful that she recognized me," Isaac said.

"Then why—"

"Because when I first arrived at Simon's house, he wasn't home, so I left a note. I don't know what became of it, but if it is found, it will connect me to him."

"Oh, Papa," was all that Anneke could say at the enormity of what she had just heard.

"But they will be able to find you in Batavia, Papa. They will still find you," Lucas said.

"I have used a false name. I do not think they will be able to trace me."

"Then it is certain you must go," Lucas said with resignation.

"Yes, and there is one other thing. I am sorry, Anneke, but I must ask that you request of Blaeu not to use our names on the map. Your mother tells me that he and Meyert are so impressed by the map that I believe he will still wish to include it in the atlas. I doubt he cares that the map would be unattributed. But if my part in the killing were to become known, Blaeu would be justifiably angry that you let his atlas be associated with a murderer. He might even dismiss you and your mother, causing you further harm because of what I have done. I am truly sorry. I am sorry that I have lied to all of you for all these years. I am sorry that this will crush your dream, Anneke."

"But why must our names be left off, Papa? Would not the surveyor be the only one who knew of the connection?"

"No, Anneke. The map shows the trail of the van Herd expedition, does it not? The details were about where we went. Anyone who was familiar with that journey would recognize this. Simon's bitterness at having lost his notes was such that I am sure that he complained of it repeatedly over the years to anyone who would listen. That could connect him to the map, and thus to me, and to you."

"But that seems so unlikely, Papa, requiring various links that may never come together! Surely it is not necessary to remove our names."

"I'm sorry, Anneke, but—"

Lysbeth interrupted her husband. "Would you take a chance that could lead to ruin for your Papa, for all of us? Would you, Anneke? Because I think that we dare not. I wanted to say that we must ask Heer Blaeu to not use the map, for what if someone saw it and asked him about its origins, but your Papa said that he could not ask that of you."

Anneke simply bowed her head. She would do as they asked, but she could not stem the tide of disappointment at the wreck of her hopes.

No one slept that night. After their parents' revelation, Lucas and Anneke retreated to her loft workroom. The room was tidier now that she had finished her work with the map. All that remained on her table were the notes, neatly stacked. She leaned over the table and, with her right forearm, furiously swept them to the floor. "How could he? How could he, Lucas?" she demanded, and flopped onto the lone chair, leaving him to lean against the closed door.

"How could he kill a man?" Lucas asked. "How could he lie to us all these years? How could he destroy your work? How could he now leave us all to deal with whatever comes? Which do you mean, Anneke?" His rage grew in intensity, though not volume, for even now he did not wish his father to overhear his anger.

"Any, all. He has lied to us, and he has betrayed Mama as surely as if he had gone to another woman's bed."

Lucas marveled at this example of deception coming from his sister. He had not guessed her thoughts would go in that direction. "I have always thought that you forgave him too much. I see that he has finally broken even your illusions."

"Oh, Lucas, be still! What good does it do for you to say that? What do you want me to say? That Papa has not been worthy of the love I have given him? All right, I say it. But I wish that I could still live with that lost vision." At this, Lucas went to her and enfolded her in an embrace, sorry now to have her see that he had been right about their Papa. Sorry that it made her suffer so.

As the hours passed, they spoke in a disjointed fashion, going back over the same thing again and again, and then allowing themselves a respite by straying to some other topic, only to return to that which weighed on them. Each repetition diminished the power of what they had heard until it seemed almost to enter the realm of the common-place, the realm of that which could be spoken of with detachment. As it came closer to midnight, the black penetrated the small window fitted between the sides of the slanted, pointing roof, and the pauses in speech became longer as each approached the threshold of exhaustion.

Finally Anneke asked, "Are you glad that our names will be taken from the map?"

"You know that I never wished mine included, never wished you to create the map. But let us not dwell on that now, Anneke." He started to pick up the papers that Anneke had strewn on the floor hours earlier. "You know, I am truly doubtful that Papa will be capable of doing what will be demanded of him, either on the ship or once he reaches Batavia."

"He didn't actually tell us the nature of what he will be doing. Perhaps he was able to gain passage without needing to work on the ship. Perhaps he somehow convinced the recruiters at the VOC that his artistic talent could be put to use for them," Anneke said, though the doubt in her voice spoke more loudly than her words.

"How would he be able to convince them of his artistic skill? He didn't use his own name, and he wouldn't dare show them any of his works. What if someone later made the connection and realized who he was? He never gained the stature as an artist that he wished, but he is known well enough that he gets commissions from time to time."

"Perhaps he was able to secure a position as some kind of clerk once they reach Batavia. At least that would be less demanding than manual labor," Anneke ventured.

"How could he have gotten such a promise in so short a time, and with no one to vouch for him?" her brother countered.

"Oh, what does it matter?" Anneke cried. "He will be miserable! I cannot imagine how he will even find his way. And we will never see him again, Lucas. Never!" Now Anneke's tears flowed freely. Lucas, too, let tears stream down his face, fatigue collapsing the wall he had always built against the love he might feel for his father.

"It is years now that I have not felt about him as I once did, but I do love him, you know. I will grieve."

"I know, Lucas," Anneke said. After several minutes, when each was lost in the mind's weary wandering, she said, "We have yet to speak of how this will affect us. Even if his part in the surveyor's death is never discovered, and everyone believes the lie of his death while in Friesland, our lives are forever changed."

"Yes, but at least we will not need to worry about our livelihood. With what you, Mama, and I earn, we will not be very much worse off. Papa liked to think of all of us as merely supplementing what he earned for the family, but we all know that it has come to be rather the reverse."

"But surely someday you will wish to marry, and I hope to find a husband, to have a family of my own. What of Mama then?"

"One of us will have her to live with us," Lucas answered quickly, as though this were a simple answer.

"Yes, one of us must. Hopefully you will find a kind wife, or I a generous husband."

After a moment, Lucas said, "If Papa is revealed as a murderer, we will all be ruined, and he will have evaded any consequences."

"Do you not think that leaving his family, his art, and his land are harsh consequences?"

"Yes, but what of us? We will suffer for his act! We may all lose our positions. Who would want to be associated with the family of a murderer? And who would want to marry into such a family?" Then, after a moment, he asked, "Do you think that the authorities would try to get us to tell them his whereabouts?"

"I suppose that is why Mama and Papa came up with the lie of his death."

"But that could easily be investigated and found to be false."

"Oh, Lucas! I can't even consider that!"

"I tell you, Anneke, the bitterness that I feel in this moment makes me wonder whether I would tell the authorities, if that were a way to mitigate the consequences that we would suffer."

"You don't mean that! Do you blame me, too, Lucas? After all, you never wanted me to make the map, and if I hadn't, none of this would have happened!"

"Don't try to take his guilt onto yourself, Anneke," Lucas said with more anger than comfort in his voice. "It was he who lied to us for all of our lives, he who acted rashly in running to the surveyor without sufficient thought, he who struck the killing blow."

"Yes, but do you remember, Lucas, that I told you some of the notes were in a different hand? I suspected something was wrong but explained it away. I did not wish there to be any impediment to what I was doing, so I put my doubts from my mind."

"I do recall that. But Anneke, you have always had such faith in Papa. You are not to be faulted that you did not expect such perfidy."

"Thank you, Lucas," Anneke said softly, relieved that, at least for now, her brother's bitterness did not extend to her.

At this, they fell silent. Neither wanted to think of an innocent man, a man whom their father had wronged, dead by his hand. Isaac had struck out in a moment he believed his life to be threatened, but that did not make him innocent. He had wronged the man for so many years, and for what? What had he even gained by keeping the surveyor's notes? Some private self-aggrandizement? Over all of these years, had he ever regretted what he had done, or had he simply glossed over the wrong of it?

After Anneke and Lucas had gone to their beds, in the hours before dawn, they could hear the soft murmur of their parents' voices. Anneke guessed that Isaac must be trying to decide what he should pack for the journey and that her mother must be helping him. She thought about what the separation would mean to these two people who had loved each other for so long, and she assumed that they must want to spend every last moment together. She wished that she, too, could be with her Papa in these last hours, despite what he had done, but felt she shouldn't intrude. It was her mother who would miss him the most. It was true that at times they lost patience with each other. There were times when they even seemed indifferent toward each other, but Anneke thought these must be the normal ups and downs of marriage. When tragedy struck, each would most wish to cling to the other, but that was not possible.

Anneke's mind wandered to a vision of a future with Daniel. Life with him could be a refuge from the complications of people such as de Groot and his wife. Perhaps she should be happy with the thought of a simple life. It wasn't that she wished to forsake her ambitions, but rather that they seemed to drift further and further from her reach, whereas life with Daniel seemed a possibility.

Everything depended on truths not being revealed. If her name became associated with Helena's infidelity, she could be ruined. Could Daniel overlook such a scandal? Perhaps, she thought, if he loves me enough. If Isaac's crime were discovered, however, could even Daniel ignore such a stain? Surely his family would not approve of a connection with the daughter of a murderer.

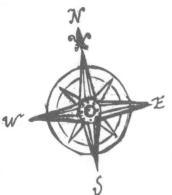

Chapter 39
October 1660

When morning finally came, Isaac carried to the street door the belongings he would bring with him to his new life. The family would not go to the ship to see him off, for that increased the risk that he would be recognized by someone who might remember that the tearful family had been on the docks when a VOC ship was leaving for Batavia. Besides, the neighbors could not see them all leave together, given the story that Isaac was traveling to Friesland for a commission.

As they gathered around him, Isaac hugged each in turn. "Goodbye, my dears! Please forgive me, and pray for me. I will pray to God each day that my name is never connected to Simon Janszoon. Do not think that I am insensible of what it could mean for each of you if my guilt were made plain."

"Oh, Papa, do not think of that now!" Anneke said. "I love you so much, Papa! I am so sorry that it is my map that set you upon the course of this catastrophe."

"No, daughter, you must not say so. It is I, and I alone, who bears the responsibility. I wished to make myself grander in the eyes of my family. I told myself that it was a harmless lie. But I should have known that a lie one tells to cover one's own wrongdoing can never be harmless. And you, Lucas," he said. As he looked up, he seemed to realize just in that moment how tall his son had gotten. "I set you upon a life for my own selfish purposes, purposes that I did not even think through to their inevitable end. I hope that you can forgive me, my son."

Father and son embraced, and Lucas responded in a husky voice, "Let us not linger on that now, Papa. I am happy in my profession. It is a good life."

"Thank you for your generosity, Lucas," Isaac said, then finally turned to his wife.

"From you more than any other, I must beg forgiveness. I know that I have wronged you, Lysbeth, always putting my ambition above all else. You have a real artistic gift, wife, and I made you squander it on useless coloring till that was all that was left to you." Her eyes filled with tears, Lysbeth embraced this man whom she had loved, this man who, even now, did not see that he belittled the life that she had led.

"Goodbye, my loved ones. I hope that we shall meet in the hereafter." Then he opened the door, walked through, and was gone.

Mother, daughter, and son stood a moment, staring at the closed door. This man who had determined all of their lives had left them. Surely that was not the last time they would see him in this life! Now that he had departed, Anneke and Lucas began to question the decisions their parents had made.

"If his name is not connected to the murder, Mama, we can write and he can return," Lucas said hopefully, looking to his mother for confirmation.

"But we will have told everyone that he was killed!" Anneke said. "Oh, can we not come up with some other falsehood to explain his disappearance? Must we say that he died, Mama?"

"Your Papa thought it best. If it were believed that he had died, there would be no speculation about him. He also said it would be easier for me to be seen as a widow than an abandoned wife. He did think of me, you see." It must have been their love for her that prevented her children from pointing out that this was but a paltry sign of their father's affection.

"But there has to be a better way!" Lucas insisted. "What if we wait longer before we tell the fabrication about his death? Could we not delay and see whether the authorities discover anything?"

"I suppose we could," Lysbeth said slowly, realizing that once again she had let her husband sway her.

"We could say his patron in Friesland is so happy with his work that he has found more subjects for him to paint, or that the landowner's friends, impressed with Papa's work, have offered him commissions as well," Lucas added. "After all, there cannot be so many artists in Friesland. It is not like Amsterdam. Papa might be seen as quite accomplished there, might he not?"

"Yes, surely that is a very believable story—perhaps even more credible than a fatal fall from his horse," Anneke said.

"Still, we could not carry on with that indefinitely. At some point we would have to explain his continued absence," Lysbeth said, her mind now working with her children's to see if they could find a way ahead that might offer a happier outcome. "Of course," she continued, "if his name came out in connection with Heer Janszoon's death, it would do no good."

"But telling the lie of his death does not prevent that from happening anyway. If they discover that it was him, that could be the time to hear that he had taken a fatal fall," Anneke said.

"But in that case, they would have someone in Friesland confirm that he had been there and that it was he who had been thrown from a horse," Lysbeth objected.

"But that would occur no matter what," Lucas said. "If we told the lie in three weeks, as you and Papa planned, and his part in the surveyor's death were uncovered, they would still wish to make sure that it was him."

"Have you thought," Anneke said deliberately, "that if we tell the lie of his death, no matter the timing, and his guilt comes out, and they check the story of his death, we will be seen as complicit. We will have lied for him so that he could escape justice."

"You and Papa didn't think of that, did you?" Lucas asked, accusing his mother now, too.

"No, Lucas." Lysbeth's voice was now steely. "We did not think of that. Forgive us for not coldly analyzing all of the possible outcomes while we were stricken with grief at our looming separation. I do see your point, though. We cannot do anything that will endanger us further."

"If we only tell the first part of the story, and not that he died, we can simply say that Papa lied to us, too. We believed him to be in Friesland on a commission. No one can prove otherwise," Lucas said.

"More lies then?" Anneke asked.

"No more than we were otherwise prepared to tell," Lysbeth said, now seemingly convinced by Lucas's logic. "Still, that explanation could not go on forever. At some point, it would become unbelievable."

"Well, then it would just be seen as a mysterious disappearance," Lucas said. "We could say that we didn't know what could have happened to Papa."

"Enough of these convolutions!" Lysbeth suddenly cried. "If his crime is not discovered, we will figure out what to do as time goes on. If it is discovered, no fiction will protect us. We will be the family of a murderer."

With this grim and inescapable reminder, the other two fell silent. Then finally Lucas said, "I must go to work. I do not wish it to be remarked upon that today I missed my assignment. All must seem as normal."

"Yes, Lucas, go. I, too, must do my work. I have some maps that I am already behind on. I cannot afford to fall further back," Lysbeth said, and left for her workroom. Even amid all of the turmoil, Anneke noticed that her mother seemed to have greatly aged.

Alone in the entryway, Anneke wondered what she should do next. Her father had said she would have to take their names off of the map. She observed with some surprise that—even with the discovery of what her father had done, his departure, their fear of discovery, and her worry that she might still be implicated in Helena's affair—she could feel sharp disappointment at what must mean the loss of her dream to practice as a cartographer.

Still, she knew she must take action. The longer she delayed, the stranger it would seem for her to ask that their names not appear on the map. She would go to Willem to ask that he inform Blaeu, though she didn't know what reason she could possibly give, especially after she had been so insistent about the attribution. Might his anger have built against her for her part in his wife's betrayal, even though, when she had last seen him, he seemed to regret the end of her work there?

Could she go directly to Heer Blaeu, or perhaps Heer Meyert? But again, how could she explain the desired change? Still, she could not wait. She had no idea what the timing was for printing the hundreds of maps which would appear in the *Atlas Maior*, nor whether individual maps might be sold before the whole was ready. If the names didn't come off and the map became known, that could, as Papa had pointed out, be the very thing that would lead to the discovery of his guilt.

Anneke put on her cloak and left the house, her feet carrying her toward the de Groot mansion. She had thought never to see the map collector again, but he was bound up with both of her problems, and she had no choice but to see whether he might be influenced.

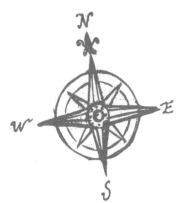

Chapter 40
October 1660

As she approached the map collector's home, it felt strange to see it so unchanged after all the turmoil she knew to have happened within. The blue door, which had so enchanted her on her first day here, now seemed to mock her. "Did you not see that within lies something that is not as it should be?" it seemed to say. When Warner opened the door to her, he let his surprise and disapproval show plainly on his face.

"Juffrouw?" he said formally.

"Good morning, Warner. I was hoping that I might see Heer de Groot."

Raising his eyebrows, Warner said simply, "I will see." Before turning his back on her, he did step aside so that she could come well in from the cold. "Wait here," he added, holding up his hand as a physical sign for her to stop, as though she might attempt an unsanctioned entry.

As she stood by the doorway, Anneke stayed perfectly still, fearful that any movement might somehow signal to Helena that she was there. Anneke most fervently hoped that she would not see the mistress of the house, although with her Papa's departure, the fear she had so recently felt here seemed somehow lessened by comparison. Even as she was grateful for each moment in which Helena did not appear, she began to dread what it might mean if Helena were absent. Had Willem banished her from the house? Had he reported her behavior to the *schout*? Had she fled of her own accord? Her speculations were put to an end when Warner returned and silently led her to the map room. After she entered, he closed the door.

Seeing that Willem was not present, she looked around at the room in which she had spent so many hours. She was appalled by what she saw. No matter which direction she turned, there was chaos. Maps were on every surface, strewn with no sense of order. Some had even fallen to the floor, and there seemed to be no one who cared whether they would be trodden upon. She recognized some of the maps as those she had worked on, but they by no means dominated the mad confusion before her. She was saddened and incensed at seeing the maps so mistreated, not cared for with the kind of reverence she had always felt for them.

Then she saw it, lying on the floor, partially covered by lesser works. It was the world map that she had worked on so recently during days of inner turmoil, not knowing when she would next be called away to accompany Helena, not knowing when Willem would discover their betrayal. The map had offered her an escape into a world which she understood, which she could control, which she could beautify. She felt that it was the best coloring she had ever done. Perhaps the intensity of her emotions had allowed her to pour her heart into the work.

The map contained no gold or silver embellishments. The colors alone defined its splendor, this map that she had done without de Groot's prying eyes, without a need to put into words what she planned to do. She had been led more by the demands of the map itself than she had ever been. Now, as she looked at it, she saw the dark blue of the sky at the top, the paint so fully saturated as to give a dramatic contrast. The earth itself was represented by two circles sitting side by side. The one on the left showed the Americas, and the one on the right depicted Europe, Asia, Africa, and Australia. Rather than coloring the oceans with a pale blue, as she often did, she had painted them white. This then allowed her to use a pale wash for the continents: yellow for the Americas, green for Africa, shades of pink for Europe and Asia. Each was then outlined in a darker shade of the color used for the interior. The decorative figures in the sky were meticulously painted, and each sat upon a white cloud, providing a contrast with the surrounding darker blue. This was her best work. She couldn't leave it here to possibly be destroyed. It wasn't hers, but she carefully rolled it up and set it on a table.

Then her eyes lit upon one of the walls. There were confused bursts of color on it, mixing as they streamed down the wall, as though paint pots had been hurled against it. There were maps on the floor beneath, now ruined by the random drops which had splashed upon them in the moment of the crash. This frightened her. She now saw an angry Willem flinging paints and sweeping maps from shelves and tables in a storm of fury. She approached the wall, and just as she was about to reach out to touch the colors, she heard a step upon the threshold.

"Ah, Anneke, how kind of you to come visit," Willem said from the doorway. She turned to see a man transformed. No longer was he the impeccably dressed gentleman, secure enough in his power to be kind to those beholden to him. She saw a man whose face was ravaged, his hair wild, and his clothes disheveled. He had not looked this way after he found out about his wife's treachery. This had happened since she had left him.

"Heer de Groot," she began, but he cut her off with a rough laugh.

"Really, Anneke? Heer de Groot, after all we have been through together? You had called me Willem," he said. As he approached her she couldn't keep herself from shrinking back, but she found the courage to say, "What has happened here, Willem?"

"Well you might ask, Juffrouw! You see before you the symbol of my life. I was proud of my wealth but even prouder of a cultured image of myself, a collector of art and cartographic masterpieces. I was not merely a gentleman merchant. I was something more. I had a fine sensibility, though I dealt in buying and selling, like everyone in our city. I had a beautiful wife to complete the image. I cared for her, in my way, and I thought that she felt the same. I suppose that she did. She cared for me in her way." Anneke stood still and silent, and so he continued.

"Perhaps you wonder how long it took for my wife's liaisons to commence. Not long, I assure you. It did take somewhat longer for me to find out about them, and longer yet for me to confront her. So, you see, Juffrouw van Brug, you were not the initiator of my marriage's demise. It is just that you shepherded it along. Well before your arrival, I had begun to despise my tolerance for my wife's infidelities, perhaps even more than the infidelities themselves.

"When you came, there was something I had never before experienced with a woman. You were intelligent and thoughtful. You were not vain of your looks. You had a fire within you for what you did, and it wasn't about money. It was about the work itself, I believed. You may have wondered at the many hours I spent with you in this room. That time allowed me to escape the sordid reality of my marriage, and at times even to put it from my mind. I admired you greatly, Anneke."

Sensing her discomfort, he continued. "No need to respond to my rantings. I simply wish to have you understand. I have done much thinking since last I saw you. When I said that I wanted to do something for you, it was meant with honest and pure intention, though I must admit now that perhaps somewhere in the back of my mind I may have hoped there might be something more between us.

"But then, Anneke, my feelings toward you began to unravel a bit when you were so insistent on the gift that you wanted, and the details of the gift. Being the man I am, I had assumed that your request would be something easy to grant. Money is so easily spent when one has a surplus. I should have known better. I should have known that you would not want something that could simply be bought." As he spoke, de Groot glanced at the maps around him, as though he could not recall why they were there.

"I have a question for you. Did you plan to use me from the very beginning? As a successful Amsterdam man of business, I should have expected it. But I didn't. You asked for the gift of my influence, and you even put demands upon it. I did not like that, Anneke, but I acquiesced. I saw myself as a man of my word, and at least in that I could retain my honor. So, you see, Anneke, my view of you had changed even before the discovery of your part in my wife's adultery."

At this, Anneke sought to protest. "But I have explained to you how that came about! Can you not see things from my position? I was no more than someone you paid to perform a task. You seemed to appreciate what I did, but how could my word possibly stand against an accusation by your wife? I did not know that she had acted thus before and that you already had reason to suspect her."

"It really doesn't matter now, Anneke. I have spent my rage and I am empty." At this last, he had looked away, but then, in a different tone, he asked, "Why have you come here, Anneke? You declared our last meeting to be the end."

"I have come for two reasons," Anneke said, gathering her determination. "First, I have come to find out whether you intend to report your wife."

Now his countenance changed from that of a defeated man to an angry one. "What business is that of yours?"

"It is my business because if you do report her, I do not see how my part in the affair can be kept quiet. There are too many people who know about it. Too many who would be happy to spread such gossip." When he didn't reply, she found herself pleading, "Can you not see that if this came out, it would mean ruin for me? Ruin even for my family? I cannot imagine that Heer Blaeu would wish to be associated with a woman who had a part in such a scandal, nor with that woman's mother. Even my brother Lucas's livelihood might be endangered by the taint. Please, before you act, think of the consequences to us! I know that this is a lot to ask, but I ask it nevertheless, because I have no choice."

"Just as you had no choice but to take part in my wife's plan?" he said sarcastically.

"Yes. Just as I had no choice then," she replied as steadily as she could.

"Well, I shall tell you, Anneke. I have not yet decided what I will do. Helena has gone to her sister's house in Delft. No doubt she has told her sister some tale of my brutish behavior. Perhaps you can take comfort in the fact that had she remained here, the irritant of her presence might have prompted me to take action. As she has absented herself, I am free to descend back into the passive self-disdain from which you had, for a time, given me a reprieve. And now you come to ask for another favor. Perhaps I shall grant it. After all, I may finally and firmly decide that I would rather avoid the embarrassment of being ridiculed by all as a man who cannot keep his wife's affections."

When Anneke made no response, he continued, "But you said that you had come for two reasons. What, pray, might the other be, my dear colorist?"

Swallowing and then looking him in the eye, Anneke said, "I have come to ask you to request that Heer Blaeu not use the name of my father, my brother, or myself on the map. We would prefer no attribution."

"My, my, I had thought you held no further power to surprise me, Juffrouw van Brug, but I confess myself to be astounded. After your insistence on that very point, much in opposition to my desire, you now wish to reverse that which caused me some discomfort to procure?"

"Yes, and I am sorry that I caused you the trouble in the first place. I remain unfailingly grateful to you for the placement of the map with Blaeu, but my family, who had not known of my request, has said in no uncertain terms that the map must appear anonymously."

"Ah, so you did not have the permission of your brother, as you had led me to believe, as I recall."

"No. I'm sorry I lied to you. I had such good intentions, but it seems that my family does not interpret things as I did."

"Perhaps I should meet this family of yours, who now intends for me to go back to Blaeu and, I can't help but think, humiliate myself a bit. Yes, I think that I should at least meet your father. He is an artist, I believe you said. Perhaps I can show him my collection," he said, in a self-mocking tone.

"I'm afraid that my father has just left on a commission to Friesland. We expect him to be gone for some time."

"Leaving you at such a time? That is a shame. Well, I'm afraid that

I must decline your request. If you wish to delete the attribution, you shall have to bring that about yourself. Now, if you will excuse me. Please, leave my home," he said, walking out of the room. No one saw Anneke leave the house with a rolled-up map in her hand.

She had completely misunderstood de Groot, but then how could she have been expected to see beneath the veneer of sophistication and even thoughtful attentiveness? Who was the real Willem? Perhaps the ordeal with his wife's continued infidelities, and, yes, her own treachery toward him, had simply revealed the man he had been all along, the man that he was able to keep hidden as long as not too many things disturbed his ordered life.

Anneke was shaken. There was no denying that, but she also began to tell herself that perhaps uncovering this Willem was to the good. She had once wished they could somehow be more to each other, although she could never define what that would have been. Now she fully knew that she was lucky to be out of his life. Well, she was out of his life if he did not report Helena to the authorities.

She walked in the direction of the printing house. It was as though her body knew what must come next, even before her mind accepted it. Once there, though, what should she do? Daniel would be surprised to see her since she had been there just the day before, and they had arranged that he would visit her parents' home that evening. How much had changed since then! How much more she had learned about what her future life might, and might not, hold!

She still wished to see Daniel that evening. She wished to see him, and more than that, she wished to tell him all that had happened. But did she dare do that? She would tell him everything about the problem with de Groot and Helena. She would confess to him her shame and her worries while still trying to make him understand how she had let herself fall into such a pit. She wanted Daniel to know, not just because she owed him that, but also because she believed he would understand—perhaps not immediately, but he would come to it. When that happened, he would offer his steadfast care. He was a man she understood, or at least believed she did. He was a man that she could count on. Tonight, she would tell him all.

No, not all, she reminded herself. She would not tell him the truth about her father. That was not hers to tell, and it could put Isaac in danger. She did not think that Daniel would report the murder to the *schout*, but he was an upright man, and perhaps he would think it his duty. Perhaps it *would* be his duty. She excused herself for the subterfuge because Isaac was her father, and she loved him. Daniel owed him no such debt. No, she could not tell him about the surveyor. She would have to explain her father's prolonged absence, and she supposed she would resort to the fiction about a commission in Friesland. She did not think she had another choice.

As Anneke entered the printing shop, Daniel looked up and saw her. She saw a fleeting look of happiness that changed to puzzlement. Today she did not wait for him to approach her but walked boldly to his press and said in a low voice, "I will see you this evening. I must speak with Heer Meyert now."

She began to walk away, not expecting an answer from him, but he said, "Heer Meyert is not here today."

"Then I will speak to Heer Blaeu if he is here," she replied, noting the look of surprise on Daniel's face, a look which clearly said that he himself would never speak so easily of meeting with the owner of the printing house. She couldn't let this deter her, though, and she walked resolutely toward Heer Blaeu's office.

As usual, his door was open, and she saw him bent over some maps on his large oak table. Behind him was an elaborate cabinet displaying exotic items from some of the far-off lands depicted on the printer's maps. She knocked on the doorframe before she could lose her courage.

"A moment!" Blaeu said without looking up. Anneke stood in the doorway, afraid to move, lest she miss his summons when he was ready. After what seemed like a long time, Blaeu said, still not looking up, "Come!"

"Heer Blaeu," Anneke began, and only then did he see her. Surprise, but not displeasure, registered clearly upon his face.

"Juffrouw van Brug," he said in a friendly manner. "How is your coloring for Willem de Groot? I know that he is quite pleased with your work."

"Oh, I thought he might have told you. I have finished with my work there."

"No, he didn't mention it. At least I don't think that he did. Perhaps I have forgotten it because the last time I saw him was when he came to give me the map of Congo and Angola. I have not had the time to congratulate your family personally, but it is really quite impressive. Heer de Groot insisted that your name be included, and I agreed, but I did ask myself whether the inclusion was only due to his being fond of his map colorist."

"I, sir, am primarily responsible for the creation of the map," Anneke said, refusing to relinquish credit, even if the truth would only be known to her family, de Groot, and this man of whom she had heard all of her life. "But it is the attribution that I have come to speak to you about. We would like to have our names removed from the map."

"Although I confess that I find your participation in the map's creation hard to believe, if that is so, why do you not wish to have your name attached to it? Are you not proud of the work?"

"Yes, I am. Very proud. However, my father thinks it unseemly for my name to appear thus, and as neither he nor my brother took an active part in its creation, they agree that none of our names should be mentioned."

"He thinks it unseemly for your name to appear on a map—with that of your father and brother, I might add—but he did not think it unseemly for you to work in the house of Heer de Groot?"

Embarrassment and anger surged in Anneke. "I believe it was you, Heer Blaeu, who suggested my name to Heer de Groot. It was my parents' trust in you that persuaded them that taking the commission would be acceptable."

Unused to hearing such a forthright answer from others, and especially from a young woman, no matter how talented, Blaeu was too taken aback to directly respond. He certainly would spend no time arguing for a course he believed would help her but which she now seemed to reject. If he didn't think the map so good, and if it weren't for the fact that he wished to include at least some new maps in the *Atlas*, he would have told her that she could keep her map, that he would not print it. As it was, he said, "Very well, Juffrouw van Brug. I will remove the names. You must excuse me now. I am quite occupied approving the other maps for the first edition of the *Atlas Maior*."

"Thank you, Heer Blaeu," Anneke said and hurried from the room.

Chapter 41
October 1660

That evening, Daniel appeared at the door of the van Brug home as arranged. When she had left Blaeu's, Anneke had told him to come after dinner so they would have a better chance to talk without the family. After Daniel entered and she closed the door against the brisk evening, she explained that her father was not home, and though she hated the deception, she repeated the lie that Isaac had gone to Friesland for what would probably be an extended commission. Daniel expressed surprise, but Anneke thought she also noted some relief. After all, he had not really come to see her parents.

Lysbeth had gone to her coloring room, saying that with Isaac gone, she felt she needed to work all the harder. Lucas had left to meet some friends he had known on the WIC ship. He said that he had arranged it a week ago, and he did not wish them to think that anything was wrong. Anneke wondered why he wished to keep company with them since he had seemed so dispirited after his return from sea. Perhaps he needed to spend time with those who had shared experiences so detached from his current life. A life so different that it could make those memories seem unreal. Perhaps he simply needed to escape his family home, however briefly.

Anneke and Daniel sat in the front room, the room that she always thought of as public since it was here that her father would speak with those who came to see his paintings or arrange for a commission. In her mind, the room provided Anneke and Daniel a sort of respectable privacy.

Whether Daniel had prepared what he wished to say, Anneke never found out, for she immediately began a long explanation of what had happened with Helena. She left out nothing, and the words seemed to pour forth unbidden. She never paused long enough for Daniel to comment or ask a question, and when she finally finished, she let out a long sigh, as though she had somehow been holding her breath the whole time she had been speaking. Looking expectantly at Daniel, she tried to read his face, but his reaction was impossible to decipher.

"De Groot's wife was meeting a lover?" was his first utterance.

"Yes."

"And you aided her in this?"

"Yes. I just explained that."

"And how many times did you do this?"

"I don't know, Daniel! I didn't keep a count."

"How could you do something so shameful, Anneke?"

"I told you, Daniel, she threatened to say that I was a thief if I didn't go along with her plan."

"This is the real reason you helped her?"

"Of course! What other motive could I possibly have?"

"You truly thought that de Groot might have believed you to be a thief, even though he had welcomed you into his house for months?"

"Yes. I feared that he would believe her. She was his wife, after all, and what was I? To him, nothing more than a lowly craftsperson he employed."

"But you said that this was not the first incidence of her infidelity. Surely that would have caused him to doubt her word," Daniel retorted.

"But I didn't know of the previous incidents then. Even if I had, de Groot might still have chosen to at least act as though he believed her, to keep up the facade of a harmonious marriage. After all, that is what he had done before."

"Did you truly feel that he regarded you as no more than another person he employed? You held no special status?" he asked. Then looking down he added, "There were times I thought that he meant more to you."

"De Groot was an employer to me, Daniel, nothing more. A way to earn money and advance in my work," Anneke said, realizing that if she did not immediately and forcefully deny his fear, it would remain with him forever. That the truth was more nuanced, Daniel did not need to know. She now knew in her heart that she wished to be with Daniel if he would still have her, and she would do nothing to lessen the chances of that. She thought of adding, "Why would you even think that?" She refrained, however. She did not wish in this moment for him to call to mind what reasons he might have had for his suspicions.

"You are certain, Anneke?"

"I was merely someone he hired to come and do work for him. My position in that household hardly held any prestige."

Daniel seemed to relax with this reassurance, not only that she had no feelings for Willem, but also that perhaps her situation was not so high above his own.

"What will you do now, Anneke? Will you go back to de Groot's house?"

"Of course I shan't! With all that I've told you, how can you ask me that?" Anneke said, hoping Daniel never discovered that she had, in fact, been to see de Groot that very day.

"Then it is finished. We need think of it no more. I do not approve of what you did, Anneke, but I can understand why you did it. We are all vulnerable to the whims of the rich."

"There is one more thing I must tell you, Daniel. De Groot threatened to go to the *schout* and tell him of his wife's adultery."

"Surely not!" Daniel cried. "She could be banished, or worse, and he would suffer embarrassment and ridicule. You said that he has kept her secret before."

"Yes, but he may have come to the end of his ability to put up with an intolerable situation. He may be willing to expose her for what she is, even if he suffers for it himself."

"Well, that doesn't directly involve you. He wouldn't reveal your part in it, would he?"

"I don't know, Daniel. That is in part why I felt I had to tell you. Even if he withholds that information, there are several people who know of it. The servants must have figured it out by now, and then there are the Hartgers sisters."

"But they wouldn't wish their names to come out."

"Celia wouldn't, I'm sure, but remember it was her invalid sister, Ursula, who informed de Groot of the infidelity in the first place. She might be willing to tell others if she wishes to cloak herself in righteousness. She seems a bitter person, Daniel. She may do it to punish a sister she believes does not treat her as she should. One might think that she would not risk her sister's wrath, being at her mercy, but it would not be the first time that someone acted recklessly to seek revenge."

Daniel seemed to be contemplating this latest revelation when Anneke added in a tentative voice, "I felt it only fair to tell you of this possibility, Daniel. If you and I should become attached . . ." Here she hesitated, as though mentioning this was somehow bolder than all that she had just confessed. "It will bring shame upon you as well if my name comes out. I will understand if you no longer wish to see me."

Daniel looked at her in surprise. "I will not forsake you, Anneke. I have cared for you from the first moments we spoke. My worry has always been that you would think my position too lowly. Not only had you been chosen to come to Blaeu's to color and receive more training, you were then sent to work at de Groot's. It seems to me now that you do not hold yourself so far above me. Perhaps you should. However, if you think us a good match, I will do all I can to make you happy." Finishing this declaration, he reached for her hand.

Anneke marveled at this man who so clearly laid bare his self-doubt and his respect for what she did. This was so different from her father, who always needed to reassure himself and the rest of the family that their efforts were paltry in comparison to his own. Anneke grasped Daniel's hand. She had chosen well.

Chapter 42

October–November 1660

Whenever Anneke tried to find a moment of peace, her worries crashed in like the relentless sea against a dike. If de Groot reported his wife, her own name would come out as well, and she and her mother would lose their livelihoods. Blaeu would be furious if his house were associated with scandal. He would not care about Anneke's excuses. He would not even listen.

Perhaps Lucas would not be dismissed. Men are not as tainted by scandal as women are, and he now had friends in the guild who would help him plead his case if need be. Yes, she tried to convince herself. Lucas would retain his position.

And Daniel. He had said that he would stand by her no matter what. When she remembered his words, his look, and the sound of his voice as he said them, she was filled with tenderness. He was a man she could depend upon. Then she had a horrible thought—what if Daniel also lost his place at Blaeu's? She told herself that Daniel was an experienced pressman. Surely, he would be able to get work at one of the other map printers' establishments, and if not there, he could apply to one of the many book printers in the city. If her part in Helena's actions came out, the notoriety would be short, lasting only until the next topic for gossip came along. The other printers would not know of Daniel's attachment to Anneke, and if they later learned of it, few would remember having heard her name associated with Helena Kregier.

Even if she escaped being embroiled in scandal, there was still her father's situation to consider. He had escaped, but his guilt might still be discovered. For this, too, her family could suffer. For this, too, they could lose, certainly would lose, their positions. Once again, she thought of the reasons that she would not tell Daniel of this. She dared not. How might he react, not only to her but to the responsibility this would place upon him? She knew him to be an honorable man, and might this very quality not compel him to report the murderer to the authorities?

No, she could never tell Daniel. If it came out, though, she did not know what his feeling toward her would be. She would not only be revealed as the daughter of a murderer, but—and perhaps this was worse—as a deceiver. She would have allowed him to ally himself with her without ever giving him the power to decide if he wished to weather a storm such as that with her. Still, she would not tell him. Telling him could hasten the moment in which she lost him.

Besides, the more people who knew the secret, the more likely it was to come out, even from some casual comment made inadvertently. In a way, she was protecting Daniel, she told herself. Lucas had already brought up the possibility that, if Isaac's crime were discovered, the authorities might question the family to ascertain his whereabouts. If Daniel didn't know, it would go easier with him—if, that is, they believed in his ignorance.

Determined to put aside these repeating worries for the moment, Anneke decided to seek out her mother. Lysbeth had seemed withdrawn, as though she were retreating into herself, and Anneke had not wished to disturb her. After a few days, though, she decided that she should share with her what had happened at de Groot's and Blaeu's. She found Lysbeth in her workroom mixing paints, though her movements were lethargic. When she looked up, the smile she gave Anneke was but the merest shadow of her usual greeting.

"Mama, how are you today?"

"As you see, daughter, I grieve for your Papa. I worry for all of us. I am angry and heartbroken and despairing in turns. I push myself to work, to get as many maps colored as I can, for fear that Blaeu will dismiss us. I hoped that work would give my churning thoughts a rest, but it does not. I have been coloring for so long that I can do it while my thoughts wander elsewhere. And even my body feels so weak, so beaten down."

"Well, I have a small bit of good news, Mama. I went to see Heer Blaeu to ask him to remove our names from the map, and he agreed."

"You went to him directly? I thought you would ask Heer de Groot to do that since it was his intervention that caused the map to be placed with Blaeu in the first place."

"I went to see Heer de Groot first," Anneke admitted. "But, oh, Mama! I have never seen a man so changed. His anger and bitterness consume him. It is mostly for his wife, and I believe that it does not spill over onto me, though I cannot know. We shall have to wait and see."

"I am afraid that all of this waiting will drive me mad, Anneke, most especially the waiting to see whether your Papa's guilt will be discovered. I shudder at every sound upon the street, thinking that it is the *schout*'s men come to apprehend him. But he has escaped, leaving us to suffer the consequences of his rash acts. Oh, Anneke, I am coming to wonder why I ever allied myself with him."

"Oh, Mama! You can't mean that!"

"I suppose that I don't. I know why I chose your Papa. I was enchanted by him. I hope that you make a wiser choice, Anneke, if you are ever given the chance."

"That is part of what I have come to tell you, Mama. You know that Daniel was here last night. Oh, Mama, I do have feelings for him. He is a good and kind man, and he cares for me deeply. I told him everything about what happened with Helena, and he did not shun me. He said that even if my part came out, he would not forsake me."

"I am glad, Anneke, that you have recognized his worth. I had liked him from the first, but the way you seemed to ignore him for weeks at a time, I feared that you would lose him. Perhaps our trials at least serve to prove his faithfulness."

"Yes, but I haven't told him about Papa."

"Of course not! And you mustn't. We must keep that knowledge to ourselves."

"Oh, Mama, what is going to happen? If Papa's connection to the surveyor is never discovered, might he not return to us someday? I don't think we should ever say that he has died. We should just say that we do not know what happened to him. Otherwise, if at some time he could come home, we would be seen as liars."

"I am beginning to think you are right, Anneke. Of course, it is too soon to even hope, but perhaps as the months pass, we might begin to."

"Could you then write to Papa and tell him to return?"

"Your Papa and I determined that we should wait a year, to be safe."

"So long?"

"What is a year when measured against the rest of his life?"

"I know, Mama, but by the time he would receive it and return to us, another year would have passed."

"Nevertheless, I dare not write before the year is up. But there is no point in debating this. For now, we live each day hoping not to hear that knock upon our door."

As winter settled in, they worried about money. Lucas spent more hours away at his work, but Anneke wondered whether it was more to avoid the anxious atmosphere at home than to gain extra income against future uncertainty. Even when he was not working, he seemed to find other places to be, places with no shadow hanging over them. Anneke was just glad he didn't frequent gaming taverns, which were popular with some of the young men and which could quickly lead to ruin. Sometimes she wondered whether Lucas disliked seeing Daniel visit their home. She had never really asked Lucas what he thought about Daniel. It was more than just that she had other things on her mind. There was also a sort of defiance on her part, telling herself that she didn't care what Lucas thought of Daniel since he had made no effort to spend time with a man who was clearly very important to her.

Anneke did not contribute to the family's income at the level she once had. She had not felt that she could ask Meyert for any commissions. She feared that she might now be seen as someone who acted in an arbitrary manner since she had come to ask that their names be taken off the map. Even to her, the reason she had given for the removal had seemed insufficient. Heer Blaeu had probably agreed to her request because it made little difference to him.

So, she helped her mother color maps, unable to see any future past this waiting present. As she colored, she couldn't help but think of the praise she had received for the quality of her map. Praise from de Groot, and Meyert, and Blaeu himself. Daniel had even told her that when word went around the shop about her family's names not appearing on the map, one of the engravers who had seen it said it was a shame for them not to get credit because it was a very good map indeed. This had given her a particular feeling of satisfaction, though it could only be bittersweet. She would have been disappointed if the map had been deemed to be of poor quality, but at least she would not have suffered this sense of injustice that her chance had been snatched from her.

Now, all there seemed to be for her was this rote coloring. She did not make the effort to put any extra artistry into these maps, for that was not called for here, and she could not afford to spend time that she would not be paid for. These were maps which would be sold to burghers newly able to afford a modest collection. The maps were not distinguished from dozens of others like them, but still, they were something that those of a certain class could take pride in.

Now and then, Anneke pulled herself from her own reveries to notice that her mother did not look well. Her skin was pale and she seemed to cough frequently. This Anneke put down to her mother's sorrow, which she could not allay, but she urged Lysbeth to rest. She need not spend so many hours coloring.

Daniel's visits provided the only light moments. Sometimes the young couple would go for a walk. At other times, they would sit quietly and talk. Occasionally, Lysbeth would join them, and Anneke found yet another thing to appreciate about Daniel in the kind and respectful way he spoke with her mother.

Daniel kept them apprised of what was happening at the printing house. The withdrawal of their names from the map had continued to be a topic of conversation. Speculation about the reason for the removal was dying down, however, aided by Daniel. Although he didn't know the true reason the van Brugs had asked that there be no attribution, he did what he could to stem the chatter at work. When someone spoke of it, Daniel would look bewildered, as though he hadn't heard there was a map that his sweetheart had been associated with, for Daniel's attachment to Anneke was now commonly known. He had happily told another pressman, confident that the news would spread. When she heard of this, Anneke again felt a surge of emotion for this man. Another might have waited awhile to be sure there would be no scandal attached to her. Not only would Daniel not forsake her, he would boldly cling to her for all to see.

For Anneke, this unfolding of her love for Daniel was always accompanied by a feeling of guilt. Guilt because she knew herself to be deceiving him in the matter of her father. Guilt because she let her desire for him to stay with her outweigh her duty to be honest with the man with whom she hoped to make a future.

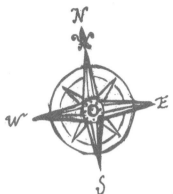

Chapter 43

December 1660

Anneke, Daniel, Lucas, and Lysbeth would from time to time wonder aloud whether the danger of a revelation from de Groot had passed. When it had been several weeks, they began to think that, if he were going to accuse his wife, he surely would already have done so. Then one day Daniel came straight from the printing house to bring Anneke and Lysbeth the news: Helena Kregier was dead. He had learned this at the printing house from his fellow pressman, Jacop, whose sister was a servant in the household. Jacop had relished telling the tale, knowing this bit of gossip would be of interest to everyone at Blaeu's due to de Groot's longtime patronage.

The story was that Helena, upon returning from an extended visit to her sister's home in Delft, had declared herself to not be feeling well and retired to her room. She had not come out for dinner. The servants were reluctant to incur her wrath if they disturbed her rest, and even Heer de Groot, saying that he imagined his wife needed sleep, did not look in on her. The next morning, when a maid finally ventured into Helena's room, she discovered Helena in a pool of blood but still breathing. The physician was called, but it was too late. By the time he arrived, Helena was gone. It was found that she had been with child and suffered a miscarriage.

"What do you think will happen now?" Anneke asked.

"I think this is the end of it," Daniel said. "Surely de Groot would see no point in revealing Helena's infidelity now."

"It is harsh to say so," Anneke added, "but her death has put an end to his torment." Then a thought occurred to her. "There is no talk of foul play involved, is there?"

"Anneke!" Lysbeth put in. "Surely you cannot think de Groot would commit such a vile act as to bring about his wife's death, and that of an innocent babe!"

"I would not have said so, but for the last time I saw him. He was as one who had lost his mind, Mama."

"No," Daniel put in before this theory could advance any further. "I do not believe there is any question but that Vrouw Kregier died a natural death."

"So, though one should never rejoice at the demise of another, you are freed from your worry on that front, daughter," Lysbeth said.

"I imagine you are right," Anneke replied. "There would be no reason for any of the servants to bring up their mistress's infidelities. It would not be to their credit."

"What of the woman who wrote the letter to de Groot? The sister of the woman who lent her home to Helena for her scheme?"

"Ursula?" Anneke said. "I cannot think that even she would see an advantage in sullying the name of a dead woman, especially since the woman's husband never acted upon the information in the letter."

"Perhaps it is the hand of God," Lysbeth said. "She died a death not uncommon for a woman, no matter whose child she carries."

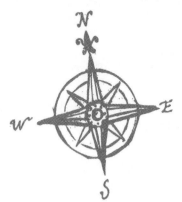

Chapter 44
January 1661

L ysbeth felt her husband's absence as a dull ache. There were moments when the cause was not foremost in her mind, but then it would come to her and the pain would sharpen. He had lied to her for years; he had held her talents and ambitions in little regard; he had killed a man and left his family to face any consequences. But still, she loved him. It was not the love of the young bride she had been, nor even of the woman who shares the joys of parenthood with her husband. Those loves had been diminished, but they were still there, underpinning her current feelings.

In thinking of the years of her marriage, she saw that she had come to view Isaac's faults as those of a beloved child. His insistence on the import of his own work, while often angering her, could also be seen as a childish reaction to cover his own feeling of disappointment in himself. She also knew that he loved her and the children. He loved them in the way that he knew how. She recalled his tenderness with Anneke and Lucas when they were young. She thought of the many nights he had sat with them at bedtime and told them tales of Africa. Perhaps one might interpret it as his own self-aggrandizement, now that she knew some of it was based on a lie. Still, he had given them something worth having: a way to imagine something they had never seen. That his stories of his trip and lost notes had ultimately led to disaster had been unforeseeable.

∾

Lucas would occasionally bring up the topic of contacting Isaac. Each time, however, Lysbeth would say that it was not yet safe. "Can you not at least tell us what name he uses, Mama?" Lucas would ask, but she always evaded the question. She did not tell her son that Anneke had told her of the conversation she and Lucas had the night before Isaac left. Although Anneke had repeated what they said to ascertain whether her mother held her responsible for what had happened, since she had secretly created and placed the map with Blaeu, this was not what had stood out to Lysbeth. She had almost absently assured her daughter that of course she did not blame her.

What Lysbeth could not forget was Lucas saying his bitterness was so great that he might be tempted to tell the authorities of Isaac's whereabouts if ever they were questioned. This Lysbeth could never allow. She would conceal the alias that Isaac had adopted, thus making certain that Lucas could never betray his father. Without the name, it would be almost impossible to locate Isaac in all of Batavia. Neither did she tell Anneke, not because she believed that Anneke would tell the authorities, but because Lucas might persuade her to tell him the name. In this way, Lysbeth told herself, she protected her husband from discovery and her children from temptation.

Slowly Lysbeth settled into a routine of living without Isaac. Her daughter's company comforted her, although she began urging Anneke to see Heer Meyert and ask if he might have something more challenging for her. Lucas's presence on most evenings, though only for dinner, also allayed the loneliness. She sensed a restlessness in him and hoped it was simply that he had taken a liking to a girl and not another urge to leave Amsterdam. Even Daniel's calming presence was a balm to her spirit.

Still, her mind would sometimes stray, wondering what might go wrong. Was there someone who might turn on them? Might Isaac's crime come to light, even now?

At night, she slept only restlessly, her mind unable to calm itself.

She dreamed not of maps, but of colors. Not of places, but of empti-
ness. Not of love, but of betrayal.

Then there was her body, which seemed to be betraying her, too.
She had ignored it for as long as she could, but now there was no
denying it. In addition to the fatigue that she had been fighting, and
which only seemed to deepen, there were times when night sweats
alternated with chills. And there was the coughing. When it had
started months ago, Anneke had questioned her about it with sincere
concern, but Lysbeth had been able to put her off, telling her it was
nothing to worry about. All that had happened since then must have
diverted Anneke's attention, and she seemed to not notice that the
cough was slowly growing worse.

When Anneke came to her one day and said, "Mama, I must talk
to you about something," Lysbeth's first thought was that perhaps she
had noticed her mother's declining health. If it was some other bad
news, she did not think she could bear anything else that would send
her mind reeling into scenes that would destroy her family. Still, this
was her daughter, and she must hear her out.

"Yes, daughter?"

"Do you remember when I told you that I had seen Heer
Vingboons?"

"Yes," Lysbeth answered slowly, stiffening.

"I did not tell you the truth about something, Mama." Lysbeth
felt a stab as though of a knife. Another lie. She struggled to keep her
voice calm as she answered.

"Tell me now, Anneke."

"I didn't see Heer Vingboons at Blaeu's. I saw him at his home."

"What?" her mother said, startled.

"It was in his public room, in his home, where he lives with his
parents. I didn't tell you because I went to see Heer Vingboons about
the map. I wanted the map to be a secret from Papa, and I knew it
would be hard for you to keep it from him if I told you about it,"
Anneke said in a rush. "Before I asked Heer de Groot to speak to Heer

Blaeu for me, I went to ask that favor of Heer Vingboons." Here she paused before saying, "And you know what his reply was."

"To ask your mother why he refused," Lysbeth said without emotion, but as though pulling at a memory from long ago, from before Isaac left. "But why are you bringing this up now?"

"Because I wondered if he might be a danger. He knows the map is of Congo, so if he sees it, he might make the connection and comment to someone about it. It seems a very slight chance, but I thought that I should tell you, Mama."

"It is good that you have come to me, Anneke," Lysbeth said, turning away from her daughter and giving the familiar answer. "I will think on what to do."

Lysbeth feared it was quite possible that Johannes would see the map once the *Atlas Maior* was published. Would he remember Anneke had gone to him about a map? Would he remember that it was of Congo? Would he imagine that it could be this one? He had refused Anneke's request. Clearly, he had not forgotten their feelings for one another before Isaac appeared to disrupt them. Did he still harbor tenderness toward her, or only resentment?

Lysbeth tried to tell herself that, in all likelihood, he would not see all of the maps. After all, the *Atlas* was to be several volumes long, with hundreds of maps. If he saw the map, how could he possibly think it was Anneke's, and even if he did, what could he gain by letting it be known that the map was from the van Brug family? Still, possibilities churned constantly through her mind, and she could not convince herself there was no danger that Johannes would somehow bring to light the connection between Isaac and the map.

She decided to speak to him, to ask him—to beg him, if necessary—never to let the connection be known. She knew this to be a dangerous path, for she would be making him aware of the very thing she hoped he would never learn. Her worries would give her no rest, however, until she had assurances from him that he would do nothing to harm her family. Lysbeth sent him a note asking him to come to her home at a time when she knew she would be alone.

Lysbeth panicked as she walked to the door, telling herself that she had been mad to take this course of action, but it was too late. When she opened the door, she saw a face at once familiar and entirely strange. She perceived the face of the younger man beneath the now fleshier countenance, which also held early wrinkles. She searched for the kindness in his eyes that she remembered, but she wasn't certain whether she could detect its remnants. At the same time, she saw a reflection of her own consternation on his face as he wondered where that young girl had gone.

"Heer Vingboons," she said at the same moment he whispered, "Lysbeth!"

She noticed the rolled canvas he was carrying as she stood aside for him to enter, and they took seats in the public front room. This was the best-maintained room of the house, and even if it weren't for her reluctance to lead him to a more intimate part of her home, she wished him to have the best impression of the life that Isaac had provided for her.

As she did not know how to begin, Vingboons asked, "Why have you sent for me, Lysbeth? Why after all these years? I look at you and fear it has something to do with failing health."

Lysbeth was startled at his ready discernment.

"No, Johannes," she said, lapsing into their old manner as he had immediately done. "I have not called you here about any illness. Rather, it is to ask a favor of you, if I have even the smallest right to do so."

"You wonder, I imagine, what my feelings toward you are. You are thinking of the answer I gave to your daughter when she came to see me about a map. You probably concluded that I harbor a grudge, but not against you, Lysbeth. Never against you! Does not my prompt obedience to your summons show that I still care about your welfare? Surely you do not think me so mean as to come only to malign you."

Lysbeth felt a prickling in her eyes at the goodness of this man she had wronged so long ago, even if that wrong was of a type common enough among young people trying to untangle that mystery of finding the person with whom they should spend their lives. "Oh, Johannes," she said. "How could I know what to expect? Surely life has changed us both in ways the other could not begin to guess. Still, I did have enough faith in you to hope that you would agree to my request."

"What can I do for you, Lysbeth, now, after all these years?"

"I ask that you never tell anyone that Anneke came to you about a map that she had created. I ask that you do nothing to connect my family to any map that you may see in the future."

With a look of bewilderment, Johannes slowly replied, "All right, Lysbeth. I agree if that is what you wish, but why? I do not understand."

"Please, don't ask me to explain. To do so would embroil you further in the situation which prompts me to request your silence."

At this moment, Johannes began a racking cough and Lysbeth saw that the changes in his looks were not only those wrought by time. She had not perceived what he had noticed in her from the moment he saw her. Johannes was ill.

"I am sorry," he said in gasping tones as soon as he could speak. "Merely a passing cough. A bother, but no more."

"Oh, Johannes, is that really so?"

"Yes, Lysbeth. It is of no import. I have been so anxious to discover the reason for your summons. I confess, I had hoped for something else."

"What could you have hoped for, Johannes?" Lysbeth said gently. "You know that I am married."

"Yes, I know. And you know that I am not." At this, Johannes opened the canvas that Lysbeth had refrained from asking about. "It is the only portrait I have ever done," he said, holding it out to her.

There she was. Her younger self, at once caressing her with her own eyes and mocking her with the passage of the years. "But I never sat for you," she said.

"It was done from memory. I have held your image in my heart all these years. When I saw your daughter, it brought that time back to me. She is like you, Lysbeth."

She looked at the golden hair, before streaks of gray had marred its glory, at her green eyes, clear with the light of youth, at full lips that had not known years or worry. "Thank you," she whispered, and he only knew what she had said by watching those same lips, now thin and pale.

There was nothing else to say. Another coughing fit seized him, and he rose to go.

"I will leave now and take my illness with me," he said in what seemed to be an attempt at lightheartedness. Then he added, "My illness and my sorrow." With that, he walked to the door and disappeared.

That evening, Lysbeth told Anneke of Johannes's visit. She did not share everything they had said, but she assured her daughter that he would stay silent about the map.

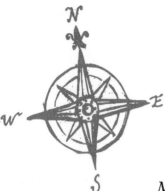

Chapter 45

March–May 1661

During the weeks following Johannes's visit, Lysbeth took to racking spells of coughing. She told herself that her condition was not worsening. She tried to work through it, hoping that if she did not think about it, she could find short periods of peace for her body while she colored. The intervals between attacks became ever shorter, and even in the moments of respite from her coughs, she felt tired and weak, for she had not eaten well for months.

When she was alone, she did not try to keep herself from coughing. Perhaps her body was trying to rid itself of something noxious. When Anneke or Lucas was home, however, she wished to suppress the hacking. It became ever more impossible to do so, until Anneke became alarmed and urged her mother to her bed. Home remedies seemed to bring her little comfort, and Lysbeth finally agreed to let Anneke send for a physician, but he offered little advice.

Lysbeth also fretted about the loss of income when she wasn't working. She would not stay in her bed alcove and constantly rose to see how Anneke was progressing with her coloring. Finally, Anneke set up a pallet in the workroom, and Lysbeth rested there. The sight of her daughter, the familiar scents of the paints, the crinkling of a map as Anneke adjusted its position—all of these comforted her spirit but did nothing to alleviate her body's torments.

Mother and daughter told each other that she would be fine, that this was something temporary, that all Lysbeth needed was rest. In her heart, Lysbeth suspected that this was untrue, and as she lay on her pallet, the sound of her daughter's paintbrush against the paper almost imperceptible, she reviewed the signs that she had not let herself heed. Now was the time to be frank, at least with herself.

She had noticed a paleness that had started perhaps a couple of years ago, shortly before Lucas had returned from sea. No one else had noticed it, or at least no one had remarked upon it. For most people, it would have gone undetected, but she was immersed in a reality where the slightest variation of color was to be noted. She knew from her work that a slight isolated change in color did not loudly announce itself as different, but when set against another color, the change became apparent. It was the color of her clothes that marked the change for her. The red scarf that had always complimented her skin now made it look an unhealthy white. She told herself that she had been cooped up too long in her house working on the maps. Green made her skin look sallow, and she told herself that it was paleness or redness that was to be feared, not this yellow look. She had not expected Lucas to see any change in her, nor even Isaac, though he, too, was steeped in the gradients of color. But neither had Anneke seemed to find anything of concern in her mother's appearance, so perhaps it was all imagined.

The fatigue had started later, several months ago, and one day she went to the apothecary seeking something that might help, though she didn't mention this to her family. She always had a ready excuse to explain away her weariness: extra time spent at her work table, the extra care she had taken to make a marzipan for Lucas's birthday, a late night spent talking with her daughter, an early awakening because she had slept the wrong way and her body protested. Even now, she told herself it was the cough that sapped her strength. When she stopped this coughing, all would be well. She told herself she was being realistic, understanding that she could not expect to immediately return to her former self, taking on all her former tasks. But at night, she willfully closed her ears to her children's whispers for fear that she would hear a note of distress in her daughter's voice, or even an easy reassurance from her son.

Then she began to cough up blood.

At first, Anneke observed that her mother always held a handkerchief to her mouth when she coughed, clutching it in a closed fist even between episodes so as to have it ready when the torment began again. But when she slept, her grip slackened, and Anneke would silently approach to discover what her mother had endeavored to conceal. It was as she had feared. The red and brown blotches upon the cloth arrested her attention, as though some misplaced colors were mocking her error.

Now there could be no more pretending, no mutual denial of the truth. Anneke spoke of it openly to Lysbeth and to Lucas, who insisted it was a mistake until he saw the proof. Anneke again sent for the physician, and this time he confirmed what they already knew. Her mother had consumption. It was not uncommon. It should be no shock. Anneke had not directly known anyone who had been plagued by the disease, but she knew people who had lost a grandfather, a mother, a friend. The physician said that Lysbeth had probably had the illness for some time, years even. Perhaps some recent incident had exacerbated the underlying weakness. It was impossible to know. And really, it made no difference.

There was little to be done. Lysbeth should rest, the physician had said, as though there were any other possibility for the woman who had already found it difficult to do aught else. He gave her something to alleviate her discomfort, but he warned against hoping anything would alter the final outcome. She had come too far.

Anneke, who had already spent most waking hours with her mother, now hesitated to leave her even for the tasks that needed to be done. She hired a girl to do the marketing for them, to prepare simple meals, and to clean the house a bit each day. Lysbeth protested the expense of this, but Anneke insisted, saying that, thanks to Isaac and Lysbeth allowing her to keep most of what she made from coloring for de Groot, she had savings. And, too, there was the money that Blaeu had paid the family when he accepted the map.

No matter how Anneke pleaded with Lucas, he chose to be gone from the house more frequently. She exhorted him that it was his duty to spend time with his mother, who repeatedly asked where he was in the evenings, though without complaint. Anneke told him he would regret it when there would no longer be a choice to spend precious moments with their mother. She said she wished him to sit with Lysbeth so that she and Daniel could visit alone in the front room, but when Lucas stayed home one evening and she and Daniel also spent the time talking with Lysbeth, Lucas said he clearly did not need to be there.

At times, Anneke tried to get Lysbeth to tell Lucas that she missed him, that she wanted to see more of her only son, that she did not have much time left. Lysbeth only said that if Lucas did not choose to be with her, she would not try to force him. Anneke asked herself whether this was some remnant of Lysbeth so often adjusting her life to Isaac's wishes or some perverted pride that would not beg her son to stay and sit with his dying mother. After a while, Anneke stopped suggesting to Lysbeth that she speak to Lucas. She stayed silent, lest she bring to her mother's mind the wound of her son's absence.

The days were hard for the two women, and both found solace in Daniel's frequent evening visits. They spoke of inconsequential things, as though the weight of the reality in the room could somehow be balanced to become something lighter. On good days, as Anneke accompanied him to the door, she would sometimes ask, "Don't you think that she seemed better this evening?" On the worst days, she asked whether he thought Lysbeth had little time left. Daniel rarely gave an answer. He would just shrug and say, "I don't know, my love," as though neither wishing to stoke her hopes nor to quell them.

Anneke had told her mother that she and Daniel wished to marry, and Lysbeth was more than happy. The two lovers had not spoken of when since there seemed to be no future time substantial enough to pin a wedding date upon it. Anneke could not think of marrying when her mother was so ill, and yet she longed for her mother to witness their union.

She was saved from her dilemma when one day her mother said, "Anneke, I would like for you and Daniel to marry while I can still see it."

Anneke made no easy reassurance that soon her mother would be better, and then they would wed. She simply mumbled, "Perhaps soon, Mama."

"Do not put me off, Anneke," her mother said with more force than she had used in days. "Speak to Daniel. Make the arrangements as soon as can be. I feel we cannot tarry."

"All right, Mama." Anneke turned away so her mother would not see her tears.

Chapter 46
June 1661

A nneke had still not told Daniel about Isaac. But now she must. She could not enter into a marriage in which there was such a gaping hole of knowledge. She would not deceive her life's partner. She would not do what her father had done.

Daniel did not yet know of Lysbeth's request for haste. She did not wish him to feel he must accept her for her mother's sake. If he could not live with what she had kept from him, if he could not join the family of a murderer, she would accept it with no rancor in her heart. Daniel was a good man, and perhaps murder was a bridge too far.

As was often the case now, Lysbeth was asleep when Daniel arrived that evening. Anneke brought him in, offered him some beer, and sat down with him.

"Daniel," Anneke began, "there is something I must tell you. We have spoken of our future as man and wife, but I cannot enter into that union without confessing something." Though Daniel kept a neutral expression on his face, she sensed a movement, ever so slight, away from her.

"You have told me of the situation with de Groot and his wife. Has something more happened?"

"No, Daniel. This is something else, something that I feared would put my family in danger."

"Did you not trust me, Anneke?" he asked, and she could hear the hurt in his voice, with just a hint of resentment. "Have I not shown that I will stand by you, no matter what?"

"Yes, and your loyalty is one of the things that I love about you, but this is a more serious matter, and though it is not fair of me to ask it, I do ask that you pledge never to reveal what I am about to tell you."

His blue eyes looked piercingly at her as he replied, "I will once again show my faith in you by vowing silence, though I know not the matter at hand."

"You know of the map that I created, and that I asked Blaeu to leave it without attribution."

"Of course, but how can that be fraught with danger?"

"It is the source of the information, and the consequences of my using it, that I will now explain."

It didn't take Anneke long to tell the story. Though it held deception and murder, it was simple in the telling, and Daniel did not prolong the tale with questions. When she had finished, Daniel said, "Would they really call it murder? Your father feared for his life."

"That is what he claims, but would everyone believe him? He would have to explain why he had gone to see the surveyor, and that very explanation would show him to be a thief and a liar. Besides, he fled, and that adds to the appearance of his guilt." Though Daniel himself had seemed to seek some excuse for Isaac's actions, Anneke was afraid he wished to withdraw his vow of silence, for how could he help a killer?

Before he could even ask, she said, "Oh, Daniel! It was unfair of me to get your promise to keep this to yourself! I release you if you feel that you have a duty to let it be known, and if you wish to break with me, I cannot rightly fault you for that, either."

After a time, Daniel said, "Perhaps a wise man would accept the offer, but who said love was wise? No, Anneke, I will not expose the secret, nor do I wish to leave you. A revelation would only serve to hurt you, your mother, and Lucas. Your father has already escaped, and his self-decreed exile is surely a hard punishment to endure. I do not see why I would compound the suffering of your family."

With that, Anneke embraced him and kissed him as she never had before, as though they were melting into one another. They talked long into the night, and at the end, she told him of Lysbeth's wish that they marry soon.

The wedding was much simpler than was tradition, in part because of the expense, but even more because of the need for haste, of which Lysbeth constantly reminded them. The announcement of the banns in church required three successive weeks. This at least gave them time to do some preparation. They chose the simplest of rings for the bride and groom, but Lysbeth insisted that Anneke get a finer bride's robe than she might have chosen on her own. There were invitations to be extended, though the guest list would be smaller than for many weddings. The house was decorated with flowers, and the chairs where Anneke and Daniel would sit were festooned with garlands.

On the day of the wedding, the procession to the Reformed Church made its way along the street. After the ceremony, everyone returned to Anneke's home, where there was ample food and drink for the guests. Hippocras, the traditional spiced wine, was served, and everyone drank heartily. As the afternoon wore on, the guests sang the traditional songs, though there were no musicians. Although there was joy, there was a subdued note to it, as everyone knew that Lysbeth's poor health was the reason for the small and hastily planned celebration.

In bed the next morning, Daniel still sleeping soundly by her side, Anneke reflected on her wedding day. It had been happy, though not unfettered. The underlying sadness that felt like a physical weight upon her heart had not left her, even for that day, though at times she could forget it as one momentarily forgets the pain from an injury on its way to healing. Anneke had seen happiness shine forth in her mother's eyes for the first time in many months, and she pondered a mother's love that found such joy in her child's delight.

Even Lucas joined in the festivities wholeheartedly and embraced Daniel, calling him "brother." Anneke beamed at Lucas and was happy to later notice him talking for a long time with a girl from the neighborhood. Daniel's parents had traveled to Amsterdam from Leiden for the wedding. They greeted her warmly, saying they rejoiced in the union and hoped that she and Daniel would travel to Leiden frequently to visit them.

When she later commented on this to Daniel, he said, "They liked you from the first moment they met you. Besides, I told them what they needed to hear, that you are the woman I love." Were their family relations really so easy, so straightforward, she wondered. So different from her own.

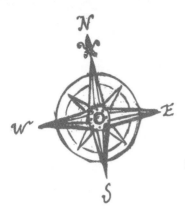

Chapter 47

July 1661

Lysbeth lasted only two weeks after the wedding. Daniel had left his lodgings and moved in with Anneke's family, but both he and Lucas were gone when Lysbeth's final moments came. On her last day, she asked Anneke to bring her the painting that was hidden between the sheets in the linen closet. She told Anneke that when Johannes had brought it for her, he had explained that he painted it long ago from his memory of the young woman he had loved.

Long after, Anneke pondered why her mother had asked for that portrait rather than the one her father had done of their family. Was it due to her own longing for the girl so lovingly rendered? Did her mother now, on her last day of life, regret the choice she had made so long ago? She had loved Isaac, and aside from his small vanities, he had been a kind and loving husband and father. Did the revelation of his lifelong deception negate all that had gone before? Did murder?

Anneke recalled how Lysbeth had told her she chose Isaac because she was enchanted by the romance of being married to an artist, but it was Vingboons who turned out to be the more successful painter. Had he loved her mother all his life? She reminded herself that Vingboons had never married. For his sake, Anneke hoped he had been able to simply keep her fondly in his memory. She also hoped his feelings had not been futilely rekindled when they met again only when Lysbeth was so close to her demise.

Lysbeth had told Anneke some of what the two had said on his one visit. Could Anneke blame her mother for wanting her to know that this man still felt a tender devotion for her? Anneke did not ask her mother for further details. Lysbeth was too ill, and it seemed a trespass upon the private life that we all hold close, even to the end.

Her final words to Anneke, spoken between tortuous bouts of coughing, surprised and touched her daughter. "I am proud of what you have done, Anneke, no matter the consequences. You created a map all on your own. I should have seen that you would be capable of it, but I did not. You astonished me." With that, the older colorist seemed to relax, as though she had performed one final duty, and she drifted into sleep. Sitting in a chair as close to her mother as possible, the exhausted daughter crossed her arms on the bed, laid her head on them, and dozed.

The sound of ragged breaths awakened Anneke, and the labored gasping grew more intense. Then it ceased. The color on her mother's face had swiftly been transformed by death.

Anneke stood to lean across and embrace her mother's frail body, already losing the heat of life. She kissed the beloved cheeks and forehead, then collapsed into the chair and let her tears flow as she grasped her mother's hand, asking her why she had to leave them.

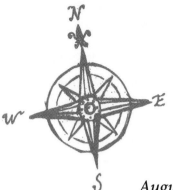

Chapter 48

August–September 1661

The haze of her mother's death kept Anneke in her own world. She knew that Daniel tried to console her. She saw him. She heard his words. Her body registered that he embraced her. But it was as though it were happening to someone else, and that someone else had no particular connection to her. She ate, she drank, she slept. Sometimes she answered questions put to her by her husband or her brother, sometimes not.

Daniel suggested that she work, knowing how much she had always loved it, how the colors had seemed to spark a magic in her soul. He said that perhaps she would feel close to her mother if she were in that workroom where Anneke and Lysbeth had spent so many hours together. It did no good. The hours with her mother that invaded her thoughts were those of her final days.

And there was something else that she told no one. She seemed to have lost colors. Everything seemed a gray to her, and she did not think she would be able to paint, even if she had the will. The only colors she kept seeing in her mind's eye were the crimson of her mother's blood, coughed up onto snowy sheets scented with sweet woodruff that could not mask the iron stench of blood, and then that final color of skin deprived of blood beneath. She struggled to name the hue.

Lucas immersed himself in work, and Anneke at first thought this callous of him. How could he think of work at a time like this? Then she came to see that his grief seemed as deep as her own, and this too, she resented. She was the one who had nursed their mother, had spent days at her bedside, had held her while coughs racked her body. Anneke found that her mind even reached back in time to find old grievances. Lucas had left them. He had left their happy trio of colorists. That it had been Isaac's command for Lucas to go to school, she put from her mind. That it was this that had made her own mapmaking possible, she ignored. Then Lucas had abandoned them all when he went to sea. That he had returned to the family when his tour was over, and that he stayed with her still, did not absolve him.

Daniel tried to speak to his brother-in-law of Anneke's unadmitted need for him, but Lucas paid him no heed. He scrambled to find ever more surveying assignments. Sometimes he was away from Amsterdam for days at a time doing a job for a *waterschap* who needed more accurate measurements of the polders under its authority. It seemed as though he sought to lessen his despair by trying to control the world with his constant calculations.

Two months after Lysbeth's death, Lucas returned home after several days at a job near Hoorn. As he sat with Anneke and Daniel that evening, he quietly said, "Papa doesn't even know."

Anneke looked up sharply, as though this mention of her father had broken through a veil. She hadn't even thought of her father. It did not seem possible to her, but it was true.

"We must write to him, Lucas! We must write to him at once. How horrible that he still thinks of her as living!" she said. "He should come home. It is eleven months since he left. It is surely past the time that anyone will connect him with Janszoon."

"I agree, but you'll have to write to him, Anneke. You were always closer to him than I was, and I trust you to know how to word a letter that will not completely crush him. Besides, I do not know the name that he has taken."

Anneke looked at him, a chill passing over her. "You, you do not know? Lucas, neither do I. Did Mama never tell you?"

"Why would she have told me, Anneke?" Lucas replied, apprehension in his voice now. "You spent so many hours with Mama. Did you never ask?"

"I did ask once, but she just said, 'Lucas will know what to do.' I took that to mean that you knew the name."

"I don't know why she would have said that. Can she have been keeping the name from us deliberately?"

"At the end she was in and out, and perhaps she meant to tell us but just forgot," Anneke said.

"It must be written down somewhere," Daniel said to them. "We just have to find it."

Over the next days, Anneke spent all her time searching. Lucas took only assignments that would allow him to return home in the evening to help, and Daniel ignored the exhaustion he felt at the end of the day working at the press and spent hours looking through the house. The three did not divide up the tasks. Each of them searched every room, every chest and cupboard, everywhere a piece of paper could have been stashed, for the other two might miss it. There was a sense of urgency for each of them, but memories rose up like specters to hamper them in their task.

Daniel did not have the years of recollections that the other two had, but he thought back to the first time that he met Anneke's parents. He had been nervous, and he had struggled to cover his unease. Lysbeth had been especially kind to him, and if Isaac was more subdued, Daniel had put it down to a father's natural reluctance to accept a possible suitor for his daughter. With time, he had felt more comfortable, and during the time when he had seen so little of Anneke because of his duties in Leiden, he had come to imagine Lysbeth, and perhaps even Isaac, as his allies. Now their children were bereft, and he must help them.

Lucas was the first of the three to go through Isaac's workroom. He came across what he knew must have been the papers Anneke had used for creating the map. She had clearly put them back after Isaac left, and he asked himself why she would have returned them then. Even more, he questioned how she could ever have told herself the notes were their father's work. A surge of anger engulfed him, for if she had but let herself doubt Isaac and had asked him, none of the following tragedy would have ensued. But she hadn't let herself doubt, Lucas thought, because she had wanted to create the map. Lucas's first impulse was to look for Anneke and ask her how she could have let this happen, but then he stopped himself. What purpose would recriminations serve? Later that night, however, as Anneke dozed on a chair, he quietly told Daniel of the papers, for he could not bear to keep these thoughts to himself. Daniel gazed into the fire and nodded.

"She let her desires blind her to the truth. Who among us does not do that, Lucas? I will care for her no less."

Lucas felt both resentment that Daniel did not see how greatly Anneke was at fault for what had happened and gratitude that his sister had found such a true and loyal man.

When Anneke went through her mother's workroom, she looked everywhere, even inside the jars that held the various supplies for making paints, though it hardly seemed likely that Lysbeth would have put something so important where it could so easily be lost or smudged. And why would she have put the information about Isaac's identity there, anyway? She can't have had a reason to hide it from them. With each new object she picked up, Anneke saw her mother holding it, using it to go about her work, perhaps chatting with her daughter as she did so. Anneke tried not to dwell on these visions, but when she came to one particular stack of papers, she sank to the floor, clutching them to her breast, and let the sobs come until she felt she could not draw another breath. The papers were the maps of imaginary places her mother had drawn for Lucas and Anneke when she was first teaching them to color. On the top was The Land of Happy Children, and Lysbeth had painted a precise likeness of each of her own.

The three searched for days, but they did not find what they sought. Though Lucas had forborne admonishing her for creating the map that caused their father to flee, Anneke could not release herself from the bitterest regret. It was her fault. If she hadn't created the map, none of this would have happened. Daniel gently told her again and again that the wrongdoing was not hers. It was Isaac's lies, and then his rash act, which had brought about his downfall. But she embraced her guilt as though it were a just punishment for an unforgivable transgression. Her father would live out his life in loneliness and fear, and they would never see him again.

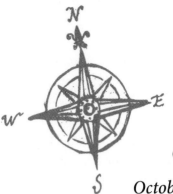

Chapter 49

October–November 1661

Anneke was left alone each day, walking aimlessly from room to room, not even noticing the chaos the three had left in their wake in their vain search for what might have been the tiniest scrap of paper. If Daniel and Lucas, returning in the evening from a day's work, wondered why she made no attempt to restore order to their home, they said nothing. Neither did they themselves take on the task. Perhaps they thought it would seem to her a silent reproof.

The weight of Anneke's grief slowly became more bearable, as sorrow must if we are not to perish. With nothing to do, she came to envy Daniel and Lucas the distraction of their work but couldn't even think of going back to Blaeu's. One day she ventured into her mother's workroom, and as though only now seeing it, cringed at the disarray. Her mother would never have tolerated such a state. Slowly, Anneke walked to the stack of maps of imaginary places, bent, and picked them up. Perhaps they could hold comfort as well as sorrow. She brought them to a table and slowly looked through them, spending a few happy moments in the past. Then she carefully straightened them and put them on a shelf.

Some of the paint ingredients had spilled, and the paints that had been mixed when last her mother worked had long since dried in their small jugs. She went out to the linen cupboard to find some old rags and brought in water. Slowly, she began to wipe away the colors of her mother's life. As she pulled the damp rag from each pot of dried paint, she saw the colors as she once had. One by one, they came back to her, lifting the gray veil through which she had seen the world, as though her mother had given her this final gift.

When Daniel returned that evening, Anneke was still in her mother's workroom, so lost in her task that she had not even thought to prepare their dinner. After calling out her name, Daniel found her. She saw the surprise on his face at finding her there. She walked over to him and embraced him. He put his arms about her and stroked her hair. "My love," he said softly. "My love."

When Daniel told Anneke a few days later that she should come with him to Blaeu's, she recoiled. He hadn't said anything about the printing house since Lysbeth's death, and she didn't think she could enter that world again.

"Blaeu's? Oh, Daniel. I cannot set foot in the printing house. The last time I went, it was to humiliate myself before Heer Blaeu," she said.

"Are you sure that he saw it that way, Anneke?" Daniel asked.

"If you had been there, you would be sure also."

"Well, someone as busy and important as Heer Blaeu has probably forgotten the conversation. It cannot have made the impression on him that it made on you."

Feeling slightly offended at Daniel's reminder that she could hardly hold a prominent place in the mind of someone such as Blaeu, she replied, "Then why ever would I go there? Surely you do not think that I should go seeking work? I don't even know that I want to. What would he give me to color? Would it be a return to the routine type of painting that I did before I went to de Groot's?" As she said this, she felt her face redden at the memory of her shame there, and Daniel's knowledge of it.

"Even when you did what you now call a routine type of work, you made it your own. You did it in a way that your talent could not be ignored. But that is not why I want you to come with me today. There is something I wish to show you. Please, Anneke, just grant me this request."

Anneke looked at this man whom she loved more each day, who so rarely asked anything of her, and nodded. "All right, Daniel, if that is what you want."

When they arrived at the printing house, everyone looked up, but their expressions did not hold the shock that Anneke had expected. Some even smiled and nodded to her, as though she had but recently come to speak to Heer Meyert about an assignment.

"Did you tell them that I was coming?" she whispered into Daniel's ear.

"Yes, I did. I thought that you would feel more comfortable if you were not greeted with astonishment. Wait here a moment," he said as he walked over to Heer Meyert. Anneke almost reached out to him to prevent him from leaving her, but she kept her hands folded in front of her, trying to disappear. She glanced at the engraver, Heer Klopper. She remembered Daniel saying his attitude was that colorists distorted the clean lines he had engraved but that he had later praised her map. She did not have time to analyze her feelings before he approached her.

"I was sorry to hear about the loss of Vrouw Plettenburg. She served the House of Blaeu honorably for many years."

"Thank you," was all Anneke could say, hoping that the engraver would walk away after expressing what he must have seen as compulsory words of sympathy. Instead, he continued. "I fear that I have misjudged the work of colorists for many years, though I always respected your mother." Anneke felt a small shock as she realized that she had never thought of how her mother was seen in the world. She had known and affected those beyond just her family and would be remembered by more than just her children. The engraver lingered for a few more moments, but as she said nothing that would encourage him to stay, he gave her a sad smile and returned to his work as Daniel came toward her.

"Come through, Anneke," he said, then led her to a part of the printing house into which she had rarely ventured. Heer Meyert stood and nodded but did not come over to her. Daniel confidently walked past him and brought her to a table on which a single map was displayed.

"Look, Anneke," he said simply.

She gazed at the newly-printed map before her. She saw land with mountains and names that she knew. She saw familiar borders, and in the sea three sailing ships. She saw the suggestion of a line that started in the middle of the west coast of the area portrayed and went toward the northeast. Along this line, the names of places were denser than in any other part of the map, and she recognized the names she had copied from her father's papers. In the corner, there were people and an elephant and a rhino, and in the middle of this cartouche, there was the name that she had written: *Regna Congo et Angola.*

Epilogue

1699
Anneke

I never learned what became of my father, but all in all, my life has been a happy one. It has not been empty of sorrow, but no one can ask that. I have had a husband who loved me and two sons and a daughter who survived childhood.

I have worked at my art, and I am in demand by map collectors. It is strange, but I still most cherish the map of the world that I colored at de Groot's and took from his home on that last day. It hangs in my workroom, though sometimes it conjures sorrowful memories.

I was eventually admitted to the Guild of St. Luke as a colorist. Though some denigrate my use of unorthodox coloring, patrons seek me out for it, and so the guild looks the other way, though they would like to control even this aspect of its members' work.

But I have never created another map. Who would trust a woman to do that? Who would come to me with the information I would need? I, who, to the world's knowledge, have never performed the magic of a cartographer. At times, I sit at my work table with a clean sheet of paper and try to recreate from memory that map that now exists in the many copies of the *Atlas Maior*. Who owns them? Who stops to ponder my map? How have different colorists enhanced or marred it?

I have thought back often on the hopes of my youth to become an accomplished colorist, to have a husband who loved me, and children to ease my later years. I remind myself that I have achieved what I had once only dreamed of. But that was before I had drawn the map. That then became my impossible desire.

I sometimes wonder if I have been punished. Punished for so many things. Punished for my part in Helena's infidelities. Punished for taking my father's notes and ignoring the fact, which I knew in my heart, that some of them were not his. Punished for keeping it all a secret, until it led to murder and exile.

I think back on all the secrets: Helena's secret of her infidelities and Willem's of having known about them, my father's secret of Simon's notes, my secret of creating the map, my mother's secret of the name my father took. What tragedies might have been averted if there had been no deception? Did the motives of those who hid the truth absolve them of the consequences?

At times I recall Lucas's first objections to my creation of the map. He had protested that it would only give new opportunities for men to savagely bleed Africa of its people. I tell myself that, though my map was new for the *Atlas Maior*, surely the Companies already had their own maps of the area, which they used to their purposes. I remember that my father always said knowledge was something to pursue, but do the lies he told negate his claim to wisdom?

I tell myself that knowledge is better than ignorance, and that in shedding light, we cannot be held responsible for how others use it. But I do not know if that is so.

Author's Historical Notes

During the seventeenth century, Amsterdam was the map-printing capital of the world, in large part due to the activities of the Dutch East India Company (the VOC) and the Dutch West India Company (the WIC). The companies maintained their own maps, and their ventures brought prosperity to Holland, as well as imported objects from the lands with which they traded, and which they colonized, including Batavia (now part of Indonesia). This global activity sparked the imaginations of the citizens of the Dutch Republic, causing great interest in the maps printed in Amsterdam, the market for which also extended throughout Europe.

There were multiple important map printers in Amsterdam at the time, the Blaeu printing house being one of these. The production which plays a critical part in the novel, the *Atlas Maior* was the largest and most expensive publication of the century. Printed over the course of several years, it came out in different languages, the number of volumes ranging from nine to twelve. There are a few new maps of places in Africa that are unattributed. It is one of these, the *Regna Congo et Angola*, which I chose to use for Anneke's map. The route of Jan van Herder in 1642 (some sources give a later date) is quite noticeable on the map, extending from Angola's northwest coast at Mols Fort near Luanda, and proceeding in a northeasterly direction into Congo and up toward the area of Mannebacanÿ.

Men, women, and even children used watercolor to enhance maps, which were, of course, only printed in black and white. The vast majority of these colorists labored in obscurity and were paid very little. The rich were able to hire their own colorists, who sometimes enhanced the maps with gold or silver. Sometimes the affluent would color their own maps as a hobby.

The coloring of the maps described in the novel is based on the coloring of maps of the period.

The idea that Anneke expresses that there are certain colors that Dutch artists seem to use came from a 1999 article by Lisa Davis-Allen, "The National Palette: Painting and Map-Coloring in the Seventeenth-Century Dutch Republic," printed in *The Portolan*, a publication of the Washington Map Society.

While I consulted countless sources in researching this book, I would like to share three which were invaluable. *Joan Blaeu and his Grand Atlas*, by C. Koeman, provides comprehensive information about Blaeu, his publishing house, and what was contained in each edition of the *Atlas Maior*. I was thrilled to discover *Daily Life in Rembrandt's Holland*, by Paul Zumthor, which gives countless details about Amsterdam during the time of my novel. Finally, the original source, *The Art of Painting in Oyl*, by John Smith, contained a section specifically about using watercolor to paint maps. While the book was written in England, and slightly after my period, I used it to describe the process of preparing the mixtures needed, and the actual application of the paint.

The Map Colorist characters

While Anneke and her family, as well as most of the other characters in the novel, are fictitious, there are several real people who play some part in the story. I have listed them here in the order of their appearance in the novel.

Rembrandt van Rijn—The story that Isaac tells the children of seeing an elephant named Hansken in Amsterdam is true, as is his claim that Rembrandt made many drawings of her. Rembrandt is also mentioned later in the novel as being able to paint people as they really are, for no one would dare question the great master.

Jan van Herder went on a mission to see the king of Congo, Nkanga-a-Lukeni, called Garcia II by the Portuguese, and van Herder's group took the route as described in the novel. This is the expedition Isaac accompanies.

Joan Blaeu owned one of the major publishing houses, which he inherited from his father. He was a shrewd, ambitious business man, and that is how I have portrayed him. Blaeu's maps appear in three of Johannes Vermeer's paintings: *Officer and Young Girl Laughing, Young Woman in Blue,* and *The Lost Letter.*

Hondius, Janssonius, and Visscher were all prominent map publishers in Amsterdam. Isaac untruthfully tells Lysbeth he has visited them to see about making a map from his notes.

Laurens van der Hem, who is mentioned by de Groot, was an Amsterdam lawyer and map collector of the time. When it came out, he had his own copy of the *Atlas Maior* colored by Dirk Jansz van Santen, and added other maps, some from the "secret" maps of the Dutch East India Company (the VOC). Van der Hem also supplemented his maps with drawings and landscapes of various places by Dutch artists of the time.

Lijsbeth Philips, our Lysbeth's acquaintance and the printer from whom Anneke gets free paper, did, along with Jan Jacobsz Bouman, publish the *Tidings from Various Quarters (Tijdinghen uyt verscheyde Quartieren)* from 1652 until 1671.

The African boy that Anneke talks about seeing at Helena's luncheon is based on information from an online exhibit by Amsterdam's Rijksmuseum. Slavery in the Dutch Republic was illegal, but bringing enslaved people from other places into the Republic was allowed. Those people then worked as servants. Often, the person brought in was an African boy, perhaps as young as six years old. In the Rijksmuseum exhibit, it says that the lady of the house often regarded the child as "a plaything" or a "form of entertainment." Sometimes these Africans, even into adulthood, wore a gold or silver collar around their necks with the crest of the family they served, to show the family's wealth and global power. The exhibit talks specifically about a boy who was given the name Paulus when he was brought to the Netherlands. He grew up to marry, have a son, and serve as a drummer in the army of Stadtholder William III.

Frans Koerten, whom Anneke thinks of when trying to find someone to recommend her work, was a colorist, engraver, and cartographer. Born in 1600, he would have been of an older generation than Isaac and Lysbeth.

Johannes Vingboons was a map colorist who worked for the house of Blaeu and also did watercolor paintings of far-flung places based on descriptions he gleaned from others, as I have depicted in the novel. He remained unmarried, and lived with a large part of his family on Sint Antoniesbreestraat, on the corner of Salamandersteeg. I have invented his love for Lysbeth and the portrait he painted of her.

Dirk Jansz van Santen was one of the few well-known map colorists, though he was probably not yet famous at the time of the novel. Some sources say that he colored for the house of Blaeu. In the novel de Groot mentions him as someone who is doing interesting work.

Judith Leyster was an artist who did genre paintings, portraits, and still lifes. She was accepted into the Haarlem Guild of St. Luke in 1633, as Anneke mentions in the novel.

Acknowledgments

In many ways, writing a book is a solitary venture, but one that is not done in complete isolation. Especially as a writer of historical fiction, I depend on the research and writing of historians. For them I am eternally grateful.

It has always surprised me that when I have contacted a total stranger, identifying myself as a novelist and asking for information about something, they have graciously replied. Peter van der Krogt, who wrote the text for the Taschen *Atlas Maior*, confirmed that the map of *Regna Congo et Angola* is still unattributed, and generously sent along other helpful information.

I was delighted to discover that my alma mater, Washington University in St. Louis, has in its Special Collections the last two volumes of the Dutch version of the *Atlas Maior*, which contain the maps of Africa. Special Collections librarian Cassie Brand obligingly answered my question about the *Regna Congo et Angola* map.

Julie van den Hout, a specialist in seventeenth-century Dutch, was kind enough to advise me on terms of address in use at the time. Any errors are, of course, mine alone.

I am not a Dutch speaker, so I was especially grateful to Johannes van der Wilk for meeting with me on Zoom and allowing me to record him pronouncing a long list of names and Dutch words. This helped me to think and speak about my characters and their setting correctly, and I was able to send the recording to the audiobook narrator.

My developmental editor, Kerri Jackson, and my copy editor, Signe Jorgenson, gave invaluable advice on how to improve my manuscript.

I am grateful to my wonderful publisher, Brooke Warner of She Writes Press, to Julie Metz and her design team for my cover design, and to Shannon Green, my ever-responsive project manager.

Linda Henley, novelist and watercolor artist gave me invaluable guidance on how one might have gone about painting a map. She went above and beyond, giving detailed ideas about the four maps that I sent her. The specifics of how my protagonist colors various maps follow Linda's suggestions.

As always, I owe so much to my family. My sister, Ellen Romano, listened to countless hours of me talking about my writing, always assuring me that she was interested.

My children, Ben D'Harlingue and Kate D'Harlingue, supported me throughout my project, always offering encouragement. My grandchildren, Liliana and Oliver Norman, to whom this novel is dedicated, always help me return to reality, and to what is truly important.

Finally, to my husband, Arthur D'Harlingue, I owe the most of all. Without his love, support, and unending patience, I could not have written this book.

ABOUT THE AUTHOR

photo credit: Sam Willard Photography

Rebecca D'Harlingue writes about women in the seventeenth century taking a different path. She has done graduate studies in Spanish literature, worked as a hospital administrator, and taught English as a Second Language to adults from all over the world. She has been in the same book club for decades, and although members sometimes disagree, there's always a lively discussion. D'Harlingue lives in Oakland, California, with her husband, Arthur, where they are fortunate to frequently spend time with their children and grandchildren.

D'Harlingue is a member of the Paper Lantern Writers. You can find out more about Rebecca, along with a book club discussion guide, on her website: rebeccadharlingue.com

SELECTED TITLES FROM SHE WRITES PRESS

She Writes Press is an independent publishing company founded to serve women writers everywhere. Visit us at www.shewritespress.com.

The Lines Between Us by Rebecca D'Harlingue. $16.95, 978-1-63152-743-2
A young girl flees seventeenth-century Madrid, in fear for her life. Three centuries later and a continent away, a woman comes across old papers long hidden away, and in them discovers the reason for the flight so long ago, and for her own mother's enigmatic dying words.

Beyond the Ghetto Gates by Michelle Cameron. $16.95, 978-1-63152-850-7
When French troops occupy the Italian port city of Ancona, freeing the city's Jews from their repressive ghetto, two very different cultures collide—and a whirlwind of progressivism and brutal backlash is unleashed.

Finding Napoleon: A Novel by Margaret Rodenberg. $16.95, 978-1-64742-016-1
In an intriguing adaptation of Napoleon Bonaparte's real attempt to write a novel, the defeated emperor and his little-known last love—the audacious, pregnant Albine de Montholon—plot to escape exile and free his young son. To succeed, Napoleon demands loyalty. To survive, Albine plunges into betrayal.

Estelle by Linda Stewart Henley. $16.95, 978-1-63152-791-3
From 1872 to '73, renowned artist Edgar Degas called New Orleans home. Here, the narratives of two women—Estelle, his Creole cousin and sister-in-law, and Anne Gautier, who in 1970 finds a journal written by a relative who knew Degas—intersect . . . and a painting Degas made of Estelle spells trouble.

Portrait of a Woman in White by Susan Winkler. $16.95, 978-1-93831-483-4
When the Nazis steal a Matisse portrait from the eccentric, art-loving Rosenswigs, the Parisian family is thrust into the tumult of war and separation, their fates intertwined with that of their beloved portrait.

Talland House by Maggie Humm. $16.95, 978-1-63152-729-6
1919 London: When artist Lily Briscoe meets her old tutor, Louis Grier, by chance at an exhibition, he tells her of their mutual friend Mrs. Ramsay's mysterious death—an encounter that spurs Lily to investigate the death of this woman whom she loved and admired.